Fyodor
Sologub

Translated
by
Vassar W. Smith

ARDIS ///// ANN ARBOR

Fyodor Sologub

Bad Dreams

Copyright © 1978 by Ardis

Published by Ardis Publishers,
2901 Heatherway,
Ann Arbor, Michigan 48104

Manufactured in the United States of America

ISBN 0-88233-128-0

BAD DREAMS

CHAPTER ONE

The beginning of spring... A quiet evening... A large shady garden at the end of town, above the steep bank of the river, at the home of Zinaida Romanovna Kulchitsky, a widow and wealthy local landowner...

Here, inside the house, in the study of Paltusov, the lady's first cousin (however, nobody in town believed that they were related), a card game was in progress. Paltusov and three other gentlemen of decent age and status in our provincial world were playing bridge. In the summer-house in the garden their wives were sitting with the hostess and talking, talking, talking.

The hostess' daughter, Claudia Alexandrovna, a young girl with green eyes, had withdrawn from their company. She was sitting on the terrace, by the fence that bordered the narrow sandy path above the bank of the Mgla river. One of the guests was with Claudia: he did not play cards.

This was Vasily Markovich Login, a teacher at the secondary school.[1] He was a little over thirty. His gray, nearsighted eyes seemed distracted, and he did not look directly at either people or objects. His face seemed weary, and his lips often formed a faint smile that seemed either lazily indifferent or mocking. His movements were listless, and his voice was not loud. At times he gave the impression of being a man who was thinking about something that he would not tell anyone.

"It's tiresome... living is tiresome," he said, and the conversation was apparently more interesting to Claudia than to him.

"Who's forcing you to live?" Claudia asked quickly.

Login noticed the irritation in her voice and smiled wryly.

"As you see, I haven't managed as yet to escape from life," he answered lazily.

"But that's so simple!" Claudia exclaimed.

Her green eyes flashed. She broke out in a wicked laugh.

"Simple? What exactly do you mean?" asked Login.

Claudia made a sharp, pointing gesture with her right hand at her temple.

"Bang!—And that's it."

Her narrow eyes opened wide, her lips shuddered convulsively, and a fleeting expression of horror passed over her face as though suddenly she had vividly imagined firing a bullet through her head and feeling a momentary pain in her temple.

"Ah!" Login said slowly. "You see, that's just too simple for me. And, after all, you don't get out of anything that way."

"Really?" Claudia asked with a morose grimace.

"I have spiritual needs, a tormenting thirst... You can't quiet such things just by the mischief of a bullet... But perhaps it's simply a childish

3

fear... a silly, ineradicable desire to live... even in the dark, even in the desert, just to *live!*"

Claudia gazed at him curiously, sighed, then looked down.

"Tell me," Login spoke up again after a brief silence, "what color does life seem to you, and how does it taste?"

"What color and taste...does *life* have?" Claudia asked in surprise.

"Well, yes... It's quite fashionable, merging the senses."[2]

"Oh, that... I suppose the taste is *cloying.*"

"I thought you'd say 'bitter'."

Claudia smiled wryly.

"No, why should I?" she said.

The ancient elms bent down their branches as though they wanted to eavesdrop on this strange conversation. But they were not listening and did not hear. They had their own affairs. They stood there unconcerned with people, impassive, unthinking, with a life and secret of their own, and a transparent sadness fell from their dark boughs as dew shaken off by the wind.

"And the color of life?" Login asked.

"Green and yellow," Claudia answered quickly, without thinking, and even with a note of malice in her voice.

"The colors of hope and disdain?"

"No, simply of unripeness and withering. Oh!" she exclaimed suddenly, as though interrupting herself. "Somewhere there must be broad horizons!"

"What do we care about them?" Login asked morosely.

"What do we care? But I feel stifled and afraid... I've noticed that lately I have a bad habit of looking back on the past."

"And what in particular do you recall?"

"Pictures—oh, lovely ones: an embittered childhood devoid of love; and youth, with the pain of envy and impossible desires... the destruction of my hopes... and of my ideals! Yes, ideals—don't laugh. All the same, they were ideals, however strange that may seem. You try to look ahead, and you see only darkness."

"And on top of all that, you feel the surge of passion," Login said in a vague tone somewhere between mockery and indifference.

Claudia started trembling. Her eyes grew dark and at the same time blazed with rage.

"Passion!" she exclaimed in a suppressed voice.

"Of course! It's not a thirst for truth that torments you, but simply—to put it crudely and bluntly—passion."

"What are you saying? What sort of passion? For what?"

"You're at the age when one gets vague impulses, an overflow of emotions; and besides, your young heart is ensnared by the demonic beauty of a charming skeptic."

"Do you mean Paltusov? If you only knew what he was in my life! If you could just imagine it!"

4

"How he helped in your development?"

"Don't talk like that," Claudia said irritably.

"Pardon me. I didn't mean it," Login said sincerely.

"When I was still a little girl," Claudia began speaking rapidly and passionately, "when he still paid no more attention to me than to any other object in the house, I was already caught up by something in him, agonizingly caught up. It was something irresistible, rapacious, like a vulture seizing a chick. Sometimes I wanted... I don't know what I wanted... I had wild, burning dreams... Still, I always hated him."

"For what?"

"How should I know? Maybe for his scornful smirk, or for his insolent way of talking, or because my mother... You know what an influence he has on her."

Claudia smiled a strange smile, somewhat malevolent, somewhat embarrased.

"Especially on that account," Login said softly. "It's jealousy, isn't it?"

"Yes, yes," Claudia answered abruptly and uneasily. "Then, I don't know how, we started being friendly. I don't remember what started it; I only recall my wicked joy. The long, eerie, passionate talks we had together —a source of new, daring, evil thoughts. An abyss of enticement opened up... But I hate it... I would like to run away from all this."

"Where?"

"How should I know? I have dreams. I'm afraid. —Of what, I myself don't know. It's like being afraid to take something belonging to someone else... But what does *she* matter to me, that distant wife of his, who doesn't live with him, whom I've never seen? Maybe she's unhappy...or has she found consolation? It's like standing before a roadblock that you're forbidden to go beyond. He scoffs at this...superstition..."

"Do you know," Login said suddenly, changing the subject, "even I was in love with you?"

"Indeed?"

Claudia gave a forced laugh and blushed.

"I thank you for the honor," she said with vexation.

"No, really."

"I don't doubt it."

Login made a slight bow to her and began talking in an intimate tone:

"Don't get angry at my words; it was hard for me to lose these hopes too. At the time I thought: why must happiness, free and unbounded, remain forbidden to me? Why not go hand-in-hand with a bold companion to the place where I envisioned new, grand expanses? Why?" he asked softly and took her slender hand with its long fingers.

Claudia did not take her hand away, but her shoulders trembled faintly, and her green eyes burned.

"Yes," Login continued, "I envisioned the grand paths of the future. Then suddenly I saw that this was a feeling nurtured artificially..."

He stood up and walked about the terrace. Claudia was silent and followed him with her strangely burning eyes. A gentle breeze was coming from the river. The boughs of the elms swayed slightly. Login stopped in front of Claudia.

"Anyhow," he said, "I think each of us has his own path to travel... hard and unknown."

"Show it to me!" Claudia exclaimed rather wildly and impulsively, stretching out her arms to him in a grand, swift motion.

"I myself wish that someone would reveal it to me," Login said morosely. "There was a time, it seemed to me... I would imagine someone with a light in his hands..."

"You have lights of your own."

"That's just the trouble, that I have none. All these plans of mine are a mirage, an urge to deceive my own mind..."

"What sort of light did you imagine?" Claudia asked sadly.

"Something unexpected... An indescribable fascination came over me... It was something un—Russian, alien to everything that's here... All the while I kept expecting that something extraordinary and impossible was on the verge of happening... But nothing happened: the days passed away tiresomely and monotonously, as always... I looked intently into myself, and within I found the same ardent but impotent audacity of all human beings, and that same dreary question about the fate of our country... Go to *him;* he'll create a heaven and an earth for you."

Claudia was on the point of replying. But the footsteps and voices of approaching ladies were heard, and Claudia remained silent.

Login returned home late at night through dark and deserted streets. He kept thinking of Claudia. An aching pity for her filled his heart.

Claudia's father had died when she was about five years old. Her mother took up with the engineer Paltusov. He was married but was not living with his wife. Mrs. Kulchitsky tried to pass him off as her first cousin. Thus they spent several years, sometimes in our town, sometimes traveling abroad. Lately Paltusov had lost interest in Mrs. Kulchitsky's fading beauty. He was attracted to Claudia. They drew close to each other in a rather strange way, as though they were at enmity with each other. Her mother had noticed their closeness. She began to be jealous. Claudia did not love her mother. But the idea of having a liason to which she had no right and which people would condemn was a thought that she found oppressive.

Even Login did not know for sure why he felt sorry for this girl; was it that her mother had never loved her and her cold childhood had deformed her passionate heart? Or was it that she had fallen in love with someone else's husband, her mother's lover, and could not understand the attitudes that were caused by this love? Or was it that Paltusov had shattered her original beliefs, and she could not replace them with anything?

Login recalled that his tender compassion for Claudia had smitten him long ago, had smitten him more strongly for the fact that he perceived how akin their natures were. Sometimes he mistook this compassion for love of Claudia. In fact this feeling of his was so intense that it even found a response in Claudia. A strange semi-frankness developed between them, a mutual testing of each other, a mutual feeling of uneasiness. They also got to be equally good at grasping each other's innuendoes. But nothing emerged from these strained relations: they could not have called their affinity love, and they did not want to lie to themselves.

Now Login thought that love could not be kindled in his heart, which had grown old before its time. Long ago he had grown accustomed to drowning any impulse of his heart in barren and futile meditations, in idle and delightful fantasies, in strange and lonely sufferings and pleasures, of which he could not tell anyone. Now he clearly recalled how quickly this surprising compassion for Claudia had been transformed into a sensual attraction; and his fantasies had given this attraction a tinge of cruelty.

He did not yet know whether this base attraction had died out, but certainly he was convinced of its illicit nature. It would be tempting to grant Claudia a year or two of torrid delights that would leave her other love, her shattered love, seething beneath their surface. But afterwards—a burnt-out feeling, despair, death... That was how the future appeared to him if he were to have an affair with Claudia... He perceived that a peaceful life with her was impossible for him; too much of the same spiteful irritation had poisoned them both; and perhaps they both had the same difficulty in loving those from whom they were separated by so much...

But why, nevertheless, did he, weary of life as he was, not seize upon this brief and seering prospect, half happiness, half delirium? What did it matter that death would follow? After all, he knew beforehand that he was approaching some agonizing abyss where he was bound to perish. What turned him away from this abyss? Weakness, or hope?

Sometimes in his reveries the pure and trusting eyes of another would open wide and an affectionate smile would shine before him. Perhaps this was a spark of pure, redeeming love, but Login did not believe it. A different, distant light would appear to him in those trusting eyes, and the abyss would seem no longer in his path...

Login lived in a little house on the edge of town. He had fixed up a study on the second storey; he also slept there; the kitchen and housekeeper's quarters were in the basement; the rooms where Login dined and received guests occupied the main floor of the house. Few did he invite upstairs to his room. This was where he *lived:* here he dreamed and read.

Bookcases and bookshleves took up a lot of room in his study. Some dozen and a half new books were on a book stand. A few of them were still uncut. Notebooks, reference books, and textbooks covered half of the desk. On top of the pile of blue-jacketed notebooks lay a slender volume of poetry with a white wooden knife inserted as a place-marker. The knife was decorated by a drawing burned into the wood.

Login walked up to the broad window of his study. Before him lay the sleeping town with its dark masses of wooden houses. From the vegetable gardens and fences dull and naive impressions of the life around him came up to Login like trustfully outstretched hands. The misty darkness of the empty streets had a moist feeling; in their silence they were alien to Login and incomprehensible to him. A feeling of something lost and no longer needed came over him.

He drew the blinds and lit the lamp. Like an ugly, annoying stain, the red blanket on the couch caught his attention.

He did not feel like sleeping yet. In the evenings he like to read for hours on end as he lay in bed. But tonight he did not even feel like reading. He went down into the dining-room and brought up some Madeira and coffee-cakes.

He kept worrying about Claudia. He poured a glass of wine and drank it slowly. Painful and absurd fantasies swarmed through his mind; then suddenly they were replaced by innocent fantasies like children's tales set in distant and peaceful valleys. Like a pendulum, his mind swung back and forth from the near and beckoning but forbidden, to the impossible but sacred and longed for.

He drank glass after glass. His innocent visions mournfully faded away, while his mad fantasies flared up all the more ardently and absurdly.

The fumes of intoxication, a languid and pleasant dizziness... His head grew heavy and drooped. Everything before his eyes was crimson and hazy.

There was a faint rustling at the door. He did not want to turn around. Was he only hearing it in his mind?

The rustling near the doorjamb was heard again. It was as though someone, brushing against the door with her skirt, had come in and was standing there now, moving around quietly near the door... But Login knew that no one else could be there. He was alone; his sullen housekeeper was asleep downstairs, there was no one else in the house, and all the doors were locked. But still, the rustling, soft but persistent, was repeated as though some impatient person were standing by the doorjamb.

Login leaned on the desk with his right elbow and looked around.

Someone was standing in the doorway. The walls of the room swayed in the haze. Reeling, Login started to get up from his seat but immediately sat down again and gazed dully at the door.

By the door stood a pretty, rosy-cheeked, young peasant woman. Her broad smile was shameless and carelessly merry. Her face was familiar to Login, but he did not immediately recollect who she was.

He kept peering intently at her—and she stood there and fingered the ends of the many-colored kerchief that she wore on her head. Her rosy face glowed, and her teeth, even and beautiful, sparkled from under her full scarlet lips quivering with a smile.

Finally he remembered. The young beauty's name was Ulyana. She was the wife of a landless peasant from a neighboring village; she worked as house-keeper for Motovilov, the honorable trustee of the high school. He also re-membered Ulyana's husband: Spirka the drunk often loafed about the streets of the town; he lived on his wife's tips and by doing occasional odd jobs. Town gossip had long borne the rumor that Ulyana was having intimate rela-tions with Motovilov. And Spiridon was beginning to believe this too. Meeting Motovilov on the street, he would look at him sullenly and insolently solicit handouts. Sometimes Motovilov would give him small change, for which Spiridon would say:

"My benefactor! I'll go drink it up to your health, and you can have her!"

All this Login remembered now.

"Why, is that you, Ulyana?" he asked.

"It's me," the good-looking girl answered softly and looked down bashfully.

But at the very same time her shameless eyes gazed boldly from under her thick eyelashes, the red flush glowed even brighter on her cheeks, and a soft, provocative laugh went rippling through the drunken air of the sultry room.

"Have you come from Motovilov?"

"No, I've come on my own," answered Ulyana, with her eyes sparkling merrily.

"How did you get here? Who let you in? Don't tell me the place isn't locked!"

"I came in right through that little window."

"What little window?" Login asked in bewilderment.

"Why, the second from the corner—and so it was left open, just as I was told at the time—that very window, yes indeed."

"But which window exactly? Who told you about the window?"

"Well, I declare! You really have forgotten! Why, you yourself told me

9

to come."

"When?" Login asked morosely.

"Why, last Sunday," Ulyana explained as though she were annoyed at his forgetfulness, "when you were visiting my master's."

"What nonsense."

"You met me in the hall, and then you said: 'Come over on Wednesday night. I'll be waiting,' you said. So here I am. There was no way to come earlier. I got away soon's I could."

"So you went through with it," Login said lazily. "What do I want with you?"

Ulyana let out a ringing laugh. Her persistent laughter teased and enticed Login. He looked at Ulyana with bewilderment and annoyance. She was so rosy and splendid. Some great heat seemed to radiate from her. Her dark braids were forcing their way out from under her kerchief. And the ends of the kerchief stuck out in different directions, and the knot was coming untied...

The rosy haze again began spreading out before Login's eyes. His head began to whirl pleasantly and languidly. The figure of Ulyana was drifting in the haze.

"Why this is a dream, a delirium!" he thought.

Ulyana took two steps forward. She stepped soundlessly and wavered strangely. The folds of her long skirt swayed and slightly revealed the tips of her white feet.

"Well then," said Login, "since you're here, my pretty, you might as well sit down."

"It's all right. I'll stand," Ulyana replied.

Her roguish eyes kept darting about the room. Suddenly she waxed melancholy, leaned her cheek on her palm, and started saying something doleful—about her drunkard husband, about her sad and abandoned state, and about her beauty, fading unappreciated. She uttered the words softly but distinctly, as though she were quickly and adroitly picking out choice grains of wheat. Her sad talk purled on ever more swiftly and sweetly. All the while she kept coming closer to Login. And now he felt her closeness, warm and languid.

"Caress me!" she whispered, then blushed deeply and trembled, and covered her face with her hands.

But her merry, provocative eyes peeped through her slightly parted fingers.

Login poured the rest of the wine into his glass and drank it greedily...

The crimson haze was spreading over the room. The lamp shone dimly and indifferently. A rosy, persistent smile...

Flowing garments were falling away... Scarlet spots flickering through the crimson haze... A warm body was so close...

Someone put out the lamp...

10

CHAPTER TWO

On weekday mornings Login was always in a gloomy mood, for he knew that he would come to the school and encounter cold, dead people who fulfilled their duty indifferently, carried out their prescribed tasks automatically, like perfect mechanical dolls. But they did not like this prescribed task, tried to spend as little energy as possible at it, kept thinking about playing cards. Login knew that from him too they expected the same soulless relationship to his work. He was obliged to be like everyone else so as not to irritate his colleagues.

There was a time when he had put a lively spirit into his work as a teacher, but he was told that he was acting improperly. In other words, he had thoughtlessly wounded some people's amour-propre, sick from stagnation and idleness; he had clashed with someone's ossified concepts—hence he had proven to be, or seemed to be, a restless, unaccomodating fellow. They did not understand why he was going to such lengths: did it *matter* to him whether they treated this boy or that boy one way or another? To end the quarrels, they transferred him to another secondary school, the one in our town—with the blandly mordant official announcement that he was being transferred "for the good of the service." And so for a whole year he had languished here in melancholy and boredom.

He got up early. Often after drinking wine at night he could not sleep well in the morning and would wake up earlier than usual.

His head ached dully: he had drunk too much. His whole body felt lethargic. In his bachelor apartment, the bright morning seemed a dreary one, lonely and sad. The housekeeper's sullen face, cratered with pock-marks, increased his melancholy.

Chaotic clusters of dim and absurd recollections filled his heavy head. He recalled the night, and the strange visit he had had... The rosy-cheeked, laughing Ulyana kept darting before his eyes.

There was no one else in his study when he woke up. He could not decide whether Ulyana *had* come or it had been a dream. He was tormented by the pangs of earlier, half-forgotten, coarse recollections. The gaping maws of two abysses had opened up for him, and he could not understand from which abyss the sad, bright vernal morning had lifted him by its impossibly innocent dawn light.

He went downstairs and walked around in the living room and dining room. He looked apprehensively at the windows. As yet no one had opened them since night. The polished gleam of their brass bolts was depressing to the eye. He peered at these bolts and there was no way he could make himself go up to the window.

Finally he was seized with angry annoyance at himself. Abruptly he

11

walked up to the window, the second from the corner, and grasped it by the bolt; with a faint scraping it slid out of its brass slot.

"It was a dream, a dream!" Login thought drearily. "Oh, no, it can't be! The second window from which corner? Maybe it's the second from the yard."

Hurriedly he went from the dining room to the living room and rushed to the second window. It had only been closed, not bolted. A brief, hoarse laugh burst forth from his throat. He threw the window wide open, and sticking his head outside, he peered avidly at something...

Down below lay the dusty grass and, a little higher, the narrow ledge made by the building's foundation; then came the grayish boards that made up the siding of the house. Had the damp and lively breeze that now blew in Login's face obliterated the traces? Or had Ulyana's long skirt swept the dust off of the ledge over the foundation? Or had there been no traces?

Login carefully examined the bare, littered ground of the road, but he found nothing there either.

After spending a tiresome morning at the school, Login returned home and set to work. Recently he had conceived of founding in our town a league for mutual assistance, with quite extensive goals. Now he wanted to draw up a draft of the statues of such a league, which he could show to those who had responded favorably to his idea.

Perhaps this project was nurtured not so much by Login's thoughts as by his troubled feelings. He was enveloped in longstanding melancholy, the coldness of a life that was self-centered and dominated by chance... Login had seen many revolting and contemptible things; he had seen the ruin of many and the stony indifference with which it had been viewed by the rest; and he was tormented by indignation, despair, and resentment. Life seemed menacing; premonitions oppressed him; misfortunes lay in wait for him. Personal happiness and satisfaction his heart rejected, and besides, they seemed hopeless to his reason; it seemed that his personal life had no foundations that could not be swept away by an absurd accident. Life swayed like a flimsy bridge on rickety supports. And then an idea that promised salvation appeared...but was chimerical.

From the beginning a doubt as to the feasibility of this idea had been lurking in the depths of Login's consciousness. Sometimes he even confessed to himself that he did not believe in it. But Login was in such great need of an escape from spiritual desolation that he could not bring himself to abandon his project without giving it a trial.

In the last few days Login had carefully scrutinized the townspeople and become well acquainted with people whom earlier he had either barely known or not known at all. By the standards of his idea he measured everything that he observed nowadays—both the people and their business. There proved to be a great deficiency. Sometimes the enterprise of carrying out a vital idea in *this* society seemed absurd to the point of being funny, and Login smiled a cold and absentminded smile.

He ate dinner alone, dressed with a certain care, then set off for the other side of town. He could breathe more easily at the place where he was going; there the people had cheerful dispositions, although they often seemed strangely alien to him.

He was going to the Yermolins, who lived on their country estate about two versts from town.[1] The Yermolin family consisted of the father, his daughter and his son. Maxim Ivanovich Yermolin had retired from the zemstvo some ten years ago; he had been chairman of the administrative board of the district zemstvo. Now he was only indirectly concerned with zemstvo affairs. These affairs were not going as they had under him, but in another direction.[2]

Login felt something kindred in the sad pensiveness that sometimes stole over Yermolin's face. But that face radiated good health and was full of that shy and simple beauty which calls to mind an expanse of fields, the countryside and the forest, where one can smell the odor of "resin and wild strawberries."

Yermolin took agriculture seriously; throughout the district he was in fact regarded as one of the wealthy landowners, not merely as one who had avoided ruin. He amazed the townspeople by the simplicity of his life, by his love for hard work, and by the heaps of magazines and books that were sent to him. He had reared his children simply and strictly. They were accustomed to hard work and were not afraid of cold and pain. False shame had no power over them; they went without shoes for days on end and in that state walked far from home. In our narrow-minded town this was, of course, condemned.

Login walked along the highway. He had just passed the last shack at the edge of town and the last eating-house, and already everything around him was quiet and deserted. The only sound that reached him was the faintly ringing thud of hammer blows coming from the squalid, blackened smithy that stuck out at an angle on the road out of town; and far ahead of Login a drunken muzhik jogged along on a shaky little cart in a gray cloud of dust, whipping up his poor little skew-bald horse, and bawling out a song, though the words to it could not be heard. Soon he too was hidden from view, and little by little the wild sounds of his discordant singing died away.

Login caught sight of the pale, sad blossoms of the water-buttercup in the stagnant water of a ditch by the road. Their thick, glistening leaves with the ruffled edges lay sleepily and indifferently upon the murky water and did not feel the warm caress of the spring air, and the sick flowers languished and suffocated in their humid and stifling abode. Radiant May was joyless for them, and joylessly did the eyes of a melancholy man look upon them...

Finally Login grew sick of the unbridled expanses of road and fields. Hurriedly he left the thoroughfare and turned off to the side, along a path that led into the bushes and through them to the river. The smell of dampness arose. The barely distinguishable, acidulous fragrance of lilies-of-the-valley made the air heady with moods of merriness and serenity. From time to time these joyous flowers showed their whiteness in the shade of the bushes and reminded Login of Anna Yermolin's carefree smile. Suddenly he felt cheerful and amused. He started picking lilies-of-the-valley, and inwardly he began chuckling at himself for actually doing anything so childish. But he felt that these innocent and unclouded moods were intimately bound to his soul, insipid though they might seem, and persecuted though they might be by the smile of Cain from the evil part of his personality.

The bank was rising. Beneath Login's feet masses of clay jutted out.

The lilies-of-the-valley were slowly wilting in his hands...

The river had formed a bend around the steep bank. The opposite bank was low-lying. There fields came into view. Part of the city was also visible from that point, and so were the green roofs of its churches, with their gilded crosses.

Login ascended the highest point of the bank. Not far away he saw the Yermolin estate: the wooden two-story house with its red iron roof, the garden, cheerfully showing its greenness, and the well-wooded park; farther away, behind the house, were the outbuildings and the vegetable garden. He shifted his gaze to the river. On the riverbank at the edge of the park he saw a female figure wearing a blue sarafan. Not far from her a boy, up to his knees in the water, was puttering around with a fishing pole in his hands. Login could not make out their faces: he saw poorly at a distance. However, he was convinced that it was Anna Yermolin and her brother Anatoly. Login armed himself with his pince-nez. It turned out that he had not been mistaken.

Anna was sitting on the ground; she was leaning her back against the trunk of a willow. Login could only see her ear and part of her back, but he recognized her by her particular bearing, by the slow and free movements of her hands, by the round contours of her shoulders, by all those barely perceptible signs which are hard to convey in words, but are so well perceived and remembered by the eye.

Login shifted his lens-equipped gaze to Anatoly. The boy was talking with Anna and smiling. The shiny visor of his grayish-white cap was cocked at such an angle that it revealed his dark-complexioned face. Illuminated by the sun, made smaller by the distance, seen clearly as he was through Login's glasses—as though framed by thin, distinct lines—Anatoly seemed as bright as if he were in a picture with the brilliant background of the blue river and radiant verdure. His white smock was pulled tight by a polished brown belt with a narrow brass buckle. Sometimes Anatoly would come out of the water and climb onto one of the rocks by the bank. His legs seemed rosy next to the dark folds of his clothing, which he had rolled up high.

The fish weren't biting much. The boy wandered in vain through the water, which was still cold. But apparently he did not feel the cold. He was used to it.

14

Login recalled his own childhood, spent far from nature, amidst the brick walls of the capital. The days had been dull and joyless; vain desires had oppressed him; his lungs had had to breathe the dust of the city; he found the hypocritical standards of modesty exasperating; evil thoughts excited his imagination at an early age. "There it is," he thought now, "life, plain and peaceful; and *I*, with my unclean past, dare to approach *them*, who are chaste."

He glared spitefully at the lilies-of-the-valley, crushed the flowers, tore them up, and threw them down toward the river. Softly the crumpled flowers fell, fluttering through the air, and scattering over the bumps and crevices of the slope. For a long time Login looked at their ruined beauty. He thought:

"Contemporary man does not like beauty in its bared aspect, does not comprehend it, and cannot stand it. Our nerves are too weak for such a simple and coarse delight as the contemplation of beauty."

Then he descended the hill and walked toward the Yermolins' park. Below, in a damp, dark spot, he caught sight of the large yellow blooms of the buttercup. With an evil grin he picked a flower and stuck it in the buttonhole of his coat; but immediately his face became sad—he threw the flower into the grass and sighed in relief.

Anna was splendidly developed for her twenty years: she had perfectly "molded" shoulders and a lofty bust. She could not be called beautiful because of her face, which though indeed pretty was too irregular for the strict categories of beauty; nor could she be a beauty in the Russian style, because of her golden, dusky complexion and her eyes, big and beautiful, but too attentive. And then there was a beautiful, strong body beneath the folds of her sarafan. Short sleeves revealed her shapely arms. Her feet showed a slight touch of tan.

Anatoly, a boy of about fifteen, strong and agile, resembled his sister. His eyes saw things with a sobriety unusual for his age, but also with an innocence perhaps also unusual for his age. We have grown used to seeing a bad and premature expression—one that is too "knowing"—in the eyes of boys that age.

Anatoly climbed up onto the riparian rock. Sadly he was saying:

"No, they're just not biting; this really is such terrible luck!"

"Evidently you caught them all yesterday," said Anna.

Anatoly rubbed his finally-chilled knees with his hands and said:

"This is a bad business... it's cruel!"

"But you keep on fishing anyway," Anna said quietly.

Anatoly blushed slightly, was silent for a little while, then replied:

"But, you know, it's not very nice for them in the water there either; they gobble each other up. Whoever's stronger is... Do you know what I imagined just now?"

"Well, what?" Anna asked.

"Do you see... that tree?"

15

Anna glanced at the willow which was bending its shaggy top over her.

"So, I'd climb up there," Anatoly recounted, "and down below the peasant children would gawk up at me, their mouths agape. And it made me sad."

"And when was this?" Anna asked.

She was smiling and teasing her brother by pretending to misunderstand.

"It wasn't, I tell you, I imagined it."

Anna burst out laughing. Anatoly looked at her with reproach in his eyes and said, "You're a merry one, you're laughing all over."

He got out completely onto the bank, put down his fishing tackle, and lay down in the grass at his sister's feet. The sun, near to setting, shone on the boy and warmed him.

"But really, doesn't it make you sad?" he asked, and he peered up into Anna's face.

She stopped smiling. She leaned toward the boy and patted him. She asked, "Why sad?"

"Why?" Anatoly repeated the question. "Here's why: they've got their prophetic dreams, bells, candles, house-sprites, the evil eye—but we're by ourselves, we're apart from all that."

"It's not that we're complete strangers to it."

"We are! We are!" exclaimed Anatoly. "Look, even if we put on burlap shirts, we won't get any closer to the common people. It would all be just a masquerade."

"Tolka, you're judging by appearances."

"No, not just by appearances," he said gaily, bursting out laughing.

"There you are, laughing away, as happy as a sparrow in the grain."

"No, you just tell me why you say, 'By appearances,' Nyutochka?"[3]

"Of course... We want to live the way of our hearts too, God's way, as they say. We'll always be *with* the common people, even though we may think differently from them.

Anatoly turned over onto his back and lay in silence for a while.

"Yes, *with* the common people," he said meditatively, then he quickly changed his tone and said with a sly grin, "though with the common people we can't really talk away as we can with..."

He fell silent, then laughed. Anna tickled him under the chin and asked:

"As we can with whom?"

Anatoly writhed with laughter in the grass.

"With somebody else," he finished in a voice ringing with laughter.

"Well, after all, it's possible to talk to anybody about anything," Anna said gently, "any little bird has its own voice."

She leaned back against the tree and peered dreamily at the distant contours of the receding bank as though they appealed to the tender feelings of her memory.

"Well, I'll tell you who is interesting to talk with, namely Login," Anatoly suddenly said quite sincerely.

Anna blushed. She said sharply, "What do you mean?"

"The point is— he can talk about various subjects. The others all talk mostly about one thing. Each has his favorite subject for conversation— and he'll crank it out like a street musician cranking out the one song on his barrel-organ.... However, nowadays even *he* has a barrel-organ to crank on."

"What a thing to say—a barrel-organ!"

"What's wrong with the term?"

"It's just that everyone talks about what's interesting to him. What's surprising about that? How would you like to see this willow suddenly sprout cucumbers?"

Anatoly laughed heartily. Then, suddenly returning to some previous topic, he asked, "But what if we should even live to see it?"

"A miracle?" Anna asked. "Cucumbers from a willow tree?"

"No, I meant if we were to live to see what must come inevitably. How happy life would be! But here's Vasily Markovich!" Anatoly shouted joyfully.

Anna raised her head and smiled. Login was descending the bank along a narrow little path. The descent was steep, and Login had to keep holding on to bushes.

The closer he approached, the more carefree his heart became. He felt again the way he had in early childhood, simple and free.

Anna rose to greet him. Anatoly ran toward him with a joyful smile.

Login settled himself on the grass next to Anna. Anatoly lay down again on the spot where he had been, and he told Login what they had been doing and where they had been that day. Login felt the charm of Anna's maidenly-tender eyes upon him. When Anatoly had finished his accounts, Anna said to Login, "We talked with Father a long time yesterday about your plans."

"I'm only afraid," Login replied sadly, "that you may ascribe the wrong motivation to them."

"Why on earth? It's clear enough, it seems: It's hard to live among unfortunate people and not try to help them."

"No, that's not it! I'm motivated by fear alone. My work as a teacher has become repulsive to me, I have no capital, I see no means before me, and I'm seeking some support for myself in life... simply personal contentment. After all, I can't just go and become a porter!"

Anna shook her head in disbelief.

"Contentment...," she started to say. "However, I don't understand why your present work is disagreeable to you. What were you expecting from it?"

"Evidently I can't convince you."

"I remember what you were saying. But, you see, it doesn't matter if the birch's bark *is* white, it still stains your fingers if you break it off. There's a dark side to everything; but, you know, a lantern won't go out merely because the night is dark."

"Life has grown oppressive to me, and I only know how to hate everything evil in it... although certainly I myself am not immaculate."

Login glanced toward the place where Anatoly had been lying just now. But he was no longer there. It had occurred to the boy that he might hinder the conversation. He had slipped away unnoticed and had again busied himself with his fishing rods.

"They know what needs to be done," Login continued. "Would that *I* knew! But now I've gotten tangled in my relations with other people and myself. I have no guiding light... And my desires are strange."

Login was saying all this in an almost careless tone, with a faint grin that strangely contradicted the meaning of his words.

"Well then, it's certainly evident," Anna said merrily, "that it's not personal contentment alone that beckons you."

"No? Why not? Sometimes it seems to me that I'd be glad to become a nice fat coupon-clipper. But the trouble with that is, money isn't what I need now... Life is frightening to me. I feel that I simply cannot go on living like this any longer."

"But *why* is life frightening?"

"It's too *dead!* We don't live as much as we play at living. The living people perish, and the dead bury their own dead... I thirst for neither love nor wealth nor glory nor happiness,—I thirst for a *living life,* without any stamp or dogma, such a life that one could cast aside all these other goals for tomorrow, in order that the unattainable goal might shine forth brilliantly."

"An impossible wish!" Anna said sadly.

"Yes! Yes!" Login exclaimed passionately. "In life there must be the impossible, and it alone has value. And, well, as for the possible... I've traveled all the paths of the possible in life, and everywhere life set traps for me. Beauty led me to vice, striving for goodness made me commit acts of folly and cause harm to people, striving for truth took me into such a maze of contradictions that I didn't know how to get out of it. Unbelief, petty, cringing, secret vice, disillusionment in something, then—powerlessness... One gets drawn to anything forbidden... We're beckoned by delights that are preternatural... well, even unnatural. We've found out the mystery too early— and are miserable... We've been embracing a phantom, kissing a dream. We've wasted the warmth of our heart in frivolity... we've sown life in the abyss, and our harvest is despair. We don't live the way that we need to; we kept losing the old recipes for life, and we haven't found any new ones. We even were brought up in a strange way: our adolescent daring was stifled lest we emerge from this medium as a man."

Anna listened attentively, though her eyes looked down at the green

18

blades of grass caressing her feet.

"I don't exactly understand all this," she said quietly. "There's so much not completely explained. Too much passion and resentment. And besides, you haven't tried everything."

"Anyway, I *am* making my confession to her," Login thought.

And he was surprised at himself and at his own frankness. Why to her, so chaste, was he talking about vices, and trustfully revealing his soul to her... the poverty of his soul? Like all chaste people, she was severe...

"And why weren't my hopes fulfilled?" he said wistfully.

Anna raised her bright eyes to him and said softly:

"We have many lilies-of-the-valley blooming now in the forests, such lovely white flowers in full bloom. But have you had a chance to see their berries?"

"No, I haven't managed to."

"Yes, and very few people have seen them."

"And *you've* seen them?"

"I've seen them. Bright red berries. And no one else, almost no one else has seen them. The greedy little children pick the flowers, then sell them."

"Hereabouts the flower is better than the fruit," said Login. "The beauty of the flower is the attainable goal for the lily-of-the-valley's life."

He remembered how, over half an hour ago, he had crushed and torn lilies-of-the-valley. He smiled so bitterly that Anna felt vaguely afraid of something. Login did not explain what he was smiling at, even though Anna looked at him inquiringly.

The Yermolins accompanied Login as he was leaving. It was late evening. The air was damp and cool. The fields were becoming covered with mist. The roadside lindens stood sad and motionless. The greenish blossoms of the elder-bushes smelled strange and sharp. The slumbering grass sprinkled dew on the feet of Anna and Anatoly.

Half a verst from the city limits a narrow macadam road split off from the main road. It was about a verst to the Yermolin estate down this road. Some hundred *sazhens* before reaching the estate, the road turned into a private avenue with ancient linden trees growing along both sides.[1] Beyond them on one side were ploughed fields, and one could see the tiny village of Podberyozye. Along the other side, the one towards the town, the linden row was the boundary to the park, which extended quite a distance from the road. In the park there were ponds like lakelets and rivulets, spanned by little bridges, and there were thick little groves and pleasant glades. After the park the garden began. Between the park and the garden, behind the row of roadside lindens and a small yard, stood the house, with a broad terrace looking onto the garden. A tall palisade enclosed the courtyard, the outbuildings, and the garden, so that, from the road, one could see only the front of the house with its two balconies—one at each end of the second story— and with the porch in the middle. The park was enclosed only by acacia bushes. There was free access to it, and the townspeople sometimes came here to stroll. Not very often, however, since it was a long way from town.

"Do you ever visit Dubitsky?" Yermolin asked.

"Rarely, and even then reluctantly," answered Login.

Yermolin laughed. His laughter was always clear and contagiously cheerful. Moreover, he was completely robust: his solid figure, his powerful hands, his spadelike beard—and his lively face, rich with a variety of expressions, his penetrating eyes, even the wrinkles of character on his well-developed forehead—all revealed a man who worked equally with both head and hand. Both of his children were like him.

"But, you know, he speaks highly of you!" he told Login.

"Dubitsky? Amazing!"

"Of course! He says that, of all the people hereabouts, only you understand him. Someone informed him," Yermolin explained, "that you allegedly said all the people around here are weaklings and hypocrites; and, you said, Dubitsky's the only one who's any good."

"Sometimes you say what you don't mean," Anna said with barely concealed agitation, and her eyes blazed.

Login looked at her brightly burning cheeks, and a proud joy stirred within him, God knows why.

"Well," he said, "Dubitsky always stands out as an individual."

"Oh, yes!" Anna exclaimed. "And how he stands out!"

"Even though he does oppress his children," Login continued, "still, he's a man of iron. But all the rest nowadays are just neurotics."

"You mean there weren't any before now?"

"People, as they always were, are ready to gobble up each other. But all of them are personally as flexible as willow switches. That man at least dares to be openly cruel."

"That's why," Yermolin spoke up again, "I have a favor to ask of you: perhaps *you* might succeed in what I'm about to ask of you."

"With pleasure, if I can," answered Login.

"Here's what the matter is: There's a teacher named Pochuyev in our district. He graduated from the local pedagogical institute not long ago. The young fellow's modest and conscientious, wouldn't even think of doing anything wrong. So, now he's getting fired from his job because he held out his hand to Vkusov."[2]

"The police chief? Pochuyev's getting fired for *that*?"

"It surprises you? See what incidents are possible in the backwoods. The police chief rides to the school and goes up to him, an *inexperienced* teacher. Pochuyev held out his hand first. The police chief started bellowing: how dare such a raw youth forget himself so! Before higher authorities he was obliged to wait for them to hold out their hands first! Pochuyev made some objection which was taken as rudeness. How can it be considered rudeness? It was simply a young man in the terribly embarrassing position of being yelled at in front of his pupils. Now it's been decided to fire him."

"How stupid!" Login exclaimed.

"A great deal depends on Dubitsky," Yermolin continued; "as Marshal of the Nobility, he serves as chairman of the school board. He can defend a teacher—if he wants to."

"But, after all, hasn't he already been fired?"

"Well, he can be reappointed, even to another school, if he can't go back to the same one. Nyuta and I have thought it over and decided to ask you to go see Dubitsky and try somehow or other to arrange it."

"I'll be glad to... Why not try? Only, is it worthwhile?"

"Why, how could the matter of where and when a man gets a place in life *not* be worthwhile? Anyway, you should be able to persuade Dubitsky; he doesn't feel kindly toward Vkusov... I would have ridden over to see him myself, only, he doesn't like me: if I intervened in the matter, I'd just spoil things."

Yermolin grinned good-naturedly and sadly.

"All right, I'll go if you find that..."

"Please, just try your hardest," Anna said affectionately, pressing Login's hand.

Her radiant eyes gazed upon him tenderly and trustfully, and it seemed to Login that they peered straight into the secret and inaccessible depths of his soul. And a pure, responding joy rose up within him and shone for an instant in the light that flared up suddenly in his dreamily weary eyes.

The Yermolins said goodbye to Login... He was left by himself. The moist stillness of the evening filled him with a bright sadness. He recalled snatches of the day's conversations, and his recollections drifted by slowly, like the flocks of clouds in the sky, where a few stars shone faintly in the light-blue vault, slightly green near the horizon. Like the sky, which repeatedly showed through the flocks of clouds, one image stood before him persistently—the image of Anna, which wafted its spell upon him... But the farther away Login went, the more painfully the poison of his ancient doubts burned in his heart. Fleeting, joyful, and useless, his dream of happiness agonizingly faded away...

Login thought of the happiness for the one who would fall in love with Anna and with whom she would fall in love. As for himself, Login was now convinced that this happiness was unattainable. Moreover, he could get along without it. His heart was cold, and no delusion of life had any power over it. He was unable to fall in love, and nothing could arouse love in him. His life would expire in loneliness. Cold and depraved was his heart. His intellect rejected carnal love and any form of lust. All his desires—both those that were socially acceptable and those that he had to keep secret—had an equally illicit nature. They all arose from a vain striving to broaden his personality, phantasmal, ever flowing, and doomed to annihilation. Woe be unto the lustful, woe be unto those who hope! Any hope deceives and any lust, in its own way, leaves behind an onerous waste. But then, happy only are those who desire—because any happiness is a dream and a delusion. He who has come to understand life is both glad of it and not glad, and he rejects happiness.

But it was ever so sweet to dream of Anna. Nor was there any envy for that other person's happiness, for the innocent happiness of the one who would take her as his wife.

Anna went into her father's study. She was all simple and pure like the water of a mountain spring. Her thick braids had been undone, and her hair came down to her waist.

It was late. Yermolin was sitting and looking through the newspapers. The mail arrived in the morning, but Yermolin had been busy all day.

On the heavy writing table covered with worn green cloth, a bronze and glass lamp burned brightly under its green shade. Everything here was plain and modest. The wide windows let in a lot of light in the daytime. The open cases along the walls were lined with books packed tightly according to their size on adjustable shelves to that no empty spaces would be left above the books. Also there were a sofa upholstered in morocco, several chairs and armchairs, some photographs in carved walnut frames along the walls, but

22

nowhere anything superfluous, no decorations or knick-knacks.

Anna pulled up a chair and sat down next to her father. She had—as Anatoly did also—the custom of coming to her father every evening. Their conversations alone, sometimes brief, sometimes prolonged, were like confessions. There was merciless frankness and stern judgment. Anna recounted her impressions of the day. This practice almost supplanted her diary. Her diaries were concise, consisting only of memoranda and brief hints: one word signified an entire event; compact formulas contained a whole series of thoughts. Only Anna herself could decipher the short entries in the thin blue notebooks.

"For some reason I'm always thinking about Login," Anna said.

"I like him," Yermolin replied, "but I don't have much faith in him."

"A great struggle is going on within him. It's like a thunderstorm that hasn't struck yet, but already you can see something like heat lightning or real lightning..."

"And hear something like thunder or a cart rumbling along," Yermolin said with a smile as he completed her simile.

"Oh, now you're joking! But, you know, he really does have a hard time. He's being pulled in opposite directions and sees two kinds of Truth at once. He's full of inconsistencies and doesn't even want to conceal them."

"Or else he doesn't know how to. Mental laziness!"

"Boldness, rather. He's like a vulture who's grabbed a chick in each foot: he can't take off with both of them, and he doesn't want to give up either one of them, so there he struggles, flapping his wings in the dust. Login hasn't been able to master complete Truth."

"And he won't," Yermolin said coolly.

"Why?" Anna asked and suddenly blushed.

"Well, because he has no real strength."

"But it seems to me..."

"He makes sound judgments sometimes, and his business will get done perhaps, though by other people. He himself is superfluous."

"Oh, no! There really is strength in him, only it's fettered."

"By what?"

"I haven't made up my mind. But it is real strength."

Yermolin smiled.

"We'll see how it shows itself."

"There's much in *him* that's bad, even wanton," Anna said quietly, as though the word burned her lips. "He needs some great impulse, some upsurge of spirit, perhaps he needs someone to warm his heart."

"That isn't you, is it?"

Anna blushed and burst out laughing.

Anna's bedroom was on the second story. In it the windows were left open all night.

Moist and gentle breezes passed over her bed in the morning. Anna woke up. A rosy light filled the windows. The sun had not yet risen, but aready the glow of dawn played across the sky. Everything was fresh and peaceful. The early morning birds were twittering. Anna quickly got up and walked to the window. A pleasant weariness coursed through her body, and the cold passed through her thin attire.

There was a birch tree beneath her window; its thin, juicy branches were drooping. The garden was still slightly misty. Thin little clouds reddened and glowed in the bright sky.

Anna went out into the garden. There was no one else around. She walked barefoot down the rather damp, sandy paths. The delightful morning coldness enveloped her. Wrapping up her shoulders in a shawl, she felt like walking somewhere far away, but her eyes still kept blinking from not having had enough sleep. She left the garden through the gate and walked in the park, down a dewy path between the elder bushes. The smell of the elder blossoms tickled her nose...

The sun was coming up: a golden rim shone from behind the blue haze of the horizon. Anna went up onto the summit of the bank, to that place where yesterday Login had crumpled the lilies-of-the-valley that he had gathered. Distant points came into view as the rose-pink and milk-white mist dissolved. The dampness and coldness enveloped Anna. It was pleasant. There was also a sad feeling mixed with the pleasure. It all went together: both the joy of life and the sorrow of life. Brisk, bold joy surged through her body, while sadness burned in her heart. Dreams and rational thoughts kept changing place with each other.

All was beautiful but seem unreal—the river with its rose-pink and dark blue waves, the whitish spots in the distance, and the red sky with golden clouds. Behind this scenery the stirring of some invisible force could be felt. This force lay hidden, arrayed itself in elegant attire, beckoned deceitfully, and led one to destruction. The waves of the river flowed on, quiet but tireless and inexorable.

"What force!" Anna thought. "Useless, indifferent to man... All Nature is either unconcerned with us or against us: the wind, blowing idly, and the beasts, and the birds, who for some reason develop all that wild and terrible energy of theirs. Useless streams, obedient to eternal laws, rush on aimlessly, and on their banks people, helpless as children, long to control this ever-moving force."

At home Anna was met by a thin, olive-skinned girl with sharp, angular movements and an unpleasantly loud laugh. She had black eyebrows and thick black hair, plaited into a braid which she wound around her head. A deep red flush glowed on her thin cheeks. This was the daughter of a former local civil servant named Dylin. He had been expelled from the service for his chronic drunkenness; then he had worked as a clerk for the county.[3] But because of his immoderate extortion of the peasants he was also removed from that post; finally he got a position as clerk for some "permanent member" of the local government. Not long ago he had drunk himself to death, leaving behind his wife and nine children. All this motley crew lived in a tiny little house next door to Login.

The girl who had showed up early this morning at Anna's was the oldest of these children. Her named was Valentina Valentinova, or, for short, Valya, which suited her better: she was still quite young and mischievous. After her father's death she had gotten a position as a teacher in the village school near the Yermolins' estate. Now she was on her way to her school from town, where she had spent the night at her mother's.

Their father's death had been a blessing for Valya's family: now he would not sell all his wife's clothes and drink away the money he got for them, and he would not be smashing everything he got his drunken hands on at home. And the sensitive town ladies had come to the aid of the fatherless children: they had fixed up Valya with her teacher's post and had gotten jobs for two of her teenage brothers as laborers in the land-engineering projects which were going on near our town; also they provided the family with clothing and food and money. The Dylins counted the Yermolins among their protectors and therefore would run to them in the hope of getting any sort of odd job or handout. Even now Valya was wearing a red blouse and dark blue skirt that Anna had given her. The shoes that Anna had bought for her Valya had left in town; here she went around barefoot, both in imitation of Anna and as a habit acquired in childhood.

"Tell me, Valya," said Anna, "you've lived next door to Login for a whole year; now then, probably, you know him well."

"Well, yes," Valya answered, with a sharp laugh which made Anna frown slightly, "as well as he can be known!"

"What do you mean?" Anna asked. "Honestly, Valya, the way you laugh!"

Valya blushed and stopped laughing. She regarded Anna with a certain timidity and reverence and tried to imitate her in every way.

"Well, Vasily Markovich hardly talks at all," she explained. "And he's very proud. And somehow he looks so..."

"How?"

"Well, sort of sad, and like he despises me."

"You're mistaken, Valya; he's not proud, and he doesn't despise anybody."

"Only, I'm scared of him."

"What on earth is frightening about him?"

"He's got the power of the evil eye."

"What's the matter with you, Valya? What do you mean by that?"

"Just that: he can look at somebody and put a hex on 'em."

"Honestly, Valya! And you're a *teacher!*"

"But it's true, Anna Maximovna, there are such eyes. It happens when a person's got a certain kind of blood. He can't help it himself, so what can you do? If his blood's..."

"Stop, please!"

"I bet you don't set any stock in sneezes or dreams either!"

"What a silly little girl you are still, Valya!"

"Some *little* girl I am! I'll soon be twenty."

"You mean, you just turned nineteen; and you're still climbing fences. Where did you get *that?*"

Anna took Valya's hand, which had a thin, red, still completely fresh cut all the way across the palm.

"Oh, I got that on Motovilov's fence," Valya explained without any embarrassment whatsoever.

"And *what* were you doing *there?*"

"We went to get a lilac."

"Over a fence, into someone else's garden, to steal flowers! Valya, aren't you ashamed of yourself!"

Valya blushed and chuckled.

"Why, what's so bad about that!" she said to justify herself. "Everybody steals their flowers, even the ones indoors; it shows how much better their flowers are. And besides, why should they miss one lilac? They've got so many it would probably have wilted without ever being noticed."

"But what if they catch you?"

"They won't catch us; we'll run away."

"Even now are you still going to run around with your brothers and sisters to steal somebody's peas just as you did last year? Really, Valya, I shall be completely outdone with you!"

"But, after all, what harm's it to anybody if we each take a handful of peas?"

"A handful each! More like entire apronfuls!"

"But, you see, it's just for fun: we do it to them; they can do it to us. Everybody goes into a turnip patch or pea garden."

"Go away! I'm entirely put out with you."

"Why, I won't do it anymore, really I won't," Valya said, laughing and trying to make up with Anna.

"All right then, but otherwise you'd better not let me lay eyes on you. Now then, why don't you go get busy with the samovar."

Valya scampered off obediently. She was glad to be of service and never refused whatever work Anna might give her. She still wanted to tell Anna the scandalous story from town today, but she did not know yet how to set about telling it. Anna did not like gossip.

Login was visiting Anatoly Petrovich Andozersky. The furniture in his study, where they were sitting, showed careful pretensions to taste and originality.

Through the open windows the crimson glow of sunset could be seen behind the pitiful squat gray houses.

Thick-set and well-fed, thirty-three or thirty-four years old, with puffy, ruddy cheeks and slightly bulging eyes of indeterminate color, Andozersky was dressed in a gray double-breasted jacket which fit tightly around his fat body. He and Login had been classmates in high school and in the university. Inclined as he was to bragging about himself, Andozersky as a youth had been disagreeable to Login, who was often awkward and shy. But nevertheless, in their school years they happened to meet each other often and even have heated arguments. After a few years the service had separated them. For some three years now Andozersky had occupied the post of judge on the circuit court for the district.[1]

"I'm surprised at you, old friend," Andozersky was saying: "You've spent just short of a year here, lived like a recluse, then suddenly, for reasons neither here nor there, you start trying to move mountains with these vague projects. So tell me, if you please, what can come of all this?"

Login grinned lazily and said:

"I certainly haven't invited you to get involved in it; I see that it's not your style."

"I know that you haven't invited me, but you yourself should know... Speaking frankly, old friend, our society still, thank God, is not ready for such things. We have no use for communism and anarchy."

"Please, Anatoly Petrovich, what are you saying? What does communism have to do with it! Get on with you! What conclusions you jump to!"

"Enough, old friend; there's no use pretending. After all, I know which way you're heading. Only, you'll see—mark my word—your own people will betray you."

"Really, you *are* mistaken; there's nothing to betray: we have no secrets."

Andozersky cleared his throat in disbelief.

"Well, that's your business. Only don't get your hopes up. I bet you're just using that society as a blind—just so you might gain time to get good and ready. And then you'll really stir up trouble."

"Anatoly Petrovich, do me a favor and quit trying to be funny," Login said in annoyance. "No one among us has any such thing in mind, I assure you. What kind of rebel am I? And who told you such things?"

"Oh, a little bird told me. Anyway, what are we here for? Why waste precious time? Let's drink up, old friend, let's have a snack with what God's provided; the talk's always merrier over a *good glass of wine.*"

Andozersky stood up, stretched comfortably, and screwed up his little eyes like a fat cat that had just awakened: it even seemed that any minute now he would start purring.

"Let's go to the dining room, brother," he invited Login.

Both Andozersky's manners and his words got on Login's nerves. He was surprised at himself: Why did he keep on visiting this dull-witted and boring man? However, after a few glasses (and the wine really was good; Andozersky knew his business on that score), little by little the giant figure of his host ceased to seem so disagreeable and vulgar. Even the imprint of the stupid but crafty man in Andozersky's smug features was now erased as it were; before Login now sat only a good-natured, cheerful man. Of course—as Login vividly remembered—this good-natured and dull-witted fellow was not to be trusted, but that did not keep him from being a very nice person.

Andozersky waxed candid: "You know, old friend, I'm getting married soon."

Login felt curious: "To whom?"

"Right now, you see, it's still hard to say to whom exactly."

Login laughed: "That means it's still a long story."

"Oh, not at all, you old crank: things are going along splendidly."

"How many likely brides have you picked out?"

"Stop, wait a minute, I'll tell you everything in order: You see, there are three of them; that is, three real ones worthy of consideration, but of possible brides in general there's a whole host hereabouts. I'll arrange for my marriage—just you wait and see. But now let's drink to my brides!"

They filled their empty glasses and clinked them together in a toast.

"Long live your three brides!" Login toasted him. "And may you get married to all three at the same time."

Andozersky chuckled.

"Now what could be better? I wouldn't have to choose any one and could have all the advantages together. Yes, brother, it's a pity that we don't go by Mahomet's law: three wives, and each one with a dowry; you'd wind up with a lovely little harem. But it's forbidden; the only harem you can acquire is one of pictures. By the way, let me show you the lot—apparently you still haven't seen what I have."

Andozersky got up impetuously, went off neighing happily to his study, and after a minute or two returned with a packet of picture-postcards. Smiling indifferently, Login looked through them.

"How about that? Huh?" Andozersky kept asking. "Man alive, that's a juicy one, isn't it?"

"Yes, only, this is all so naive, elementary."

"Well, see if I show you anything again!" Andozersky said in an

28

offended tone and gathered up his cards.

"Anyhow, what about your brides?" Login asked.

"Brides? Here they are, then: first of all Nyuta Yermolin, a lovely little girl. It's a shame, though, that she's been brought up in such a strange way. But a worthy objective. Eh, what do you say?"

"A lovely girl," Login said reluctantly.

"What's the matter, brother? You haven't fallen in love with her yourself, have you?"

Andozersky winked at Login and made his face show an expression of cunning that hardly suited his puffy cheeks and expressionless eyes.

"Look, don't get the idea of winning her over for yourself: you've taken to going there often for some reason."

"Well, that's where I've taken to going."

"However, she really isn't your type."

"And how do you know what my type is?"

"Oh, I just know. She's not for you; a girl who's a bit daft and sharp-witted needs a husband with character, a practical man; and then, old friend, mighty little good will come of it if two dreamers marry each other."

"Mercy, why would I be trying to win over one of your brides? Do I look like a Don Juan?"

"Who knows you dreamers? Still waters run deep. However, don't you even think of it: nothing will work out for you there; I declare to you, that little girl is head over heels in love with me. Whenever or wherever we meet, her little eyes start twinkling."

"So that's how it is! Well, I congratulate you," Login said with a grin.

"Her little eyes start twinkling," he thought, "only, why indeed?"

Andozersky leaned back in his chair and complacently stroked his multi-colored vest, which covered a belly of moderately sizable dimensions.

"Yes, brother, I've already investigated it thoroughly. Maybe even, come tomorrow, the wedding arrangements will come off as big as life. Only, right now I'm still looking and comparing. The other two maybe would be a little more fun, even though they're not quite as well-to-do."

Login kept sipping the wine from his glass, hastily and in small swallows.

"Any fly," he was thinking, "can stick its filthy paws into anything it wants to."

"Number two," continued Andozersky, "is Netochka Motovilov, quite a lovely young lady, don't you think?"

"Yes, Netochka is lovely," Login answered lazily. "She even has a calling."

"To what?" Andozersky asked, even with some alarm.

"To get married."

"Precisely... Her papa, to tell you the truth, is some rogue—of course, that remark's just between the two of us."

29

"Well, now, I'm not about to go off gossiping."

"They're mad at you, by the way."

"Who?"

"The Motovilovs. Because you keep giving their Petka D's."[2]

"Oh, that..."

"You must know he's taking the matter up with others. But, of course, that's your business. Still, everything would be better... oh, if, for example, you started courting Netochka, and, I daresay, if you were a little easier on her little brother. A splendid girl, damn if she isn't... Her papa's got a tidy little fortune, even if it was amassed dishonestly."

"It's just a pity that it'll have to be divided many ways."

"Why, that's no problem, there's enough for everybody. And, you know, the old-timers remember how, twenty-five years ago, when he first showed up hereabouts, he was wearing a ragged overcoat and worn-out boots,—oh, a manifest scoundrel. He was the manager of some fool Petersburg woman's estate. She put her faith in him completely. Nowadays you'd think he's a paragon of virtue, the way he talks! 'Blessed is the man in word but utterly unscrupulous in deed,' as the seminarists say."

Andozersky guffawed.

"She had some nice timberland. He wiped it out completely, and he pocketed the money. Then he married a rich widow. Somehow, quite soon after that, she kicked the bucket, and she had willed all her capital to him. He married his second wife. A lot of other nasty things have been spread around about him. It's said that in fact that will was forged. Even some completely improbable things keep getting said."

"And you want to have such a man for your father-in-law! And you'd chase after such a dowry!"

Login got up from his place and paced about the room. He had long felt a strange revulsion for Motovilov. His every manner seemed hypocritical to Login. Motovilov was a prominent man, and quite indefatigable, and everywhere the townspeople filled the air with the incense of their praises and esteem for him. Finally Login could not even hear the very name of Motovilov without getting irritated.

"What does it matter!" Andozersky said in vexation. "After all, I bet even you wouldn't refuse a pretty little sum of money, would you? And his daughter's nothing to sneeze at. She's quite lovely. Here, let's pick a bottle and drink to her."

Andozersky set about looking through the bottles and seriously examined each one, holding it up to the light. He paused and looked as though Login's words had displeased him: his ruddy cheeks constricted as sternly and firmly as their fat puffiness would allow; his bulging eyes glared angrily toward the place where Login had stopped by the window. He selected a somewhat cheaper wine, a rather inferior brand, and muttered through his teeth: "Here, we'll try this one; it's also a fine little wine."

Login grinned.

"Well, anyway, so how are matters going for you on this score?"

"No doubt about it, old friend, for quite some time the little girl's just been going into ecstasy at the sight of me!"

"Oh, ho! So you've won her!"

Andozersky again grew lively and talked merrily:

"In this place, brother, the young ladies all but fight over me, their mothers too are always thinking how they could catch me for their daughter's suitor. Another fish would have gotten fried long ago, but, brother, I've got the knack. No one's going to pull any tricks on me. Anyway, as for Netochka, it so happens that her papa would be very glad to get me for a relative: it would come in handy for him."

"Indeed?"

"There's some business... Well, now as for the matter at hand... Finally, there's number three. She's also just fine for a bride—Claudia Kulchitsky. A girl that's full of energy and quite intelligent."

"Indeed, smarter than both of us put together."

"Now I don't know about that," Andozersky replied pompously, "but she's certainly no fool. Just the other day she said to me: 'I could live with you; you're not a bad fellow.' A very passionate young lady—I'm just afraid she might run off."

"From you?"

"She won't run away *from* me! I'm afraid she might run to me all of a sudden. That girl's just too fantastic! One look from me, and she'd come and say: 'I'm yours forever.' But I haven't decided yet who's best."

"So that's how it is! But, anyway, why would she have to run away? After all, she is of age, isn't she?"

"Yes, but she's so eccentric: let her think up something, and it's as good as done. She has some little capital of her own—it was left by her father. Her mother was trustee for her and squandered a good part of the daughter's money once she got to carrying on with Paltusov. He's about as much her *cousin* as you're my wife!"

Andozersky laughed gleefully at the comparison he had made.

"He was one of the nihilists," Andozersky continued. "And he got his tail salted. It's said that he had to make a rapid-fire exit from the service: Either he lied himself into a mess or he got caught embezzling. However, he did manage to rake up a pretty penny. At first he and Zinaida Romanovna lived lavishly, went kicking up their heels through all those places abroad. Nowadays they've had to cut down a good bit on their spending. He's taken up speculating—I say this strictly in confidence—and he conducts his business very efficiently, even though not altogether honestly. He's as wise as Solomon."

"But isn't it so that 'a clever man cannot help but be a knave?' "

"Naturally! He's had his nose into more things than any dog around...

31

And he's nobody's fool when it comes to having a love affair. He's set his sights on Claudia now that he's fed up with her mama. The mother's jealous, and the daughter irritates them both to the *nth* degree. Just tell me this, old friend: What makes Claudia so alluring? After all, she's *not* a beauty—green-eyed, pale, and such hair that it's actually not black but blue. What *is* there about her?"

"What is there about her?" Login said pensively, returning the question. "An inexplicable, alluring charm, something enigmatic and supple."

"Precisely, supple like a cat. And ever so wicked."

They sat there long after midnight, talking now of the present, now of the past, mostly of the present: they did not have a lot of reminiscences in common. Login mostly listened, Andozersky did the talking, mostly about himself, and if he did talk about others, then it was always in such a way that he himself stood in the foreground. He was one of those people who are bored when the conversation is not about themselves and who become cross when they are not praised or when someone else is.

It was a warm and bright night outside when Andozersky came out onto the porch behind Login. Their footsteps and their voices rang out in the keen stillness of the street. Andozersky was pleased with his attentive listener and with the conversation, which had been interesting—at least for him; and the little rough edges on the evening were forgotten in that special surge of friendliness that hosts always feel when they see off guests who have stayed with them until quite late.

"I would walk out farther with you," he was saying; "the weather's nice, and it's fun chatting with you; but I've put away a lot tonight. I'd better go fall into bed."

Login felt a slight dizziness from the excess of wine that he had drunk. The vague outlines of houses, fences, and trees swayed as though ruffled by the breeze. But the coolness of the night tenderly embraced him and soothed his burning head. Having arisen with a sweet feeling of rapture, the moon, sinking into the west, tenderly looked over the jumble of his wild thoughts. Login began to feel unusually light-hearted and merry: new forces began churning within him; unknown, mysterious strings rang softly in his heart, as though a transparent song were being born there, filling him with the charm of its sky-blue melody.

Login crossed over a long and rickety bridge. Its narrow foundations dolefully murmured something to the river currents. Login turned and went along the high bank, where the fences of orchards and vegetable gardens extended. Deep in thought, he passed the turn to the street that he would have to take to get to his house—and he went on farther.

Here it was absolutely deserted. The vegetable gardens and orchards still continued on this bank, but beyond the river grain fields and forest began. The air was suffused with warm and moist fragrances. The river babbled in its gravelly bed, wide and shallow. One could hear from afar the murmur and splash of the streams at the mill pond, where green-haired and green-eyed mermaids dwelled, lurking on the bottom. Archipelagoes of stars twinkled in the clear and cloudless dark-blue sea of the heavens. The nocturnal semi-darkness grew thicker in the distance and lay down in dreamy silhouettes, and the mist beyond the river enveloped the lower part of a grove from which individual bushes stuck out in front and showed darkly.

Login noticed that he had gone too far. He looked around and realized that he was standing by the Kulchitskys' garden. The tall trees watched attentively from behind the fence, and their branches did not stir.

Login leaned his back against the fence and gazed at the undulating mist. Something eerie was taking place in his mind. It seemed that the stillness had a voice, and the voice was sounding both inside him and outside him, and it was comprehensible but not translatable into words. His soul was heeding this voice and opening up completely, and drowning in infinity...

It was not the first time that this sensation had overcome Login. In his life there were moments of great feeling, when questions of existence—questions that at another time would appear so menacing, so agonizingly incomprehensible—now seemed easily solvable. He acknowledged himself as truly merged with the world, which ceased being external; and the moment was complete, like an eternity. And as it crowded into his mind, everything in this world was merged and reconciled in a unity that, at another time, would have seemed absurd: sounds took on coloring, smells assumed bodily shapes, and forms rang out and smelled sweet; the intoxicating rosy whisper of the river, the sweet, light-blue trembling of the birch boughs, and the bitter, green sighs of the wind, and the dark-violet, slightly salty echoes of the sleeping town embraced and kissed him like mischievous elves. It was madness, irridescent, sharp, and ringing, and his soul found it sweet to open up completely and dissolve in the unbridled stream of it.

But footsteps, the rustle of a dress, and a hushed conversation were heard in the garden: two people were walking and talking. Then the footsteps stopped, a bench board creaked, the voices abruptly fell silent for a minute... Again the sounds of words were heard, but the words were elusive to the ear. Only once in a while some word or other could be distinguished. A dream put a meaning of its own, sweet and languid, into these words. Login did not want to go away.

A woman's passionate voice, Login dreamed, was saying:

"Love draws me to you, and my heart is full of joy, sweet like sorrow. The malice of life frightens me, but to me our love is joyful and agonizing. Bold desires are flaring up within me—why, then, is my will so powerless?"

"Dear one," answered another voice, "from the horrors of life there is one salvation—our love. Do you hear? The stars are laughing. Do you see? The blue waves are breaking on the silver stars. The waves are my heart, the stars are your eyes."

33

At this point Claudia spoke to Paltusov in a hurried and uneven voice, and her flashing eyes stared straight ahead:

"Do you still keep thinking that I've come here because of you? Malice drives me toward you, do you understand? Only malice alone, and nothing more, absolutely nothing. You've no cause to be happy over it! There's no reason to rejoice! And why are you torturing me? I would have dared, understand, I would have dared everything, but I don't want to because it's disgusting to me, it's entirely disgusting, both you and everything about you."

Paltusov leaned toward Claudia and stared anxiously into her eyes.

"My dear," he said in a slightly hoarse but quite pleasant voice, "listen to me..."

Claudia quickly moved away from Paltusov and interrupted him:

"Listen to me," a mocking note rang out in her voice, "little words like 'my dear' and the other syrupy little words that you've apparently borrowed from Irina Avdeyevna you can keep to yourself, or save them for... well, even for your first cousin."[3]

"Hm, yes, i.e. for your mommy," he said touchily and sarcastically, "for your adored mommy."

"Yes, yes, for my mommy," she replied quietly.

Both the resentment and the tears could be heard in her voice.

The voices fell silent for a moment; then Paltusov again started talking, and again Login lent his ear to the deceptive whisper of a dream.

"Put away your doubts," the voice of her beloved rang out in Login's dreams, "let sorrow be for others; let us take our happiness; we shall be cruel and happy."

"I curse such happiness, evil and merciless," she replied.

"Don't be afraid of it: it will gently lead us away from evil life. This love of ours is like death. When the heart is full of happiness and bursts in an excruciating rapture, life will fade away, and it will be sweet to give it up for an instant of perfect bliss, to die."

"It would be sweet to die. I have no need of happiness. Love, death—it's all one and the same. To melt away quietly and blissfully, to forget the phantoms of life—that is the heartfelt rapture of dying!"

"For the one who loves, there is neither life nor death."

"Why do I feel frightened and hopeless, and why does my love torment me like a hatred? But our bond is inseparable."

"Bitter are these fruits, but having tasted them, we shall be as gods."

And so they spoke of intimate, personal matters in the garden.

"Believe me, Claudia, you're a prey to needless doubts. You're afraid to take happiness where you've found it. Oh, my child, dear child, you can't possible still be so superstitious!"

"Yes, the happiness of revenge is an accursed happiness, and it was even born in an accursed moment," Claudia answered with restrained passion.

34

"Believe me, Claudia, if you should decide to refuse this happiness which you curse—however, you won't reject it—but *if*... oh, I would find enough courage within me to remove myself from life: I can't live without you."

"To die! That's what I want more than anything! To die! To die!" Claudia said quietly and as though in terror, then she fell silent and bowed her head low.

A hard smile flickered on Paltusov's lips. With an inconspicuous movement he wrapped up his throat, then he spoke up insistently:

"We still have a lot of life ahead of us. Even if we just have a few moments, let them be ours. Then, afterwards, each of us can go his own way—you to a convent to pray away your sins, and I... to somewhere a bit farther on!"

"Oh, what have you done to me! It's revolting even to think about myself. Oh, I never was happy; but at least I had hope. Even if it was silly, still, it was hope; and I was so sincerely religious. And all that has died within me. My soul feels empty—and frightened. And my faith was torn from my heart so quickly, almost without a struggle, like a tree without roots. Without a struggle, but with what horrible pain! Can I love you? I always hated you, even at that time when you paid no attention to me. Now even moreso... But all the same, I'll probably follow you if I want to vent all my hatred upon you. I'll go. But why? To enjoy myself? To die? To drag out the convict's barrow of my life? I read that a certain convict chained to a wheelbarrow decorated it with many-colored designs. Have you any idea why?"

"What strange thoughts you have, Claudia! What's the point of this rhetoric?"

"What's the point?" she repeated sadly and listlessly. "What did he do it for? After all, it didn't help him," she continued in compassionate sadness; "he still loathed his wheelbarrow. With tears in his eyes he pleaded to be unchained from it. It doesn't matter, though, how much anyone begs for something!"

"Believe me, Claudia, the time will come when you will regard these tribulations of yours as an absurd dream, although, I don't deny, all this is sincere, youthful... What's to be done? The fruits of the tree of knowledge all in all are not sweet; they're bitter, revolting, like bad vodka. On the other hand, those who have tasted them shall become as gods."

"That's all just *words,*" said Claudia. "They won't change anything in the fate that's in store for us. Enough of this; it's time to go inside."

In Login's dreams the words rang:

"Delight is fleeting, joy will wither and grow cold, just as your hands grow cold with the wind from the river. But let us pick our happy minutes like roses, pick them with greedy hands, and through their resounding death a spectral veil will be thrown open, and there will flash before us the

35

sanctuary of our love, the unattainable non-being. And afterwards, let the folds of the ghostly pall fall heavily again, let a dead force exult—we shall have left it for blessed repose...

"Something inexplicable is trembling in my soul. A feeling that happiness and joy and earthly amusements are pale and feeble things! My innocent hope is so far away, so greatly exceeded by the abundance of my passion! Childlike faith is cancelled out by the uttermost ecstasy of unattainable love. Memory of the past, disappear! Shades and phantoms are dissolving and fading away, my soul is expanding and growing brighter; idols of old are overturned without a struggle before the dawn of love, without a struggle, but making me overflow with sweet pain.

"To love is to embody the impossible of life in a life that is impossible, to broaden one's own existence by a mysterious union, while trying to hold back the headlong change of transient conditions by a sweet deception.

"I thirst so for life that I am ready to become a slave to another, just so that I might live in him and through him. You, who have freed my soul from the glimmers of life's oppressive phantoms, take it: take my soul, free like the blowing of the breeze; take it, that, in its emptiness, it may feel the powerful breath of life. I shall follow you anywhere, whether to delight or to die or to drag behind me the minutes and years of needless existence,— I shall follow you, yours forever...

"The old behests will be fulfilled: we shall be as gods, wise and happy— happy like gods."

A cool breeze was beating persistently against Login's face. He came to, and his reveries were dispersed. In the garden it was absolutely silent. Slowly Login went home. Along with him went someone else, invisible, close, frightening.

As he went onto the porch of his home, in front of the locked door he felt—as he sometimes did at the end of a trying day—that someone was soundlessly calling him. He turned around. Before him stood the bewitching night, mute, inexplicable, calling him somewhere—to a struggle, to a heroic deed, to happiness—how could he guess? He was thrilled by the blissful feeling of *being*. His black thoughts paled and died away; something new and meaningful poured into his chest like a deep breath of exhilirating air... Joy glowed in his heart like dawn in the sky—then suddenly died.

The night was ever so sadly quiet and hopelessly clear. The same damp chill as always blew from the river. It was boring and cold in the empty streets. Wretched little hovels dozed sullenly in the mournful darkness.

Login felt his heavy head whirling. There was a ringing in his ears. Melancholy gripped his heart, gripped it so that it became hard to breathe. It took him a while to stick the key into the lock, open the door, somehow make his way to his bed, and he did not at all remember how he got undressed and went to bed.

36

He fell into a restless and fitful slumber. Miserable dreams oppressed him all night. One dream remained in his memory.

He saw himself on the shore of a sea. Shaggy, white-capped waves were breaking on the shore, right onto Login, but he had to go forward, against the sea. There was a sound shield in his hand, a heavy one, made of steel. He was pushing back the waves with his shield. He was walking over the exposed stones of the bottom, the moist stones; and in the crevices between them, hideous slugs were swarming. Beyond the shield the waves raged and stormed, but Login was proud of his triumph. Suddenly he felt his arms grow weak. In vain he strained every nerve, in vain he first transferred the shield from arm to arm, then leaned against it with both arms at once—the shield was shaking, bending rapidly, falling... With a laugh of victory the waves rushed upon him and swallowed him. It seemed to him that he was suffocating.

He woke up. Church bells were tolling...

CHAPTER FIVE

Claudia and Paltusov entered the house through the terrace. Inside, it was quiet and dark. A flood of revulsion suddenly twisted Claudia's tightly pressed lips. Her hand trembled in Paltusov's. At the same time she realized that for some time she had been neither listening to nor hearing what Paltusov was saying. She stopped and leaned her head toward him, but she still did not look at him. His words rang with passion and entreaty:

"Claudia, my angel, forget your childish fears! Enjoy life while you're alive... It's *good* to love, my darling!"

Abruptly she turned to him—and found herself in his arms. His kiss burned her lips. She pushed him away and shouted:

"Leave me alone! You've lost your mind."

A door slammed somewhere. A reddish light began flickering on the wall of one of the farther rooms—but Claudia and Paltusov did not notice any of this.

"You kissed my mother with those same lips... What vileness! You deceived me, you managed to convince me that I loved you; but it's a lie! I didn't love you, but my hate for my mother; now I've realized that. But you, you—how you've humiliated me!"

Hurriedly, as though he were chasing her, she fled from Paltusov. Gloomily he gazed after her and smiled mockingly.

Paltusov was about forty-five. He was well-preserved. His long, wavy, deep-chestnut hair made him look like an artist. A few little gray hairs showed up on his temples. His face bore a stamp of perpetual irony, somewhat worn-out, though, from being used too frequently. His was the face of a man who is, no doubt, clever, but who has grown accustomed to admiring himself for being cleverer than the people around him, and who knows something that they are still not old enough to know: he regarded people in the same way as a sixteen-year-old adolescent regards twelve-year-old boys, whom he scorns for their age and for their childish games. Sometimes it even seemed that he had managed to become rather obtuse in this constant and ingenuous self-adoration.

Claudia went quickly through the dark rooms. The light of a candle made her stop: She raised her head. Before her stood her mother in an ugly white dress with a great many little flounces. A candlestick swayed in Zinaida Romanovna's upraised hand.

"Come to my room," she said solemnly; "I want to talk with you."

"What does she want?" thought Claudia. "A confrontation in the middle of the night; she can't put it off until tomorrow!"

With her brows knit angrily, she followed her mother into her mother's boudoir, which was lighted by a little rose-colored hanging lamp.

38

Zinaida Romanovna was some five years younger than Paltusov. In her day she had been not bad-looking, maybe even beautiful. But hers was that transient, gypsy-like beauty, which quickly loses its bloom. Now there remained the restless desire to be desirable—she constantly had to resort to cosmetics. However, in the proper lighting she was still quite a stunning woman. Her low, finely chiseled forehead handsomely crowned her small head. Her lower jaw projected forward slightly. She had green eyes, like her daughter, and a body just as shapely and supple.

Claudia resembled her mother, as it often happens with daughters whose mothers do not love them as much as they should: Claudia had the same low forehead, only just the slightest bit higher and not set in such a straight line as her mother's; and she had the same slightly protruding lower jaw.

"You want to talk with me, now?" Claudia said half-questioningly.

Zinaida Romanovna stood before her with her arms crossed on her bosom and looked at her with frightened hatred. Her thin lips were dry from agitation; they trembled and moved soundlessly. The fingers of her right hand kept drumming on her left elbow. Claudia knit her thin brows and stared fixedly at her mother's nervous hands.

"What are you doing, Claudia?" Zinaida Romanovna began. "I've been patient for a long time, but my patience is wearing thin. Tell me, what's the meaning of all this?"

With a sharp movement of her arm she pointed somewhere off to the side.

"I don't understand you," Claudia answered, indifferently, it seemed.

"You don't understand! It's only a minute after you stated that, out of hatred, you've made another woman's husband love you!"

"You eavesdropped!" Claudia said scornfully.

"How naive you are! Should I lock myself up during your intimate talks? So you hate your mother—what a barbarous way to feel!"

"Why should I love you?"

"Why? Well, at least because I bore you and suffered over you. In order that you might see the world, for several months I went around ugly and couldn't be places where I could enjoy myself. When your time came, I cried out in pain like a washerwoman in torment. I assure you, it was all very coarse and inelegant. When you're a mother yourself, you will experience that on your own. But, that in fact is what *love* will lead you to."

Claudia turned red in the face. Her eyes blazed with anger. She turned to go. Her mother restrained her.

"No, wait! My words are no cruder than you actions. Do you know what we have that men need? A sympathetic soul? Beauty? Cleverness? All that's nonsense, my dear—it's just something to spice it up a bit—we just whet their appetite with these things, so that later on they can find out how sweet forbidden fruit is. So then, you'll take your pleasure, up to the limit if

39

you like, until you reach the point that you begin to hate your darling. Those mad, vile kisses will become revolting. And then comes retribution for that 'paradise on earth': your lover absconds, and *you*... if you're not married, you can simply die of shame, or run to some shelter that'll look after you confidentially, and you can leave your child to strangers. Or you can kill it before it's born, risking your life as well as your health. That's what the punishments for *love* are!"

Claudia tried to tear herself out of her mother's hands and kept turning away from her livid face, but her mother held fast to her arms and did not let go of them. Her voice was lowered almost to a whisper, and its hissing sounds made a cutting noise to Claudia like the blows of a knout as they fell harshly on an aching body. Claudia made for the door; the door opened inward, and therefore it was to no avail that Claudia grasped the doorknob with the hand which she had freed with great effort: her mother threw all her weight against her, pinned her against the door, and peered into her face with wild eyes that burned like those of an enraged cat. They were both breathing heavily.

Finally her mother fell silent. Claudia let her arms drop and wearily leaned her back against the door.

"And why the hatred for me?" Zinaida Romanovna spoke up again after a brief silence. "I gave you everything that you need, a good upbringing, and your capital saved up, everything in fact... Yet you still lacked something."

"Your love!"

"What tenderness! It hardly suits you."

"Maybe. In childhood I got used to your being stern and was afraid of you. I thought then that you enjoyed making me suffer. I was hardly mistaken. Only, you petted me when company was around."

"Oh, Claudia, God has punished me through you. Oh, if anyone else ever endured so much in life. I am not guilty of anything before you. I'm your mother, and a mother cannot help loving her own child, in spite of all the insults and abuses."

"What kind of love is *that?* Even now you would gladly have murdered me. But you know that that won't do you any good. You're simply afraid, that's all."

"Enough, Claudia. What should I be afraid of! I've grown used to your threats. When you were still a little girl, you threatened to drown yourself. Childish threats! Nowadays every schoolboy hurls them about. When you're a bit older, you'll realize that maternal love can manage even without displays of affection. You should be grateful to me for everything good in you."

"How strange: For the evil in me, I myself am at fault, but I'm obliged to *you* for anything good in me?"

"Of course you're obliged to me!" Zinaida Romanovna exclaimed. "You're mine altogether. We're both stubborn, we both won't stop at anything. It's my very self in you that I hated and feared!"

"But you hated me all the same!" Claudia said with a mean smirk.

"You and I have clashed just now. It hurts us both, and neither one of us wants to yield. But you must yield! Yes, it's true I was all but ready to murder you; however, you can go to him right now. And *he*–oh, they don't really appreciate love of self-sacrifice. His wife is a saintly woman, and he abandoned her. I have that sin upon me. But now he's even lost interest in me–and I can't live without him. Oh, Claudia, I tell you, leave him alone, or it'll be bad for both of us. I beg you, leave him alone."

Unexpectedly, she fell on her knees before Claudia and grasped Claudia's knees with trembling hands. Claudia bent down to her.

"Get up! My God! What are you doing!" she said in dismay.

Zinaida Romanovna quickly got up.

"Just remember, Claudia, what I ask of you: Leave him alone, or watch out. I'm ready for anything!"

By her burning face it was obvious that this outburst of hers surprised even her: her expression showed a curious mixture of pride, shame, and bewilderment. Impulsively her hands came to rest on Claudia's shoulders and trembled convulsively. Her burning gaze was riveted on her daughter's eyes.

Claudia moved away slightly. Zinaida Romanovna's arms fell down.

"I'm tired," she said. "Leave me alone; I can't stand any more."

Zinaida Romanovna sank down in exhaustion on the chaise lounge. Claudia waited a little while.

"Surely it'll start up again in a minute," she thought with annoyance; "the finale is still not effective enough for her."

Finally she went up to the door and put her slender hand with its long fingers on the brass door-handle. Zinaida Romanovna raised herself up and watched her daughter with avid curiosity, as though she saw her in a new light. Suddenly she stood up, and, with quick steps, she walked up to Claudia. She embraced Claudia and glanced at her face.

"Claudia, my angel," she said in a pleading voice, "tell me the truth: Do you love him?"

"You know," Claudia answered, stubbornly looking downward, past her mother's face, which was inclined towards her.

"No, you yourself tell me straight out, do you love him? Yes, you do love him or no, you don't?"

Claudia was silent. Her eyes looked stubbornly at the brass handle, which gleamed from under her pale hand. Her mother looked up into her eyes.

"Claudia, just do say something! Do you love him?"

"No, I don't," Claudia said at last.

Her green eyes turned toward her mother with an enigmatic expression. Zinaida Romanovna looked at her miserably and distrustfully.

"No, you don't love him," she repeated quietly. "Claudia, this hurts me very much. However, there won't be any more of this, will there? It was just an outburst from your fiery little heart, wasn't it? A mean joke, right?"

Claudia put her palms over her burning cheeks.

"Yes, of course," she said, "he was only joking and having fun with me. You've no reason to take these jokes so seriously."

"Claudia, have more faith in me. Forget your sombre thoughts. You will always find a sincere friend in me."

"Why, I suppose, really, I'm yours as ever," Claudia said after a brief hesitation. "I want to believe you—only, I'm afraid to: I'm not used to it. But, still, it's comforting just to believe *something.*"

Claudia limply held out her arms to her mother.

Zinaida Romanovna fitfully embraced Claudia and thought:

"What burning cheeks she has! Really, the little girl is seductive, though not beautiful by a long shot, *I* was much better-looking at her age; still, youth is a great factor, especially such passionate youth."

Then she kissed her daughter's cheeks and lips. Claudia's lips quivered. An awkward, embarrassed feeling stirred within her, as though she had been caught in some act of deception. She bowed and kissed her mother's hand. Zinaida Romanovna took her chin in her slender rosy fingers, which still trembled slightly, and kissed her forehead. Her mother was so close that Claudia was all but overcome by the reek of her mother's perfume, which she detested.

Claudia could not get to sleep for a long time. She felt stifled and ill-at-ease, and her cheeks were still blushing. At times an unbearable feeling of shame made her huddle in her pillows to hide from the nocturnal shadows, which kept staring her in the face inquistively and mockingly. The cover weighed heavily on her chest, but she modestly hid her arms under it, and pulled it over her head, still higher and higher until the tips of her toes were exposed; then she quickly drew in her feet and wrapped them up in the cover.

Then she was overcome by a whole swarm of thoughts and feelings. She could not resolve their strange contradictions. She kept throwing off the blanket, sitting up in bed, and listening keenly to the indefatigable quarrel of irreconcilable voices. Disconnected fragments of contradictory thoughts at times would dominate her consciousness, crowd out each other, then return, with no sense at all—vain, insistent, and powerless in their impassioned quarrel.

"But what, just what is it? Am I afraid to tell the truth even to myself?" she thought, and immediately she decided that she was not afraid. If the truth had appeared to her right then, she would have accepted it without hesitation, whatever it might have been. But neither in the realm of thought nor in the realm of feeling was there any answer to her persistent searching.

When she called forth the image of Paltusov in her mind's eye, her heart ached with vague, inexplicable feelings. What was it, love or hate? At one moment it would seem that she loved him passionately, then she would feel a flood of dark malice. At one moment her heart would long for his death, then it would grow faint with pity for him.

She kept asking herself whether what seemed love to her might not really be either pity for his passion or pride over his love for her; and whether what seemed a hatred for him was not really her own passionate anger over the fact that she could not have the happiness that had been forbidden her and kept being rejected by her. Or was this succession of agonizing feelings, was even this actually love? Or was it only a vindictive feeling, of petty spite, and had the attempt to cultivate love in her heart resolved itself in a burst of mad hatred for the man who had frivolously revealed to her the means for a sweet and easy revenge for the old offenses she had borne in childhood? And could it be that these oddly pleasant waves that at times coursed through her troubled soul were only the captivating music of a satisfiable vengeance and of self-induced passion? Or were all of these false explanations? Was the truth perhaps somewhere much deeper, and was it much more complex? Or was there a simple and clear solution to these doubts, and did she only have to open her eyes in order to see it?

And what should she do now? Wait and see what time would bring her? Its rippling waves were slow, but they rushed along with treacherous swiftness toward the final, indubitable solution to the riddles of existence.

To wait! Every day of fruitless expectation was bound to increase her interminable torments, to reinforce the insoluble muddle both inside herself and in her relations with those people whose fates were so agonizingly and absurdly interwoven with her own. No, not one day of waiting! In whatever way it might be, she had to take action!

The resolution to act, to go forward, quickly ripened within her. Plans took shape, bold unfeasible plans—her reason laughed at them, but what of it! Nevertheless, she would be taking action...

It was already light when she fell asleep. The twittering of the early morning birds came to her in her troubled slumber, in which she caught fleeting glimpses of the rosy reflections of the morning sun...

CHAPTER SIX

Because it was a holiday, Login's morning was free. Login lay on his couch, dreaming... He kept having dreams that were torrid, tempting, agonizingly wanton. Sometimes he would suddenly feel joyful: Anna's image would weave its way into his dreams—and they would become cleaner, more peaceful. He could not combine *that* image with any unclean idea.

He felt annoyed upon hearing the sound of the doorbell. Rather hastily he went downstairs lest the early guest manage to come up to him. In the livingroom he saw Yury Alexandrovich Baglayev, who, in the circle of his drinking companions, was usually called *Yushka,* even though he held the office of mayor. He was a little older than Login. Red-cheeked, light-haired, short and stout, with a light-colored beard of very venerable appearance, he seemed somehow all soft and pudgy. He was rarely sober, but also he could rarely be seen insensibly drunk; his nature was strong—he could drink up a great deal of vodka. His means of making a living were dubious, but he lived openly and cheerfully. In this town of our his wife was renowned for her hospitality; the dinners at her home were excellent, though by no means lavish; and there was no end of guests in the Baglayev home. Especially a lot of young people hung around there.

At this time Baglayev already was reeking of vodka, and he was not at all steady on his feet. He gave Login a bear hug and cried out:

"Friend, help me out! My wife's not letting me have any vodka; she's hidden it. And we spent the night on a binge, got good and sloshed commemorating Lyoshka Molin."

Login, dodging his kisses any way he could, asked: "What happened to him?"

"What happened to Lyoshka Molin? Did you just come from the moon? Or have you really not heard anything?"

"I haven't heard anything."

"Eh, you conspirator! You sit around and make up plots, but you don't known what's going on around here. Why, the dogs have been barking about this for a whole week now, and yesterday they even nabbed him."

"What did they nab him for? Tell it to me sensibly, then I'll understand."

"Friend o' my heart, I've *got* to take the edge off this hangover; set out the vodka decanter, and I'll tell you all there is to know about it."

"You better drink wine; I don't have any vodka."

"What do you mean, you don't have any! What's the matter with you, fellow? What are taverns for?"

"You know that they're closed; they won't open 'til noon, and right now it's all of ten o'clock."

44

"Oh, Mother of God! How can they be that way? I can't go without something for this hangover. I'll *die* if I don't get a snort of vodka!"

Baglayev's face looked so frightened and dismayed, that Login started laughing.

"Why, Yury Alexandrovich, did you remember Ogloblin's little verse: 'If you keep it up all morning, what'll become of you towards evening?' "

"What's wrong with you? Can't you see I'm clean as a whistle? But I've just got to get one under my belt."

"Here, wouldn't you like to have a snack?" Login suggested.

"Cross yourself! As long as the supply wagons are rolling, I won't have a snack without vodka! I haven't just come from a desert island!"

But there was some vodka after all, and Baglayev blossomed.

"There now," he said joyfully, "I know you just fine. Not for nothing did I come straight to you. How can there *not* be vodka in a decent home? Yes indeed, it's a shame about our *marimonda.* "

"Now what in the world is a *marimonda?* "

"You don't even know that? Why, it's him, Lyoshka Molin."

"Now, who nicknamed him that?"

"He himself did. Brother, he's just got the idea he can swear at anybody. You think he doesn't call you anything? Don't give me that, brother; you're mistaken!"

"So, how has he nicknamed me?"

"You really want me to tell you? You won't get mad?"

"Why should I get mad?"

"Well, look here. He calls you a 'blind devil,' that's what."

Login broke out laughing.

"Well, that's not hard to figure out," he said. "Well, but just what does this word *marimonda* mean?"

Meanwhile, Baglayev had already poured his third glass of vodka.

"Why, here's what it means," he set about explaining. "He says: 'I'm so ugly no girl could fall in love with such a *marimonda;* with *my* mouth I couldn't even catch flies!' Only, he was still a great skirt-chaser—why, he wooed *all* the unmarried girls. And he was really smitten with our Yevlasha. He's a teacher, she's a teacher—so he got the idea that they were a match. He completely sets his heart on her, but she completely turns her *back* on him. But he won't give up. Well, it's well-known, she lives at my house. I had to take up for her. But, anyhow, he's done for, and all because of his female connections. Oh, brother, our Lyoshka's out of our sight now, and a roguish lad he was!"

"Well, what happened to him? Tell me sensibly at last, or else I'll put away the vodka."

"Wait, wait!" he cried out in a frightened voice: "Desperate man! Really, how *can* anyone joke about such things? I tell you in all honesty: they put him in jail. Well, are you satisfied?"

And Baglayev set about filling his glass.

"In jail? For what?" Login asked in astonishment.

Login happened to have met Alexey Ivanovich Molin, a teacher in the town school. Molin was a great carouser and card-player, but nevertheless it seemed strange that he had landed in jail.

"Wait a minute, I'll tell it to you in order," said Baglayev. "You know that he was living at the home of Shestov, the real young teacher?"

"I know."

"But do you know why he moved to Shestov's?"

"Well, why?"

"You see, nobody wanted to have him as a lodger anywhere any more: he raises hell; that's one thing."

"Well, Yury Alexandrovich, it seems you were right in there helping him."

"How do you mean? Brother, he was a past master on that score. We raised ˜uch hell that it got hot in heaven. And the next thing is, he's such a skırt-chaser it's simply frightful: if his landlady's young, he can't keep his hands off of her; if the landlady's daughter shows up, he starts pawing her. And so he was driven from one lcJging to another. It finally reached the point where nobody wanted to rent a room to him. Well, then he latched on to Shestov: 'You've got a place,' he says; 'That aunt of yours and her son,' says he, 'can make room.' Well, now, Shestov respected him very much; brother, he's such a modest fellow: he and Molin went out together all the time and drank vodka."

"And that's what you, your Honor, the mayor, call *modesty?*"

"Get this straight, silly: he did in fact drink vodka out of modesty; the others drink, so how can he refrain from joining them? Anyway, on this matter Shestov couldn't refuse him, so Molin was allowed to live with them, albeit against the old lady's will. Well, so what do you think happened then? He lived with them about four months, then, look here, such a funny thing occurred that it's really quite astonishing!"

"Well, Yushka, did you have any part in this story?"

"Wait, I'll tell everything in order. I don't meddle in bad business. We were visiting at Lyoshka's the other day. A respectable group of us had gotten toɡ ›ther: I was there, and the pawnbroker with his wife, and Bynka, Gomzin, and someone else. We played cards; then the pawnbroker and his wife left, since they had won; but we stayed and visited a little while, old buddy o' mine, until, oh, about three o'clock in the morning."[1]

"A little while!"

"The main reaon's that our hosts got so potted that they slid under the table, and, well, we certainly didn't disturb their rest; rather quickly we drank up the remains and then went home. And here's where the funny thing happened. Right at the crack of dawn the old woman hears Lyoshka going into the hall, and from there into the kitchen. And he stays in there a long time for some reason. Now, their maidservant, a fifteen-year-old girl slept there in the kitchen. Do you sense what that smells of?"

"Well, go on."

"Well, the old woman began to worry why he was taking so long. So she got dressed and marched straight to the kitchen. She's just gone into the hall, when Lyoshka comes out of the kitchen, and of course, he's drunker than hell. He banged into the old woman with his shoulder, didn't even see her, and lumbered off to his room. Well, then she goes into the kitchen. She sees Natalya sitting on her bed, trembling, wild-eyed. You get that? You understand?"

Baglayev winked at Login and started chuckling with mellow laughter.

"What a vile thing!" Login said in disgust.

"No, you just listen to what comes next. In the morning Natalya goes running to her grandmamma. Her grandmamma lives with her on Vorobinka."

In our town Vorobinka is the name of a small island in the river Mgla, an island that is covered over with wretched little hovels.

"She and her grandmamma went to the police inspector. *He* showed them the door, but he himself went to Molin. Well, you know how it is: Molin should have paid off the inspector right away, and the whole thing would have ended then and there. But he got stubborn."

"Staunch fellow!" Login said sardonically.

"A real blockhead," said Baglayev. "He was thinking they wouldn't dare try anything. But he hadn't come across the likes of them before. Yesterday the investigator suddenly appeared at Lyoshka's; they made a search, and then they nabbed Lyoshka. And you can't imagine what rumors have gone around now, it's amazing; it's claimed Shestov and his aunt put Natalya up to it."

"Now, on what account would they have done that?"

"Well, they might have, out of envy, since the high officials in the service wanted to make Lyoshka an inspector—Motovilov was working on it. And folks are mad at the investigator; they say that he too acted out of spite because of Mrs. Kudinov: he's having an affair with her, and Lyoshka once cursed her out. So that might have something to do with it."[2]

The day turned out hot, as days seldom are in our place at this time of year. There were no clouds in the sky, no motion in the air, no moisture in the earth. The sun hurled its harsh rays at the earth that lay defenseless before it. In an open spot one could see how the sky had a smoky haze at the edges. There was a smell of burning in the air; a forest fire was smoldering in the distance. It was sad to behold the young grass which had fought its way up here and there on the unpaved and dusty streets and now was languishing from the heat, drooping, growing yellow and dusty.

People moved along lazily and sleepily. Anyone who could would stay hidden in the shade and idleness of his bedroom. Young ladies under white umbrellas would occasionally pass by on the streets as they went on their way to or from a swim. Maidservants in many-colored scarves would be lugging sheets behind them. Here came Mashenka Ogloblin, a young girl of the merchant class: she was holding her umbrella high; that way her gold bracelet would be seen. She would not take off her bracelet even while swimming.

The splash of water in the swimming holes kept lulling the smooth-streamed river. The slow waters caressed and sang lullabies to the bridge that stretched out over the river. Both the bridge and the street were empty. Only, sometimes a frantic traveler's rattling tarantass would be drawn along over the bridge's rickety planking, or someone's ordinary droshky would go dolefully jingling along—and the disturbed bridge would start creaking plaintively in its midday drowsiness.

A little after one o'clock Claudia went out of her garden gate onto the street. In the morning she had thought of something that must have been of great significance to her. She had hastily written Login a note without either salutation or signature:

"Perhaps what I am writing to you will surprise you. But recently you were saying that I am possessed by sudden, fantastic impulses. Now such an impulse—rather a necessity—compels me to do something decisive. I need to see you: it seems to me that you can say to me the magic word that will set me free. Right now I am going up onto the rampart, to the summerhouse. If I meet you there, you will hear something interesting."

As she sealed the note, she realized that she was acting carelessly, but by now she neither would have nor could have changed her intention; something was urging her on.

And there she was ascending the rampart, and it did seem to her that there something would be decided and completed.

The rampart had been raised in olden days, when our town was subjected to raids from foreigners. It enclosed the town square, which was shaped like an extended quadrangle. The rampart was a little less than a verst in width and some eight sazhens in height. Formerly, they say, it had been higher, but it had grown weary of standing and had collapsed. Only its outlines would remind one of its past design. It had blunt ledges on the long sides and minutely protruding bastions on these two ledges and at all four corners. It had a peaceful and even a cheerful look about it: not for nothing did the townspeople like to stroll here in the evenings. About halfway up the rampart two terraces extended, one on the exterior, the other on the interior side, and each about two sazhens wide. Both these terraces and the slopes of the rampart were overgrown with grass. On top of the rampart a narrow little footpath had been beaten out. For thoroughfare into the fortress, two gates had been made in the eastern and the northern side of the rampart. Beneath their brick arches it was damp and gloomy, and sounds reverberated easily.

In the middle of the fortress was an ancient cathedral with its white walls and green, slanted roof that gave it a cheerful appearance making it seem not so old as it really was. The onion-dome cupola with its rusty cross rose up above the sanctuary of the church. To the west of the cupola, on the slopes of the roof, two little onion domes stuck out, each about two *arshins* high.[1] These domes were like applies on thin little legs, apples with a point added at the top. They were so incongruously small that they seemed like strange birds that had migrated from somewhere; hence, one could even imagine that all of a sudden they might jump onto the ground and go hopping off on their thin little legs.

South of the cathedral was a stone jail; its walls shone brilliantly white. The warden's vegetable garden clung to the foot of the rampart. The pale prisoner looked out from behind his bars at the red and blue rags which were drying on a fence, looked at the greenery on the rampart, at the blue sky, at Claudia's pale-yellow attire as she walked along the upper path at a quick pace—and at the birds, which, to his eye, flew by a great deal faster and seemed like black dots or multi-colored streaks.

The buildings of the local garrison stretched out over the area north of the cathedral: a two-story brick barracks, a wooden stable, and a tidy little stone house, the office of the garrison commander. Here also were vegetable gardens. Figures of soldiers flashed by in their red shirts, and they seemed peaceable people. But by the barracks wall a cardboard figure of an enemy with a painted gun stubbornly stood by itself in the weeds—an object for target practice.

Between the barracks and the eastern gate of the fortress, a quadrangular pond lay stagnant, with the surface of its water as still and dull as lead. It watched everything passing by above it and kept angrily silent. It was getting overgrown with green duckweed around the edges.

The southern base of the rampart was separated from the river by a yellow strip of road. At this spot the river was shallow, divided into two streams, and encompassed Vorobinka. Vegetable gardens and grassy vacant lots embraced the base of the rampart on the other three sides.

A summer-house in a little plaza on top of the short southern side of the rampart impressed one with its beauty; it was brightly painted and ornamented with fretwork in true Russian style. The seal of the province was painted on all six doorways of the summer-house. The summer house had been built to honor a recent official visit from the Tsar: from it His Imperial Majesty could admire the town. It was decided to preserve the summer-house, both for its beauty and as a monument.[2]

Login and Claudia met on the rampart's footpath, exchanged a few words, walked on into the summer-house, then sat down in silence. Claudia kept tapping the wooden floor with her umbrella and squeezing its ivory handle. Login gazed at the town absentmindedly.

From here the town was pretty. The birch trees at the foot of the rampart did not block the view. Even though the poplars had had their tops chopped off, their upper branches still somewhat obscured one's view of the town. But the poplars grew only on the eastern terrace. There were none here.

The central part of town by the large bridge could be seen as plainly as the back of one's hand. The green gardens by each house; the violet, dusty expanse of streets half hidden by houses; the grayish clusters of wooden hovels with red, blue, or gray roofs sometimes bright after a recent painting, sometimes dull and faded by the rain; brown hedges and fences that leaned in all directions: all this was beautifully blended and gave the impression of a quiet and peaceful life. The occasional harsh sounds from below did not fly up this far. The tiny figures of people now and then passing by seemed silent and motionless; horses' hooves, as it were, did not clatter over the stones of the abominable pavement, nor, so it seemed, did the wheels of a tarantass rumble as it moved slowly through the market place; people, gesturing as they met each other, resembled marionettes in a puppet show.

The river curved in beautiful expanses. It formed little swimming holes. In some of these, where people were bathing, the water was splashing. Here and there boys were catching fish and, for this purpose, even waded out into the river itself. In the distance, beyond the last shacks of town, white foam gleamed, watery sprays sparkled in the sunlight, and the bodies of swimming children glistened. But even the ringing shouts of the children did not reach here.

It was absolutely quiet here. Only sometimes a bee would buzz pompously as it flew by, and the wind would rustle in the thick, prickly, and tangled grass and would babble with the branches of the birch trees which crept up the inner slope of the rampart and were absolutely unable to reach the top. But in fact the wind today sprang up only now and then, and feebly at that, not as on other days.

"I don't like to be here in the evening, when people are strolling about," said Login, "but in the daytime, when there isn't anybody."

Claudia looked up at him. The flicker in her eyes was sombre, as though she had had to force herself to listen to his remark; she then asked:

"You don't like a crowd?"

"I don't like being in a crowd, making up part of a crowd."

"But without a crowd places are empty... and dull."

"But why be in a crowd? To contemplate the Kalmyk faces? Crowds around here always have an Asiatic look: uncouth bodies, non-European faces... It's true, Europe ends there, at the border."

"And our land is what, Asia?"

"No, just simply a sixth of the world... Anyway, it's good that this rampart was heaped up. It lets one enjoy the innocent pleasure of getting up ever higher and higher, away from the flat ground. It inspires the soul. One can breathe proudly and happily when the town, with its dust and dirt, is far below one's feet. After the trivia and nonsense of day-to-day life, this is the only place where one can come and find comfort."

"There are other comforts in life," Claudia exclaimed.

"Like what?"

"Loving, feeling passion, burning your candle at both ends, fulfilling every moment by struggling ardently for what you want."

Login smiled faintly.

"How are *we* going to do that? In this nervous age no one has the strength to accomplish anything. With the temperament of a disillusioned frog, how can we go in for adventures?"

Claudia's face turned pale. She asked impetuously:

"How have you kept living up to this time? Now you have your idea, and it gives you a reason to live. But what did you do earlier?"

"I sought the truth," Login answered quietly.

Even he could tell that Claudia was under a considerable strain. His face assumed a sad and serious expression.

"The truth?" Claudia repeated the word in amazement. "And just what is it?"

"I haven't found it; I merely made the mistake of getting entangled in controversies."

"You haven't found it!"

"Right. I haven't found it anywhere, neither on the main highways nor on the remote country roads. And there's no point in seeking it."

"Why?"

"Clever people say: 'There was truth on earth, but not within our memory.' "

"A witty slogan!" Claudia said scornfully.

Login looked at her sadly and thoughtfully. He said:

"But perhaps the truth might have been found, but there wasn't enough patience or love, and my strength was not sufficient."

"Truth! What is it to be found in? All this is pedantry!" Claudia said in annoyance. "You have to live, simply live, hasten to live."

"Why is that so absolutely necessary?"

"Listen, I wanted to see you. All this was terribly indiscreet of me. But I can't go on waiting! I want to live, to live in a new way, even if it should bring me sorrow, as long as it would be different. Any why such bookish views on life? Take it as it is, and whatever you get your hands on along with it."

"Excuse me, but I think you're mistaken about me, and even moreso about yourself."

"Indeed? I'm mistaken?" Claudia asked in a voice that was suddenly faint. "Perhaps."

"I mean to say that even in our present life there is a great deal of value."

"You may be right; I don't know. In childhood even I had everything that everyone else had, everything you'd expect, even pleasant reassuring thoughts. I waited, with such radiant hopes, for the time when I would be big. Well, now I *am* big. And this business of living has turned out to be hard. And my hopes have vanished imperceptibly, like water evaporating from a saucer. Only the big questions of life remain. And people everywhere are all alike, dull and useless to me. And everything everywhere is uninteresting, this whole routine of life, and these boring habits. And my thirst always keeps growing."

"Why, that happens to everyone. We appease this thirst by working, by striving for independence, for dominion over people."

"Work! Independence! What for? I want to live on life, not on ideas."

"Work is a law of life."

"Oh, those words! Perhaps they're clever words, but forget them. After all, I don't live between the covers of a book: I've got a real flesh-and-blood body; I'm young, high-spirited, nimble. I'm stifled by resentment and despair. The thought of staying here frightens me. All that I'm saying, I feel, is disjointed and incoherent; I'm not saying what I need to; I can't get the words together... I need to go away and burn up, burn up all the old in me."

"I understand you. Life has its own unbreakable laws. It throws people together, and there's no point in resisting it."

"Indeed? You do think so? It was quite absurd of me, asking you to come here. And do you know why? So that I could say: Take me."

Her pale face was trembling all over with excitement and passion, and her eyes stared unflinchingly at Login. Their queer, frightened expression attracted him with a strange fascination. A sweet and passionate feeling began to seethe within him, but in his consciousness there was something cold that sadly and sternly kept suppressing his excitement and prompting him to give restrained answers. As he uttered them, he felt that they were silly and feeble and that each of them tore up something, committed something irreparable. He said:

"Take a deeper look into yourself, test yourself."

Claudia did not listen but continued:

"Take me, even if only for a while. Break my heart, then abandon me. It will be sorrow, but it will be life; now, however, there's no way out, as though I were standing before a blank wall. Even if you don't love me, it doesn't matter; just save me! Have pity upon me, make me feel loved!"

"You're mad, Claudia Alexandrovna. And what good will it be to you if I get infected with your madness?"

Claudia blushed all over. She said:

"I know, you're saying that because you already love—Nyutochka."

"I? Love Anna Maximovna? Oh, no... hardly... But why..."

"Yes, perhaps even you yourself don't know it, but she has captured you with her quick little eyes, her clever sayings, which she got out of books, and her affected simplicity—the coquetry of simplicity."

Login laughed slightly.

"Now, now, I wonder what girl doesn't have something of the coquette in her!"

"Don't argue: It tantalizes your dirty imagination—a rich girl going around with her bare feet on the dusty roads. That simplicity exceeding the limit, a way that nobody else anywhere ever acts—how alluring and interesting it must be!"

"You're being unfair!"

"I thought you were more original than to get attracted to a girl (whose head is as empty as the palm of my hand and who's as sweet as almond candy)—just because her half-addled father stuffed her with ideals (not that she understands them any too well!) and because he trained her not to be afraid of the dewy grass!"

"Maxim Ivanovich is a clever man."

"Oh, he could be a mental marvel for all I care! But, listen: I'm prettier than Anyutka and more daring than she! And what's so fine about her? Everything about her is ordinary—the healthy country maiden."

"She has real redeeming courage," Login said with conviction, "and not that furious but impotent daring that speaks so blatantly in you."

"What are you saying! I'm braver than she is; I'm not even afraid of what frightens Nyuta. Here, do you want me? I'll come to you. I'll..."

"You're a beauty and you're brave," Login interrupted. "Maybe you're right; maybe I do love her— but even you, you too love someone else."

"Indeed?"

"It's time that you should love. Go to him with that burning passion."

"Can you really not know that women do not forgive what you've done just now?"

"I just gave you good advice... If you'd needed a vulgar surrogate for love..."

Claudia stood by the exit from the summer-house and put on her gloves. Her eyes and Login's met. An insane hatred was reflected in Claudia's face. She quickly walked out of the summer-house.

About four o'clock in the afternoon Login was sitting in the living-room of Dubitsky, the Marshal of the Nobility. The host, a tall, fat old man in a military coat (he was a retired major general), kept looking at his guest with a gracious but self-important air, and his great weight pressed down hard on the springs in his broad sofa.

Here everything was in strict decorum. The heavy furniture had been arranged near the walls in irreproachable order. Everything gleamed with absolutely military spotlessness: the parquet floor was as shiny as a mirror—in fact there was not one speck of dust on it; the furniture shone as though it had just been varnished, and, on the cornices on the walls, the gold leaf looked as though it had just been applied, the brass and bronze as though they had been polished just an instant ago. A solemn stillness reigned in these quarters. Although Dubitsky had a lot of children, not the slightest rustle could be heard anywhere, except maybe an occasional cautious shuffle of footsteps somewhere not far away.

It was hard for Login to talk about the matter for which he had come. He knew that to succeed he would have to say something that would please the general, but playing the hypocrite disgusted Login. Now he felt annoyed with himself for having taken on this awkward mission. However, he had to say something, for Dubitsky was looking at him more inquisitively by the minute, and the phrases that he uttered in his hoarse voice were becoming more and more disjointed.

"Please excuse me for the imposition, Sergey Ivanovich," Login said at last: "I've come to you to ask a favor."

Dubitsky's sullen face with its low forehead and narrow eyes did not show the least surprise, and he quickly replied:

"I noticed!"

Login smiled wryly and wondered, "How do I look like a suppliant?"

"You want to know why?" asked Dubitsky, and he did not wait for an answer, but explained: "If you had not come with some request, then you would have crossed your legs, but as it is, you've kept them side by side."

Dubitsky guffawed, and his whole enormous torso began swaying from his hoarse, oppressive laughter.

"I must say," Login replied, "Your Excellency's powers of observation are quite keen."

"Yes indeed, my very kind Vasily Markovich, I've seen people in my time. You'll live to be my age and won't have a tooth or a hair left, but I'm not at all a complete wreck yet, as you can see."

"You're remarkably well-preserved, Sergey Ivanovich; you're still a long way from being old."

"Yes, indeed, I'm a staff of vintage wood. In my time people weren't as they are now. Nowadays, pardon me for saying so, people have all become milksops; but in my day, dear fellow, they were tough as nails. Well, so what can I do for you?"

Login began to explain the purpose of his visit. Dubitsky interrupted him at his first words and even began waving his arms.

"Yes, yes, I know! Pochuyev, the former teacher; how could I not know about such an outlandish young fellow! Oh, he's fired, fired! I don't care if he has to search the world over for a job, I'm not having anything to do with him."

"But, Sergey Ivanovich, since it was the first time he did anything like this, I would ask you to be lenient on the young man."

"What are you saying to me about 'the first time'? Will you also demand lenient treatment for whoever bumps off a man for the first time? Or to your way of thinking, to the *new* way of thinking, is it not the thief who is guilty but the man who was robbed? Huh?"

"Your Excellency, the young man's fault—if it can be called a fault—lies only in his lack of experience."

"If it can be called a fault!" exclaimed Dubitsky. "Could you happen to have any doubt of it? It was disrespect for his elders, it was a bad example for the boys. They need to have subordination instilled in them."

Dubitsky angrily pounded the arm of the chair with his fist.

Rather feebly Login spoke up again, "He wanted to greet the police chief, he wanted to show respect for him, only he didn't know how to do it properly. And besides, really, it's no great fault. So he held out his hand first—how could *that* hurt or offend anybody?"

"No sir, he was very wrong! Today he treated the police chief too familiarly; tomorrow he'll disregard an order from his own chief, and then, you'll see, he'll even get involved in turning out propaganda. No, in such positions as his, we need *loyal* people!"

"Of course," Login continued, "our police chief is a highly respectable man..."

Dubitsky cleared his throat, not really indicating either agreement or denial.

"We all know that Peter Vasilievich quite deservedly enjoys our general esteem."

"So far as police chiefs can be esteemed," Dubitsky said sullenly.

"But, Sergey Ivanovich, wouldn't it have been better if he had been magnanimous and left the matter alone and not gotten so angry at the young fellow? And then, after all, it could have happened that Peter Vasilievich set himself up for it."

"In what way was this, allow me to ask?" Dubitsky exclaimed menacingly.

"Your Excellency, I'm only letting myself make an assumption. It could have happened that Peter Vasilievich, with that genial physiognomy of his, entered the classroom a little bit 'lit up' (as we say), and let out some salutation in that French dialect of his, something like: 'Mercy and bonjure, mess infants, yenonder-shish!'[1] You can understand why the teacher felt a lot less timid."

Dubitsky guffawed loudly and hoarsely.

"Could be, could be," he repeated in intervals between laughing and coughing. "Our chief of police, to tell you the truth, is some clown. In my opinion he's got no business sticking his nose into the schools—he can't collect any of our unpaid taxes there. But at any rate, there's nothing I can do about it: Pochuyev's fired."

"Your Excellency, you can change it if you only want to."

"I'm not the only one to decide about that."

"But, Sergey Ivanovich, who on earth will go against you? You have only to say the word."

"I don't know. It serves him right. He can't stay in that school: the students would think they could get away with misbehaving."

"But couldn't he go to another school?" Login inquired with careful deference.

"To another? Well, we'll think about that, maybe. But I don't promise anything. Yessir, my very kind Vasily Markovich, discipline is the first thing in life. Our people couldn't get along without it. We need to go back to the good old days. Where, let me ask you, do they have strict morals? In the East, that's where. Respect for elders, obedience... Here, let me show you my piglets; you'll see what obedience is."

Login's heart sank as he anticipated an unpleasant scene. Dubitsky rang the bell. As soundlessly as a shadow, a young housemaid appeared in the doorway. Her apron was snow-white and faultlessly neat. She looked at Dubitsky with frightened eyes.

"The children!" he ordered in his commander's voice.

The maid disappeared soundlessly. Not a minute passed before the children appeared from the same doorway. There were two schoolboys, one fourteen, the other sixteen, a nine-year-old boy in a little sailor jacket, three little girls of various ages from ten to fifteen. The little girls curtsied, the little boys clicked their heels for Login, and all six stopped side by side in the middle of the room, lined up in order of height. They were well-fed and big for their ages, but their faces showed a somewhat timid, somewhat dull expression. Their eyes were dull but uneasy; their cheeks were rosy, but their lips quivered.

"Children, attention!" Dubitsky commanded.

The children froze: their hands were held motionless at their sides, their feet were held together, toes apart; their eyes were riveted upon their father.

"Start dying!" the second command followed.

57

All six feel down on the floor at once, fell as flat on their backs as if they had been knocked down, without sparing the backs of their heads from getting banged against the floor; then they started rolling their eyes and stretching out. Their arms and legs twitched convulsively.

"Die!" shouted their father.

The children grew still and lay motionless, rigid like corpses. Dubitsky gazed triumphantly at Login. Login took off his pince-nez and carefully examined the faces of the prostrate children; these faces with their wide-open eyes were so imperturbably calm that it was disquieting to look at them.

Dubitsky again gave them a command: "Sneeze!"

Six corpses sneezed in unison and again grew still on the impeccably clean parquet.

"Attention!"

The children jumped up, as though they had been tossed up from the floor on springs, and they took their places at attention.

"Laugh!"

"Cry!"

"Dance!"

"Spin around!"

Their father commanded—and his children laughed obediently and even very heartily, wept (albeit without tears), danced zealously, and spun around tirelessly. And all this they performed all together and identically. At the conclusion of the performance they lay down on their bellies at a command from their father and crawled out of the livingroom one by one, the little ones first. Login sat there speechless and looked at his host with amazement.

"Well, how about that?" Dubitsky asked in triumph when the children had crawled out of the room.

A faint rustling in the next room was heard for a brief while; there the children were getting up off of the floor and withdrawing quietly to their own lairs. There was something terrible in their noiseless disappearance.

"Yes, that is extraordinary obedience," said Login. "Just like that, at your command, they would eat each other up."

A shudder of revulsion ran down his spine.

"Indeed they *would* eat each other up!" Dubitsky cried out in a delighted voice. "And they wouldn't leave any bones behind. But they get plenty to eat. I don't starve them: they're fed in the Russian manner, quite enough, it would seem, on both buckwheat kasha and birch kasha.[2] They won't get fat and lazy; and they get lots of fresh air."

Login rose to leave. He felt sad.

"Now that's how discipline should be," said Dubitsky. "It's better to beat one senseless and teach a hundred than to rear two hundred blockheads and nincompoops. But are you leaving already? Have dinner with us, won't you? No, you don't care to? Well, do as you wish: 'Freedom for the free, heaven for the saved.' "[3]

When that same noiseless, aproned maid had just helped Login into his overcoat in the entrance hall, Dubitsky, taking up almost all the space between the doorposts with his broad figure, appeared in the doorway to the anteroom and said:

"So be it. He's young and green, and should have gotten a good whipping, but your Pochuyev will receive a teaching position,—only because of you—but, anyway, so be it."

Login started to thank him.

"You needn't, you needn't," Dubitsky stopped him. "I'm not a merchant-benefactor.[4] What I've wanted to do I've done. You just tell him that he'd better keep his nose clean and his best foot forward. Otherwise, it's all over for him! And then no entreaty of any sort will do him any good, none—by God—none!"

Login went straight from Dubitsky's to Yermolin's. Several people had gathered there to talk about the society which they proposed to establish hereabouts according to Login's idea. Login had set about writing a draft of regulations. Today it had to be read through and discussed.

When Login arrived, three people besides Yermolin and Anna were sitting on the terrace: Shestov, Konoplyov, and Khotin. The voices of Anatoly and Mitya, Shestov's first cousin, rang out in the garden; the boys' bare feet flashed merrily on the grass. It seemed to Login that Anna raised her bright eyes more than once to greet him. The folds in her sarafan hung down straight. There was something amazingly serene about them.

Yegor Platonovich Shestov, a young teacher working in the same school as Molin had worked before his arrest, was a short, thin youth with light blond hair and blue eyes. By reason of his youth (he was 21) he was still innocent and had not lost the boyish quality of blushing with any deep emotion. He was inordinately bashful and indecisive—as though he never knew what he had to do and sometimes, perhaps, did not know what he wanted and what he did not want. Therefore he was inclined to be submissive to anyone. When he went visiting, it was hard for him to decide when to leave: he would always wait until the rest of the company got up to go. If there was no guest besides him, he was prepared to stay on endlessly; when he finally noticed that his hosts had become bored to distraction, then he would slink off after his cap in such embarrassment that it looked as though he were trying to steal it. Thereupon, they usually would ask him to visit a while longer (although they would really have been glad if he had left); he would refuse once, mutter, "I really mustn't," or "I should have left long ago," and would end up by staying. When the hosts would yawn and show no further signs of wanting to keep him around, then he would leave, tormented by the thought that he had stayed too long and talked no end of rubbish. The latter point worried him not without good reason: he was very much at a loss for words in conversation and had to wring them out of himself whenever he was in some situation where he absolutely *had* to talk about something, and sometimes, in a fit of distraction caused by his bashfulness, he was capable of saying something quite tactless: at one time he might mention priests who went around stuffing their pockets—and a priest would happen to be present; at another time he might start talking about "old maids" around maidens who could be offended by such a phrase; or he might take to thumbing through an album and, not knowing that a certain portrait was of his host's mother, would ask the lord of the house:

"Who's this old lady who looks like a rabbit?"

At that, the host would answer in annoyance:

"That's, well, somebody I know..."

And he would start talking about something else. Always, after any such escapade, Shestov would instantly grasp what the matter was, and he would blush furiously: he would not have intentionally said anything distasteful to anyone.

Since, in spite of all this, he was impeccably honest, was quite fond of reading books, and, for all his bashfulness, passionately loved talking and arguing with anyone over questions that interested him and was, moreover, prepared to reveal his most cherished convictions and most ardent hopes to any chance fellow in conversation, it is understandable why he seemed disagreeable in the company of *favorable* and *respectable* people.

Savva Ivanovich Konoplyov was an instructor in the local pedagogical institute. He was tall and scrawny like a weed, to use a popular simile. His face was encompassed by a shaggy red beard, the sort that makes a person look like a monkey. He had on a black coat that was quite worn and was shiny at the elbows; under his coat he wore a blue calico shirt with a red worsted collar. His gleaming, darting eyes, swift awkward movements, rapid, indistinct speech (such a swarm of words passed through his mouth that he sometimes even spattered people with saliva) all made him look like a maniac, like someone who had just gone off of his rocker. His cheeks were too sunken, his chest inordinately narrow, his hands extraordinarily long, bony, and large-veined. It was immediately obvious that he was both fussy and muddleheaded.

Ivan Sergeyevich Khotin was a small local merchant. He wrote verses and recited them, much to the delight of our petty-bourgeois and minor civil servants. In town he had only one rival, and that was also one of the merchants—young Ogloblin. The latter, however, was more educated, had finished high school, whereas Khotin had not completed his studies in the *uyezd* grade school. Ogloblin's verses were printed in a provincial sheet and sometimes even appeared in some weekly published in the capital. Khotin's endeavors to get his work published were unsuccessful. Khotin was hurt and became convinced that, without someone's official patronage, you could not even break into print. Although barely literate, he was a person full of enthusiasm and loved to dream. His store was faring poorly: he did not feel quite himself behind the counter. He was about forty. He had a long black beard. He had a considerable bald spot on his head.

Login had gotten to know him through his verses. Khotin had brought his verses to him: Login had told him his opinion. Khotin seemed interesting to him: the statements that he made showed a seething, implacable thirst for justice. He would talk about town affairs with sorrow and concern. But Login knew that Khotin was one of those "schlemiels" who are fated to make a mess of whatever business they get involved in.

In spite of the absentmindedness that had come over Login lately, he generally maintained a remarkable degree of psychological insight, a well-established, inborn quality, as it were,—at any rate it had developed without any conscious effort on his part. He was rarely mistaken in his estimation of people. Even though his new plan was making Login seek out people, nevertheless, it had not made him blind to their faults. These people that had gathered at Yermolin's were the only ones who had become interested in the matter, each in his own way, so that with them it was possible to "make a beginning."

"If we only *can* make a beginning!" thought Login.

For they would immediately be faced with a struggle for their right to work under different conditions.

"What new have you heard?" Konoplyov asked Login when the latter had said hello to everyone.

"The townspeople, you know, are only interested in one thing: they're delighted at the scandal."

A scornful expression passed over Anna's face. It seemed to Login that her eyes dimmed. Immediately Login regretted that he had begun with such a remark, but suddenly this feeling inside him gave way to a malicious delight so strange that it startled him.

"Yes, that case of Molin," Khotin said, "is a foul thing. It's got all our petty shopkeepers in quite a bad temper."

"That Molin of yours is scum!" Konoplyov cried out to Shestov. "I always said so. And furthermore, the girl, to tell you the truth, is a slut."

"No, you're mistaken," Shestov said, blushing. "Alexey Ivanych is a very honorable man."

"Why, of course, honorable people always do such things!"

"But, really, he's absolutely innocent in this matter."

"Well, so much the better for him. But how do you know?"

"Why, he assured me that it was so."

"And that's all. A lot of proof that is!"

Konoplyov slapped his kness with his long arms and guffawed.

"Molin wouldn't lie," Shestov objected strongly. "He's an honorable and intelligent man and knows what he's doing, and his pupils respect him."

"Oh, get on with you! He's an out-and-out scoundrel!" Konoplyov said resolutely and even with irritation. "You just liked to hang around with him! I'm glad that at least one hypocrite has been unmasked."

Shestov was very much distressed by these cutting remarks about his colleague and was on the point of saying something more in reply. However, Yermolin intervened in the conversation; up to this time he had been silent and had been watching Shestov affectionately and sadly with his wistful blue eyes.

"Let's not quarrel because of him," Yermolin said in a conciliatory voice. "Whether he's guilty or not, it'll all come to light."

Somewhat bashfully, somewhat pensively, Anna gazed down at the ground and said quietly:

"Even talking about him is unpleasant. It always embarrassed me to look at him: he's so insolent and clings to everything, like a cocklebur."

"And gives everybody insulting nicknames," said Khotin.

It was evident that he remembered one of these nicknames, perhaps one that pertained to someone in the present company,—and he could hardly keep from laughing: his face showed a glimmer of that wicked feeling that overcomes many of us when we recall how people have laughed at or insulted some friend of ours.

Shestov turned scarlet. It occurred to Login that Molin could have applied some crude nickname to Anna, and that made him furious. Quickly he looked at Anna. Her lips quivered faintly in disgust. She extended her arms forward as though she were forbidding any further discussion of the matter. Her gesture was peremptory.

"Here's more important news," said Yermolin. "In our province, they say, there have already been some cases of cholera."

Khotin sighed, shook his head, and said:

"That wooden barrack, obviously, wasn't built in our area for nothing."

"A plague on your tongue!" Konoplyov cried angrily. "Why do you croak such things!"

"Croak or don't croak, it's upon us already. Have you heard what the common people are jabbering?"

"Well, what?" asked Login.

"They claim for a fact: the barrack was built to exterminate people, that healthy people will be strung on boathooks, and living people will be put in a grave and covered over with quicklime."

"But still the cholera's for the better," declared Konoplyov.

"How on earth is that?" Khotin asked in really a rather sensitive tone.

"Oh, in that they've at least cleaned up the town a bit."

All were silent. No one wanted to say anything more about the cholera. It was still far away, and the bright spring day with its joyful greenery, with its gentle and merry rustling of branches and carefree chirping of birds, did not believe in cholera and hastened to live its own present life. But that conversation made Anna remember another distasteful matter, but closer to these flowers and sounds of spring.

"Vasily Markovich, have you been to Dubitsky's?" she asked Login, and, anxiously awaiting his reply, she inclined her handsome figure in his direction and leaned with her bare arm on the edge of her chair.

"Yes, indeed I have. Pochuyev will get a position, but in some other school."

"Well, I say, thank you ever so much!" said Yermolin, and he firmly pressed Login's hand. "How did you manage it?"

Anna looked gratefully at Login, and, in an affectionate gesture, her hand came to rest on his. Because she looked so radiant, Login felt that it would be better if he did not recount the scene to her; but, mastering himself, he told in detail everything that had happened.

"A fine fellow, the general!" Konoplyov exclaimed in sincere delight.

Khotin shook his black beard in disapproval. Shestov blushed in indignation. Anna asked coldly and sternly:

"Just why are you so pleased?"

Konoplyov became slightly flustered.

"How about that! Isn't that some discipline! It couldn't be bad, could it?"

"It's stupid. What pitiful children!"

"You shouldn't get terribly indignant about *everything;* wouldn't it be better to save your heart for better feelings?" Login said with a grin.

Anna blushed so fiercely that even her neck and shoulders turned red, and her eyes became wet.

"What feelings could be better than indignation?" she said softly.

"Love is better," said Shestov.

Everyone looked at him, and he blushed in embarrassment.

"What is love!" said Anna: "There's selfishness in any love; only hate can sometimes be unselfish."

Sharp, metallic notes rang out in her voice; her blue eyes turned cold, and the flush quickly disappeaed from her dark cheeks. Her bare arms lay serenely crossed on her knees. Shestov looked at her, and he even began to be somewhat fearful because of what he had said to her: to him this barefoot girl in a sarafan seemed so stern, as though she were accustomed to manifesting her own will.

"Here now," said Login, "of course, you've been indignant for a long time, but have you done a lot about it?"

Anna raised her calm eyes to Login and stood up. Her hand came to rest on the terrace's wooden railing.

"Do you know what needs to be done?" she asked.

"I don't know," Login answered firmly. "Sometimes it seems to me that people who get indignant at tormentors are simply jealous of them: they resent the fact that others inflict pain, whereas *they* don't. We like to hurt others."

Anna looked carefully at Login. A dark feeling welled up inside her. Her cheeks turned a burning red.

"Well now," said Yermolin, "hadn't we better get down to business? Vasily Markovich will read us..."

"Wait," said Konoplyov, "let's write down everything. Paper will take anything."

Everyone started laughing. The sudden laughter surprised Konoplyov. He asked:

"What's the matter? No indeed, ladies and gentlemen, wait a minute; I'm not implying that... Here's what I want to say: It's important to know right away the very essence of the matter, the main idea, so to speak. Here I, for example,—I got into this, actually, after the others; they told me about it, but perhaps they didn't tell me everything."

"Savva Ivanovich is a stickler for getting the complete details," Khotin said, laughing softly.

"Well, why not? It's always of interest to know what's what and why."

"In that case," said Yermolin, "we shall ask Vasily Markovich to give us a brief oral statement of his idea, if he doesn't mind."

"Not in the least. I'd be glad to," Login replied.

Dreamily he gazed ahead at some place beyond the maples in the joyfully flourishing garden and said slowly:

"Nowadays everyone is complaining that life is hard."

"It really is hard!" Khotin said with a sigh.

"Not being capitalists," Login continued, "we as a rule have to live from day to day."

Had he looked at Anna, he would have noticed that she was suddenly embarrassed at something; but he did not see anything, and he said:

"When someone is sick or out of work, or the head of the family dies, it all eats up one's savings in a hurry. And besides, how can one save anything? Often, for some reason, even the very process of saving up money is unattractive."

"Oh, in what way?" Konoplyov asked suspiciously.

"There's something miserly, contemptible about it."

"Why, don't say that. If you can save up a pretty penny, then you can be your own master and not have to depend on anyone."

"That's for sure," Khotin agreed, pensively stroking his long beard.

"Maybe that's so," said Login, "but savings alone can't be enough. Let's even consider savings banks. They have tremendous amounts of capital, but so what? You open an account, but that doesn't afford you any relationships with the other depositors. Once you've exhausted your account, you're helpless: the bank won't grant you a loan on any terms."

"That's what loan companies are for!" said Konoplyov.

"Yes, that's good, but it's limited; money isn't always enough help. Sometimes personal assistance is needed, or a doctor's advice, or a lawyer's, or help in finding a job, or something else. We need to form close links between members of society, as in a family, where all help one another."

"Some family that would be!" said Khotin.

"We'll make a fine one," Anna replied with a tender smile.

"A great many people," continued Login, "have to put up with not having enough of the essentials, and, moreover, they often cannot find a job. Yet there are no superfluous people."

"Indeed, as if there were no superfluous mouths," Konoplyov argued.

"There aren't any," said Login. "If by his very presence a new worker increases the supply of labor, then by the same token he increases the demand for others' work. A person cannot go through life without the help of others, it's clear: the natural condition of the individual is poverty. But, on the other hand, the natural condition of society is wealth, and therefore society should not let its fellow members go without work, without bread, without all these things of which there would be enough for everyone if all lived a life of mutual help. In our town, for example, you could find quite a few people, both plain and educated, who are unemployed, and they are needy in many respects. They can unite. They could figure out in advance how much work would be needed for a year, and they could do the work for each other. Each will do what he knows best: a cobbler will sew boots..."

"And drink like hell," Konoplyov said, sticking in his two bits worth.

"So let him drink, as long as he does his share of the work," said Yermolin.

"But he'll have a lot of work," continued Login. "On the other hand, many will be doing their work for him: a doctor, and a lawyer, and a carpenter, and a locksmith, and a teacher and a baker. A union of mutual assistance will be formed, where each will be needed by another, and each in a brotherly way will be disposed to helping others, and they, by the same token, will always give him help and support; all will be at home with each other as neighbors and friends. For every one who wants to work, work will be provided. And everyone will enjoy the greater conveniences of life, the opportunity of not living in those rats' nests where most of them live now. And there's another advantage: in such an organization based on neighborly cooperation, there would be no need for expensive middlemen such as merchants, landlords, and entrepreneurs."

"He's lukewarm to the idea and doesn't really believe in it," Anna thought suddenly, and she leaned all the way back in her chair and looked at Login in amazement. "No," she thought again, "I'm mistaken, of course!"

"And what if the members fall out with each other?" Konoplyov asked.

"That may very well happen," Login replied. "But it's no great problem: the malcontents will leave; the other wranglers will submit to the general opinion, they'll see that that's to their advantage."

"You'll need capital," said Khotin. "Without money you can't build even the most trifling things."

A pragmatic consideration hardly suited him: his face always looked so dreamy and absent-minded.

"Every person in and of himself is capital," said Login. "Of course, many will turn up with their own instruments."

"And money will turn up," said Anna, and she blushed again.

She was overcome by a strange feeling of awkwardness; she began peering into the garden, and put her hands on the terrace's wooden fence. The flowers that smelled so placidly of spring restored her tranquility.

"A thread from everyone in the *mir*," Shestov began to say.[1]

But by now he had been silent so long that he did not get it all out in time; his throat had gotten dry, and the sound came out hoarse. Shestov became confused, began to blush, and did not finish the proverb.

"The main thing is," said Yermolin, "for a beginning we must have strong-willed people, so that they have faith in the cause and influence others by their convictions."

"The people will turn up," Khotin said with a look of assurance, and he stroked his beard as though he had these people in his beard.

"Just get a trough...," Shestov began again, and again he fell silent in embarrassment: he saw that Anna was smiling.[2]

"By pooling our resources we can get machines," Login went on to say. "The work will be more productive and less tiring... We'll put in electricity. Right at their fingertips people have a great deal of kinetic energy that they never use. We'll establish our own public library. We'll keep exchanging our different kinds of knowledge. We'll organize journeys..."

"To the moon," someone said quietly. Login did not catch who it was.

Login shuddered slightly and realized that he was dreaming out loud.

"Why to the moon?" he asked in annoyance. "I meant just around our own country. Otherwise we won't even know it as well as we should."

"One more question," Konoplyov said quickly. "Will there be a printing press?"

Thereupon his face assumed an expression as though this were the matter of greatest interest and importance to him, and his dark eyes stared at Login in expectation.

"Well, if we need one, why not?" Login replied. "Other towns have them, so why shouldn't we?"

"In our town? What do we have to print?" Anna asked with a smile: "A town news-and-gossip sheet?"

"It's absolutely necessary," Konoplyov said enthusiastically: "Hereabouts there are quite a few institutions, both public and private ones, that need printed forms, accounting books, advertisements, and who knows what else. Finally, we can print books."

"What sort of books? Credit and debit?"

"Well, I'd also print something I composed myself—it's almost ready."

"That passes for a book," Yermolin agreed, with a barely perceptible smile.

"That printing press," said Anna, "is going to be like a greenhouse for nurturing provincial books."

They decided to read aloud and discuss the rules. The boys returned to the terrace, and Anatoly asked that he be allowed to read the draft.

After each paragraph had been read, arguments arose, most of them ever so absurd. While often not understanding each other, Konoplyov and Khotin argued more hotly than anyone else: Konoplyov liked to argue, Khotin wanted to show his own practical sense, and both proved themselves equally muddle-headed. Yermolin and Anna tried to help them figure things out and hardly succeeded at this. Shestov did not talk much; however, he got greatly excited and kept blushing. The boys did not go away but listened attentively; Mitya glowed with delight and got cross at those who misunderstood things. Login was silent and watched all the while with his dreamy eyes that barely discerned objects. But he did see that Anna's affectionate eyes sometimes came to rest on him, and he enjoyed feeling their look upon him. Sometimes it seemed to him that her pure trustful eyes were laughing at him. Indeed, he could never entirely free himself from a mocking attitude toward his own plan and toward himself, its author.

When the reading was over, they still argued for a long time over the name of the society. Konoplyov proposed calling it a force, Khotin—a company, Shestov—a brotherhood; and they did not agree on anything.

"It'll be terrific what things we'll git done with this society!" Khotin exclaimed with sudden inspiration. "We'll show 'em how to live honest. Just let us set this thing up all right, we'll teach *them* who's first rate!"

And he furiously threatened some imaginary person with his fists.

Login suddenly scowled: a caustic smile flickered on his lips.

"Nothing will come of this," he thought for a moment and began feeling melancholy. But aloud he said:

"Yes, of course, if we go about it sensibly, it has to become a reality."

"The father," he was thinking of the Yermolins, "is such a dreamer, as is his daughter. He believes in my plan more than I myself do. He believed in it at once, before I'd hardly said two words about it. But, still, after so many thoughts, I almost do not believe in myself! How fine and full of vigor Yermolin is! His eyes shine every bit like a young man's; one can't help but envy him."

"Anyhow," Konoplyov said fussily, "I'm not about to waste time doing nothing. I'm just about to have a book ready for printing. More than anything else I need a printing press. This solves the problem nicely. Here I've written a book. To print it I need money. But with our own printing press I can do it for free—an obvious advantage."

"Well, not entirely for free,"Login said, frowning and smiling at the same time.

"Yes, yes, I understand: paper, printer's ink. But those are only details, they'll be taken care of."

"You have a lot of work as it is," said Shestov, "yet you still find time to write."

He regarded with great respect the fact that Konoplyov was writing.

"It can't be helped; I have to write," Konoplyov replied with a smug pretense to modesty. "No one else has said in print what needs to be said; hence, we have to come forth and say it."

"And may I be so bold as to inquire what your book is about?" asked Login.

"It's against Leo Tolstoy and atheism in general. A most complete refutation, reduces it to smoke and ashes. There were earlier refutations, but not so thorough. I've included everything. I'll smash them to smithereens as Danilevsky did to Darwin.[3] And it's against science."

"Against science!" Shestov exclaimed in horror.

"Science is rubbish! They ought not to have it in the schools," Konoplyov said in excitement. "Everything about it is false. Even arithmetic lies. It is said: 'Give away all that thou hast, and it shall be repaid thee an hundredfold.' But what does arithmetic teach? To subtract, so that less will remain! Nonsense! That's against the Gospel. To hell with it!"

"Along with the schools?" asked Yermolin.

"Schools aren't for teaching arithmetic!"

"Then what are they for?"

"For instilling good morals."

"In your views on science," said Login, "you go much further than Tolstoy."

"To listen to your Tolstoy tell it, it so happens that, before he came along, all were fools and didn't understand anything; then he instructed everybody and revealed the truth. He tempts the weak! He should be hanged!"

"I daresay, you aren't any too fond of him."

"His books should be burned! On the square, by the executioner!"

"And what should be done with his readers?" Anna asked with a smile of amusement.

"Everyone who reads him should get it with the knout—in the market place!"

Anna glanced at Login as though she had tossed Konoplyov to him.

"Beg your pardon," said Login, "but did you read him?"

"I? I read him with the aim of refuting him. I am a mature person. I've gone through all that myself: I was an atheist, I was a nihilist, I was ready to rebel. But nevertheless, I matured. God enlightened me; He sent upon me a grave illness—it made me consider and repent."

"You've simply done so because it's so fashionable nowadays," said Shestov; Konoplyov's words had made him extremely indignant.

Konoplyov looked at him contemptuously.

"Fashionable? Explain that, please!" he said angrily.

His thick lips kept twitching nervously.

"Well, yes," continued Shestov, growing agitated and blushing; "there used to be such an epidemic of free-thinking, and then you tried to keep up with everyone else, but now the wind's blowing in a different direction, so you too..."

"No, excuse me, I didn't just try to keep up with others; I passed through all that sincerely."

"Tolstoy also did—sincerely."

"Tolstoy? He's disturbing the blessed people in his old age."

"Your book certainly will expose him completely," Anna said in a conciliatory tone.

"That's not good enough for him! He must be impaled, and flayed!"

"Unfortunately, the measures proposed by you are a bit out of date," said Shestov. He tried hard to make his words sound sarcastic but failed to do so: he blushed all over, and his voice kept cracking and breaking—he was very much offended on Tolstoy's behalf, and he now hated Konoplyov with all his heart.

"A bit out of date!" Konoplyov drawled mockingly. "Why, nowadays everything's coming apart at the seams, both the family and everything else. There's only debauchery: divorces, love affairs! It would be so much sounder if we lived by the Domostroy rules."[4]

"Yes, by the Domostroy rules, i.e. an unruly wife..."

"Should be flogged with the lash!"

"Fine—for who's holding the lash; not so good for who's under the lash," said Login: "Anyone seeks what's good for himself, but what's not so good he leaves for others. So does a wife."

"No, that's not at all so. A wife is a frail vessel; she's the weaker, and therefore her obligation is to obey her husband."

"Here you say that the wife is the weaker," said Anna. "But what if it happens that a wife is stronger than her husband?"

"It doesn't occur!" Konoplyov said resolutely.

"You don't say!"

"Even if she may be stronger in body, still she will be inferior in mind or character. The husband is the head of the family. Take Dubitsky—he's a model family man; he keeps his in obedience..."

"A monster!" Shestov exclaimed.

"Then just take our mayor—oh, he's a real laughingstock. I'd put his wife in her place."

"You wouldn't succeed at it," Khotin objected, laughing a little.

"Don't worry! And then there's the police chief's wife: Is that any good, I ask you? Her husband has to borrow money, yet she dresses up lavishly. She's no young filly; it's time she settled down and behaved respectably!"

CHAPTER TEN

The three of them, Login, Shestov, and Mitya, were returning from the Yermolins'. They had declined to go in the carriage which had been offered them, whereas Konoplyov and Khotin had preferred to ride.

Mitya was tired after the day. He wanted to sleep. Sometimes he would rouse himself, run down the road, then again plod along slowly with his head drooping.

It was quiet along the highway. By this time the sun was touching the hazy strip along the horizon. From somewhere off in the distance came the doleful refrain of a song, slow and alluring. Large yellow dandelions along the edges of the road swayed on their long and leafless stems. Fat marsh-marigolds showed their brilliant yellow here-and-there in the meadow. In a copse, a lonely wood-goblin began its brief, bored cackling, then fell silent.

Shestov marched down the road with such a lively step, as though he had actually just accomplished some heroic deed. Login grinned as he listened to Shestov's enraptured exclamations. Login kept remembering how, as they had said goodbye, Anatoly had pressed his hand firmly. He had looked at Login then with shining eyes and glowing cheeks. The boy's delight had pleased Login and amused him.

"A tempting toy for children and for old men who are young unto the grave,"–thus he now defined his project.

"What a superb idea!" Shestov exclaimed. "Oh, it's just splendid that without any great upheavals we can establish an intelligent way of living–and so soon!"

"An intelligent way of living in Glupov," Login said quietly.[1]

"Remember Bellamy's *Looking Backward*," continued Shestov. "When I was reading it, I kept thinking all the while that it was something a long way off, almost impossible. After all, he was considering things a hundred or so years ahead. Why, what else will people have to enjoy a hundred years from now? Their ideals will perhaps be a bit better than ours. But this cause of ours can be achieved even now! It can begin right now!"

"Of course, right now," Login said morosely; "we'll just go home and completely change our life."

"Well, not literally right now... But, no, right now, right away we can be talking about it, getting people together to work with us, working out the regulations. The authorities will allow it, you know."

"If anybody wanted it authorized."

Shestov looked carefully at Login, as though he were wondering whether or not it would be allowed, then he again strode briskly and confidently.

"After all, there's nothing wrong or illegal about this. Still, there's some question as to how they'll look at the matter. Now, one of my friends was writing to me that clubs have not been allowed in their town: they got only a few members and none of the local authorities. But we'll recruit a *crowd* of members."

"We'll hardly get a dozen."

"Why on earth do you think that?"

"Indifference—the worst enemy of any movement."

Shestov fell silent for a little while.

"Oh, if I could only have a bit more faith in myself," thought Login. "With his enthusiasm this boy would warm up anybody... if only the circumstances weren't what they are."

By this time Login was well enough acquainted with the story that engrossed the town and with the mood of certain influential personages, that he could foresee that Shestov's participation would not facilitate putting the plan into effect. Rather the contrary: it would be impeded because Shestov was a participant in it.

"But nevertheless, we'll struggle through," Shestov said resolutely.

A proud feeling rose up in Login's heart, a feeling like that in the heart of a warrior before battle, a warrior who is not sure of victory but treasures his honor.

"We'll struggle through," he said cheerfully.

And faith that was as strong as his lack of faith in his project sprang up in his heart, and yet it could not overshadow his gloomy distrustfulness.

"His delight is good in itself, apart from any possible results," he thought of Shestov. "That delight is aesthetic!"

There really was something beautiful and touching about the young enthusiast. The road where they were walking, with its gray, beaten thoroughfare and narrow ditches along the sides, stretched out dustily amid the depressing landscape that was so wearisomely monotonous; with its harsh and deserted expanses beneath the faded green sky, with all its boring appearance, it strangely and sadly highlighted the young teacher's childish delight. The stunted birches along the sides of the road did not listen to his exclamations, but shook their drooping branches, rosy now in the sunset, and did not awaken from their eternal sleep. The wind made the coarse dust of the road fly up in delicate clouds, blue-gray, deceptive. When the dust at Login's feet would rise up, he seemed to see through it someone hazy and evil.

"What a good soul Yermolin is!" Shestov went on in his raptures. "What an amazing girl Anna Maximovna is! Their Tolya is a remarkably bright boy, not like you, Mitka!"

"Just listen to you!" Mitya muttered crossly. "Everybody's so remarkable to you!"

"Konoplyov's a very clever man too, but he just gets horribly muddled."

"What are you saying!" Login said in annoyance. "What do you mean 'clever'? He has a head full of onion stew instead of brains."

"Oh, no, you really hardly know him yet!"

"He says he was a nihilist. Well, he's a nihilist even now,"

Login did not go straight home. He gathered that the townspeople would be gaping at the jail, where Molin, the arrested teacher, was being kept; and he felt like going to have a look at that.

He was not mistaken. On the rampart he came upon lines of people strolling along that little road above the river, from which the jail was visible. Some would stop in front of the jail and look down at it from above; they tried to guess which window Molin was sitting behind. They were hoping that he would show himself; someone assured them that Molin talked through the window with his pupils in the afternoon. But he did not appear now. The curious townspeople argued over which window belonged to his cell.

Login met acquaintances of his, heard fragments of conversation, merry laughter, jokes—quite stale, as usual,—all about the prisoner. Some who were a bit more common cursed Molin roundly and made fun of his having landed in jail; they were delighted by the thought that here, even though the fellow was a gentleman, he had been put in jail nevertheless. But Login detected neither any sympathy for the prisoner nor any ardent condemnation in the statements of the people who tried to imitate "ladies and gentlemen": the sleepy crowd had seized upon a funny story, was amused by it, and that was all.

Today an even greater audience was here, trying to imitate the gentry in attire, but with strange results: Ladies' hats that were hardly becoming to their wearers; cropped manes over tinted eyeglasses; loud, many-colored ties under pocked, ugly mugs; tight shoes on huge, ugly feet; and efforts to imitate the gentry not only in one's conversation, but even in one's very thoughts.

Some young ladies, fidgety but apparently startled by something, were giggling; some very young, gauche, and free-and-easy civil servants hovered around them—one posted himself opposite the young laides and even walked backwards that way. Dark-skinned, pock-marked Lt. Gomzin with his sparkling white teeth walked by dashingly with Mashenka Ogloblin, who fashionably kept shaking her pretty, stupid little head to show off her gold earrings, and kept waving her chubby, stubby-fingered little hands so that people would see her gold bracelets. Her brother, the fat young merchant, ran bustling by in a crowd of incoherently noisy young folk; each phrase of his was swallowed in their enthusiastic neighing. Here Valya Dylin and her younger sister Varya darted by; they were pursued by two unsightly youths who were students at the pedagogical institute; in the mild, moist air the squealing and crackling notes of the merry girls' loud laughter rang out sharply.

There were also people on the square below, between the cathedral and the jail. But they were not trying to hide their curiosity under the pretense of having come here for a stroll; these were the working people, who only took a stroll to the tavern or to the bar. They kept walking by sullenly, lingering before the jail's iron gates; they were gloomy, despondent figures in soiled, patched clothes: grubby, ragged and dumbfounded little boys; various craftsmen; a shoemaker with shoes down at the heels, dirty all over, and full of holes, and his fingers blackened from cobbler's wax; a red-faced butcher, whose clothing smelled of blood from the steers he had killed; a tall, scrawny, pale joiner, whose strong and bony hands swung through the air and longed for the plane that had been left at home. These people were talking quietly but angrily—in fragments of ominous threats and mysterious aphorisms.

"Why, what are you doing here, Kudinov?" Login asked a ruddy-faced, long-nosed schoolboy who was running around in the crowd on the rampart road, looking curious and excited.

"Oh, my mama sent me to see what's going on here," Kudinov explained frankly.

Three postal clerks stopped on the rampart opposite the jail windows. Drunk. One of them, a lame man with an expression of concern on his round, ruddy, whiskerless face, tried to persuade his comrades to move on, and he smiled in embarrassment. He muttered:

"Quit, fellows! It's quite disgraceful and really bad. What does it amount to, really? The devil with it! It's nothing to marvel at! Let's get going, really and truly, let's get going!"

The other two, scrawny, pale, stupid and insolent characters, restrained him, grabbed him by the arms, and yelled out, turning toward the jail:

"Lyoshka, old friend, light o' my life, show yourself! One-and-only friend, why don't you stick out your ugly mug, you stupid beast!"

Finally, though, the sensible companion prevailed upon them (they drank for the most part at his expense and therefore obeyed him somewhat). They went on their way, laughed uproariously, reeled, cursed. They were not as drunk as they imagined, and could have held themselves up straighter, but they felt like swaggering.

The foppish young taylor Okoyomov, who walked like a pair of scissors on his bowlegs, bounded up to Login and suavely held out his hand to him. He reeked of pomade and spirits of mignonette; a little green tie with rose-colored spots stuck out on his thin, prominently veined neck; he had on a ginger-colored bowler hat, a neat little turquoise vest, and tight, checked trousers. He made and mended clothes for Login and therefore would come up to talk with him on the street. Login knew that Okoyomov was silly, and conversations with him were no longer amusing.

"Why, just look," Okoyomov said scornfully, "what absolutely be-nighted people: they're surprised, and at what? What's there to goggle at! What's the difference? What'll they see? And what's so special about it? Well, so let's say they did throw an intelligent man in jail for a breach of morality. But, I ask you, is that really any great rarity?"

"You mean, it isn't a rarity?"

"What do you mean! Why, they don't read the newspapers, but if you just pick up, say, *Son of the Fatherland*, even there, in every issue, you find more than enough about all kinds of crimes; it makes you so sick you just don't want to read it, so finally you don't pay any attention: things like how somebody killed somebody or cut his throat or poisoned him—pah!"

"But here one of our folks got caught," Login explained, "and *everyone's* interested."

"Of course, " Okoyomov agreed, "since, you might say, there aren't any higher interests or amusements in our blessed town, they in fact feel flattered by this circumstance. Why, psychopathic behavior is in style nowadays in the capitals and in the big cities. After all, I myself, you may happen to know, like you, lived in St. Petersburg; I learned my trade there."

"And did you see a lot of psychopathic behavior?"

"Yessir, it's as if psychopathic behavior is, shall we say, a very fine and delicate thing. It means, 'I'll just do any damned thing I want to, and don't you interfere with my right.' Well, but, say you didn't do the least little thing to humor them, then right away you'd better hold on, look out, and take off; otherwise that temper of theirs would go off right lively, just like a pistol-shot. So you better just put up with them if you're one of the rest and are a simple fellow without a case of nerves. Very smart! Those gentlemen approve of it very much."

"Well, and how about you?"

"What, sir?"

"You approve, I believe, of psychopathic behavior?"

"Me?"

"Well, yes, you."

"Ah, how can I tell you; it is, of course... But just let us suppose somebody kills because of his psychopathic condition; then, nevertheless, there'll be great agiturbances because of him, and I don't respect that. I much more revere everything being quiet, peaceful, and decent."

"That means, you wouldn't kill people?"

"Why on earth would I? Let 'em live."

"But you would kill a fish; I saw you this morning."

Okoyomov turned red: that morning he had been very sloppily dressed indeed.

At this point they encountered Tolpugin, a young police officer, one of the least in rank and influence; on the other hand, he was renowned in the city as an expert bookbinder. He was a little fellow, very thin, curly-headed, lisping, and covered all over with dust and a bit of glue. It was obvious that he was happily concerned and busy with some of his special work. He was slightly out of breath with excitement when he said to Login:

"Congratulate me, I've been promoted."

"Oh, so you're now a..."

"Collegiate regithtrar!" Tolpugin said with pride, and his pock-marked face beamed.

Login congratulated the new collegiate registrar.[2]

"Why, don't you have any work for me?" Tolpugin asked.

"Just come see me any day now; I think we can find something."

As soon as Tolpugin had taken care of his business profitably, he too began talking about Molin. He nodded his head toward the jail.

"He'th getting fat there now," he said, transported with delight. "Why, you know, they built the jail right on the main thoroughfare!"

The pastry cook with his family—his wife, and his son and daughter, who were both village schoolteachers—walked past Login, dark and solemn like leisurely ravens. Had Login been alone, then they would have spoken to him. But they despised Tolpugin and Okoyomov, whom they considered beneath them.

The hubbub of faces and the nonsense of the conversations wearied Login. He shut his eyes tight. Out of the darkness Anna's dusky face arose before him with her eyes downcast in embarrassment and with a scornful grimace on her indignant lips. And it drew him away from these people— from these *good* people. He left the rampart and took a horse-cab. He felt tired. His head was beginning to ache.

He recalled Shestov's enthusiasm, and it warmed Login's heart. Without noticing it himself, he began to dream of how his concept would become a reality. Dream after dream swarmed through his head. The objects of the real world disappeared. And then to unanimous applause at a meeting of the members of his society, he had just concluded a speech about opening a classical theater with moderately priced general admission in our town, when suddenly the droshky lurched violently, Login bounced up and down with the springs of the seat and almost fell out. They were riding onto the bridge. A board was sticking up from the poorly laid planking—it had almost turned over the droshky. It seemed that the whole bridge creaked and rocked under the mangy nag's hoofs. Login turned pale.

"It'll collapse, it'll all collapse," he thought in sudden panic.

He felt a dull pain in his right temple: something cold and hard pressed against it. The barrel of a revolver would have felt the same way. He raised his hand, brushed away the invisible barrel with an irrational gesture, and smiled like a man who is done for.

"Going home, Vasily Markovich?"

It was Baglayev's voice he heard. Baglayev was walking toward the droshky. He was, as usual, noticeably less than sober. The driver, accustomed to stopping frequently (i.e. whenever his passengers wanted to visit with someone that they met on the way), stopped the horse; there was no reason to hurry in our town. Login pressed Baglayev's chubby hand and said:

"Yes. Just now I almost fell out of my cab on that town bridge of yours."

Baglayev laughed and showed his rather decayed teeth.

"Oh, why, how is the little bridge?"

"Just fine, needless to say!"

"It'll collapse, brother, it'll collapse. They just repaired it this spring, but next time the floating ice will carry it away."

"You don't say?"

"Why, I guarantee it. They just did a hasty patch-up job on it. It won't hold up even now—it'll be absolutely *kaputt-kranken*.[3]

"Hah, some mayor you are! Why should such a thing make you happy?"

Yushka started giggling then tried to invite Login to his home for the evening. Login declined.

The driver crossed over the bridge slowly, as ordered, and took Login through streets paved with agonizingly large cobblestones. The droshky rattled and shook Login. He gloomily looked around him.

The houses with their windows set up high, right under the very roof, had a stupid look, like senseless ugly mugs whose hairlines began almost at the eyebrows. Grubby little shops, noisy bars, silly signboards—"Craftsman of the Hatter's Trade" Login read on one of them.

Wild, disjointed, tormenting thoughts kept cropping up. Life seemed absurd. It was strange to think that he was the one experiencing all this for some reason. An anguish of reminiscences oppressed him.

"Why has this chaos and this confusion fallen to my lot? And why am I what I am? What bliss it would be if, at will, I could abandon this repulsive shell and move right into the body of, oh, even that ragged and grubby little boy, or that stout merchant so morose and pensive! Why the niggardly fate of having only one life?"

A sudden din and uproar drew Login's attention. He was riding past Obryadnin's tavern, which was a favorite spot for the local petty-shopkeepers. Right now a fight had broken out there. Suddenly the doors of the tavern flew open with a crash and a clang. A drunken gang tumbled out of there, howling savagely. A tattered muzhik with a crimson face and bloodshot eyes lunged at the droshky. The driver fended him off with the whip. The drunk roared out in pain but cravenly desisted.

Login was swiftly borne away from the crowd that murmured behind him.

CHAPTER ELEVEN

The morning was gay and happy, Shestov sat by the window. He was overcome by vague, troubled feelings. There was nothing to do at the school, since today was a holiday. Sometimes he would pick up a book, then toss it back onto the table next to him—he didn't feel like reading. Absentmindedly he looked out at the unpaved street, where gray fences stuck out, chickens wandered, brownish-green grass grew, and yellow umbrellas of celandine clung to the fences. He kept "setting" himself to thinking about Login's project. But in spite of himself his thoughts kept going off in another direction.

His comrade who was now under arrest he greatly respected for his "intellect," for his scornful opinions of everyone, and for the fact that Molin was some five years older than he. Now Shestov was sorry that Molin had been "taken into custody." Nevertheless, he had an uneasy feeling toward Molin as he recalled how Molin had raged when he finally realized that he was in serious trouble. In the room that Molin had occupied, the wallpaper, torn and soiled, hung from the walls in ragged strips, and chairs lay about bent and broken; these were the results of a violent outburst: the evening before his arrest, Molin had come home late at night from some place where he had been warned of what was impending; then for a long time he had stormed about the room, vehemently cursing somebody, hurling the chairs around with a crash, and throwing against the walls anything he could find. Shestov had told him:

"Look, Alexey Ivanovich, it's quite late; my aunt's asleep."

"Oh, God damn you and your aunt!" Molin had yelled, and smashed a light chair of beech wood against the floor with a powerful blow.

Shestov had discreetly withdrawn to his own room and had done nothing more to hinder Molin's loud outbursts of anger. That fury had even enhanced Molin in the eyes of the naive youth: "Why, then, he must be innocent if he's so indignant." But still he was annoyed: "But why smash up the chairs?"[1] He remembered that having Molin as a lodger had been very unprofitable: he cost them too much and did not pay them enough, so that lately they had wound up owing money to the shops; but Molin still wasn't satisfied with his food every day. This extreme finickiness of his was driving Shestov's aunt, Alexandra Gavrilovna, out of her mind, and she kept saying:

"Pearls before swine!"

Shestov reproached himself for these petty thoughts and tried to drive them away.

He was so used to respecting Molin's intelligence and honesty, that he felt bound to believe him even now; and Molin *did* keep assuring him that he was innocent. However, as soon as Shestov tried to view the matter impartially, then he became immediately and beyond doubt convinced that Molin had done that of which he was accused. And not only had he done it,– a person could do *anything* accidentally–but in fact Molin had just such a temperament, such inclinations, and such views, that he was quite capable of doing it deliberately. This conviction hurt Shestov, like a betrayal of their friendship.

But they had not really been friends–they just went drinking together, whereupon Molin never missed the chance to show off his own superiority. And Shestov did not argue against that, but he began to suspect that this was a poor friendship. And ever since he had learned to drink vodka almost as well as Molin, he had begun to notice that there was nothing superior about it. Already he listened mistrustfully when Molin said rather proudly:

"Hereabouts I'm considered a kind of district Mephistopheles!"

But Shestov tried not to let his thoughts about his comrade go too far: he had really been quite smitten and captivated by Molin from the very beginning, two years ago.

If Shestov, in his uncertain state of mind, had seized upon an extraneous idea in order to distract himself, the effort was a desperate one. The idea could not dispel his former thoughts, albeit great was his enthusiasm for that idea and for its author.

Suddenly Shestov frowned in vexation: outside he saw Galaktion Vasilievich Krikunov, a teacher and inspector of the school where Shestov worked. It was obvious that Krikunov was coming to see him; in fact he even began unbuttoning his overcoat when he noticed Shestov at the window.

Shestov considered Krikunov an evil and hypocritical man and hated his ingratiating manners, his sanctimoniousness, his servility before important people, his bribe-taking, his unfair treatment of pupils, and his petty embezzlement of State funds. Lately, through certain minute but doubtlessly reliable signs, Shestov had begun to suspect that Krikunov had come to hate him. The only reason for this could have been certain indiscreet remarks that Shestov had made when "among friends," i.e. in the circle of young men who drank with Molin. But since the most cutting of these expressions had been said in a conversation with Molin tête-à-tête and in such a place where no one could have eavesdropped–on the road outside of town–and since Krikunov had grown quite violently ill-tempered, Shestov suspected that Molin had conveyed all this to Krikunov's wife, and that, at the same time, he had perhaps attributed to Shestov certain caustic comments of his own at Krikunov's expense. In keeping with his habit of giving everyone slighting nicknames, when Molin was in his own little drinking circle he never called Krikunov anything but an icicle or a lollipop. Shestov had not brought himself to talk this matter over frankly with Molin, partly because of his own bashfulness, partly because he was afraid that Molin would be insulted if he mentioned these suspicions of his.

With a heavy heart Shestov went out into the entrance hall to meet

Krikunov.

"Hello, hello, good morning," said Krikunov. "Here I am to see you, Yegor Platonych, like it or not; do be hospitable."

His voice, with its weak, nasal tenor, seemed so vile to Shestov. He blushed as he shook Krikunov's hand and awkwardly replied:

"Hello, very glad to see you."

"Alexandra Gavrilovna, dear lady! It's been ages and ages since we've seen each other!"

Alexandra Gavrilovna, a thin and hearty elderly woman of about fifty who was quite tall, looked down hostilely at the small, gaunt, stoop-shouldered figure of her guest and said:

"You don't come to see us very often."

"Don't have time to, dear soul, not the least little bit of time," answered Krikunov, and he made his face (with its sharp little eyes) assume an expression of concern. "Well, now, I've run over just for a minute on business. I did want to have a talk with you yesterday after mass, Yegor Platonych, but, apparently, you weren't at mass yesterday, were you?"

Shestov followed Krikunov into the livingroom. Alexandra Gavrilovna did not follow them. Krikunov gathered up the tails of his neatly tailored coat and sat down in an armchair, slowly pulled a silver snuffbox out of his pocket, then turned it around (with obvious satisfaction), thumped it on the lid, opened it, and took a pinch with great relish. (He had learned to dip snuff in order to quit smoking: it was cheaper.) Then he sneezed loudly and sweetly. His quick little gray eyes darted around, glancing at the corners of the large, rather sparsely furnished room. He began speaking in a long, drawn-out manner:

"Here now, let me brag a little to you: I received this gift from a former pupil. Volodya Dubitsky sent it to me; I've gotten him ready for military school; he passed all his exams extremely well; his father was very grateful to me. Yessir, Yegor Platonych, even if I'm just a poor simple soul, still I'm somebody too."

"It's a pretty snuffbox," said Shestov.

"Why, it means a great deal to me that he remembered me this way himself; his father says that absolutely no one put him up to it."

Krikunov showed Shestov the inscription engraved on the inside of the silver lid, then read it aloud, distinctly and with emotion:

" 'To dearly esteemed Galaktion Vasilievich, from his grateful pupil, Volodya Dubitsky.' "

"A fine lad Volodya!" said Shestov.

"Yes, he has remembered an old man, brought him comfort."

Krikunov was not old; he was around forty, but he called himself an old man, obviously, for sentimental effect.

"And yet," he continued, "you young people think it's really funny; in fact even you are smiling..."

"Mercy, Galaktion Vasilievich, it's not funny at all—entirely the contrary; that is, I mean to say that I fully share your feeling that it is very touching."

"Yes, he has brought me great, great comfort. He even sent me his own little card."

"Also inscribed?"

"Of course, inscribed," Krikunov said irritably.

His tiny little eyes flashed, but the sweetness of his recollections consoled him; in a delicate feline manner he repeated:

"Inscribed! Dubitsky himself brought it yesterday. He came to see me quite casually. We visited a while, not talking about anything in particular. Suddenly he hands it to me. It touched me very much. Sinner that I am, I all but started crying. Now, isn't that something to treasure? That he remembered me himself, remembered me all by himself, the dear little boy!"

Shestov forced a smile.

" 'Oh, such,' I say, 'such a glorious occasion you've made for me, Your Excellency, such a glorious occasion! From now on,' I say, 'I shall never ever ever part with this little snuffbox. I shall always carry it with me whenever I go anywhere. At home I'll dip snuff from my old birch box; but, just let me go somewhere, and I'll grab the silver one, so the good people can see it. I'll brag to everybody, Your Excellency,' I say: just as I've said with you here today. 'When I'm about to die,' I say, 'I'll order 'em to bury this snuffbox with me, Your Excellency.' "

Krikunov tenderly sniffed some tobacco, sighed, and raised his rascally eyes toward the ceiling.

"Along with the little note?" Shestov asked.

Krikunov instantly snapped:

"With *what* little note?"

"Oh, from Kalokshin."

"Yessir, both that note and this snuffbox, I daresay!"

The note that Shestov mentioned had the following history: Last winter two officials had come to town to inspect the institutions of education: the assistant administrator of the school district and, with him, the inspector of the district, who had come in order to investigate the details thoroughly. The first of these men had behaved majestically, had awarded more or less protracted attention only to time-honored personages; the younger employees he had stunned with the laconic nature of his questions, the imposing quality of his remarks, and his awesome glance like a bolt of lightning. One evening the younger of the two inspectors, the more accessible one, had had to convey some sudden order from the assistant administrator to Krikunov. In order to avoid summoning Krikunov in person to his quarters (he did not have time for that, as he was getting ready for a most interesting bridge game), the district inspector had written Krikunov a brief little note on a scrap of paper, almost the sort of paper that was used for wrapping. In his excitement Krikunov had taken this letter as a sign of great favor: it was a note signed by hand, and in it Krikunov had been addressed by his first name and patronymic.[2] Let us assume, the inspector got it mixed up and called Galaktion Vasilievich Vasily Galaktionovich, but that happened, of course, because he had so many concerns to cope with. What was most touching of all, the note began with the word "Dear"! Moved to the depths of his soul, Krikunov had shown the note to all his colleagues and declared that when he died he would request that the note be buried with him; long after that, he had gone around to everyone he knew, showing off the note and repeating the same will-and-testament, then putting the note away; so by now he had talked about it ad nauseam. Finally he caught wind of Molin's rather coarse gibes that, in as much as Krikunov's civil service career was still a long way from being over, by the time he did die his coffin would look like a wastepaper basket, since it would be stuffed with these little slips of paper and a sucked-out lollipop. Krikunov was cut to the quick, and stopped talking about the note.

Lately Shestov had noticed that Krikunov considered *him* the author of the *indecent analogy*. Now Shestov caught on to the fact that he had just given Krikunov reason to be even more convinced of it.

"Why, what did I do that for? Oh, I always act so stupid!" Shestov fretted.

"Yes, Yegor Platonych," Krikunov grumbled, "it's quite all right that my coffin will look like a waste basket, quite all right. God grant that every man may ultimately lie in such a basket!"

"Why, yes, of course, every man!" Shestov said, and he himself did not know why he said it: it just slipped out. "But God also grant that it'll be a long while yet before you're laid to rest."

"Ah, Yegor Platonych!" sighed Krikunov. "Troubles are everywhere. How many times I've requested that I not have to keep charge of the school, that I could become just a plain teacher. But, no, our superiors ask me to stay, and the parents do too... Evidently, I'm still needed. Well, what can I do? I'll serve while the Lord gives me the strength."

"Of course, why go away when you're so well liked."

"Precisely, Yegor Platonych, my dear. You're still young, but you've asked me... Oh, well, I've stayed long enough. It's time I made my way around to the various homes. I've got business to do, you know."

"But why are you hurrying? You should stay a while longer."

"I don't have time. The mail I have to send off tomorrow—oh! But wouldn't you do something for me? So here's what sort of business it is: I was just at Motovilov's."

Krikunov's little eyes again began glancing evasively at the corners of the room. A look of sweet but evil anticipation flashed in them, as in the eyes of a cat when it smells its prey from afar. Shestov looked at him and sat still.

"So, then, Alexey Stepanych asks you to come to see him."

"When?" Shestov asked faintly, miserably.

"Oh, why, right away if you can."

"Did he tell you why?"

Krikunov grew restless, fidgeted in his chair, and stood up. "I don't know for sure. But I think it's about this case..."

"About Molin?"

"Yes, on that very matter."

"Well, all right, I'm going."

"Why, that's fine, that's just excellent. Now you listen to me, Yegor Platonych: don't you argue with him."

"What do you mean? I'm not about to argue with him."

"No, you see, if he proposes that you do something, you understand, then don't you refuse."

"What on earth is he going to propose?"

"Oh, I was just saying that, mostly as something to think about. I don't know anything certain—I'm just wishing you well, and in general, that all this could somehow be handled a bit better. I just ask you, please, do me the favor, Yegorushka Platonovich!"

Krikunov patted Shestov on the shoulder, pressed his hands sentimentally, and gazed at him with his sly, greasy eyes; for greater tenderness he had even wanted to use the endearing form of Shestov's patronymic, only he did not manage to do so.[3] Shestov felt very embarrassed and very ridiculous.

Motovilov was also honorable trustee of the town school. Because of certain petty gossip he did not like Shestov.

Shestov put on his new coat sprayed with ylang-ylang perfume, which cost about a quarter[4] a bottle, and went off to Motovilov's with the courage of a second lieutenant who is going into battle for the first time and, because he has had a bad dream, is convinced that he will be killed. Along the way he tried to think about other subjects, preferably pleasant ones.

He did not have far to go; it is no great distance to *any* place in our town. In ten minutes Shestov was standing by Motovilov's house. It was a wooden, two-story house, squat and ugly. It had a balcony enclosed with stained glass. A shop and storeroom were on the first floor, living quarters on the second.

Shestov considered that it would be more appropriate to walk on farther as though he were merely taking a stroll and then just turn around and come back from the next corner, then go in. So he did. But he had not yet reached the designated corner, when he suddenly decided that he had shown his independence well enough—and he swiftly turned back. About three steps from the porch he wondered if it might be better not to go in. After all, he did not want to see Motovilov, Motovilov wanted to see him, and what business was it of Shestov's anyway? Anyhow, he stopped at the porch. And once he had stopped, how could he *not* go in? Moreover, somebody might have seen him as he stood by the porch. Should he not go in, they would think he was afraid to. He suddenly blushed at that idea, ran up the porch steps, pulled the brass bell-handle, then, going through the unlocked outside door, he disappeared from the view of anyone who might have been watching him.

The door upstairs was opened by a maid. In the first room that he entered after the anteroom, he happened to meet the host's oldest daughter, Anna Alexeyevna. She was a young and nice-looking girl, an object of his secret fantasies. But he had never had the pleasure of her attention: he was shy with young ladies. He was even somewhat afraid of Neta, considered her derisive, though actually she was merely risible. But never before had she been so austere as she was today: Neta barely glanced at him, barely nodded her head in response to his awkward bow or respect, turned away disdainfully, and walked on in silence. The maid was smiling derisively. Shestov's heart sank, and he quietly made his way into one of the sitting rooms, where the maid suggested that he wait for "the master." He had to wait some twenty minutes, and that time seemed very long.

The sun was still not high. It was bright but depressing in the little sitting room with its two windows, dark furniture, and flowers in the corners and by the windows. No voices or motion from the inner rooms could be heard through the open doors. Several times Shestov tried to leave, several times he walked up to the doorway—and stopped. Finally he had quite made up his mind to leave, and went out of those rooms. But after going through two or three rooms, he met Motovilov.

"Ah, it's you," Motovilov said, offered his hand without halting, and walked on ahead.

Motovilov was tall and fat. He had the habit of swaying slightly as he walked. He had a small head, a low, slanting forehead, thick, graying curly hair, a pointed beard largely flecked with gray. The back of his head was wide, his cheekbones were handsomely prominent. In conversation he would lean with one ear toward the person with whom he was talking—he was hard of hearing.

He indicated an armchair for Shestov by the coffee table; he himself sat in one on the other side. The slanting rays of the sun illuminated the many-colored tablecloth upon which were a red china ashtray shaped like a crayfish, and a short, ponderous lamp. Motovilov kept drumming his pudgy fingers on the table. Shestov remained silent and withdrawn.

"I wanted to have a talk with you about Alexey Ivanych's case," Motovilov began; "you lived with him; you know more about it. What do you think, is he guilty or not?"

"I don't know," Shestov answered undecidedly. "He himself says that he's innocent."

"That's right. You must admit, we're all more disposed to believe Alexey Ivanych than that girl. Alexey Ivanych, as the saying goes, is not averse to hitting the bottle. But it is too bad that your aunt ventured to testify as she did. It's quite a pity."

"Yes, but what do I have to do with it?" said Shestov, and he turned red all over.

"It seems to me," Motovilov said imposingly, "that, as his friend, you should have been concerned lest any harm come to Alexey Ivanych. That's especially important for your sake, in view of the unseemly rumors that are going around town to the effect that you were involved in the beginning of this thing."

"They're stupid rumors!"

"So much the better. But I shall not hide from you the fact that these rumors are stubbornly persisting. Of course, your aunt's testimony has already been given, but it can be changed."

"Why, then, the investigator can conduct another investigation," Shestov said in confusion.

"But he can also *not* conduct one. I advise you to persuade your aunt to report to the investigator in person and state to him that her first testimony was, so to speak, not exact, that she did not hear that door at that place, well, and so forth in general, so that it should be evident that it is impossible to tell whether Molin went into the kitchen or not."

"Alexey Stepanych, I talked with my aunt about this matter," Shestov said in a trembling voice.

"Very good, well, so what then?" Motovilov asked sternly.

"She, of course, won't consent to that. Everything was exactly as she testified."

"Well, you must persuade her, even if you finally have to force her."

"How could I *force* her?"

"Yes, literally force her. You support her and her son at your expense; her son is exempt from tuition in our school—and she *must* appreciate that very much—she ought to listen to you."

In the rays of the sun the china crayfish on the table reddened like Shestov and bashfully hid under his trembling fingers.

"So it turns out that I must, so to speak, intimidate her, turn her out of my home if she won't do as I say?"

"Yes, as a last resort, hint at it, give her to understand it, even state it outright. It is very important for your own sake; this whole filthy incident can even affect your service record."

Motovilov gave his voice and his face the imposing expression that he loved to assume.

"No, Alexey Stepanych, I can't do it."

"You are wrong. You will regret it later. As you make your bed, so shall you lie."[5]

85

"In my opinion, that's really dishonest—to testify falsely."

Shestov stood up. He was trembling with sincere, pure-hearted indignation.

"No, you've misunderstood me," Motovilov said with dignity. "I cannot have advised you of anything unjust. Look at this gray beard of mine. I was merely asking you, in the name of honesty and justice, to influence your aunt to give the right testimony instead of a wrong one."

"Oh, so *that's* how it is!" exclaimed Shestov.

"Yessir, that's how it is. Your aunt has her own views, but, in our general opinion, this is nothing but blackmail, and it will come to light, I can assure you. And if your comrade, to our general regret, suffers because of your perfidy, then you, believe me, will not gain anything for your career in the service."

"Why are you threatening me with my job?"

"I am not threatening, I am warning you."

"Well, fine; we have nothing more to talk about," Shestov said with sudden determination, bowed awkwardly, and rushed out.

It was getting on towards evening. The sun was close to setting. The weary sky mellowed, relented, and covered its fearsomely gaping wilderness with a blanket of tender hues. But the tenderness was deceptive: light clouds, as transparent as a spider web, smoldered and caught fire, like thin yarn.

A garrulous, many-hued, and ever-present crowd whirled along the rampart's narrow roads. Barefoot little peasant children were busily selling lilies-of-the-valley. It was no longer crowded down in front of the jail: the crowd's curiosity had worn off.

Login was sitting by himself in the summer-house. He had a headache and felt melancholy. His thoughts came in disjointed fragments. Maddeningly, the people passing by blocked his view. At last, far away, he caught sight of a bright yellow straw hat with white and yellow feathers. He had recently seen this hat on Anna. He stood up and went in that direction; it seemed that he turned that way accidentally—and he joined the company where Anna was.

Present here were (other than Anna, he noticed them only when they greeted him) Neta Motovilov, elegant and merry; and a delicate-complexioned young man who kept hanging around her—a young man painstakingly neat and conservative in his attire, a young man with his hair combed so that not one pomaded,perfumed hair was out of place, a young man with a closely trimmed, black beard, a courteous smile and oily little eyes (his name was Ivan Constantinovich Bienstock, he worked in the law-court, he was busy looking for a bride, and everything that remained of his salary after paying the rent he spent on clothing, perfume, and on maintaining a decent appearance in general: he spent little for food, since he preferred to be someone's guest every day); and, accompanying Anna, Lt. Gomzin, one of those people whose wits would hardly set the world on fire (he had a pock-marked, dark-tan face and white teeth, which he obviously was proud of, since he kept letting out sounds that resembled neighing, all the while taking pains to show off his teeth.) Then there was Motovilov in a light, gray cloak and with a heavy cane in his hand; arm-in-arm with him was his second daughter, fifteen-year-old Nata. Thus had the name Anastasia been altered for the sake of euphony and brevity.

Nata was still an ungainly and awkward little girl. She still wore short dresses, but tried to conduct herself with poise and was ashamed of those awkward, almost boyish movements that sometimes betrayed her age. She no longer liked to be regarded as a little girl, but she still turned as red as a cherry when she was addressed as Anastasia Alexeyevna. Now she sat looking crossly at Bienstock and at her sister; her pale face was frequently covered with a blush of annoyance. Suddenly she disliked her Mordvinian costume—she thought that its colors were too loud.

Sometimes Bienstock paid attention to Nata also. He was saving her "just in case," "in reserve," and told his friends:

"Just wait a while, she'll be quite a dish."

It happened he was offended when Molin assured him that the Motovilovs really would only let him marry "tubercular" Nata, and even then only because she was "deaf." Molin liked to tease his drinking companions in a rather crude way. In this instance he was not entirely correct: Nata was not deaf and she did not have tuberculosis—but there were days when blood came up from her throat, or her nose bled, and then she began to be hard of hearing.

Login returned with them to the summer-house. They sat down on the benches. It seemed to Login that they were all bored but were all pretending to be having a good time.

Bienstock told Neta something under his breath, probably something funny: he smiled very convincingly and sometimes even giggled and chortled a bit. Neta laughed and, when the others weren't looking, raised her hands to her cheeks: Login managed to observe that she kept pinching her cheeks so that she would not be pale. She was wearing a hat that had a wide brim with a pink lining, so that her face would have a rosy hue.

Gomzin was entertaining Anna with stories, as is typical of soldiers. Not only his face, but even his whole body was turned toward her in extraordinary civility. His beautiful teeth shone splendidly.

Motovilov was leaning with crossed palms on his silver-headed cane set between his feet, which were spread apart; he was telling Login incidents which were bound to prove that he was a local figure respected by all, and that his labors were so very beneficial to society that he simply could not even begin to tell everything about them. At the appropriate points Login, almost mechanically, would make remarks proper to the occasion. He kept asking himself: "Anna couldn't really be interested in Gomzin's cock-and-bull stories, could she?" She was conversing with him as though it brought her great pleasure.

"That garrison warrior," thought Login, "is simply stupid and is very pleased with himself. He imagines that his uniform and his courtesy are irresistibly charming. She ought to inform him that he's a dim-wit and in the reserves besides."

He felt annoyed. Anna's dress, with its light fabric, pale yellow-green color, and bright yellow belt, displeased him. To him the white lapels of her bodice seemed too large, the feathers on her hat too yellow and too wide, and the bow of pale yellow ribbons on the milk-white handle of her red, light umbrella seemed too luxuriant, ill-matched with the thin straps of her sandals that she had put on over her bare feet.

Motovilov suspected that Login was not listening as attentively as he should. Motovilov attributed this to flippancy and free-thinking on Login's part, and he redoubled the habitual impressiveness of his intonations and of his countenance.

"Vasily Markovich," Neta said when Motovilov had come to a pause in his stories, "I heard that you're organizing a charitable society hereabouts. Is that true?"

"And from whom, permit me to ask, did you hear this?"

"Ivan Constantinovich was just telling me."

"Yessir," Bienstock affirmed with a courteous smile, "Shestov visited me just a little while ago and enlightened me on this account."

"That's terribly, terribly fine," Neta babbled. "We have so many poor people, and we're going to help them—how splendid!"

"It's not exactly charitable..."

"Yes, yes, I understood everything perfectly," Neta interrupted; "they won't be helped for nothing, but only if they work. They can weave charity baskets."

"Or gather charity mushrooms," Anna added, smiling.

"Yes, yes, mushrooms, or possibly berries too."

Motovilov knocked his gold ring against the head of his cane and began speaking impressively:

"Charity, of course, is a sacred thing. We are all obliged to help a poor man as far as our means allow. True Christians certainly do so, I am convinced of it. Who could bring himself to deny a piece of bread to a man who is honest, but impoverished through misfortune or weakness, and holds out his hand with tears in his eyes? One must needs have too hard a heart to think only of himself. But it is best to perform acts of charity in such a way that the left hand not know what the right hand is doing. Yet public charity is a very difficult and—if I may so express myself—even a delicate matter: it requires, in the first place, great experience; in the second place, a knowledge of local conditions, quite a great deal in general."

"Absolutely right, as you were so kind to say," Gomzin agreed obsequiously, turning his delightfully grinning teeth and his respectfully bowed figure toward Motovilov: "Both experience and a knowledge of local conditions, and, mainly, an influential position in society."

Motovilov bowed his head pompously.

"Yes, precisely, an influence on society. In fact, that is exactly what I meant to say."

"Influence on society," Gomzin chorused and yelped servilely.

"Now let us take that free dining hall of ours for example," Motovilov continued. "We organized it on a practical basis, and it has proven a real blessing."

Login knew of this dining hall which the bored ladies of our town had organized at the municipal alms-house. Here some fifteen beggar-women were fed each day through the patronage of these ladies. Smiling, he said:

"There's a slight misunderstanding here. I didn't even dream of intruding upon charity and other good deeds: Why, indeed how can I? I'm ashamed to say, moreover, that in fact I can't afford it. The matter's more simple."

He set about explaining his project. Motovilov listened with strict attention. Login spoke briefly and ineptly, unwillingly as it were. It was disagreeable to expatiate on his plans before Motovilov.

Anna watched Login attentively. Her brows arched slightly, as though she were trying hard to figure out some idea of hers. Neta was disappointed and clenched her dainty teeth in vexation. She reproached Bienstock:

"Why on earth did you tell me something entirely different?"

"I understood it that way myself at first. But I must confess, I didn't listen to Shestov very carefully. I had been working in the afternoon, I had a splitting headache, I wanted to go for a walk, but then he came—terrible!"

Anna embraced Neta and said with a laugh:

"Oh, you philanthropist! Just wait, in the winter we'll organize *tableaux vivants* again for the benefit of the poor, but in the meantime you can do a week's duty in the charity dining hall. The old women kiss your hands and call you a princess."

Login felt annoyed that Anna was amused both at how Bienstock had understood Shestov's words and at how Neta and Motovilov had regarded the matter. He perceived something else in Anna's disposition, something that had been provoked by the feebleness of his own words: it was conveyed by the quiet tapping of her sandals against the floor of the summerhouse.

"I am not taking it upon myself to judge the feasibility of your project," Motovilov said with a redoubled air of impressiveness; "of course, all this is fine in theory, but in practice it is a different matter. I shall merely be so bold as to remark what trouble you risk encountering hereby: In what way are you guaranteed against your society's being invaded by a corrupting element, by sluggards and parasites who only think about how they can work a bit less and get a bit more? Such drones, even if they will do a job, do it badly."

"If you fed me, for example," Bienstock remarked flippantly, "and clothed me and supported me that way, for free, for absolutely nothing, would I want to work? Tell me, please, what for?"

"Oh, don't you judge everybody else by your own standards," Nata impetuously interrupted the conversation.

That remark came out suddenly and sharply. Nata blushed deeply when everyone looked at her. Everyone started laughing. Login smiled with restraint. Anna looked affectionately at Nata and thought:

"Poor little bird, you'll never fly."

"You're right, of course, Nata," said Login. "The people who live in town should not judge this by their own standards: we've grown used to

90

diffused living and get along superbly without manual labor. But for a working man, to be without work is death."

"No," Motovilov objected, "without work he'll just go to the tavern to drink up his last copeck."

Anna glanced at him calmly. Her lips trembled scornfully. Her bright eyes turned toward Login—and suddenly he did not feel like arguing with Motovilov. He realized that it would hardly be to his advantage to have Motovilov against him on the matter that he was contemplating: Motovilov would rush in and wreck it, the old shark! Login said:

"But I rather agree with your opinion, Alexey Stepanych. That point, naturally, should be taken into consideration."

"Yessir, absolutely," Motovilov said with a self-satisfied air. "The matter must be kept under strict control. Without a manager it cannot get anywhere. We Russians cannot live without someone's leadership to guide us. And, if you will excuse me, I shall deign to give you some more advice as an experienced man who has lived in the world for some time—if, of course, you would care to hear me out."

"I'll listen to your advice with the deepest gratitude," Login said with a courteous smile.

But inwardly he seethed with annoyance.

"You recall, of course, how the fable writer said: 'Be careful in your choice of friends'?" Motovilov asked with an expression of profound wisdom on his sly face.

Login noticed how, upon hearing this prelude to the promised advice, everyone tried to make his face look serious and perceptive. Anna alone smiled derisively, but, then, perhaps it only seemed so: after half a minute her face was calm again; her hands rested motionless on her knees.

Gomzin showed Login his teeth and said with an air of profundity:

"A sterling principle. Krylov composed his fables very wittily."[1]

"*His*, and no one else's?" Nata cried out fervently, losing control of herself.

"Nata!" her father restrained her, speaking sternly, under his breath.

Nata calmed down, but her eyes flashed at Gomzin. Motovilov continued:

"So I shall say straightway that you ought to choose your colleagues more carefully. We have to admit, not everyone is capable of being a good partner. With some it is easy to be duped; trust my experience. Do not think that I am saying anything of the sort that I could not repeat around whomever I would. Yessir. I am a straightforward man. I dare think that it is not for no good reason that I enjoy respect. I shall not mention any individuals, but I consider it my duty to warn you."

Login pulled impatiently at the black ribbon of his pince-nez. He burned with hostility toward Motovilov, and the imposingly pompous figure of the old hypocrite was becoming unendurable. He said firmly:

"Shestov is incapable of any act of perfidy—he's young, innocent, and honest."

"Young people are not the only ones who are good," Motovilov said touchily, "but, as I already had the honor of explaining to you, I am not mentioning any individuals, and I am not forcing my opinion upon anyone—I dare not: you perhaps are so fortunate as to have acquired a great knowledge of the world and a great intellect, and you've absorbed quite a few books, but I am telling you how it appears according to my perhaps imperfect reasoning—and I am speaking in general."

In his irritation he kept tapping his cane in time to his words.

"Ah, in general... I was thinking... Anyhow, I am grateful to you for your advice," Login said coldly.

"That will do for today," he decided, bowed to everyone, and set off for home.

The sun had gone down. The western sky glowed like the face of a child who was out of breath from running about. The eastern half of the sky was flooded with shades of soft-red, lilac, and pale yellow. The air was quiet and sonorous. Its light rustling was suffused with a sad reverie. Evening glimmered transparently and twilight descended imperceptibly. A moist and dreamy stillness lay over the river. With a gentle, whispering sound like that of children's lips kissing their mother's hands, the smooth ripples splashed against the damp sand of the bank. On the bank, the little red star of a campfire began blazing merrily in the distance; a fisherman's boat could be seen there.

As Login descended the rampart, he felt a mood of peacefulness and bliss come over him.

"Why?" he wondered in surprise, then: "There's the answer!" Anna's smile flickered before him.

"How could I be annoyed at her smile? Here it warms me, and I bear within me a testament of peace."

A song resounded through the clear, mild air. On Vorobinka a ragged crew of fellows was sitting right by the water. It was they who were singing, and singing exquisitely.

Login went by way of the island: it was closer that way. When Login had crossed the bridge, a big, tall fellow in tattered clothes, with down-at-the-heel shoes and no socks, separated himself from the community of singers and approached Login. He began speaking, and he reeked of raw vodka. He tried to give his hoarse voice a pleading tone.

"Kind sir, let me be so bold as to trouble you with something. By your countenance and by the elegance of your movements, I observe that you are an intelligent man. Do not refuse to help people who are also intelligent, people who are of society, but who have fallen into misfortune and are compelled to earn their sustenance by the back-breaking work of an unskilled

92

laborer."

Login stopped and stared at him in surprise. He said:

"You express yourself too eloquently."

"I perceive the underlying meaning of your remark. You deign to imply that I've, er... that I've *tied* one on."[2]

The big fellow slapped himself on the spot where he had once been in the habit of wearing a tie.

"From sorrow, kind sir, and because of the climate, and as both a precaution against and a relief from colds. I have seen, as have these nestlings travelling and singing with me, I have seen better days. But 'the beautiful days of Aranzhuyets have passed!'[3] I was once a legal investigator. But afflictions of the heart and the unfairness of my superiors plunged me into an abyss of misfortune, where indeed I remain without hope of escape. And those wandering with me are also from among the mighty of this world: one is a former police superintendent; another is a former civil service senior clerk, and the third is a former nobleman banished from the capitals, though more or less without being guilty. A most noble, high-ranking company!"

"But where are you traveling to?" Login asked.

"We work in common on improving the routes of communication, but the local engineers, if you'll pardon my saying so, are crooks. But, of course, they are also most noble!"

"And what exactly is it that you want from me?"

"I request any amount of money as a loan, not by any means as alms."

"All right, I'll give you something as a loan, as you put it. But are you always in *that* condition?"

"I frankly confess: almost continuously! As a noble human being!
    Narrow morals aren't our feature,
    And the sign (that we'd not think
    To conceal) of Russian nature
    Is—It's Russia's joy to drink!
A quotation from Nekrasov."

"But, anyhow, are you ever a bit more sober?"

"In the mornings, sir, and on compulsory fast-days as well."

"So then, at that time, won't you come to my place some time?"

"Do you happen to be a writer?" the ragged man asked, winking slyly.

"No, I'm not a writer. I have something else in mind."

"At your service, sir."

Login explained how to find his place. The big fellow heard him out, obviously tried to memorize it, and then said with a broad smile:

"Please don't trouble yourself with explaining; I'll just find it. How, you may wish to know? Here's how: There are some benefactors that take in cats and holy fools; there are especially some benefactresses like that, such tender-hearted ones; but as for such citizens who would care to set eyes

93

on the likes of *us,* they are no more than one in a billion. When *we* come, then people thereupon look as though we might steal something; they chase us off without ceremony because we are, if I may say so, a hopeless lot. So, just let me mention your High Honor's name, and I'll find your place even without the address."

Login silently heard him out, frowned, then walked on.

"Your High Honor!" the ragged man called out to him. "What about the assistance you promised to lend me?"

Login stopped, pulled out the money, and said:

"I don't care, you can drink it up."

"Of course, without delay, but to your precious health, O generous, generous and kind sir. The Lord reward you! I shall repay you at the very first opportunity. Serpenitsyn!" Thus he gave his name, tipped his ragged cap which was gray from the dust and dirt, and clicked his heels. "Pardon me for not having an I. O. U. to give you."

The big fellow returned to his partners, and the notes of the song resounded again. They came from the heart, and the sound was produced lovingly. The public on the rampart listened to the singers. Those sounds teased and tormented Login.

"Poetic design, artistic fulfilment... and the singers are drunkards. Wild and beautiful!"

He returned home. Through the open windows in the neighboring building, loud voices could be heard: now Valya was quarreling with the student who courted her.

"Some home owner you are!" Valya's voice carried all the way to the street. "One good kick, and your whole wretched house would fall down."

"And do you think that Andozersky's going to marry you?" said an angry youthful tenor in reply. "You're even glad to let him amuse himself with you."

"Well, you're a fool; you call yourself a pedagogue, but you're just a little boy; why, they still make you stand in the corner."

"No one would *dare* try to make me stand in the corner! You're a tutor, and you own pupils lambasted you!"

"You're lying! He pasted me with a snowball, but he didn't mean to!"

CHAPTER THIRTEEN

Login was sitting in his study. Everything about the room made it gloomy: the dark-green wallpaper; the rose-bordered, coarse linen draw curtains that hung by brass rings on brass rods over the three narrow windows facing the street; the low ceiling covered with yellowish paper; the dark-green Lyonese carpet. The brief light with which Anna's smile had blessed the day was fleeting, and the flower that had blossomed by her white feet now had withered.

There were a bottle of Madeira, white bread, roquefort cheese, and a slender little glass on a German-silver tray on the table near the couch. Login drank a glass of wine while standing, poured another glass and carried it to the desk. For several minutes he sat there in deep thought. His head burned and whirled dizzily. He felt that it would be a long time before he could get to sleep. A sad craving drove him to the wine.

Lately it often happened that he spent nights entirely without sleep—nights of oppressive fantasies, disjointed recollections. Something had gone wrong with him. His conscious life had grown muddled—it lacked its former integral relationship with the world and other people. The slightest occasion was enough to make him suddenly start thinking and feeling differently, and then the thought and feeling that he had just abandoned would seem odd to him.

Scenes of the past sped through his mind on these sleepless nights. At times his attention would rest on one of these scenes—and its contours would become vivid, irritatingly distinct.

It seemed strange to identify himself with the boy on whom he looked back from the mountain of experience and weariness. Recollecting, he would see himself rather extraneously. It was not that he could clearly observe that other person of whom he thought when, through the mutual inaccuracy of language and thought, he would say: "I was," or "I did." It was like sticking one's head out of a window and trying to peep through the adjacent windows or up under the eves, where the gray birdsnests cling, or into the windows of the other stories; the house would be seen not altogether from the outside, but one would still feel that he was not actually inside the house.

Thus he beheld the red glow waxing then waning on his cheeks, the stern, slightly wavy lines in his face, and his figure all thin and frail, but not as distinctly as one remembers completely extraneous objects. He vaguely remembered the really strong, heartfelt emotions that he had experienced in the past. On the other hand, sometimes something, external and petty, but connected with some feeling that he had strongly experienced, would stand out sharply in his memory.

There were certain circumstances that seemed entirely lost beyond recall. It seemed that many links in that chain of the impressions that once flowed over the threshold of consciousness in orderly waves had now become lost, had sunk into the general dark mass of his past life—and similar links became fused like two converging streams. Consciousness, a will-o'-the-wisp, toiled over this jumbled mass and by its glimmerings made what is called the conscious life.

It seemed to Login that the contents of the mind had no unity, no wholeness, that the disintegration of his mind had begun long ago and was now nearing its completion. There were days when his thoughts and feelings traveled a path of joie-de-vivre—everything gloomy in life was forgotten. There were also life's cruel periods: unbearable anguish gripped his heart, and all the graves in his mental cemetery gave up their dead; at such times his awareness of the other, better world in his mind was wiped out.

But more often, the light of consciousness would burn on the bridge between the two halves of his mind, and what he felt was an agony of indecisiveness. The bridge's foundations rocked and cracked under the pressure of the waves of life, and the will-o'-the-wisp of consciousness sometimes illuminated their white-foamed crests and the terrible swaying of the foundations. Sometimes this light shone on thoughts that were happy and full of hope, but the strength for living belonged to that man of old who had committed wild deeds, rushed about like a mad beast before his amazed consciousness, and longed for tribulations and self-torment. The more oppression built up in life, the more powerful and more prolonged was the triumph of the liberated Id.

"Isn't it obvious," Login sometimes thought with a strange gloating, "that my Ego is quite a pitiful pretension to an existence that is ever-flowing and self-renewing like the water between a river's banks, which themselves are immutable only in appearance."

Login opened one of the desk drawers and pulled out a letter which he had recently received. He had not yet answered the letter. It was from his best friend, with whom he conversed almost frankly. Now he carefully reread all four pages of the letter. Then he sought out his stationery, moved his armchair a bit closer to the desk, and began to write—about his project. He sat at this task for a long time, sometimes drawing the pen swiftly across the page, sometimes leaning back in his chair and thinking hard. At times he would pick up his glass and drink a bit.

Cold air poured in from the street through the open window. It was quiet in the town. From far away came the sounds of the river, chattering by the mill-pond; there a restless mermaid babbled loudly and laughed and wept, and her green braids spread out over her whole body.

He had completed the letter. He finished the wine in his glass. The coldness of the glass and the taste of the wine brought him a delight in which he would be wholly absorbed for a minute. Then he would grow sad again.

He paced about the room several times, poured the rest of the wine from the bottle into his glass, then sat down again at the desk to reread his letter.

Reaching the place where his will was mentioned in the event of his project's failure, he smiled sadly. He thought:

"A suicide's will—a bunch of papers with the traditional request not to blame anyone for his death. I say, a lot of good *that* is! People are used to being curious, even amused by any sort of event, including suicide. The reasons are sought out and noted carefully—for the sake of statistics. And the suicides humbly submit to a procedure irrelevant to them and leave behind explanations for their deaths. Someone will write a whole letter—to his friend or to his betrothed—with the secret aim of portraying himself in the tragic element of his end. How silly! However, on those occasions the people, probably, are horribly distracted and reason poorly.

"If it should come to my having to kill myself, I would try to make it look accidental: quite a few unfortunate accidents do happen!

"But it would be best of all to disappear altogether inconspicuously, without a trace: to drown in the ocean, to poison oneself in an inaccessible cave. Later on the bones and skull might be found, and such trash might be put in an archeological collection."

The uncomfortable sensation of a dull pain in his temples kept returning ever more frequently. He leaned back in his chair. His pallid face seemed calm. He heard a quiet laugh ring out behind his back. He recalled Anna's laughter. A damp chill went through his body. Glancing at the open window, he thought:

"It ought to be closed."

But he did not feel like getting up.

"No, I'd better do that later," he decided; "otherwise it'll get stuffy."

He drank some Madeira and again took up the letter. For some reason, several points reminded him of Motovilov—and each time, hatred and contempt for that man flared up within him. He was surprised at the way he had ended the letter. He wondered:

"Why is it I thought to affirm that I believe in my own idea? After all, it's just logical that if I did not believe in it, I wouldn't have started thinking of fulfilling it. A bad sign! Or is it really too soon in life for me to tell the halflight of dawn from the twilight of the distant future?"

All the while that he was sealing and addressing the letter, he kept hearing the strange incessant laughter. The dull ache in his head spread farther and farther. It seemed that something alien was standing behind his back.

Suddenly he realized that he felt frightened. With a forced smile, he overcame the queer feeling, wheeled about.

"It's the river," he concluded, stood up and closed the window. It became quieter in the room—the noise of the water resounded more dully and more faintly behind the window pane.

He finished the wine, felt warmer and happier. He lit a candle, put out the lamp, got ready to go to bed. He walked up to the bed with the candle in his hands.

The blanket lay on the couch in heavy wrinkles and covered the pillow. The shadows of the wrinkles contrasted sharply with the red color of the blanket. It was spread out in a strange way on the couch: it was humped down the middle and lay flatter near the sides. Near the foot of the couch was a long mound shaped like legs; it extended to the middle of the cover. At the pillow it also was elevated and rounded. It was as if somebody had gotten up under the cover and was lying there quietly, without stirring. Login stood still before the bed and raised his right hand with the candle in front of him, as though he wanted to shine the light down on something more conveniently. In his pallid face, his gloomy eyes burned in painful perplexity.

The soft, persistent laughter rustled behind his back. His thoughts took shape slowly and laboriously, as though he wanted to remember or figure out something, and the effort to do so was excruciating. But it seemed that he was beginning to understand.

There, under the cover, lay someone frightening and motionless, exuding coldness. Login felt that coldness against his own face and body. It was the coldness of a corpse. There, under the cover, decomposition had not yet set in. But its lips had grown blue and heavy, its motionless eyes were sunken.

Login was held fast by an uncanny numbness and was unable to lift up the cover. The candle's red light rippled over the red blanket. A whitish mist began moving in, creeping in from all sides, and through it only the red blanket gaped with its dark wrinkles. The mist trembled and laughed soundlessly but intelligibly. Login imagined the corpse's face: it was—his own face, horribly pale, with dull-leaden hues on the sunken cheeks, untouched as yet by decomposition.

Here lay a corpse still unburied and wandering the earth, where it was active only part of the time, like the sunshine; it had lain down here and was resting in peace without dreams. And Login knew that it was he himself lying there motionless and dead.

"An absurd fantasy! I must get control of myself!" Login's pale lips whispered.

His hand reached out toward the blanket. But the mist grew thicker, clouded up now over the blanket, and laughed maliciously and mournfully. The candle was shaking in his numb and heavy hand. Login felt it wearisome and frightening to lie like a motionless, unburied corpse and to wait. A crimson light kept shining through the cover. Its heavy folds were crushing his powerless body. Someone was standing over him and, with wildly-burning eyes, was peering at his body covered by the red blanket. Someone's hand kept coming to rest on his chest, feeling it through the blanket, trembling—

and his chest felt several rapid and feeble thumps. How strange and wearisome to keep waiting, when one cannot move at all.

The cover was being raised—cold air streamed over the corpse's face bathed in a cold sweat. A horrible inhuman strain pierced him through and through. He raised himself up from the pillows...

Calming his overwrought nerves by a tremendous effort of willpower, Login set the candle on a little round table and paced the room from corner to corner. The mist that had obscured his vision began to disperse. Login went up to the couch and quickly put his hand down onto the blanket. There was a soft pillow under the cover—and that was all...

"Really, I should see a doctor—I've been having an unbearable headache the whole day."

He undressed and threw back the cover.

"Why is there that depression in the pillow? Oh, yes, I did that with my hand... But it's as though a head had been lying there."

He put out the candle and lay down. The red of the blanket also went out. It was dark. Only the windows showed dully white—a monster's eyes fixed in attention as it lay in wait for its prey. The mermaid laughed in the distance.

Login wanted to lie down in the same way as "he" had just been lying under the cover. A slight shudder went through his body.

"It'll be warmer this way," he thought, and he covered his face with the blanket.

Login lay face-upward. The cover kept pressing heavily on his chest and face. Again it seemed to Login that he was a cold and motionless corpse. A horrible anguish gripped his heart. He was seized by a passionate craving for air, light... The cover had to be thrown off... But a numbness held him fast, and he lay there immobile. The terror and anguish died away. He lay there cold and serene and looked through the heavy cloth with dead, closed eyes.

A man was sitting by the desk, with his back toward him, and the man was given over to sad thoughts. And it was strange to Login, and he did not understand why that man was depressed while his dreams and hopes, slain before their time, turned cold here in his dead body. Everything was decided and finished, there was nothing more to think of, and with his heavy gaze he summoned that other person to him; the dead body summoned and waited for the man.

Login imagined how this man stood over him and peered with wild eyes at the red blanket. Then Login knew that it was he himself standing over his own corpse. And he heard his own strange sentences.

"Lie there, disintegrate faster, don't hinder me from living. I am not afraid of the fact that you have died. Do not laugh at me with your dead smile, do not say to me that it is I who have died. I know that—and am not afraid. I shall live by myself, without you. If you yourself had not died, I would have killed you. For you (for myself, you correct me,—so be it, it doesn't matter) I saved a good aluminum-cased bullet. Make room for me, disappear, let me live.

"I want to live, and I haven't lived, and I don't live because I drag you around with me. Oh, if you only knew how oppressive it is to drag my own heavy and horrible corpse around with me. How cold and serene you are! How horrible is your rejection of me! How incontrovertible your silence is! Your dead smile tells me that I am only an illusion of my own corpse, that I am like the little weakly flickering flame of a wax candle in the yellow and motionless hands of a deceased man.

"But that cannot be the truth, it must not be the truth. I am myself, constant and whole. I do exist apart from you.

"I hate you and want to live anew, apart from you. Why should you always be with me? You don't enjoy life. You're obsolete now. You're my burdensome past.

"Why don't you disappear as snow melts away in the springtime, as clouds melt away at noonday? Why do you keep pouring the putrid poison of the hateful past into the divine nectar of my impossible hopes?

"Disappear, tormentor, disappear before I smash your dead skull!"

He lay there motionless. And it was eerie, and pleasant, to torment the man who was out of his mind from melancholy. His soft laughter rang out in the room and reminded him that it was only he tormenting himself.

He imagined again that he was standing over the bed in the dark room; he was cursing the dead body—then he was chilled by an agonizing terror. The darkness stifled him with its fierce embrace, picked him up, and threw him into the abyss. The voices of the abyss laughed dully. He kept falling down, down, down... His heart stopped beating. The laughter died away in the distance. Stillness, darkness, absence of thought, then heavy and dreamless sleep.

Login threw back the cover. His pallid face pressed tightly against the pillow. His breathing was rapid and quiet. With its dull eyes night looked through the window panes at his weary face, at the smile of hopeless bewilderment that hardened on his lips.

CHAPTER FOURTEEN

The Kulchitskys were having an evening party. Although Login did not arrive late, almost everyone else was already there. The ladies' and girls' elegant formal dresses came into view; there were people familiar and unfamiliar to Login, young and old people in dinner jackets and frock coats.

Quiet, sad outdoor noises like the wistful murmur of water over the rocks behind the mill-pond still echoed in Login's mind. The specters of gray houses in the rays of the sunset died away in his slumbering memory like fragments of an old dream. The light-colored wallpaper of the rooms, in which the evening light from the windows mingled sadly with the dead smile of the lamps, created for nearsighted eyes the illusion of agonizing immobility, like that in a dream.

He moved about from room to room, exchanging greetings. He felt that every face he encountered reflected a distinct type of disposition. Traits of vulgarity and obtuseness were painfully predominant. The most disagreeable impression was made by Motovilov's family: his fat little wife with her vulgar manners, mean eyes, coarse voice, green dress, and gaudy shoulder-straps; his sister, sallow and scrawny, also wearing green; Neta, looking rather stupidly coquettish, wearing a pink decoletté gown Nata, with her restless, provocative smiles and in a full, ugly white dress with a huge triple bow on the sash; his teenage son—with rotten teeth, a green complexion, slobbery smile, and sunken chest—being too familiar in his courtesies to the little ladies a bit younger than he.

He also encountered nice people. There were the Yermolins, father and daughter. Login suddenly felt the boredom swept away by someone's smile. A dreamy, quiet feeling remained. He felt like going off by himself amidst the crowd, sitting in a corner, listening to the noise of voices, giving himself over to his thoughts. Reluctantly he entered the host's study, where an argument could be heard and the guests who smoked were crowding together.

"Oh, the Holy Ghost on crutches!" shouted the treasurer Svezhunov, a fat, bald, red-faced man.

"We're all talking about Molin," Paltusov explained to Login.

"Yessir, I am prepared to shout it from the rooftops, that the investigator's actions are disgraceful: to put an innocent man in jail for personal reasons!" said Motovilov.

"Could it really have been only for personal reasons?" the engineer Sanotsky asked in a careful tone.

"Yessir, I affirm that it is because of personal conflicts and nothing else. I say that straightforwardly. I am a fiend for the truth. And, you will see, it will come to light: the truth will always be revealed, no matter how people try to trample it into the dirt. We all vouch for Molin; I offered whatever bond could be required—that man continues to keep him in jail. But it is horrible—to treat an innocent man like a criminal! And all because some little tramp was bribed to slander him!"

"Best of all," said the police chief Vkusov, an old man with a dashing figure but a senile face, "would be to give that girl a good old-fashioned whipping, yenonder-shish!"

"I hope," continued Motovilov, "that we shall succeed in bringing this disgraceful matter to the attention of the judicial authorities and in bringing the actual perpetrators of this vile blackmail to the attention of the school authorities."

"But isn't it better to wait and see how his trial turns out?" asked Login.

"Would you rely on a jury?" the treasurer Svezhunov asked rudely and derisively. "A bad prospect, old man: our shopkeepers will condemn him out of spite and won't even begin to listen to the case as they should."

"How has he made them so angry?" Login asked, smiling.

"Not he personally," the treasurer muttered in confusion.

"Excuse me," Motovilov interrupted. "Why, do you consider it just to lock up an innocent man in jail?"

"In any event," said Login, "agitation in behalf of the prisoner is useless."

"In your opinion, it so happens that we are engaging in unscrupulous agitation?"

"Mercy! Why should that be so! I'm not saying—why, you're intentions are beautiful. But good intentions, I think, aren't enough. However, the truth will come to light—you're convinced of that—what more do you need?"

"For us the truth is plain even now," said Father Andrey, the old archpriest who held classes both in the high school and in the town school, "therefore it pains us on behalf of our colleague: a man is suffering unjustly. He is no stranger to us, and besides we feel sorry for him in many ways as a human being. We can only be amazed at that truly villainous calculation that was achieved through professional envy. The case is clear; why, indeed there can be no doubt about it."

"An action unworthy of a nobleman," said Malyganov, an instructor at the pedagogical institute. At one minute as he listened to the conversation, he would give Login a sly wink; at another minute he would bow respectfully to Motovilov.

"A bad fellow, your Shestov," Father Andrey said to Login. "For Heaven's sake, he once took it into his head to call my cassock an overcoat! Doesn't that beat anything you ever heard of?"

"And have you heard," Paltusov asked Login, "what he called our venerable Alexey Stepanych?"

"No, I haven't heard."

" 'Kindly observe,' he says, 'the honored   fixture   that we have in our school.' "

"And his own esteemed superior," said Motovilov, "Krikunov, who is respected by us all, he deigned to call an icicle."

"Not inappropriately," Paltusov said with a laugh.

"Of course," Motovilov went on imposingly, "Krikunov does have a rather thin figure, but why should one mock venerable people? Extreme disrespectfulness! When he encounters my wife or daughters on the street he will not always favor them with a bow."

"He's nearsighted," said Login.

"He is an atheist," Father Andrey said sternly. "He admitted it to me himself, and with all the complications, i.e., accordingly, even in his political attitude. And that aunt of his is quite a vicious beast, in fact almost an Old Believer."[1]

"Mauviais!" said Vkusov.[2] "The whole community objects to him. Now Krikunov—there's a teacher! You needn't worry about turning your son over to the likes of him."

"But what if he pulls your son's ear off?" asked Paltusov.

"Well, to each as he deserves," Vkusov countered. "Otherwise, it'd be simply impossible in that school, such brats, all *infants turribles.*"

"Slaves and despots at the same time," thought Login.

Again a vindictive feeling welled up in fierce paroxysms inside him, and again it was concentrated on Motovilov.

"Say what you will," Paltusov said suddenly, "Molin's a fine lad: a master at drinking, and certainly nobody's fool when it comes to the girls."

"Why, that certainly is idle talk on your part, Yakov Andreyevich," Motovilov said reproachfully.

"What? Oh, yes... Well, then, gentlemen, I'm not going against the community."

"However," said Login, "your opinion, apparently, does not coincide with what the community has decided."

"The voice of the people is the voice of God," Paltusov laughingly excused himself. "However, for the stomach's sake, shouldn't we get down to some serious drinking?"

In the diningroom was a little table prepared with different kinds of vodka and hors d'oeuvres. People drank and partook of the hors d'oeuvres. Police chief Vkusov amused the company with his "French" dialect.

"Let's take a crack at it—hey!" he mumbled with his toothless mouth, then he drank some vodka, tried the hors d'oeuvres, and talked: "Yenondershish! That's Studentese, the way the students in St. Petersburg talk."

"But what does it mean?" Father Andrey kept asking with a loud laugh.

"Je ne siais pas, irreverent Reverend," the police chief would reply. "So, then, je mangera ce petty poissonlet. Eh-hey! C'est joli, c'est tres joli," he approved of the little sardine that he had devoured.[3]

And his wife, sitting in the living room, where the gales of laughter reached her, said:

"Well, I just know that's my comedian amusing everybody. Our whole family is terribly merry: I have a sanguine temperament, and my daughters are such little gigglers. Oh, don't let your name land on their tongues!"

"You're so full of life, Alexandra Petrovna," Zinaida Romanovna said languidly; "you should be back on the stage right now."

"No, I've had enough of it; I've earned my pension, and thank God!"

"She was an 'extra' and none too good at that!" Motovilov's sister, Yulia Stepanovna whispered in her sister's ear.

The latter peered sternly and haughtily at the former actress, actually not even at her, but at the gauche cut of her red dress; that, however, did not trouble the police chief's wife in the least.

"What roles did you play?" the actress Tarantin asked with an air of naivete. She was pretty, wearing a bit of make-up, but still half-girlish.

The local ladies cherished Miss Tarantin for her talent but especially because she was from a "good family" and had been "given a proper upbringing."

Gomzin was sitting opposite her and getting ready to turn her head with compliments, but for the time being he softly clacked his teeth. His dark face was bowed down over his dashing but rather stoop-shouldered body, and his eyes gazed carnivorously at the actress; at a distance it seemed that he was licking his lips, languishing in oriental decadence.

"When I was a Miss," a rather young lady was saying in another corner of the room (with her upraised eyebrows she had a face like that of a Palm Sunday cherub), "we once went to a masquerade."

"With your broom," said the treasurer, who had just popped out of the dining room.

"Oh, what's the matter with you!" the lady exclaimed with a blush.

Anna was sitting next to the lady who had just recently been married. Anna's shoulders were exquisitely covered in broad silk-muslin flounces. Her dress was the color of delicate peach skin, a soft gold all over, which cast slight golden reflections on her tan face and neck. Her skirt was embroidered with large yellow tulips down the right side, and they looked as though they were falling out of her dark-red velvet sash. Her gloves and fan were cream-colored. She had on light little white dancing slippers. A slow smile came to her red lips. There was expectation in her wide eyes.

The sounds of an intimate conversation reached her from a secluded corner.

"We haven't seen each other for so long, Mikhail Ivanych," Yulia Petrovna, Vkusov's daughter by his first wife, said in a voice of affected sweetness. She was a girl with a masculine face, a red nose, and a little black mustache. She was tall, large-boned, but skinny.

The person with whom she was talking was a teacher named Dvoretsky, a fat little squab with a face like that of a salesman in a fashionable shop. He was not happy with the conversation; he kept turning red with annoyance, huffing and puffing and glancing from side to side, but Yulia Petrovna kept blocking his way with her enormous feet and the heavy train of her light-blue dress.

"Yes, it has been a long time," he answered wryly.

"You know, we were almost like bride and groom."

"What of it?"

"Why couldn't it be that way again? After all, you did make me a proposal."

"No, I didn't."

"Not you, just Irina Avdeyevna in your behalf; it's all the same thing."

"No, it's not the same thing."

"Papa will give you as much as you asked for."

"I didn't ask for anything; I'm not a miser."

"He'll even add two hundred rubles."

With these words Yulia Petrovna's rather coarse voice sounded almost musical. Dvoretsky remained adamant. He answered with annoyance:

"No indeed, Yulia Petrovna, and don't you mention money to me. You have a suitor: you pay court to Bienstock, go and entice him with your money, but leave me in peace."

"What's the matter with you, Mikhail Ivanych! What kind of suitor is Bienstock! It's just that you're courting Mashenka Ogloblin."

"Miss Ogloblin's not the girl for me."

"How about me?"

"No, that was two years ago. And during that time you've changed, and besides, I know my own worth. So you leave me alone, please. You're after the wrong man!"

Dvoretsky stood up resolutely. His face was red and angry.

"You'll be sorry, but it'll be too late," Yulia Petrovna said in an ominous voice as she moved her feet back and gathered up her gown.

"Damn beanpole!" Dvoretsky muttered as he walked away.

Login entered the living room. Anna's smile again seemed to him both irritated and sweet. He wanted to make his way through to Anna, but Claudia stopped him. She gave off the fragrance of Coeur de Jeannette. She asked:

"You're not playing cards?"

"Some card player I am!"

They were standing alone by the doorway. Claudia nervously kept pulling and straightening her bodice's draping, which was arranged in transverse folds and fastened at her left shoulder, under a cluster of tea roses.

"We're going to dance, and you... Listen," she whispered quickly, "do you despise me?"

"For what?" he said just as softly, then added aloud: "I don't dance."

"Then what are you going to do? Be bored?... Do you despise me very much? Do you consider me a nymphomaniac?"

"I'll watch... Enough of that! Why should I? Despising others is a waste of time in my opinion—I haven't done it in ages."

Mrs. Vkusov had heard his last words from the place where she was, and she interrupted the conversation:

"So you think that dances are a waste of time, do you? Oh, you young fellow!"

"Some young fellow I am! I'm one of the old folks—like you."

"Thank you for the compliment, only, on my part I don't accept it."

"Vasily Markovich is an old hand at paying the sort of compliments that won't make you jump for joy," said Marya Antonovna Motovilov.

Someone began playing a quadrille on the grande piano. A general movement took place. Some dancers with their free-and-easy gestures suddenly appeared and got busy looking for partners. Very skillfully two or three military coats twisted and turned with their lady partners. Dancers in civilian clothes took their partners in tow. They kept moving their shoulders from side to side as though they were pushing their way through a crowd. The girls and ladies who were already dancing wore a look of bliss.

Login peered absent-mindedly at the absurd figures in the quadrille. The young man who was directing it kept shouting unintelligibly.

"He doesn't know how to breathe the way he should, the rascal, so he keeps shouting the same thing!" Login thought.

The quadrille was over. Login made his way through to Anna, sat down next to her, and said:

"These kind people make me tired!"

"Why do you call them kind?" Anna asked, smiling affectionately at him.

"Why not ask each of them what he thinks of himself? They would all turn out kind and good. But if you were to tell them that nowadays there *aren't* so many good people that every backwoods hole might be teeming with them—how furious these kind people would get!"

"Perhaps each only considers himself good?"

"Fine, if they do..."

"That's hardly fine!"

Anna broke out laughing. Login said, smiling:

"After all, what's so amusing about that? What if all the people that I know are good people, then it's not hard to get among good people? I know them, however, the scoundrels! But if—then everyone would so consider the matter and willingly award each one a diploma for goodness. But just imagine that the good people are few! That means it's hard! Why, suppose only I am good, the rest are villains. But, oh, how difficult it would be for me to sustain myself in such a position! It's just for that reason that any criticism angers them."

"Only them, and not you or me?" Anna asked vivaciously.

"Well, there was a time that I thought I and many of my friends were altruists, but for what reason? I would accept as proof the mere fact that we could speak eloquently on lofty themes. Now 'altruism'—even that lanky little word itself—seems absurd to me."

"You consider yourself an egoist?"

"Everyone's an egoist. People are merely deluding themselves at their own expense when they assert that unselfish love is possible."

"There now, it's unfair to think that: as soon as I've stopped being an altruist, then everyone has to be an egoist."

"However, I am ready to make a concession. Let there be altruists— so the word itself won't disappear. But, really, it's nothing more—like overeating."

"How can one distinguish good from evil?"

"How can one distinguish warm from cold or hot? Probably, through our adaptation to circumstances, every good results from something that seems evil."

"But that is moral alchemy."

Then the piano rang out again, one couple after another whirled around the ballroom. Gomzin dashed up to Anna with an exaggerated verve. Smiling, Anna put her hand on his shoulder.

Login watched the dancers with a detached air. The ladies' cheeks glowed, their eyes glistened; the women's bare shoulders were beautiful, but the gentlemen, as Login saw them, were indecent: red, sweaty, cheekboned faces, black clumps of hair dangling over flat and wrinkled foreheads, and the expressions of courtesy and zeal in their bulging eyes. Gomzin was looking past Anna's ochre-yellow lace *bertha* to the spot where it was fastened to her bodice with a dark-red *chou;* Anna smiled merrily. It all seemed silly to Login.[4]

Anna returned, then she immediately went off to dance with a young man in a baggy frock coat. Login did not know the young man's name, did not even know his social status, but they thought that they knew each other and even chatted when they met.

Login would have liked just to have left that dusty ballroom where the music and the candles were so tiresomely merry, but Anna sat down next to him again and said:

"If they knew how to make gold out of lead, what would gold be worth?...—No, thank you, I'm tired," she replied to a man inviting her to dance. The *man* was worn out and looked wet and pitiful.

Hiding her smile with her embroidered fan, Anna watched him with her laughing eyes while he sought out a partner. Then she looked inquisitively at Login. He smiled and said:

"Gold would be a bit cheaper, but it would not be available to everyone."

"Indeed?" Anna asked in disbelief.

She put her fan down in her lap. The name Anna was embroidered on it in yellow silk between two sprigs of lily-of-the-valley. Login looked at that name and said:

"Psychological alchemy will in fact achieve the same thing. A 'divine spark' has been found in fallen souls, but on the other hand, ideals have been dethroned. And here the sharp distinction between the good and the evil has been eroded: we have come to sympathize with evil and, at the same time, are indifferent to what formerly appeared sublime. We've lost our naivete, and with it our happiness."

"As if happiness were invariably silly!"

"The elect do not seek happiness, and do not have it."

"Why?" Anna asked. Her eyes looked up at Login in surprise.

"Happiness is not for them. Blissfulness, for them, is a vile feeling. How can one enjoy what chance has presented us, when everywhere there is so much sadness, so much suffering!"

"There is a delight in suffering," Anna said pensively.

"Now where have you learned that?"

"From experience. And happiness always has to be won."

"But, then, do only the strong attain it?"

"Of course," said Anna.

To Login the determined set of her lips seemed cruel.

"And the weak? Should we trample the weak in order to acquire happiness? I think it better to be conquered. And even the naive happiness by which the human herd is satisfied,—how hard that is to attain! You can either fight your way to the tropics through a blizzard in the steppes or warm yourself by the fireplace. But people freeze to death on the steppe, and by the fireplace..."

"The heart grows stale," Anna quietly finished for him.

"Yes, the heart grows stale."

"See how good I am at making rejoinders!" Anna said, laughing.

Her face quickly shed its momentary pensiveness.

"A philosophical discussion in an inappropriate setting," Login replied, trying to match her tone for ending the conversation. "Do you know whom I find most likeable of all this company?"

"Who?" Anna asked, slightly knitting her brows.

"Baglayev."

"Not really! What's good about him; Always chattering, lying."

"Yes. I like him because he's the most ingenuous of the scoundrels. He has nothing on his mind except what comes to his lips."

A young lady with pale eyes came up to Anna and started talking with her. Login walked off and encountered Andozersky.

"I'm looking for a dancing partner. Aren't you dancing?" Andozersky asked him with some concern.

"No, why should I?"

"You're just impossible, old friend—why're you such a stick-in-the-mud! Follow my example. Why, just now I've had to get cracking with Netochka."

"Oh, and why?"

"Well, I just have to teach that little actor a thing or two; Pozharsky—he's gotten ideas about courting her. And what kind of fellow is Pozharsky? Just a petty bourgeois named Frolov from Bouy, and a drunk to boot! What scum!"

"What's the difference! A Frolov is a Frolov."

"Oh, yes! Yes indeed, and anyhow, all our local actors are just such tramps, such down-and-outs. A community will get fed up with them, they'll stop putting on their performances and shove off for another town, on Shanks' mare, barefoot, with their boots hanging on a pole. Well, I'm going to look for a partner."

Login went up to Neta; she was talking with a young lady that Login did not know. He sat down next to Neta, bent down close to her ear, and quietly asked:

"Who's better: Pozharsky or Andozersky?"

Neta turned her eyes on him and tried to make them show a stern expression. Login kept smiling calmly, and he persistently looked her straight in the eye. He asked:

"Who seems better for you?"

"Listen, you mustn't ask such a thing," Neta answered, slightly drawing out each syllable for emphasis and trying to maintain a tone of sternness.

"Come, come, now; just why mustn't I?"

"Why? Really, only you could ask such a thing."

"But, anyhow, who's better?"

Neta started laughing. With a feigned grimace, she said:

"Andozersky is your friend."

"Oh, I won't betray you."

"Yes, really? Oh, how happy you've made me! I was so afraid of it."

"So, then, who's better?"

"You know your friend is conceited and incredibly boring for his age," said Neta.

She made a willful grimace.

"Yes. And isn't Pozharksy nice and witty?"

"He's lovely!" Neta exclaimed sincerely.

"But don't you know his real name?"

"That's a strange question!"

"Pozharsky's his stage name. His real name is Frolov."

"I didn't know."

"A petty-bourgeois from Bouy. There's a town called Bouy in the province of Kostroma."

"So, what of it?" Neta asked, blushing and getting annoyed.

Out of habit, in her confusion she pinched her cheek so hard that a distinct little spot was left on it.

"Just... a propos," Login said, grinning indifferently.

Neta fell silent. Login walked away.

"I'm carrying on some strange conversations today," he thought.

Pozharsky was the foremost actor in our theatre. He bore the entire repertoire on his shoulders: in *The Inspector General* he played Khlestakov and sometimes the mayor as well; he also played Hamlet, in fact any role that he had to. He cut capers in musical comedies, died in tragedies, sang satirical songs, recited verses and dramatic scenes on the Jewish, Armenian, native Russian, and any other way of life in the variety shows. Offstage he was a sprightly lad, could drink as much vodka as he wanted, hardly got tipsy in spite of it, and was the life of the party among the drunken merchants, whom he masterfully kept beating at *"knock-off."*[5] Molin was the only one who could compete with him in this art.

The public loved Pozharsky. The theatre would always be full at his benefit performances, and expensive presents would be brought to him: at one time a silver cigar-case, at another a magnificent dressing gown with tassels and a skull-cap. But he did not have any money—all that he acquired through his skill or from playing cards he drank up immediately. To his good fortune, he had always had some tender-hearted widow who would care about his personal comforts. Now Neta had smitten his heart in earnest: he was drinking less than usual, and for some two months now he had had nothing to do with his last mistress.

CHAPTER FIFTEEN

The second quadrille was over. The air had become hazy. It reeked unpleasantly of perfume and later of aromatic resin as well. The middle of the ballroom was deserted. The pastel colors of the maidens' gowns seemed misty. The gentlemen had managed to guzzle several glasses of vodka apiece, but many of them behaved in a more and more aloof manner toward the ladies during the intervals between dances; only, their eyes acquired a greedy look. Several beardless youths timidly hung around the young maidens, tried to be more free-and-easy, and kept blushing deeply. Their eyes gleamed, their smiles were banal.

Pozharsky whispered passionately to Neta:

"If only at rare intervals, even if at a distance, to see you, so that I can carry off your dear image like a sacred object in my memory and pray to it—that alone would be for me the bliss that life is worth living for. You alone have treated me like a human being and not a buffoon."

Neta cast tender glances at the actor. She said:

"But hereabouts they respect you so!"

"Respect me! Yes, I daresay they even love me as a clown, as a comedian. No one cares that a human heart also beats in the breast of an actor. When we're on the stage, we make people laugh and cry, and they applaud us. But in society—they despise us."

"Oh, that's not true!"

"Dear, dear child! You still don't know people—they're mean and ungrateful. An actor, in their opinion, is always striking a pose, his feelings are not genuine, and all his actions are foolish tricks. Let an actor slip on that parquet—the entire hall would rock with laughter: the comedian just played a trick!"

"But not all people in the world are mean, Vitaly Fyodorovich."

"Yes, yes, that's right. Take for example Mr. Login—Hamlet, prince of Denmark; he wouldn't laugh—because he despises the whole world, not merely actors. Then there's the noble father, virtuous Yermolin—his mind soars too high for him to admire any sort of actor... But begone, dark thoughts! Let the crowd command: 'Laugh, clown!'—you stand before me, a little white dove in a flock of black rooks!"

Neta looked at the actor with admiration and compassion; her thin rosy lips smiled in deep emotion; her blond curls quivered over her cheeks, which she had pinched hard on the sly.

Login said to Andozersky:

"It seems Netochka finds Pozharsky fascinating."

"Why, it's nothing of the sort," Andozersky answered self-assuredly.

"But, look how sweetly they're talking to each other."

111

"Well, I'll just scare him off."

Andozersky walked up to Pozharsky, unceremoniously clapped him on the shoulder, and said:

"Well, why talk idly here! Let's go, brother, let's have a drink."

Pozharsky quickly glanced at Neta and shrugged a shoulder. His quick grin and triumphant look said to her:

"See there, I'm right."

Neta blushed and looked at Andozersky with angrily flashing eyes. Pozharsky stood up, struck a pose from *The Inspector General,* and said carelessly, like Khlestakov:

"Let's go, my friend, let's drink up."

Then he gallantly bowed goodbye to Neta and went off behind Andozersky. With saddened eyes Neta watched them go out. Her white fan trembled and fluttered convulsively in her little hands.

"First it's official inquiries, then it's something else," the police chief was explaining to Login, "it won't take less than a year."

"Distressing," said Login. "Who of us in the civil service knows where he will be in a year."

"What's to be done about it? Attendez-vous a little. You can't even build a decent chicken coop if you try to rush things and do a sloppy job of it. 'Mieux tard que jamais,' the French say."

"What, brother? Are you always talking about that society of yours?" Baglayev, who had just come up to them, asked with a giggle: "Are you enticing the powers that be into your heresy?"

"Oh, we're just talking about the latest development in that matter," the police chief answered for Login.

"Give up all that dreaming-and-scheming, brother: nothing will come of it. Let's go do something better, like have a good chug-a-lug to the health of our good old police chief."

"As far as being up to doing it, we're up to it; only, why won't anything come of my plans?"

"Well, here, I'll tell you, in one instant I'll tell you a secret. Well, hold on to your glass," Baglayev said when they had entered the dining room and made their way through to the little table with the vodka. "Look, first I'll pour you some of the rowanberry stuff; nothing better in a cholera epidemic. But, then, tell me, who am I—eh?"

"A laughing-stock," Login said in annoyance and drank a glass of vodka.

"Well, you're the one who's wrong on that score, before good witnesses too! No, better let the police chief say who I am."

"You, Yushka, are the head of the town, yenonder-shish; the chef de lia ville, as the French say."

"No, not that, but the prevot des marchands," the treasurer corrected, punched Yushka in the belly, and guffawed, shrieking and squealing.

"Blast you," Yushka snapped, "you could punch a little easier. I'm a pudgy fellow, I get hurt easily. Well, so there, brother, I'm the head of the place—that means, the favored person, the mastermind of the whole town. How could I *not* know our society? Brother, we're solid citizens, old sparrows; you won't catch us with chaff; we won't go for your bumptiousness, there's never been any of that with us. Why, for isntance, if I should announce that I'm going to give birth to a child tomorrow, the whole town would gather at my house for the performance, we'd get crocked to the gills, but in the morning we'd again be clean as a whistle, ready again 'for a valiant exploit, my friends.' Is that right or what, treasurer?"

"Right, Yushka, you're a clever head, full of brains."

"There, precisely! Well, fellows, our task isn't a great one: let's take a drink, then another one—so that the cholera won't get to us."

"All that's true, Yury Alexandrovich, but tell us, why do you drink such a lot of vodka?" Login asked.

"Well, I'll be damned! What do you mean 'a lot'? I only drink a mere trifle—and that only for one perfectly good reason: fellows, I just like to keep the cups clean."

"It's impossible, you know, not to drink," interrupted Ogloblin, a fat and fussy, red-cheeked young man in gold eye-glasses. "A time like this— a man loses heart, he wants to forget his troubles."

Meanwhile, at another corner of the table, Andozersky was drinking with Pozharsky.

"Let's have another one, then," Andozersky said morosely.

He glared spitefully at the actor's rose-colored necktie, carelessly tied and sitting a little askew on his impeccably neat shirt-front.

"Let's have another, my friend, whatever may happen," Pozharsky replied light-heartedly.

He reached for a bottle and began singing in a falsetto:
Here amid the slumb'ring woods
And the fields live we;
All the mighty of the earth
Aren't as happy or as free.

"Why, brother, you're not getting ready to marry, are you?" Andozersky asked.

He looked askance at the threadbare elbows on the actor's jacket.

"As it's been rightly observed, Signor, the public scarcely encourages dramatic talents; marriage is a most excellent means of avoiding tuberculosis of the pocketbook."

"Hm, but where is the bride?"

"We shall find a bride, most esteemed sir: as long as there be suitors, God will punish each with a bride—such is the course of us suitors."

"Why, have you set your sights on a merchant's daughter?"

"Why necessarily a merchant's?"

113

"Well, a shopkeeper's then?"

"Why in the world a shopkeeper's? With my pleasing talents and with my cute little mustache, I can win the heart of a real young lady for all time—I'll swagger by her, make wicked eyes at her, and she'll fall."

"Well, brother, bend the branch as far as you can," Andozersky said with a mean little laugh.

The actor made a face like that of a steward in a realistic drama.

"Mercy, sir, you see fit to offend me, and for no good reason. I'm not such an ordinary fellow. How am I not adequate? Indeed I have the figure and courage and courtly manners, and besides, I haven't gotten my head broken. No indeed, do me a favor, let me hope."

"You're walking down another man's path, you're treading on ano-ther's man's grass; be careful not to get your neck broken."

The actor imitated a stupid character in a folk play, set his feet apart, smirked dull-wittedly, and said:

"Eh? This, that is, er—what exactly do you mean? A little ol' trifle like that, for instance, never occurred to me. Looky, uncle," he addressed Gutorovich, an old man who acted in comic roles, "for no reason in the world the master's so cross he's made me afeared. How've I distressed him? Oh, Lordy, I didn't mean to."

Gutorovich's wrinkled, decrepit face contorted itself into a grimace that was supposed to represent the humble submissiveness of a drunken muzhik, then he began to mumble, shaking his head and waving his hands like a drunk and showing the black remnants of his teeth:

"Ah, Vitashenka, my one best friend, let's sing a little song, let's really cheer up His High Excellency, the impartial judge."

"Well, let's sing it then, O Elder."

Andozersky muttered something unkind, then walked away from the table. Pozharsky and Gutorovich put their arms around each other and, staggering around in front of the table, began singing in mock-drunken voices:

> Hey, young Bossie, your frolics should end;
> You're a grown young heifer!
> Calves to birth you should be carrying.
> What on earth would you be hoping for?
> Hey, you, Tolya, you, Tolya, old friend;
> You're a grown young sour-puss!
> Why, we wonder, aren't you marrying?
> What on earth would you be hoping for?

The actors were surrounded by the company of slightly tipsy men. The military commandant's merry wife mingled in the midst of the crowd; she drank two glsses of vodka with a young second lieutenant to whom she was making advances. Everyone was having a good time. For the onlookers' amusement Gutorovich imitated several persons in local society at interesting

114

moments in their lives: Dr. Mataftin as he examined cholera patients at a respectable distance and trembled in fear; Mokhovikov—the haughty head-master of the pedagogical institute—as he paced about his classes with an inaccessibly-pompous air and with his hat in his hand; Motovilov as he talked about virtue, then let it slip about the bargeful of goods that he had stolen; Krikunov as he prayed to God—and then boxed little boys' ears.

"I'll be damned!" Baglayev cried out. "You'll make us split our sides."

All this finally became unbearably revolting to Login. He left. Gutoro-vich winked at the merry audience over him, bent his back, and whispered:

"What a shame—a man has to walk the earth upright. He has to get up on a pedestal, even a tiny one; otherwise, you know, it just won't do, gentlemen."

The "gentlemen" laughed gleefully.

Login entered one of the sitting rooms, where the resounding laughter of young ladies was heard.

"Here too, no doubt, I'll encounter something vulgar," he thought.

He saw Andozersky—the latter had somehow managed to make the girls laugh. Claudia was among the young ladies. There were no other men here besides Andozersky. It seemed to Login that Andozersky had become embarrassed when Login caught sight of him; he abruptly ceased his lively narrative. The merry, laughing eyes of the young ladies turned toward Login. Claudia looked at him provocatively; something hostile shone in the depths of her narrow pupils, and the green flames of her eyes burned maliciously.

"We were just talking about you, Vasily Markovich."

Then she moved her chair back slightly so that Login could sit in the next chair, which had been covered by the folds of her skirt.

"Speak of the devil!" a little curly-haired Miss with the face of a pretty little boy said merrily.

"Curious that you found anything interesting to say about me," Login said lazily.

"How could we help finding it! Anatoly Petrovich was just saying..."

"Why, it was a joke," Andozersky said, trying to dismiss the matter.

Claudia looked at him in amazement. In confusion Andozersky turned to the serving girl who had just come up to him with a tray, and he took an orange. Immediately he felt that the orange was too large and that choosing it had been a mistake. It annoyed him. Claudia continued calmly:

"He was saying that the members of your society will have to make secret vows in a dungeon, in white robes, with candles in their hands, and that they will have to burn signs on their backs as proof of eternal member-ship. And whoever betrays you will be condemned to death by starvation."

Login let out a short, harsh laugh. He said:

"What a sad joke! Why, however, it's not a bad thought: a certain vow should be taken, though why on earth a secret one? It could even be an open vow."

"Just what sort of vow?" asked Claudia.

"A vow not to slander one's friends."

"Well, now, you know, I was joking," Andozersky said in a carefree manner.

"Eat the slander for dessert," said Claudia.

She pointed out to Login the maid, who was holding the tray of fruit in front of him.

Login piled a lot of fruit onto his plate indiscriminately and set about eating it. His thin nostrils kept quivering nervously.

In the next room Motovilov and the police chief were having a hushed conversation. Motovilov was saying:

"I greatly dislike Login."

"And why?" Vkusov asked in a cautious tone.

"I do not like him," Motovilov repeated. "I have a reliable opinion; I would not cut him down for no good reason. Believe me, that society of his is up to no good. There is something suspicious about it.."

"Societie, yenonder-shish," Vkusov said in a melancholy tone.

"Believe me, it is only a pretext for propaganda against the government. That gentleman must be unmasked."

"Hm,... let's wait and see."

"In the school too, you may know, he is positively dangerous. The pupils flock to him, and he corrupts them..."

"Corrupts them? Oh, yenonder-shish!"

"With his propaganda."

"Aha!"

A sly and cunning expression passed over Motovilov's face as though he had suddenly conceived of something very convenient. He said:

"And I cannot even guarantee that he is... Who knows what he is like! He keeps aloof, lives by himself; the servant's downstairs, he's upstairs. I feel uneasy about it. You know what I mean; you are a father yourself; your son in high school is a *handsome boy.*"

"Have you heard something by any chance?" Vkusov asked uneasily.

"If I had not heard something, I would never have allowed myself to speak of such things," Motovilov said with dignity. "Believe me that without sufficient grounds—fully sufficient, you understand—I could not have brought myself to..."

"What are you gossiping about?" asked Baglayev, coming up to them. Motovilov walked away.

"Well, we've just been talking about Login," the police chief said sadly.

"Ah! A clever man! Haughty! Always the same! Brother, he despises us, and with good reason! We're swine! However, he's a swine himself. But I love him, I swear to God I love him. He and I are great friends. We're as thick as thieves."

Vkusov looked at him pensively with his dull eyes, shook his head, and mumbled:

"C'est vrai! C'est vrai!"

CHAPTER SIXTEEN

Login was looking for a place to set down his empty dish, and he wandered into a little room that was half-dark. Two melancholy eyes peered at him from a mirror. He turned away in annoyance.

"My dear, what angry eyes you have!" he heard a saccharine voice say to him.

Before him stood Irina Avdeyevna Kudinov, a widow about forty years old, wearing picturesque make-up and trying to look younger than she was. After her husband's death, she had been left with a teen-age daughter, a son in the gimnazia, and a nice little house. She had dubious means of making a living: a small pension, fortune-telling, match-making, some confidential affairs. She dressed fashionably, richly, but too gaudily (Anna compared her to a woodpecker). She went everywhere. She kept thinking of getting married again, but it had not yet worked out.

"Why on earth are you so sad, my dear? Hereabouts there are so many eligible maidens, one lovelier than the next, and you let yourself be depressed! Ay-ay-ay, and still a young fellow! For an old woman like me it would be excusable, but just look how merry I am! I run around   like quicksilver."

"What kind of old woman are *you*, for heaven's sake, Irina Avdeyevna! But I have been enjoying myself very much today."

"Somehow it doesn't look like it. You know what I'll tell you: it's time for you to get married, my precious."

"You'd find a match for everybody!"

"That's right; why be so sour about it? Let me, and I'll get you married right away, to *any* girl. Which one do you want?"

"What kind of bridegroom am *I*, Irina Avdeyevna?"

"Well now, why not? *Any* girl, as God is my witness, would... You're well-educated, explosive."[1]

Andozersky came up to them. He unceremoniously interrupted:

"Don't listen to her, brother. You want to get married? See me about it: I have some small knowledge in these matters."

"You're taking bread out of my mouth," Mrs. Kudinov said affectedly. "Shame on you, Anatoly Petrovich!"

"You have enough for the rest of your life. You have a pension."

"Is my pension large? A pension in name only."

"Brother, I'll find you a match for free. I don't need the money to buy silk dresses. I'll fix myself up, and I won't forget you either. Only, mind you," he whispered mysteriously as he led Login away from Mrs. Kudinov, "most of all, my claim is to Nyutka; watch out, don't go after her: she's mine."

"Then why are you jealous of Netochka's attachment to the actor?"

"I'm not jealous, but the actor's just let his eyes roam where he shouldn't—to get that merchant's snout of his on Easy Street.[2] Then too, anyway, I need her just in case. So be it, I'll tell you confidentially: there's not much hope of getting Nyutka—she's a stubborn little girl!"

"Then why are you saying that she's yours?"

"She's in love with me up to her ears—that's certain. But there is a hitch—some sort of foolish principles. She and I had a strained conversation the other day. And, well, she and I still have a lot of haggling to do over something: you're my friend, so you won't interfere."

"Of course, I won't."

"Well, good. Hey, you could do better in hiring a housekeeper."

"What kind?"

"A young one, of course. Ah, you lone wolf! Well, old friend, I'm going off to dance again."

Login was left alone in the little sitting room. Mentally he tried to assume the role of suitor to Claudia or Neta. His heart turned cold at these thoughts.

Neta was a fickle, simple-hearted child, but a very nice one. However, no sooner did he try to imagine Neta as a bride and wife than cold indifference immediately destroyed his mental picture of the nice, rather silly, spoiled little girl stuffed full of worn opinions and cliches.

"Now Claudia's different. What force and passion and thirst for life! And what helplessness and dismay! A recent storm has swept through her heart and devastated it, as indeed once happened to me. Both of us are seeking a solution and our salvation. But there is neither a solution nor salvation. I know it, she has some premonition of it. What could we do together? She thirsts all the more for life, I'm beginning to tire of it."

Those were his thoughts, elated one moment, cold the next, and his mood was the same. As long as he recalled Claudia just as she was, it was pleasant to think of her: the vivacious sparkle of her eyes and the sudden bright flush on her cheeks warmed and caressed his heart. But he had only to imagine Claudia as a wife—the charm faded, vanished.

Another image, the image of Anna appeared to him. A vision clear and pure. He did not want to think anything about her or imagine her in any other way: it was as though he were afraid of frightening away the dear image by prosaically interlacing it with ordinary thoughts.

He shut his eyes. He envisioned the blue sky, white clouds, quietly rustling fields of rye, and, on the narrow strip between them—Anna, her happy smile, her suntanned face, her light dress; her slender, suntanned feet stepped soundlessly through the dust of the road, left behind their soft tracks. He opened his eyes: the vision did not disappear at once, but grew pale and hazy in the tiresome lamplight; the dear smile grew dull, lost its shape. Then he shut his eyes again in order to restore the wondrously beautiful vision. There was the music's persistent strumming, the dancers' stamping, the young conductor's hollow voice... but above all this uproar a gently mocking smile shone, and suntanned hands moved in time to the music and gathered blue corn-flowers and a red poppy.

"I daresay, you aren't having a very good time: it seems you've gone to sleep," he heard a quiet voice say over him.

He opened his eyes: Claudia. He stood up. Calmly he said:

"No, I wasn't asleep, but for some reason I did start dreaming."

Claudia's green eyes shone with a burning brightness.

"Dreaming about Nyutochka?"

"A person can dream about anything in idle moments," Login replied.

He forced a smile, with a feeling of awkwardness that was strange for him.

"Happy Nyutochka!" Claudia said with a light sigh and an ironic smile. "And I'm ready to bet that you imagined Anna just now in a field, among flowers, in utter simplicity. Tell me, did I guess right?"

Login frowned and clamped his teeth on his lower lip.

"Yes, you guessed it," he confessed.

"Nyutochka enjoys the sunshine. The sweet little flowers and butterflies," said Claudia, and she kept rapidly opening and closing her fan and pulling on its lace trimming. "But she is now dressed up for the ball. Aren't you sorry about that?"

"Why indeed?"

"You see, even Nyutochka cannot stand above fashion. Silly, isn't it? It would be better if we had to dance barefoot, right? Anyhow, I beg you not to doze off: we'll be having supper in a minute."

The music had stopped. The people noisily had made their way to dinner.

The company dined in two rooms: in the large dining room and in the little room next to it. In the large dining room it was spacious and orderly. There were gathered the married ladies and the maidens, some venerable, bored-looking elders, and the young gentlemen, who were obliged to sit with the ladies and amuse them.

Andozersky sat next to Anna and took up her time zealously. Miss Tarantin, the pretty actress, kept affecting naivete and lisping, showing her glistening, white, even teeth. The apathetic Pavlikovsky kept her diverted with stories about his greenhouses. Bienstock was saying something amusing to Neta. Nata kept flashing angry eyes at him. Gomzin wasted his favors on Nata. Every time that Nata looked at his grinning teeth, the whiteness of which was revolting to her (Bienstock had yellowish teeth), malice would well up inside her, and she would say something impudent, taking advantage of her rights as an *innocent little girl.* With stern zealousness Motovilov kept sermonizing on virtues. The military commander's wife kept sipping wine in small swallows and vowing that, if she should get the chance to become rich through poisoning someone, then she would poison him if it could be done without anyone else's knowing.

Motovilov was horrified and vehemently exclaimed:

"You are slandering yourself!"

The decrepit military commander and both the elder Motovilov women talked quietly about housekeeping. Dubitsky told about how he had commanded a regiment. Zinaida Romanovna pretended that that was interesting to her. Claudia and Yermolin began arguing quietly but vigorously about something. Paltusov and Dubitsky's wife—she was glad that her husband was sitting some distance away from her—talked about the theatre and about flowers.

In the little room the company was crowded together, merry, and drunk. Here were only men: Father Andrey was slightly tipsy; Vkusov incessantly kept exclaiming, one minute in Russian:

"Buddies, I'm pickled!"

Then in French:

"Frerekins, je suis pickle!"[3]

"And forgot his wife, I say," Ogloblin made it rhyme for him.

The treasurer was telling cynical anecdotes; Yushka was there, as red as a beet; Pozharsky and Gutorovich were not getting tight, although they were drinking more than anyone else. Sanotsky and Fritz, the inseparable pair of engineers, were present. There were five more, gentlemen with graying hair and insolent looks. And Login also found himself here.

At this table they were all drinking a lot, as though they had all been dying of thirst; they chose the beverages that were somewhat more potent, and they poured them into the largest glasses, without concern for the fact that the dregs of a different drink were still on the bottom. They ate greedily and sloppily, smacked their lips noisily, talked loudly, kept interrupting and insulting one another. The conversation was such that, drunk as they were, even they would at times lower their voices so that the ladies would not hear. At such times, the circle of those conversing would move together, those sitting father away would lean across the table, the others would bow their heads; for a short time it would become quiet; only a hasty whisper would be heard. Then suddenly gales of uproarious laughter wculd fill the crowded room and make the ladies in the large dining room shudder.

"Some anecdotes!" Father Andrey said with a rumbling laugh. "Listen, fellows, I'll tell you a better one, an actual experience that happened to me. What a dream I had the other night! I see myself in some sort of garden, and there are all these fir-trees in that garden, and there are little icon-lamps hanging on the fir-trees. Oil's been poured in the lamps, the little wicks are floating, the little flames are flickering, so everything looks fine and orderly. Then I see servers bustling around those lamps. As soon as a lamp goes out, immediately a server takes it down. There I stood a while and looked, and then I ask, 'What is it,' I say, 'that these lamps are for?' The server then says: 'These aren't mere lamps. They're human fates; where a flame is burning brightly, a man still has a lot of his life left; but where there isn't much oil,' he says, 'it'll soon be the end for that person.' At that, fellows, I was scared worse than I am before the archbishop. However, I got up my nerve and then I ask: 'Well then, Sir, may I find out which lamp here is mine?' He led me to a certain little fir-tree. Several little lamps are hanging there, all burning brightly, but one is just barely flickering. 'There it is,' he says, 'that one is yours.' I started trying to find some remedy. I see the server's got his back to me. Very quickly I stuck my finger into someone else's lamp; the oil, I knew, would cling to my finger. I shook off a drop into my own lamp. The little flame came to life again. And so I did it several times: as soon as he would turn his back, I'd put my finger in someone else's lamp and then in my own. I kept dripping it in gradually. And dripped in quite a tolerable amount, only all of a sudden I got careless, got in a hurry, and got caught. The server (Blast the luck!) turned around and sees me a-poking my finger in someone else's lamp. How he started screaming! 'What are you doing? And what are you sticking your hand in there for?' And then, fellows, just as he whopped me on the mug, right then I woke up."

Great rumbles of laughter went around the table.

"And what did it turn out to be? It was my wife slapping my face in a fit of temper."

When the guffawing had died down, Baglayev tried to begin a story:

"Well, now, gentlemen, when I was serving in the Forty-second Artillery Brigade..."

"You're lying, Yushka," shouted Sanotsky. "You never served in the artillery."

"Well, that's a fine thing to say! I never served—indeed!"

"And at what university did you get your education, you head full of brains?"

"At Moscow, of course!"

"But I heard in effect that you were expelled from school in the fifth grade."[4]

"Spit in his eyes, whoever told you that."

"You do the spitting: he's right here—Constantine Stepanych."

"Kostya, friend, was it really you? You could bring yourself to say such a thing?" Baglayev said reproachfully.

"We know what you're like, head of the town: a notorious liar," Ogloblin replied. "Here, you'd do better telling how little boys run away from the alms-house."

"The alms-house is an abomination!" Baglayev said with renewed vigor. "The filth! The disorder! They all steal! The old men and old women get drunk. The little boys run around without any supervision and get into mischief."

"Wait a minute, wait a minute, you brainy head," Sanotsky shouted. "Whom are you denouncing? Who's in charge of the alms-house?"

"You know who: the head of the town, the mayor."

"And who's the mayor?"

Laughter went around the table.

"Clever, Yushka!" the treasurer said, going into raptures. "You forgot that it's the mayor."

"I didn't entirely forget."

"He just sensed that they'll ride him for it, yenonder shish!"

"They won't ride anything! But I don't want the place that way myself. And I'm going to straighten out that alms-house!"

"Tell us why the little boy at your place took to his heels," Ogloblin said to pester him.

"Because he's a rascal: every year he runs off. Last year he ran away and acted like a fool. He was caught in the Summer Garden, under a bush, and was brought back to me and thrashed; and now he's gone again as usual, 'way off into the woods—he sensed it was spring. The good-for-nothing! Why doesn't somebody knock his head off!"

"Why, did you recently tan his hide as an advance installment or something? Or did you do it for no reason at all?"

"I didn't give him anything in advance, but he hasn't been doing well in school! Krikunov made a complaint, and I dealt with the matter."

"By giving the boy a hundred hot ones?"

"Nothing like a hundred, but fifteen altogether. In fact I was present when he was whipped."

"Did you hold him down, then?"

"Fool! I don't even care to talk with a fool!"

Laughter went around the table, but Yushka was furious and grumbled:

"I am the mayor. My business is to deal with matters, that's what! Not to hold someone down."

"You-roach-ka, you rogue!"[5] Father Andrey called out. "Would you like a butt to smoke?"

Login persisntely kept silent, gazed at the drunken faces, and shuddered in acute anger and melancholia. Every word that he heard pierced and hurt him like a red-hot needle. He drank glass after glass. His consciousness was dulled. His anger dissolved into a vaguely oppressive feeling.

At last supper was over. Through the noise of chairs being moved back, the stamping of feet, and the merrily excited murmur of conversations, the sounds of music were heard: the young people were getting ready to dance some more. But the drowsier guests were bidding goodbye to the host and hostesses.

Login and Baglayev walked out together onto the steps. Yushka kept hanging around Login and babbling something. On the porch Login held out his hand to Baglayev and said:

"Well, we have to go our separate ways."

"Why, silly? I say—let's go get drunk."

"Well, look here, we've *had* some little bit to drink! And besides, where can we go at such a late hour?"

"I do know of a place; I'll take you there! Silly, they'll let us in!" Baglayev said convincingly. "Do you think I've gotten away from my wife for nothing? Let her dance the mazurka all she wants to, but we're going on a binge. Come on now, I mean it, let's relive the good old days!"

Login thought it over, then followed him. Soon Paltusov caught up with them. Giggling, Yushka asked him:

"Well, Ox-eye! Have you abandoned your guests?"

"Oh, to hell with them," Paltusov said gloomily. "Your wife missed you, so I promised to find you..."

"And fill him up," Login concluded.

"And deliver him home."

"Oh, really?" Baglayev giggled. "But I just went home—you might find me there any minute now. Like hell!"

"I'll say I didn't find you," said Paltusov. "I have a headache; I'd like to have a drink."

"That's what we're after!" said Login.

"I can't go without drinking," Paltusov explained. "To live in Russia and not get drunk is just as impossible for me as it is for a fish to lie on the bank and not suffocate. I need a different atmosphere. Whew! Hell! Even streetlights here are few and far between... Police chiefs, zemstvo chiefs—just the smell of them makes me sick."

In Login's consciousness everything wavered and grew hazy. Somehow it all became an "I don't care." With a feeling of dull pleasure and wearisome lack of will, he walked behind his friends, listened to their sentences and their muttering. Their footsteps and voices reverberated dully and sluggishly in the stillness of the night.

In the tavern, which they visited via the back door, drowsiness began to overpower Login. Everything became as in a dream: the back room weakly illuminated by two palm-oil candles; the stout, barefoot tavernmistress in an unbuttoned housecoat (she whispered something unintelligible and scurried about like a bat, with bottles of beer in her hands); and that beer, tepid and unpalatable, which he swallowed for some reason.

Paltusov was saying something frank and sad about his love and his trials and tribulations; unwittingly he let Claudia's name slip out twice. Yushka crawled over to kiss him and cried on his shoulder. Login perceived life's great anguish and wanted to tell how strongly and unhappily he had loved: he would have liked to have Yushka start crying over him. But the words did not fit together, and besides, there was no use talking about it.

"Zinaida!" Paltusov exclaimed. "I never loved her, but now I hate her."

"A delicate lady!" mumbled Yushka.

"Her affectedness! Her provincialism! It's beyond my endurance. She doesn't have that bouquet of aristocracy, without which a woman is a wench. Oh, Claudia! Only I can appreciate her. She and I are kindred souls."

"Lively girl!" Yushka said in approval.

Paltusov fell silent, put his elbows on the table, which was wet with spilled beer, and hung his head in his hands. Yushka moved up to Login and whispered:

"Here's a remarkable man, brother, I tell you. He alone understands me down to the last detail, brother,—a clever number, the rascal. He could steal Panama and not get caught. No, brother, don't tell me otherwise, he's a genius!"

A policeman looked in at the door. The hostess started whispering fearfully:

"Didn't I tell you! God, that's all we needed!"

"Can it!" Yushka babbled in alarm and looked pop-eyed at the policeman.

"Please don't get upset, Your Honor," the policeman said reassuringly. "I just, er, came 'cause, you know... the light; but long as it's just some fine gentlemen that I know..."

The fine gentlemen whom he knew gave him twenty copecks apiece and ordered the hostess to serve him beer. The policeman was "much obliged" and left. Yushka began tossing off contemptuous remarks at the expense of the police. But their mood had been spoiled. They sat for a while in silence, sucked up the rest of their beer, then left.

Login did not remember what happened after that. He regained consciousness at home, by an open window. Faces and images kept swarming by. A new feeling was mounting in him.

"It's envy of Andozersky," he thought, and he himself was surprised at the thought.

He did think that Andozersky was rather stupid and vulgar, even rather vile, and he was terribly angry at Andozersky. But suddenly the fat and hypocritical figure of Motovilov sailed forth from the darkness, and Login began to tremble all over and was inflamed with the ancient malice of Cain. Again there was a corpse lying on the bed, and again Login began to feel chill paroxysms of terror.

Suddenly Login felt a flood of insuperable malice, and he moved determinedly toward the hateful corpse.

"I'll step over it!" he whispered hoarsely, and he squeezed the heavy folds of the cover in his hot hands.

He fell into a deep, dreamless sleep. Near dawn he suddenly became conscious as having been awakened. A shrill wailing echoed in his ears. With the clarity of actual vision there appeared before him a vault, a window with bars on it, a maden's naked body, torture. Someone bright and evil was saying that all was well, and that there is great elation in suffering. And under the blows of the knout, blood spurted from the white, crimson-striped skin.

CHAPTER SEVENTEEN

Mr. Yermolin and Anna were on their way home. Their barouche rocked along smoothly, the wheels rolled noiselessly on their rubber tires, and only the horses' hooves could be heard clopping swiftly and rhythmically over the fine gravel.

The pre-dawn glow was already beginning to grow lighter. The still, moist treetops were catching and reflecting a barely perceptible tinge of rosy light. Somewhere nearby a nightingale was wearily and languidly whistling the last notes of its tender little song. A bat, up past its hour, flew near the barouche, turned around sharply in mid-air, and rushed away.

Anna and her father were conversing in broken phrases. Her eyes were drowsy. Various impressions would stand out clearly in her mind then fade into one another. The cool breeze's delicate touch would suddenly take her mind off of her recollections of the loud, oppressive scenes at the evening party, and then all that peaceful stillness of misty fields and dark trees, everything dear and familiar, would draw near to her. At such an hour, usually too early for waking, all these peaceful and familiar scenes seemed somehow enigmatic and illusory.

Heretofore Anna had had a clear outlook on the world, had felt a love for Nature, had had rational explanations for the natural phenomena, and had not been troubled by the unknown or incomprehensible in nature. But this spring was a stranger, unlike all the rest, and it pervaded everything with terrors and mysteries. Nothing, apparently, had changed in Anna: her views on life and the world were as bright as ever. But her dreams had become troubled, and her fancies, contrary to all her past, were sometimes directed towards the useless and the impossible. In former days she had clearly seen both her relationship with each person that she happened to encounter and her feelings toward each of these people. But now she inwardly felt a presentiment of something new, undetermined as yet. The vagueness of her thoughts and feelings oppressed her. With unwonted timidity she left a certain realm of impressions unexplained for the time being. However, since her thoughts kept turning to this realm unwittingly, accidentally, and ever more frequently in the course of time, then a single definite word for all this did in fact suddenly occur to her at times, and at such times she would begin to burn all over with a bashful and joyful and eerie feeling. But she still would not rely upon this definite explanation, and, all disturbed, she would sigh softly, and her bosom would heave.

Now, in the rosy chill of early dawn, Anna enjoyed giving herself over to the moist touch of the softly blowing force against which she was borne down the stillness of the road. With its fragrant blossoms, the mountain ash foreboded sorrow, but forthcoming sorrows did not frighten her.

Suddenly the shadow of unpleasant memories fell across her face, which was slightly pale from fatigue, and she said quietly:

"The young people around here have such a depressing way of having a good time!"

Yermolin looked at her with kindly eyes—in them lurked an age-old sadness. He answered:

"At least it's good that joy, even of that sort, has not dried up."

Anna shut her eyes. She bowed her head sleepily. A light sleep came over her, but, after a minute, something awakened her, an indistinct sound. She straightened up, looked at her father with wide-open eyes.

"Have you been asleep?" Yermolin asked affectionately and smiled.

"Dozing. Was someone singing?" Anna asked, listening carefully.

"No, I didn't hear," answered her father.

All was quiet. The driver, dozing, swayed back and forth on the coach-box. Without hurrying, the horses trotted down the familiar road.

"So I just fell asleep," said Anna. "It seemed to me that the sun was setting, and someone was singing 'There's More Than One Path in the Field.' And, it seemed, I was walking on a country road, and I wanted to move toward the one who was singing. He just drew me to him with his song."

"Go, dear," Yermolin said pensively.

Anna blushed. She looked at him with amazed, sparkling eyes. She asked:

"Where?"

Yermolin gave his head a shake, passed a hand over his face, and said:

"Where? No, I didn't mean anything. I've been dozing off too, it seems."

Smiling, Anna shut her eyes. She leaned back. It was comfortable and pleasant to lie there, to rock back and forth, to bask in the coolness of the pre-dawn air.

The shadows of the trees kept passing over her face; they alternated with rosy shafts of light from the incipient dawn. The trees kept spreading out, becoming thicker, coming together in clusters, gloomily evading the rosy, still rather faint rays of light.

And again Anna was dreaming, this time that she was walking in a strange, gloomy valley, among dark, forbidding trees. A weak, unsteady light flickered between them. Grim foreboding filled her with a feeling of depression.

Suddenly Anna noticed that everything around her was coming awake: the old trees, broad-leafed and tall, and the young grass, hard and glistening, and the pale green moss, and the timid forest flowers—all came awake, and Anna felt upon her their oppressive and hostile stares directed at her from all sides. Everything was watching Anna, and everything was motionless and silent. Horrible was the enmity of the silent witnesses. Anna went on. Her feet moved with difficulty; she went on alone, went on hastily. Then she

128

knew that there was nowhere to go, and her feet were growing heavier and heavier. Then she was falling—and she opened her frightened, weary eyes.

The horses were snorting—they sensed the nearness of their stable. The coachman stirred, waved his whip. Her father looked at her, smiled affectionately. Anna responded with a smile, but she did not feel like moving, and her eyes closed again.

"Here we are at home," said her father.

He held out his hand to help her out of the barouche.

Anna threw off her clothes, stood by the window, leaned on one shoulder, and, with her whole shapely body, gave herself over to the caresses of the cold air. The garden let its juicy and dewy branches tremble joyfully. Swiftly and merrily the sky was turning scarlet, and its tender glow was widely suffused over the duskiness of her face and the contours of her nude body. With a sudden joy she awaited the first rays of the sun.

Anna gazed intently at the dawn blazing in the sky, but a light reverie crept upon her without her noticing it, and it covered her eyes like a golden mist. Her eyes closed.

She dreamed of a golden meadow all covered with sunlight and surrounded by low brick walls. Little boys in red capes and little girls in blue skirts were running about on the well-mown grass. They were batting a large ball back and forth with the agile blows of their sticks, and it kept flying up high. The children were laughing. Their silvery laughter pealed forth, a sound of bells, unceasing and even.

At first Anna enjoyed watching their game. She felt like joining in— she would have done it more skillfully. But soon their laughter grew tiresome. Anna looked closely at the children and thought:

"Why do they have such pale, mean faces?"

She raised her eyes toward the brick walls—they were interminable; nothing could be seen beyond them; only the tiresomely monochromatic, faded-blue sky rose above them. Anna looked at the children again. Nothing had changed in the boring monotony of their merry game—but suddenly Anna became frightened.

She knew that something horrible was approaching, and each time that the ball flew up, her heart constricted in horror. Amid the monotonous tinkling of the joyless laughter, the horror kept mounting.

She knew that she had to do something to break the fatal spells, but she could not move. Like one overcome by lethargy, she strained every nerve, but in vain—and she grew immovably rigid in the midst of the bright-green meadow.

She saw the ball descending directly upon her and growing larger... She made a final desperate effort—and opened her eyes.

Her heart was pounding so fast that it hurt, her body was trembling, cold, but soon her terror gave way to joy. The sun had just risen; however, everything around was still quiet but for the little early birds chirruping in the bushes.

Anna was amazed at her dreams. She would have liked to go out into the park, toward the river, but sleep weighed upon her, and she reluctantly walked up to the bed.

Covering her chilled shoulders with the blanket, she felt a languor and a weariness throughout her body, but it seemed to her that she could not get to sleep. However, she had hardly laid her cheek on the pillow when her eyes closed and she fell asleep.

She spent less than her usual time in bed and woke up several times during that time. Before each awakening she dreamed new dreams, strange things for her—formerly she had slept soundly and had almost never had dreams. Then it seemed that she had been dreaming all night and waking up constantly.

She dreamed of a dense grove. Bushes were crowded together between the tall trees; she could see the yellow pods of the acacia, the red spurge-flax and mountain ash. Little mounds were covered with wondrous flowers. Bright-colored wooden crosses and stone slabs were barely visible from behind the thicket. It was bright, quiet, sad...

She dreamed that savage hounds were roaming in a dense forest, barking furiously, sniffing the ground and the bushes, tracking down somebody... Pale, frightened, he was hiding behind a tree. And she was riding horseback into the forest and did not know what she should do.

In yet another dream, she saw herself by the bed of a sick child. She raised up the cover—there were dark spots all over the child's body. The child lay still, looked at her with eyes full of reproach. Anna asked him:

"Do you know?"

The child was silent. He was still quite an infant and did not know how to talk—but Anna saw that he understood and knew. Someone was asking her:

"Whose fault is this? And how can it be remedied?"

Anna was frightened, and she woke up.

Then she beheld herself in a rocky desert. The air was stifling, crimson and hazy; the soil was red ashes. Anna was carrying a man on her shoulders—a motionless, cold burden. He was wounded, and thick, sticky blood was dripping on to Anna's shoulders' She held his hands in her strong hands—his hands were pale and familiar to her. She was hurrying and anxiously looking ahead, where a dim light appeared through the haze.

The wounded man was saying to her:

"Leave me. I'm done for, you save yourself."

She heard the sound of pursuit, an uproar, laughter. He whispered:

"Put me down, put me down! You can't get me out of here."

"I'll get you out," she whispered stubbornly and hurried onward. "Somehow I *will* get you out of here."

Her feet were as heavy as lead, she was moving slowly, and the pursuit was drawing near. Despair! Her strength was giving out—and then she woke up and again noticed with alarm the rapid beating of her heart.

CHAPTER EIGHTEEN

Gossip spreads quickly in a small town like ours, in fact, the dirtier and the more improbable the gossip, the more quickly it spreads. Motovilov had only to have a word in private with Vkusov at the Kulchitskys' evening party, and on the next day Motovilov's sudden fabrication was already going around town, passing as unquestionable, and encountering objections from no one.

On that same day, the gossip reached Claudia. Valya was the bearer of it; she sometimes came running to the Kulchitskys' too, where her family also found help.

Claudia heard her out, raised her brows, and said:

"Nonsense! Valya, how *can* you repeat such vile things without being ashamed!"

Valya broke out laughing and assumed a sly look. When she had gone, Claudia fell to thinking.

"Nyutochka too will find out," she considered gloatingly; "she'll be hurt, and won't believe it. But maybe she *will* believe it? Or will she doubt it? Or will she not find out at all? Valya won't tell her,—she won't dare, or else will she start talking and Nyutochka not want to listen?"

For a long time Claudia stood by the window, screwed up her green eyes, and smiled insidiously. The day was clear and calm, the sky cloudless, the trees green and fresh; the warm air licked at Claudia's pale cheeks, and the stern inexorability of bright Nature helped bring on her evil thoughts.

At last a gleeful, determined smile lit up Claudia's face. She sat down at her beautiful desk that was cluttered with glistening, fanciful knickknacks, cleared a place for the paper, pushed back her wide sleeves, took the pen in her hand—and let out a ringing laugh. It was careless laughter, like that of a boy before some funny bit of mischief. But her eyes burned wildly.

She set about tracing the letters on the stationery; she tried to diverge from her usual handwriting. In every way possible she changed the position of the paper and of her hands, first bent then straightened her back, leaned her head to one side then to the other, jumped from the chair at times, knelt on it, and, while doing all this, trembled and blushed all over and soiled her fingers with ink.

When for a long time the letters did not turn out as she wanted, she gritted her teeth, pounded her fist on the table. When it did seem that the matter was going successfully, Claudia suddenly started laughing and pressed a hand over her mouth lest anyone in the garden or in the other rooms should overhear her merriment. She took a match and burned the sheet that she had covered with writing, then she fell to work on another.

The more leaves that she destroyed, the more difficult the attainment

132

of her goal seemed, but the calmer she herself became. Her face paled more strongly than usual and took on a stubborn expression. After several hours she decided that haste makes waste, and continued laboring persistently; she patiently noted the slightest differences and reinforced them through much careful exercise.

Late at night she saw that she had indeed attained something, but that, all the same, she required something more. On the second and the third day she sat in her room without a break, and her task went on ever more slowly, more calmly, and more assuredly.

Toward the evening of the third day she was satisfied with her labor: before her lay a sheet that would not have to be burned.

She leaned back in her chair, lifted her white hands over her head—the sleeves fell from them down to her shoulders—and she stretched wearily. Her face was pale and calm. She walked up to a mirror. For a long time she looked straight into the eyes of her own reflection, with a cold, irresistible look, neither smiling nor exultant. It seemed there was no expression of any kind on her face, it was immobile.

Having peered long enough, she smiled indifferently, let her gaze fall to her white hands. On them were ink spots—she set about washing them off.

Then she knelt before the open window, and for an entire hour she stayed like that, rigid and motionless, and she peered at the clear sky and the bright foliage.

The letter came to Anna in the mail with the town's postmark on it—something that was a rarity in our little town. The handwriting was unfamiliar.

Even the first lines made Anna blush furiously. She dropped the letter on the floor in disgust, and with her brows knit angrily she walked up to the window. The day before her was clear and calm, and she overcame her repulsion, picked up the letter, and carefully read it through from beginning to end. It was filled with the sort of details that may not be conveyed here, details concerning the allegedly authentic escapades of Login. At the end were cited certain insulting and cynical words which Login supposedly had said about Anna while in the presence of several people.

For a long time she sat before the letter that she had read, and kept looking at the white clouds sliding across the sky. Her cheeks burned, tears welled up in her eyes. Her thoughts were diffuse, but, like those white clouds, irresistibly drawn in one direction. The more she peered at them, the lighter and more exultant she felt at heart. When the oblique rays of the peaceful sunset fell across her dress, someone invisible said quietly and benevolently:

"Their sun is setting, but your shadow is before you!"

Listening to these strange words, which came over her mind like the ringing of church bells over the broad fields at evening, Anna stood up; her radiant eyes on the point of tears began to shine both joyfully and sadly.

"Just what I need," she said quietly, and humbly bowed her head.

However, she wanted to know her father's opinion—she was obedient to him in everything. She brought the letter to her father, gave it to him in silence. Yermolin read it.

"Whoever did this must really wish you well," he said when he had come to the point where the signature should have been.

Anna stood silently before him and watched anxiously. Her dress, yellowish white with rose blossoms and a very high waist, extended almost without a fold to her bare feet. Her sleeves, rolled up high above her elbows, left her arms bare as they hung motionlessly at her side.

"Do you believe it?" Yermolin asked.

Anna shook her head in negation.

"And one shouldn't believe it," Yermolin decided. "It cannot be the truth, it must *not be the truth.*"

Anna knelt before her father and put her head in his lap. Yermolin saw that she was crying, but he knew that her tears were tears of joy. She said:

"I'm glad that you do think that. No, I think as you do; you have shown me in which direction I should go, and I shall do what you tell me."

That night Anna dreamed that she was flying. Light, almost incorporeal, she rose up from the bed and hovered quietly, face upward, just below the ceiling. She descended a little when she reached the doorway, then rose up again in the next room. It was pleasant and eerie. She slipped out the window quietly into the garden. It was a dark night. The lanes kept their secret and their silence as she passed along under their aged boughs. Someone watched her shady flight with his dark eyes. An ancient stone vault suddenly rose above her; she slowly ascended to the top of its wide, gloomy cupola. Beyond its narrow windows the dim, rose-colored dawn was breaking. The vault parted and melted away; a dim light streamed all about. The dawn shone palely. The heavens seemed faded, ancient. Brilliant streaks, like cracks, suddenly cut through them. Another instant—and it was as though a curtain had fallen away from the sky. Anna looked down; the peaceful valleys were rejoicing in the sunlight. A boy was blowing on a silver pipe. His rosy cheeks were puffed out. The sun blazed on his pipe—and there was an ineffable joy in this.

Login had little required work. The school year was coming to an end, exams had begun.

Good relations had been established between Login and his pupils. He had a knack for attracting youths and boys, although he had never been concerned about that. Perhaps the students at the school were drawn to him because he liked to be with them, and he sincerely wanted them to come. The gentle and unhardened features of their faces pleased Login as did their peculiarly nonadult way of talking.

"They're still developing," he thought, "and we're beginning to fall apart. They're taking from life everything that they can, to themselves and for themselves; we, weary under the weight of our load, unburden ourselves, throw to the wind as much as possible. Then if someone profits from our wastefulness, we call it love. How inexpressibly good it would be to grow little, to become a child, to live on impulse—and not to ponder over life!"

His dreaming painted naive pictures—but his reason peevishly destroyed them. Envy arose for children's mood of joie-de-vivre and even for their light and fleeting sorrows. At times he felt like being severe with them, but he would only be gentle.

Sometimes it seemed that he ought to be more aloof from little boys. Evidently this was not difficult. It only required that he be like all the rest, that he regard the students as machines for turning out notebooks with mistakes. But that failed right away: however morose he might be at times, he looked at them and desired something of them. And they came to him as though from custom or from necessity.

It displeased his colleagues that the students kept going to Login; they said that it was not the proper thing. *They* would not have had anything to talk about with the students. They only conversed enthusiastically about the town's petty affairs and spread gossip as worthless as backyard trash.

During these days rumors about the Molin case were circulating. Absurd rumors were passed around. People were not embarrassed at the obscene details—the conversations among the teachers always included such details, since there were no ladies present.

One morning in the teachers' lounge at the high school, Antushev, the history teacher, said as he stood by the window:

"Our venerable one is riding somewhere in a barouche."

The curious Father Andrey began to bustle about: "Where? Where?"

Everyone crowded by the window. Only Login and Ryabov, the teacher of classical languages, remained seated. Ryabov was a tall, emaciated fellow in blue-tinted eyeglasses. With his sallow face and sunken chest, he was one of those figures of whom people say: "Horrid! His shoulders are narrower than his forehead!" He kept coughing softly, smiling caustically, and smoking cigaret after cigaret with a desperate haste, as though his life depended on the quantity that he smoked. Winking slyly, he whispered to Login:

"They've turned like flowers toward the sun."

"Our house is in such an out-of-the-way spot," Login answered, "that hardly anyone will drive by here."

Ryabov, he knew, was a great gossip and loved to ascribe whatever gossip he spread about anyone to being either something absolutely preposterous or else his very own words.

"Why, you know, he's coming *here!*" exclaimed Father Andrey.

"A fine figure he cuts with that major's belly of his!" Ryabov grumbled.

"Why, don't you like him, Eugene Grigorievich?" Login asked.

"I? Mercy, why do you ask me that?"

"Well, it seemed so to me."

"No sir, I don't have any reason not to like him."

"In that case, I beg your pardon."

Ryabov looked at Login suspiciously, smiled his cadaver's grin, patted Login on the knee with a wooden movement of his cold hand, and whispered:

"We all have no objection to tripping up one another, old fellow, only why shout about it?"

"That makes sense!"

All sat down in their places and talked in whispers, as though they were expecting something.

After about five minutes Motovilov appeared. He was in uniform. His formal, navy-blue semi-caftan, made when Motovilov had been a bit thinner, was too tight on him. The brilliant color of his fat red neck highlighted the golden embroidery on his velvet collar. His sword stuck out awkwardly underneath his caftan and beat against his fat legs as he walked. Motovilov had a solemn look. He had a white glove on his left hand; in the same hand he held the other glove and a three-cornered hat. Behind him entered the headmaster, Sergey Mikhailovich Pavlikovsky, a man with an indifferent, anemic face, not yet old, but sickly.

"It smells like a speech!" Ryabov whispered to Login, then rushed past him toward Motovilov.

There was a general commotion as the teachers vied for precedence in getting to Motovilov. They bowed respectfully, smiled sweetly, and shook Motovilov's pudgy hand with reverential care.

"Even I had the honor of being included," Ryabov said to Login, again in a whisper. "But why are you standing there like a stubborn so-and-so? See, with them making such a wall, he won't even notice you."

But Motovilov did notice. With an extraordinarily dignified gesture, he parted the crowd, and, with his hand extended, he took two steps toward Login. The teachers looked at Login with envy.

"I am especially glad," said Motovilov, "that I have found you here too. You will get to know our common cause, toward which our thoughts and, I daresay, our feelings are directed. In all probability you know something about it already."

"Apparently I don't as yet," Login objected.

"Certainly you do—I am speaking of unfortunate Molin's case."

"Oh, that! Sorry, I had no idea that that was a common cause."

"You have become familiar with it through persons with a special interest, but now listen to us, people who are unbiased."

With his heavy gait Motovilov walked up to the table, stopped in front of it, and looked meaningfully at the teachers. Login noticed a large sheet of paper rolled up like a pipe in the headmaster's hands. Motovilov began speaking:

"Gentlemen, it gives me great pleasure to see almost all of you here. We have succeeded in forming an amicable family. If by my own modest endeavors I have been able to help in the matter of our mutual unity, then I am very proud of that. I have always been of the opinion—and our much-esteemed Sergey Mikhailovich, as far as I know, agrees with me—that my obliation does not consist merely in making contributions. I have decided to hope for a more, so to speak, intimate relationship with you, gentlemen. It seems to me, I meet with your full sympathy on this path. I do hope that I am not mistaken?"

"We all highly appreciate your cordial participation in our affairs," Father Andrey replied obsequiously. "And indeed, how could we not appreciate it? You're perhaps the cleverest man in our town. I may be an old man, but I gladly listen to your accounts, and I learn something—without constraint I say: I truly learn something."

"The phrase-monger!" Ryabov whispered to Login.

But Ryabov's sallow face, turned toward Motovilov, was contorted, like the ingratiating faces throughout the rest of the group, in the same grimace of servility.

"I thank you," Motovilov said and shook Father Andrey's hand. "It goes without saying, that I have tried to establish the same sort of relations in the town school too. But in the last few years my intentions, unfortunately, have begun to fall on barren soil. A pernicious element, if I may use such an expression, has intruded into my amicable family of teachers. I do hope that I shall be permitted to speak bluntly. The young people often suffer from too high an opinion of themselves."

Motovilov sternly cast a sidelong glance at Login, then everyone else looked sternly at Login.

"Yes, young people are not always respectful enough," Login said with a smile.

"It is not a matter of respect alone. However, we people of the old style think that even respect for people worthy of esteem is a matter hardly out of place. The municipal grammar school's venerable inspector, Galaktion Vasilievich, more than once has expressed his wish to retire from his position. I have been trying to persuade him to the contrary. More than once I have even pleaded with the authorities—in private talks—to give him a promotion, which this hard-working man has fully earned. I received a promise from them. Then, just when there appeared a possibility of filling the vacancy for the position of inspector, a claim to it was made by another party, who had no right to expect it, since he had rendered no meritorious service of any sort, had in fact only been in the service some two years, and was much too young. In the school there was also another candidate, one fully deserving—and look! He has now been eliminated by means of a disgraceful slander."

"That *is* a tragedy," Login said, smiling, "to be both a villain *and* a

137

victim."

"I can only be amazed at your... opinion on this extremely serious subject," said Motovilov, and he peered significantly at Login.

Login did not answer. His hatred for Motovilov was beginning to torment him again. Motovilov continued:

"Gentlemen, I think that we are obligated to come to the aid of our colleagues."

"With cards and wine," Ryabov whispered to Login.

"Stop whispering," Login said quietly. "After all, he might take offense at it."

"All decent people with whom I have spoken about it think that Alexey Ivanovich is the victim of an intrigue. You are familiar with his noble character and his high moral principles, so I am convinced that I shall find in you the same such sympathy. Alexey Ivanovich is absolutely crushed, and we must console him. Father Andrey has just been to see him and will confirm that he is weeping."

"Yes, he is weeping," Father Andrey said dolefully.

All showed expressions of sympathy on their faces.

"We must expose this matter for what it is; otherwise it will lie upon our consciences. We have prepared a collective statement to the public prosecutor, that we are all convinced of Molin's innocence, that we ask him to release Molin, and we set all our stock in him."

"We are getting him out on bail," the headmaster explained.

"Let me ask one of you gentlemen to read out the statement, and afterwards, let those who want to do so sign it. Only those who want to do so."

Ryabov thrust himself forward and read the statement aloud. All listened through it attentively, made their faces look sympathetic, then pushed forward to sign it. Off to the side stood Motovilov and the headmaster, who had both signed earlier, and Login.

"I'm very sorry," he said, "but I cannot join in. How *can* I vouch for him?"

"Do as you wish!" said Motovilov.

"Now if it were about his prowess at drinking—I know what he's like on that score. But will the statement benefit him?"

"They cannot fail to weigh our opinion very seriously in the case." Abruptly turning away from Login, Motovilov addressed the others: "Gentlemen, I can convey some sorrowful news to you: cholera is indeed in our vicinity. Yesterday two men and one woman were taken ill."

The teachers exchanged frightened looks.

"It's all right," Father Andrey said encouragingly. "It won't get to us. By the way, I've been sent three lovely kegs of the distilled stuff—splendid vodka! You are welcome to come try it at my home tomorrow."

CHAPTER NINETEEN

Andozersky was visiting Login in the evening. They were sitting in the summer-house in the garden, drinking tea, and talking. Valya, her next oldest sister Varvara, and their friend Liza Shvetsov were laughing and running around in the yard next door. Liza was the daughter of a local private attorney, a man of petty-bourgeois origins, semiliterate, and almost always drunk.

Andozersky kept watching Valya with his gluttonous little eyes.

"An appetizing morsel! Look how she keeps buzzing about!" he whispered to Login. "Only, hands off—it's all mine! It isn't for you; I've already started to work on this little job."

"But what about your three brides?"

"Hey, I'll handle the brides in due course: when the time comes for me to get married, then I'll have a respectable dinner; but for now this'll do for a pleasant pastime."

"So that's what it is! Ah, you're just a skirt-chaser!"

"I do have that fault," Andozersky confessed modestly, while winking immodestly at the girls.

"Why, could you really prefer *that* girl?"

"Come, come now, old friend, I'm not a prude. Why, what do you think? She's just jumping for joy. Here, you'll see, I'm going to start talking with her right now."

Andozersky started talking with the girls and opened the garden gate for them. The girls evidently were very pleased. Granted, they feigned modesty and did not enter the garden; nevertheless, they certainly did not go away from the gate. Login even noticed that Valya blossomed in delight each time that Andozersky would start talking with her.

After chatting with the girls for half an hour and making them laugh with his simple little stories and jokes, Andozersky said softly to Login:

"Why there's something all right there. These common folk, the little girls, don't appreciate the everyday stuff that they're offered in abundance, and therefore it's time for me to retire honorably."

Login felt sorry for the poor girl and wanted to warn her. After a year he had managed to size her up, even though she was home at her mother's place only on her days off, since she worked in the village.

Valya was an utterly simple, frivolous girl. Besides her textbooks, which she understood poorly, and three or four novels that she had somehow got her hands on, she had not read anything. It goes without saying, that Valya had very few abstract concepts, and that her ideals were hardly sublime.

Povery had not dispelled the desire to make merry and to dress up fancily. Valya certainly was no stranger to this desire, as indeed neither was Varya, her sister closest to her in age. At home, when there was no company present, they went around in everyday dresses and barefoot, but when they headed for town, whether for a stroll or to go visiting, then they dressed up fancily and made themselves look pretty, as genuine young ladies ought to.

Valya already had a suitor. They had not exactly come to complete agreement, but somehow everyone contrived to tease them and call them bride and groom as though they had.

Her suitor was Yakov Sezyomkin, a pimply, curly-haired fine fellow in his twentieth year. He was a student at the local pedagogical institute who would finish his course of studies that spring.

The lower middle-class youth, with whom Valya and Varya were associated, broke up into couples at a very early age: a seventeen-year-old "gentleman" would choose a fifteen-year-old "lady" and hang around with her. These bonds were hardly lasting: sometimes the lady, sometimes the gentleman would be unfaithful to his "object" in order to enter into a new union. Hence arose quarrels, trouble-makers, scenes of jealousy.

Both Valya and Varya kept having to get even either with each other or with their girl friends because of some boy friend. Indeed such tiffs occurred as could have seemed quite serious to an outsider. Similarly, the two sisters together would sometimes attack their best friend and most frequent visitor, pretty little Liza Shvetsov, and, in the innocent simplicity of their disposition and in the passion of their temperament, they would give her a beating, "straighten her hair-do," as they expressed it. Liza would shriek and run away from them in tears and rage, declaring that she would "never set foot in that house again!" Two or three days would pass, and Liza would be at the Dylins' again, going merrily about the yard after she and the sisters had embraced one another.

But the sisters had never had cause to envy their girl friends over Yakov Sezyomkin: he courted only them, in turns, sometimes Valya, sometimes Varya, and never gave the other girls the least hope of his favor. By right of longstanding acquaintance, the sisters unceremoniously called him *Yashka,* sometimes even to his face. They were neighbors: Sezyomkin's mother kept a little house, a half-delapidated hut on chicken legs next to the vegetable garden that belonged to the Dylin holdings. This poor little house frequently was the object of gibes which both sisters mercilessly heaped upon poor Yashka.

As a matter of fact the sisters almost always quarreled and exchanged abuse with Yashka, although they maintained a high esteem for his mind and his knowledge.

"He's brainy," they said of him.

Sezyomkin himself bragged of the fact that he was clever and the he was a pedagogue. Sezyomkin's conceit and touchiness especially aggravated the sisters: they mocked him to their hearts' content, and they infuriated him by doing so. But, nevertheless, he was drawn to their abode like a fly to honey.

Valya alone had been his sweetheart for the last year: he had been courting only her. Varya had been mocking him more harshly than usual; Valya was beginning to stand up for him.

Somehow, without noticing so themselves, they had progressed to having intimate conversations: they had started planning how they would live when he had finished the institute; when they met alone, they would hurriedly kiss each other, and thereupon both would blush to their ears and bashfully lower their eyes.

But all that had changed when Andozersky had taken notice of Valya. Valya got the idea that Andozersky was in love with her and wanted to marry her; she would then be a lady of society. That flattered her imagination. Moreover, Andozersky himself was a handsome man and more respectable by far than a callow little youth who was still in school. What was Yashka? A mere boy, a raw youth! And the other was a real gentleman and a handsome man.

Valya grew cool toward Yakov. At first he was bewildered, then he became angry; he began keeping an eye out and making inquiries, and he found out after all what the matter was. That certainly was not hard to do in our town, where everyone knows all there is to know about everybody else.

Yakov made an effort to prevail upon Valya:

"Listen, shameless eyes," he said, "after all he's not going to marry you. He's just talking idly, serving you twaddle on toast—and you're gobbling it down! He's going to catch you like a pike on spoon-bait, then you'll howl like a stuck hog."

But the sisters, without caring, made a laughing stock of him . In his sorrow Yakov took to drink. That was still during the Easter season. Each day he would begin drinking first thing in the morning and would be quite drunk by noon.

It went on like this for several days.

Finally his comrades began trying to talk him out of it:

"Cut it out; you could get expelled, you know."

"Now I don't care," Yakov answered glumly with his curly head dangling over the vodka. "Let them expel me. I've come to despair. I'll plop into the river—and that'll be the end of it.

There's no one left for me to love,
There's no one left for me to pray to!"

He declaimed these lines, let his head sink onto the table, and began sobbing bitterly.

His friends stood around with solemn faces. They were transfixed with awareness of the significance of what was happening: they contemplated how ruinously a rejected love affects a proud and mighty soul. However, they

141

were all drunk.

The rest of the students at the institute regarded their drunken comrades' riotous behavior with respect. But even so, it was not enough: they longed to accomplish some great exploit all together.

On the fifth day of their holidays, a band of the institute's students who had gotten slightly tight went carousing through the town's streets, making the town resound with their bold songs. One of them was holding a bottle of vodka in his hand; another was lugging a chain of bagels that had been dragged through the mud. In the cathedral square they sat down on the ground in a circle, joined arms, and began singing "Down along the Mother Volga." Yakov led the singing. Their voices, rough from overdrinking, could be heard far off, like a wild roar.

The townspeople were outraged. Two anonymous denunciations flew to the head of the school immediately. But their authors had been over-zealous, had written a lot of absurdities, and, moreover, had contradicted each other in their respective testimonies. The denunciations were thrown in the wastebasket. The denouncers were expecting a general investigation—and waiting most impatiently.

On the next day, before yesterday's heroes had managed to take a drop to ease their hangovers, they were obliged to have an accounting with the headmaster of the institute. The accounting was brief but impressive. Those students who had come to the brink of despair were restored to their former, not so desperate condition and stopped getting into mischief.

Only Sezyomkin still got drunk every Sunday at his own home, a bit further away from the headmaster's eye.

Meanwhile, Valya gave herself over in earnest to her wild fantasies. Indeed, how could she help but dream? After all, she had only gotten her position thanks to the public sympathy evoked for the Dylins by the death of their father. Earlier, our public school inspector could in no way have acknowledged simple little Valya as qualified to occupy a teacher's post.

"Mercy," Alexander Ivanovich Ponomaryov would say, "what sort of teacher is that: she runs around barefoot to fetch water in buckets! And besides, she didn't learn her own lessons very well. A silly little girl and nothing more! And with no manners at all! Besides, I have candidates from the pedagogical institute, young men of splendid upbringing: when one of them talks with his superior, he keeps his hands at his sides and stands at attention. This I understand right away. I needn't worry about the school—he would establish exemplary discipline there. But should I appoint *that* little trick, I'd get no thanks at all! Besides, I have girls as candidates too, well-bred young ladies from good families. But, pardon me, I cannot entrust a school to the likes of her."

The inspector spoke decisively and with conviction because the influential persons in the zemstvo and in town thought the same thing. As for himself, he was a man quite indifferent to school questions, really because of his own ignorance: in youth he had distinguished himself not so much by achievements in his studies as by his modest behavior; in fact he had been appointed to his present position because of his piety, whereby he had managed to attract the attention of some personage. Manners and upbringing were also of little concern to him: up to the present time he himself had maintained many rather simple habits. Our inspector was very efficient and dependable and very slow-witted at his job. He tried in every way possible to guard the schools against disloyal elements: he allowed no indulgences for teachers who did not fast on Wednesdays and Fridays, and a certain school mistress' wearing a red dress was cause enough for her to be dismissed from her position.

When the Dylins' disastrous situation became the talk of the town, it was unanimously decided that Valya had to be given a position. The inspector did not object, and gave Valya a position at fifteen rubles a month.

"Serve as an assistant for two or three years," he said to her kindly, "and then we shall make you a teacher too."

Valya was in ecstasy and ardently set about her task. The little boys, her pupils, dumbfounded little animals with grimy paws and dirty noses, were dull-witted and muddled-headed, but they wanted to learn and worked hard at their lessons in every way possible in order to "get somewhere." The lessons, of course, were difficult for the ill-versed and inexperienced Valya, but her work prospered, somehow or other.

On the other hand, it was hard for Valya to get along with the teacher. Sergey Yakovlevich Alexeyev was a man of uncouth and stupid appearance. He had a low, narrow forehead, was bullnecked, and his face was overgrown with wiry dark-red hair. With their characteristic bluntness, the Dylin sisters, who had known him earlier, had nicknamed him "Stupe." Valya's trouble was that he had reasons to be displeased at her appointment and regarded Valya as an enemy.

There had also been an assistant in his school before Valya. The teacher and the assistant had calculated that it would be profitable for them to combine their salaries and live together: In the country forty rubles a month was a tremendous amount of money; they could save up a tidy little sum for their old age if they would stash away a little each month. They got married last year, the week after Easter. Lizaveta Nikiforovna moved from her peasant hut to the teacher's lodgings in her schoolbuilding. Sergey Yakovlevich's two heretofore bleak rooms took on more of an atmosphere of home and hearth—and the teacher was in bliss.

Having received for the first time both his *and* his wife's salary at the zemstvo office, and feeling richer than Rothschild, Sergey Yakovlevich decided to go full tilt on a spree, not, however, in bachelor style, but like a decent family man. To this end he bought some Yeliseyev port, a whole bottle for a ruble and twenty-five copecks, and spent the change from the two

143

rubles on a real find—various snacks, namely some stale Swiss cheese and a sausage that had been brought from the capital half a year ago and was slightly coated with a whitish layer of mold. Having loaded his pockets, he walked down the streets in a holiday mood to which the superb weather corresponded. Transparent little clouds were gently melting and sinking away in the blue wilderness; behind their green matrix the young birches on the boulevard let their white trunks sway back and forth and their thin little branches babble at length; the merry dust wound about and went up in whirls and clouds and did not want to calm down: the river lapped playfully, sending tiny ripples over its entire breadth, and the sun's rays upon it were broken up as though someone had scattered a whole handful of new, silver ten-copeck pieces. That simile entered Sergey Yakovlevich's mind, and, leaning on the railing of the bridge, he mused:

"So what if they really were ten-copeck pieces there? Would I go gathering them up now? Eh, why should I stop to take the trouble, get down into the water, and risk catching cold!"

The acquaintances that he encountered congratulated him and kept making friendly winks at the left pocket of his overcoat, whence the wine bottle, wrapped in white paper, was sticking out. Sergey Yakovlevich would smile, pat the pocket where the wine was, then the other pocket, where the money was, then declare:

"You know, I just can't. I'm hurrying home."

"Yes, yes, of course," they would answer him, "your wife, I daresay, will be on tenterhooks."

And to that they added more of the various encouraging and witty remarks pertaining to the situation at hand, according to the rules of good etiquette.

Sergey Yakovlevich even encountered the inspector, who also congratulated him.

"Well, now you'll have a better time of it," he said.

"Ever so much better, Alexander Ivanych, sir."

"Your little family of teachers is going to increase..."

"Hee-hee," Sergey Yakovlevich giggled bashfully and gleefully.

"By autumn," Alexander Ivanovich finished saying.

"Hee-hee, it won't be time by autumn, Alexander Ivanych."

"Why won't it be time? We already have a girl candidate."

"Girl candidate?" Sergey Yakovlevich babbled in embarrassment and bewilderment.

"Yes, we have one! Of course, things will be the same for the summer; let your spouse make use of her salary—it'll come in handy for you in fixing up your household. But as of autumn we're appointing an assistant for you."

"But why, Alexander Ivanych? After all, my wife doesn't want to leave her job. She'll stay, I mean, just why shouldn't she stay?"

"What's the matter, Sergey Yakovlevich? It really can't be that way, can it?"

"But why?"

"Because it's not the proper thing. What sort of teacher can she be if she's married. She'll have to look after a house and children. Besides, others need a position too. Lizaveta Nikoforovna has found her place."

For Sergey Yakovlevich it was like falling out of Heaven.

In a state close to dark despair, he headed homeward, jolting along on the hard seat of his shaky tarantass which bounced along on its high wheels over the deep ruts in the clay road.

The unbearable dust got into Sergey Yakovlevich's nose and mouth and blinded his eyes; the sun, setting in the west, stared him straight in the face, stupidly and indifferently. Riding was very uncomfortable. The pigeons annoyed him with their monotonous cooing. And besides, he remembered that Lizaveta Nikiforovna was not at all as pretty as he had thought before the wedding.

"I guess I've hung a real goody around my neck," he thought resentfully: "A rag, a bone, and a hank of hair! Sans teeth, sans eyes, sans taste, sans everything! No-good face, no-good skin, blind as a bat, and ugly as sin!"[1]

It insulted him to think that he was bringing the wine for her.

"Isn't that too much?" he thought, and he set about uncorking the bottle with his pen-knife. He passed the time on the road by eating and drinking what he had bought. He reached home in a bellicose mood and provoked their first domestic brawl.

Sergey Yakovlevich oppressed Valya and tried to show her that he was her superior. Lizaveta Nikiforovna would needle her. The priest, who taught religion, behaved diplomatically at first, but he favored Sergey Yakovlevich: the teacher kept vodka on hand, Valya did not. Valya lived in a hut that belonged to a peasant to whom she paid five rubles a month for room and board. Sergey Yakovlevich lived like a respectable family man; one could even have a snack at his place after class.

So once when Valya was present at one of these snacks, the good father in a friendly way decided to take her to task for poorly following the example of her elders.[2]

"You have spoiled them, Valentina Valentinovna," he said reproachfully as he sipped vodka with a loud slurp. "You haven't been here long, but you've spoiled them. That's not good!"

"But how on earth have I?"

"It was different under Lizaveta Nikiforovna. They were quieter than the water and humbler than the grass. You just cannot manage without measures of sternness, my dear lady!"

"Of course you can't," Lizaveta Nikiforovna said soundly.

"But what if I don't have to punish them!"

"Well, you're letting them get swelled heads—and they've just gotten

145

out of hand."

"But what if there's no reason to punish them, Father? What then?"

"Why, that's wild goose with dressing!" said Sergey Yakovlevich.

"Hm, no reason!" the good father continued. "Here's an example for you: some rascally little boy comes to your class with grimy paws; what do you do then?"

"I'll send him to wash up," Valya replied.

"And if he shows up the same way the next day too?"

"Well, why then, well, I'll send him to wash up again."

"No, Ma'am, that's only a waste of time. Now you just ask our head of the family here how he acts in such cases, or else you can be very stubborn and let everything go its own way."

"Hee-hee, yes Ma'am, you ask me, then the thing will improve. Thank God, it's not my first year at the school."

"Well, just how do you act?"

"Well, here's how: without a harsh word, I'll send that sloven outside and order him to pour sixty dippers of water over his hands."

"That's in the winter?"

"Yes Ma'am, in the winter. Most likely he won't care to do it a second time."

"Oh, brother, he *won't* care to!" the good father affirmed. "So, then, young school-mistress, on such matters you consult us people of experience."

"In my opinion what you made him do was silly," Valya said, blushing deeply.

"Really?" exclaimed Lizaveta Nikiforovna. "Imagine that! We simply had *no* idea!"

Shortly thereafter an incident occurred which made the priest assume a manifestly hostile attitude toward Valya.

When the priest would come to hold his class in her section, that with the younger children, Valya would go home. Once, during the good father's class, Valya found it hard to relax at home and returned to the school earlier than usual. In the hallway she heard the priest's shouting and a little boy's wailing. She opened the door. An astonishing sight presented itself to her.

The priest was savagely thrashing a boy with the rolled-up skirt of his cassock; with his other hand he had taken the boy by the hair—the boy was howling and writhing. Another boy, who had been punished, was standing on his head by the stove; his feet had been lifted up onto the stove, his body was hanging at an angle with his head downward, and his face, turned toward the floor, was covered by his tangled hair, which had fallen over it. The boy stayed there as though rooted to the floor, leaning hard against it with his fingers spread far apart.

Hearing the click of the door as it opened, the priest released the boy that he had been busy with, peered sternly at Valya, and asked:

"What do you want?"

146

"What are you doing?" Valya cried, blushing to the point of tears. "You ought to be ashamed of yourself!"

She rushed to the stove and set the little boy on his feet. The boy was panting heavily. His face, so flushed that it was almost blue, showed a dull expression of fright.

"Allow me to ask you, Miss Teacher's assistant, by what right do you interfere in my acts of instruction?" the priest exclaimed, standing up ominously straight.

"By such a right that you'd better not dare do such things any more. Have you gone crazy or something?"

"So that's how you talk in front of the pupils! You'd have them rebel against me! Well, you will remember this! I'll make you eat humble pie. I shall not stay indebted to you!"

The good father left, slamming the door terribly. The little boys sat there scared to death. They thought that, most likely, the reckless schoolmistress would be condemned.

Thus began Valya's conflicts with the teacher and with the priest, conflicts that made her cry more than once. The priest's daughters also became her enemies; in fact once in the springtime they tried to throw tobacco in her eyes as she was walking past their home. Sezyomkin was some help to her with his advice: for example, he gave her a prescription for treating stupidity—which she left around for Sergey Yakovlevich and thereby highly insulted him. But when she quarreled with Yakov, then she no longer had anyone to give her witty advice.

When Andozersky had left, Login went down into the garden again. The girls were still in their back yard. Login walked up to the gate.

"Listen, Valya, would you like me to tell you some news?"

The girls started giggling.

"Oh, do tell me, please," Valya said, pursing her lips in an affected manner.

"There's going to be a wedding soon."

"Oh, really? Oh, how interesting! Whose wedding?"

"You mean, you haven't heard?"

"Right, I don't know."

"Andozersky's getting married."

Valya blushed.

"It can't be!" she exclaimed.

Login smiled.

"And why on earth can't he get married?"

"Who's he getting married to?" Varya asked, looking derisively at her sister.

"Well now, I can't tell you that. However, it's to a rich girl."

"To a rich one?" Valya asked, repeating his words and trying to look

147

indifferent. "You don't say!"

"Yes, indeed, to a rich one. However, he's doing it for love."

"But who's he getting married to?" Valya persisted.

"No, I'm definitely not going to tell. You guess it yourselves."

"Oh, I'll get wind of it!" Valya exclaimed.

She blushed still deeper and took off running home.

CHAPTER TWENTY

Anatoly would often come to see Login. He had managed to weave a web of common interests between them.

"Tolya, you do look like your sister," Login said once. The boy at that time was examining the wooden knickknacks on the desk. He laughed and said:

"I must look a lot like her, since you said the same thing to me just yesterday."

"Did I? I'm often very absent-minded, my friend."

"My sister and I have wide chins, don't we?"

"What do you mean by wide? Look at what a fine young fellow you are—the very picture of health!"

Anatoly blushed bashfully.

"I've come to you on business. May we talk about it? I'm not keeping you from anything, am I?"

He had read extensively about a flying machine and had got the desire to build one according to the illustrations. They discussed at length and in detail what would be needed for the construction of such a machine. Their talk was also about other subjects.

As he saw Anatoly off, Login again thought that the boy looked like his sister. He suddenly felt like kissing Tolya's rosy lips that smiled so tenderly and trustfully. He affectionately put his arm around the boy's shoulders and said:

"Come around with your interests a little more often."

"Thanks for taking care of me," said Anatoly. "That's what the local petty bourgeois say to their hosts as they leave," he explained with sparkling eyes full of joy; then he said quietly: "But there's a lady coming to see you."

Then he ran off down the porch steps. Login admired the sight of Anatoly's white clothes and the quick flashes of his sun-tanned legs, bare from the knees down.

Down the wooden sidewalk on the empty street, Irina Petrovna Ivakin, a teacher in a village school, was coming towards Anatoly. Login had met her two or three times in all. Her school was some thirty versts from the town.

Login escorted Miss Ivakin to the living room. She was a little old maid, as bony as a carp, and with a hectic flush on her cheeks. Easily excited, she talked rapidly in a cracking voice and accompanied her talk with restless movements of her whole body. She began talking:

"I have come to you in order to point out to you a matter which is most essential for our area. I have heard about your plans from Mr. Shestov. He is an extremely decent gentleman, but, unfortunately, afflicted by his milieu and his own modesty. I am fully convinced that he has been falsely

149

implicated in the Molin case through the intrigues of the archpriest Andrey Nikitich Nikolsky, who is Shestov's personal enemy because of his religious convictions. But let's talk about that later. Right now I must say that it is imperative that we publish a newspaper."

"A newspaper? Here?"

"Why, yes. Why on earth does that surprise you? It is imperative that we have a local organ of public opionion in our remote, God-forsaken hole."

"Why has public opinion become so necessary to you all of a sudden?" Login asked with a grin.

Miss Ivakin got all excited, blushed deeply, and started coughing.

"Mercy! How can you talk about it that way? Here you are laughing. You're well off in town, but what about us in the villages, in the very centers of an army of ignorance and superstition, where we, the school-masters and school-mistresses are the lone pioneers of progress!"

"We can hardly help you with that newspaper of ours, and besides, the means..."

"You definitely can," Miss Ivakin drummed on: "The direction of school business depends largely on people living in town. Here live the eminent people who are responsible for the entire course of the campaign in the name of public enlightenment, and they must concentrate all their attention on the state of the public schools."

"All their attention indeed!"

"Without fail. A school in a village is an outpost established in a hostile camp, the outpost which alone might be able to breach the Great Chinese Wall of our people's ignorance. But instead of getting any help, it is ignored completely. It's enough to make you despair."

"But is it possible the school officials don't visit you?"

"Over the two years that I was in charge of a school in Kudryavets, for example, only once was I honored with a visit from my lord the inspector; however, that visit was only an examination of the school's achievements, with no attention whatsoever to the intrinsic order of the school."

Login was beginning to grow tired of Miss Ivakin's inordinately rapid chatter. He said limply:

"It must be, they trust you."

"I have behind me fifty years of experience and a certain knowledge of school," Miss Ivakin continued, "that has indeed helped me against either losing my head or shaking off the dust from my feet and running away without looking back. Personal matters are probably the reason for my having been forgotten, although, in my firm opinion, on such a matter as national culture one ought to put aside personal misunderstandings until a more opportune time. For example, I could not gain full sympathy for such a useful and extremely noble undertaking as 'The Society for the Protection of Useful Birds,' made up of schoolboys and recently founded by me."

"How's that? I don't understand. 'Useful Birds Made up of School-boys?' " Login asked with a grin of annoyance.

"No, on my initiative the schoolboys formed a society for the protection of useful birds, whose nests are mischievously destroyed by some boys."

"Ah!"

"Can you imagine, even such a bright individual as Mr. Yermolin referred to this matter without the proper sympathy—even though he does acknowledge the society as useful, still he doesn't regard it as any sublime or ideal matter."

"And how does Anna Maximovna regard this matter?"

"She's too young. She still just smiles when one talks with her about such serious questions. She only knows how to reap grain and launder her kerchiefs, but questions of the highest order are scarcely intelligible to her."

"You don't say!"

"But, nevertheless, I founded that society. I'm not about to let it founder, not for anything in the world!"

"That speaks well of your energy."

"Our duty is to devote all our strength to the hallowed cause of enlightenment. It is not so startling, that one must struggle with the uncouthness of the masses—that's natural; the startling thing is the sad phenomena that the persons—whose duty is to work for the spiritual enlightenment of these masses and to support the institutions striving toward the same great goal of elevating the masses—act exactly to the contrary: they undermine these institutions, try in every possible way to discredit them in the eyes of the people, with no qualms about using either backroom gossip, filthy insinuations, or outright slander for this purpose. I'm talking about the priest in my village, Mr. Volkov. That's a man you can't see through right away, an absolute chameleon. He showers favors upon you, presses your hand, but at the same time tries to cut you down in every way, even writes captious denunciations against you. I would not have started stirring up all this filth if I did not consider myself morally obligated to expose that man's tricks."

Miss Ivakin would have jabbered on for a long time. However, Login morosely and insistently cut her short.

"Listen, Irina Petrovna, don't you write verse?"

Miss Ivakin was taken aback.

"But what on earth does that have to do with it? I don't understand... No, of course I don't write poetry."

"You know what? You should wait a while... even for balloons."

"What? For flying balloons?"

"Look, when piloted balloons will fly everywhere, then, even without a newspaper, your outpost—as you kindly express it—will be stronger, I guarantee you that."

151

"But what *is* this about waiting?" Miss Ivakin babbled in bewilderment.

"At this time no newspaper of any sort will be of help, so quit worrying. Go meekly about your business, and wait for the balloons."

"With dynamite!" Miss Ivakin whispered, glancing in terror at Login's morose countenance.

"With dynamite?" Login asked, repeating her words in amazement. "Come, come, there are things stronger than dynamite, beyond all comparison."

"Stronger than dynamite?"

"Why, yes, of course."

"But... how, then... it can't be done without a revolution, can it?"

"Why, what revolution?" said Login, then to console Miss Ivakin he added, "Anyhow, we'll think about a newspaper too."

With a terrified look on her face, Miss Ivakin got up to say goodbye.

"Her brains are addled," thought Login.

He could hardly hae foreseen what would result from his inadvertent remarks about balloons.

Miss Ivakin left thoroughly terrified. She recalled the conversation in most gloomy colors: Login had sat there frowning, said almost nothing, bitten his lips, smiled sarcastically, then suddenly—the mysterious words—balloons, and on them something stronger than dynamite. Miss Ivakin was afraid even to mention it. She told only two or three trusted friends upon whose discretion she could rely. Yet, on the very next day rumors circulated, one more absurd than another, and they disturbed the town.

People began to say that someone had seen a balloon flying from the Prussian border (which is quite a few versts away from our town). Some said that one balloon had been flying quite close to the ground and that German officers had been dropping pamphlets from it, but the muzhiks were picking them up and taking them to the constable without reading them. Others were saying that it was not pamphlets, but a whole lot of counterfeit bills, and the muzhiks allegedly had hidden them away and were intending to pay their taxes with them.

It was also said that the people riding in the balloons were not officers, but young fellows in felt hats and red Russian peasant shirts, were drunk, and were singing subversive songs, something between "La Marseillaise" and the Kamarinsky song.[1] The treasurer Svezhunov asserted that the drunks in the felt hats had come, not in balloons, but down the river in boats, that they had been singing about Stenka Razin's cliff and had brought a nude girl with them; all this, the treasurer asserted, he had seen with his own eyes while bathing in the river, and now, according to his words, the young fellows were sitting in the restaurant in the Summer Garden, were drinking and singing, while the girl was dancing—with a red flag she was prancing. Many went to the Garden, but did not find the young fellows, and the waiters assured them that no strange nude girls had been there. The deceived

152

would rush back to the treasurer and reproach him.

"I played a joke, my dear fellow," Svezhunov would say, then laugh loudly.

But the lower classes were disturbed and worried gravely.

The sun was setting in the west and striving to shine through the terrace of the Yermolins' home. It kept thrusting its dull rays between the pleats of the linen curtains. Anna's dusky cheeks were aflame. A thoughtful smile colored her lips, and they curved like the valves of a rosy clamshell. Her hands rested wearily. She was wearing a dress of striped vicuna wool. In the sun's rays, the black satin ribbons of her sash and the bow at her collar seemed coated with a rosy touch as soft as pollen. Both her formal dress and her white feet, barely visible underneath its hem, feet like those of the forest princess,—in fact everything about her was like a fairy tale, like a lovely dream come to life.

Yermolin and Login were having a lively talk. It was one of those endless discussion that Login often carried on with the Yermolins. His uncertain views were so sadly contrary to the Yermolins' distinct opinions, that he himself felt his mental desolation but did not want to renounce his own point of view.

They heard footsteps in the garden. Anna listened carefully to them. Smiling to Login, she said:

"Our numbers are increasing."

"If, as it seems, I recognize those footsteps," he said quietly, "it's not those with whom I'd care to stand in the same ranks."

It was Andozersky and Mikhail Pavlovich Ukhanov, the court investigator, who had come. Locally Ukhanov was considered extraordinarily clever, mainly because he had always disparaged Russians and Russian ways. He was becoming bloated by some sickness, his face was pale, and he seemed not long for this world. He still flaunted his long black hair. Andozerksy was paying the Yermolins a visit not only because he had his sights on Anna, but also because, as a member of the judicial profession, he considered it his duty to adhere to the society of educated, independent people, even though he was bored if there was no drinking, dancing, or card-playing. After all, at heart he was drawn to influential people who determined their own fates and those of others.

To the Yermolins' question of how things were, Ukhanov began talking about the difficulties of investigating Molin's case. He recounted:

"One gets the impression that someone is trying to obscure the matter. The witnesses talk complete nonsense, as though they have been intimidated or bribed."

"Why, who on earth would bribe them?" Andozersky interrupted.

"Who? Russians, it's well known,—let one undertake some dirty trick, and there'll be others behind him. Now I *am* convinced of Molin's guilt, but in town folks are complaining and grumbling against me."

"He's a good lad—his friends are indignant in his behalf."

"That's just it: his friends are a bunch of sly birds. Motovilov, for example—now there's a habitual criminal. He's feathered his nest, doesn't have to steal any longer. But he breaks the law in other ways: he bribes witnesses, sets himself above the law. Even the children that he has are degenerates."

"Well, now you have gone too far!" Andozersky said, cutting him short.

Ukhanov angrily fell silent. Login said:

"But it is the truth, in this matter all the people in town are dancing to somebody's tune; they're afraid even to think for themselves. It's some kind of terror: some are intimidated, others are flattered senseless. Here's how I heard someone praise Miller the other day: '... a splendid fellow, an honest man—he's so indignant at the investigator's actions in the Molin case.'"

Everyone laughed. Yermolin remarked:

"Many of them are convinced that they're doing a good deed, they're rescuing him."

Login and Anna were sitting at the chess table by the window, in the evening's rosy light that was beginning to burn out. Anna was playing carefully, as if she were working; Login played absent-mindedly. While Anna was considering a move, he would look sadly at her head bowed over the chess board and at the lofty bundle of her coiffure. A thought completely apart from the game oppressed him, a thought which he could not express in words—as though there were some problem that he *had* to solve, but the solution was not forthcoming. He knew that she would make a move, raise her eyes, and smile. He knew that in her trustful smile and her bright eyes he would catch a glimpse of the problem's solution, simple but strange and incomprehensible to him. More than anything else, what oppressed him was this awareness of alienation, of an indestructible barrier between them.

When his turn came to make a move, he would devise intricate and risky combinations. Anna's responses were simple but strong; they brought him the delight that a player feels in the game. He could not put together a clear plan for himself now—he got carried away by ideas that were inconsistent and unreliable; in such a case he could have won only if he had been playing with an unskilled or hot-tempered player. But Anna continued to play surely and carefully.

He saw at last that his pieces were scattered around absurdly, while the blacks (Anna was playing with them) kept together systematically. He made a move that was careful but at the same time weak. After her move in response, Anna said:

"If you're going to continue like that, you'll lose soundly. You're just giving up."

"Giving up? No, but in my situation the Asiatic fatalist who is fond of chess would say, 'The wise man knows the will of the Almighty. I am bound to lose.' "

"We can't tell for a while yet."

"I am bound to lose," Login said with sadness in his voice, and he made a risky move.

Anna shook her head and quickly responded with a daring sacrifice. He started to raise his hand to take her queen, but immediately he sat down calmly again. Anna asked:

"What on earth is the matter?"

"It's all the same, I'm checkmated," Login answered listlessly. "I have to give up. Only he who believes wins, and only he who loves believes, and only God can love; but there is no God, so, it must be, there is also no love. What is called love is only a futile striving."

"Reasoning like that, no one is likely to win."

"And no one does win. Indeed, it's not only winning or victory—life itself is impossible. If you'll permit me, I'll tell you a certain childhood recollection."

Anna bowed her head in silence. She leaned back in her chair and closed her eyes for a moment. The chess board with its pieces appeared distinctly before her, then began sliding, and melted away. Login was saying:

"I was twelve years old. I was taken ill. And just before my sickness or when I was convalescing (I don't remember very well), I had a dream that something insufferable had befallen me, and I was responsible for it. And I had to fulfill this impossible thing, but I couldn't fulfill it. I hadn't the strength. It sounds insipid when told in words, but the impression was indescribably horrible, incomparable to anything—all the sky and its stars had, as it were, collapsed on my chest, and I had to set it back in place because I myself had dropped it. And I would whisper crazily in my delirium: 'I destroyed a thousand birdnests—I can't go out and play.' I often remembered it later, but always much less vividly than I had experienced it. That impression was so astonishing that I later tried to recreate within me—to create a nightmare artificially. I've suffered some strange dreams, agonizing ones and delightful ones, but that particular one has not been repeated. Now, after having striven so long and persistently for life and having wasted so much of it, I understand that prophetic dream: life—its necessity and impossibility—has stifled me."

"The impossibility of life! Why, people live..."

"Live? I don't think so. They're dying gradually—and that's all that life is. You'd just like to capture one exquisite moment of life—and there isn't any, it's perished."

"What arrogance! Why demand of life what it doesn't have and cannot have? How many generations have lived their lives—then died humbly."

"And they were convinced that it had to be that way, that life has a meaning? But let it be proved that life has no meaning—and life will become

155

insufferable. If the truth becomes known to everyone, no one will want to live. The more knowledge and intellect there is in society, the more noticeable it becomes that the sources of life are drying up. That's why people of our age are so sympathetic toward children: we envy them their naive simplicity. People say, 'I'm living for the children's sake.' For the children's sake! Formerly people lived for their own sake and were happy, as they knew how to be."

"Because they were stupid?"

"It was said long ago: 'Blessed are the poor in spirit.' "

"Then what will there be later on?"

"What? Later on it's worse. Great Pan is dead and will not rise again."

"On the other hand, Prometheus has been freed."

"Yes, yes, he has been freed. Mad with pain, he roars and thirsts for vengeance. Soon he will see that there's no one on whom he can take vengeance. Then he'll plop down to sleep forever."

"What an unexpectedly crude ending!" Anna exclaimed.

"What's crude about it? It's the natural thing."

"No, I disagree with that. Life does have a meaning, and besides, if it doesn't, we can even have an absurd life and be happy with it."

"And what is the meaning of life?"

Anna put her elbows on the table, leaned her head on her palm, and was silent. The flounces embroidered with fine cotton lace on her long, luxuriant sleeves drooped like two sallow wrists. She smiled and looked at Login. Her trusting smile radiated joy and happiness; she promised bliss and plunged one's mind into the quiet calm of selflessness. It seemed to Login that his mind was dissolving in this radiance of youthful joy, that a death-like oblivion, soothing and longed for, was descending upon him.

"The meaning of life," Anna said finally, "is only a human concept of ours. We ourselves create the meaning and put it into life. The point is that life should be full, then it has both meaning and happiness."

" 'A thought once uttered is a lie,' " Login recalled.[2] "Besides, wasn't the very fascination that possessed him a delusion? Wasn't it one of those traps that have been laid everywhere by life? " Sadly he said:

"So, then, we put the meaning into life; it doesn't have its own meaning. And fill you life as you may, nevertheless, there will remain in it empty places that will expose its aimlessness and impossibility."

"You're stubborn, you must have the last word," Anna said gently as she set the chess pieces back in place. Her hands were used to putting things in order.

"All people are stubborn," Login answered in the same tone while gazing tenderly at her thoughtful face. "They can only be persuaded of what they like. They don't even believe what is most obvious—death. They even want to live again in the next world."

"Even she will die!" Login thought suddenly. "And every death will

156

be met without terror—and then will be forgotten!"

Sharp spurts of pity, terror, and bewilderment passed through his mind. He felt something perish, something young and happy that had stirred in his heart for a moment.

"A moment of happiness has died—and will not rise again!"

Something had faded, flown away. The moments kept dying. It was melancholy and painful.

CHAPTER TWENTY-ONE

A little after midnight Login, Andozersky, and Ukhanov went out onto the porch. There was a droshky by the porch: Andozersky had ordered his driver to come for him. But they dismissed the driver; the night was warm and quiet—so they went on foot. The fine gravel of the road gleamed in the moonlight. Mr. Yermolin and Anna walked out with their guests for half a verst, then returned home. Andozersky began telling bawdy stories; Ukhanov was not to be outdone. Their voices and laughter offended the pure stillness of the night, and the moist air shuddered in embarrassment and displeasure. Imperceptibly, Login lagged behind and entered the woods. The places here were memorable to him: he loved to be in these woods.

"Halloo! Halloo! Where have you gone off to?" his companions' voices echoed from the road. "The wolves will eat you up!"

Login did not answer, and continued going deeper into the brush. Soon the voices fell silent and were replaced by the distant but clear voice of a nightingale. The birches sympathetically inclined their silent bought toward him, brushed their moist green leaves against his face as though asking him what it means to live and love, while feeling sorry for their own unconsciousness. He walked on—and sweet visions went around in his head. At every turn the winding paths reminded him of the dear image of a girl with trusting-bright eyes. It was as though her white shade could be glimpsed before him in the shafts of light between the branches; it seemed that her footprints were still visible on the trail.

He went up to that plot of grass by the stream, where last year he had first seen Anna and been seen by her. His mind was full of thoughts about her and was warmed by the tender hope of love. Before him shone the smooth surface of the noiseless stream that flowed here in a broad and narrow bed. It reflected the trees, but did not see them, and was sad. The old oak, under which Login had once seen Anna, protruded from the darkness with a kind of tense and concealed uneasiness, as though the desires born in someone's fiery blood now coursed anxiously through its lifelessly heavy trunk and almost overcame its submissive slumber. Something indistinct showed up darkly under the tree. Login walked up to it.

By the tree lay a thin little boy in ragged little pants, worn out little boots, and a canvas shirt with bells and crumpled brass buttons. His face was gentle and innocent, and seemed to have a bluish pallor because the moon was separating the trees' upper branches with its cold rays and admiring it. His short chestnut hair fell over his forehead in uneven locks. Hugging his knees, with his hands stuck into the alternate sleeves, he was breathing rapidly and uneasily and was sometimes muttering in his sleep. On the ground next to him was a little empty cylindrical collecting-box

158

made of lathed pine.

Login thought that this probably was the runaway little boy from the alms-house, over whom people had been taunting Baglayev. The exhausted expression on the child's face showed that he was worn out and starving. It was obvious that he could not be left here. Login nudged his shoulder. The boy opened his eyes. Login said:

"Better be getting up, brother: it's time you went home!"

The boy raised himself up to a sitting position. He was trembling feverishly, he was hot and perspiring all over. Login asked:

"You live at the alms-house?"

The boy began moving about restlessly. He began babbling:

"I don't want to, don't have to, I *won't* go to the alms-house."

"What else is there, then? It's no good spending the night here, brother,—it's damp."

The boy was silent, and his whole thin little body slumped forward as though in slumber.

"Let's go. I'll take you to my place," Login said and tried to pick him up.

The little boy grasped the tree with his weak arms.

"Why, what's the matter? I won't give you back to the alms-house. Do you have a father?"

"No," the boy whispered, dropping his arms and taking a good look at Login.

"A mother?"

"No."

"Then, whom do you have?"

"Nobody. Leave me alone. Let me go," the boy whispered, tried frantically to get up, but stood up rather weakly, then lay down on the grass.

"Why, what on earth is the matter?" Login repeated. "Now that I've found you, you're mine, and I won't give you back to the alms-house. Let's go."

With Login's help the boy got to his feet. He swayed helplessly and apparently was failing to comprehend matters and was losing consciousness. Login picked up the boy in his arms. The boy felt himself in the air, stretched out his arms and put them around Login's neck. Login carried him. The boy dozed; he got warm; he smiled. Then he opened his eyes and looked at Login.

"Don't you give me back to the alms-house," he said suddenly.

"All right, I won't give you back."

The boy closed his eyes and was silent.

"I'll earn my keep," he spoke up again.

"Well, fine, get some sleep."

"I can walk myself," he said after another brief silence.

Login set him on his feet. The little boy grasped Login's hands.

"My name is Leonid, Lenka," he said and huddled against Login's legs.

Login raised up the boy's still, pale face with its eyes wearily shut.

"You're a traveller, eh!" he said.

The boy was silent. Login hoisted him onto his shoulders.

"However, he's not a light burden!" Login thought as he approached his house. "I'll be lucky if he doesn't die right on my shoulders."

Lenka did not die, but he was sick. He lay in bed for several days; he began growing delirious at times, but everything turned out all right. Login summoned the doctor, and the latter treated the boy with medicines. It had to be determined what the child's status would be in the future. Login stated his wish to adopt the boy. There appeared to be no obstacles. However, everyone with whom Login happened to speak of this was surprised and asked:

"But what do you need him for? Children are nothing but trouble; even people's own children make them lament."[1]

Login too was surprised then, and he replied with the question: "But what am I to with him?"

"What indeed! After all, he *was* in the alms-house, wasn't he?"

"But I promised him that I wouldn't put him back there: he doesn't want to go."

"Just look, what touching affection! For a good-for-nothing little boy!"

In fact there was no one in town who was not astonished at Login's strange undertaking.

"He's making a fool of himself!" prudent people would say.

And those who by this time had heard the gossip spawned in Motovilov's conversation with Vkusov would exchange *very significant* glances.

Only the Yermolins were not surprised and not angry at Login. Anna once did say to him with a smile:

"You're going to get it because of Lenka."

"From whom?"

"From everyone around here. Had you taken the boy to use him for odd jobs, had you been a merchant or a craftsman, then it would have been understandable. But taking a strange child upon yourself merely because you can afford the extra expense—*that* is a marvel for them. Wait and see: they'll praise you highly, but in such a way that it won't do you any good."

Lenka began to recover; he took up a portion of Login's time each day and created something like a family environment for him. Lenka was meek and helpless, was confused over his new status. He listened timidly, then began to talk about the town school, which he attended. Later he took to looking at the pictures in the books and would try to copy them, but he would not show his drawings, was shy in general, and did not talk much. But

160

sometimes a forthright mood would come over him, and suddenly, apparently without any cause, he would set about telling Login his memories.

Anatoly would often run over to see him. Lenka was also shy with him at first, but he soon got used to him. Little by little they became friends. Anatoly was held in great respect by Lenka, and Lenka would obey him unquestioningly. That was good for the "softening of their dispositions," Tolya would say.

Praskovya, Login's pock-marked and sullen housekeep, was highly indignant: she had to work more. In her conversations with the neighbors, the Dylins, she called Login's treatment of Lenka pampering. When Lenka was back on his feet, she tried to put him to use in the kitchen so that he would not be loafing around: she would make him shine boots and run errands. The boy would obey if he was not at the disposal of Anatoly. His whole capacity for resistance, it seemed, had been completely exhausted by his running away.

The Dylins sympathized with Praskovya. Like everyone accustomed to being poor and making use of hand-outs, they were envious of someone else's good fortune. What could have been given to one of their brothers or sisters was being squandered on a "trashy little brat!" It seemed a swinish trick to them. The fact that Lenya, when he felt like it, could settle down in any armchair and even on the sofa enraged the poor little boys and little girls who slept wherever they could—on the floor or on benches,—covered themselves with rags, and wore pitiful tattered clothes. Therefore they teased Lenka and insulted him when he would appear alone in the yard.

"Jealous!" he called them.

Rumors that disturbed the townspeople continued circulating in the town. There had been cases of death from cholera. The story about the balloons became implicated in the rumors about the cause for the cholera. It was said that mysterious people were flying about in balloons and were dropping poison into rivers and wells, and that was causing the cholera. But later it was thought that the balloons had come from England: the English had contrived to exterminate the common people, later they would come to wage war; the English, allegedly, had even bribed the doctors. Little gangs of burghers began strolling about near the cholera barracks; they kept looking angrily at the medics and cursing softly. The medics assumed an air of strained indifference. They waited in vain for patients: those who had fallen ill were hidden by their relatives, or simply were not allowed to be transported to the hospital—it was thought that they would be exterminated inside the barracks. Drunks began to be encountered more often on the streets.

Someone started a rumor that Molin had flown out of prison on a balloon. A crowd of lower class people assembled at the jail and began making a racket under the window of the warden's room. It turned out that

Molin was still there. But many said:

"Of course, he *will* escape," the gentlemen said all together.

"He's not such a fool as to go into penal servitude!"

Yushka Baglayev, as head of the town, got the idea of demonstrating his efficiency and ordered that several freight wagons be painted black: he was thinking of transporting cholera patients to the barracks in these wagons. When the wagons were ready and Yushka was inspecting them, he was suddenly inspired, and ordered that white stripes be painted along their edges. The gloomy carriages appeared on the streets and threw the townspeople into a state of depression.

Login's name kept getting drawn into the town's gossip, and, without his knowing about it, he became notorious in town. On the lowest levels of society the conjectures about Login were altogether absurd. It was said that he was the one who went flying on the balloons at night, when everybody else was asleep, but he could not be seen, and the balloon could not be seen: something like the *shapka-nevidimka*.[2]

"What balloon!" said the old women. "Why, he flies around on a fiery serpent."

"Maybe that's how it is," others agreed.

"Or else he just straddles a broom and takes off."

It was said that Login apparently was gathering people together into a secret covenant and was placing the mark of the Antichrist on them. These rumors stemmed principally from the shops: the merchants had hated Login's project as soon as they had heard of it.

Motovilov was especially interested in the rumors about Login. He too had a store in town, and therefore Login's project angered him. Apropos of the town's rumors, Motovilov had an intimate conversation with the headmaster of the high school. The headmaster listened to Motovilov apathetically, then expressed his opinion that it was necessary to wait for "actions," but meanwhile everything was in order. Motovilov remarked that waiting for actions would, very likely, be imprudent, that the headmaster would have to have a talk with Login and expose him. The headmaster grinned but agreed. However, he did not hasten to demand an explanation from Login.

Each time that Login went out onto the street, the people that he encountered would watch him with special attention. Some would stop and follow him with their eyes. Hostile and fearful were those looks! But Login did not notice them; he was immersed in his own plans and dreams. More and more often the hope of happiness began to glow within him, like the dawn breaking over ruins. The image of Anna would flash before him, her voice would ring in his ears. But something dark cast a flickering, troubling shadow over his heart. Someone hazy, elusive, evil, kept mocking his cherished dreams.

Login's melancholy eyes and his taciturnity sometimes startled but did not frighten Lenya. The little boy would look up at him and try to understand something, but to no avail as yet.

In the evening, when Login was sitting at the tea table, Yushka Baglayev came in, tipsy and red-faced as usual. He announced:

"Business first! Tomorrow we're going to a May Day picnic. You agreed? Why should you always be poring over something! You need to loosen up a bit."

"Tell me first, who's going," Login asked lazily.

"Silly!" Yushka exclaimed. "You certainly won't be bored—after all, I'll be there with you."

"In that case, how can I help going!" Login answered, grinning.

"Well, since that's that, let me have some vodka."

"I just poured you some tea," Login said, pointing to the steaming mug in front of Baglayev.

But Yushka demanded vodka until he got it. Seizing the glass with trembling hands, he accidentally knocked it against the side of his mug and spilled half the vodka into his tea. Login reached for Baglayev's mug and said:

"Here, let me change your tea."

"What's the matter with you! What is the matter with you! One good thing can't spoil another."

"Where was it you took a drop today, mayor?"

"You know where—at home, at dinner, polished the glass clean, and just now while I was walking over here, I got fanned by the breeze, and here I am again, clean as a whistle. Yushka Baglayev, mind you, is never intoxicated."

"True!"

"Brother, I slipped away from my wife and came to you on the sly," Baglayev whispered: "She's jealous of me and Valka."

"But Valentina's not in town today."

"Well, then, do have a talk with my old woman."

"But, one must suppose, you've given her some cause for jealousy."

"Why, tell some more lies!"

Yushka had hardly managed to toss off two more glassfuls, when out on the street resounded the loud cries of Josephina Antonovna, Baglayev's wife:

"I know he's here, the scoundrel! I'll tear his guts out!"

Yushka jumped up and cringed against the wall. His bulging eyes showed terror. He pressed his elbows against the wall as though he wanted to burrow into it. Rolling his bloodshot eyes, he whispered:

"Have I ever got my tail in a crack! Hide me, hide me away somewhere: she'll ransack every nook and cranny."

Login walked up to the window. Moving her whole body nervously, Josephina Antonovna cried out:

"Aren't you ashamed, Mr. Login! Where have you hidden my husband? But don't worry, I know where he is and whom he's with."

Mrs. Baglayev's dark face was twitching nervously in a thousand angry grimaces. She had brought along Bienstock, who tried to conceal his wary and slobbery giggling, and Eulalia Pavlovna, a faded maiden with a merry smile and frowning eyes. She was a teacher at the junior high school for girls.

"Now, now, Josephina Antonovna," Login tried to persuade her: "Your husband's safe at my place; I certainly won't let any harm come to him."

"Oh, you're even laughing!" Mrs. Baglayev said, growing even more excited. "Just what is the meaning of this! That you've fixed up a brothel at your place, or something?"

"Why, come in and see for yourself, Josephina Antonovna."

"You give me my husband, but I won't go to you."

"Well, Yushka," Login said, walking away from the window, "clear out, don't prolong the scandalous scene."

Seeing that Login intended to hand him over, Yushka instantly turned savage, and, advancing on Login, he muttered:

"What? Turn me out? I'll fix your snout for that."

"Oh, go on, go on, swaggering won't do you any good."

Yushka cooled off just as quickly. Login stuck Baglayev's hat on his head for him, took him by the arm, and led him outside.

"Here's your husband," he said to Mrs. Baglayev, "and I swear to you, there was no one with us besides Svetlana."[3]

"I know the likes of you," Josephina Antonovna grumbled back at him. "One could cry bloody tears for all that you men can be trusted. It's lucky for you that I know for sure that that little butterfly Valka is in the country today."

"Then why on earth did you make such a scene?" Login asked, knitting his brows in annoyance.

"And why didn't you give him back to me at once. Well, anyway, let it pass. Don't forget, now, come to the picnic tomorrow."

With a carefree look, Yushka bid goodbye to Login and whispered to him, while making a wink at his wife:

"Her nerves, you know!"

"There, you see," said Lenka when Login had returned, "he's absolutely afraid of his wife, but she still hasn't scared him enough to make him quit drinking vodka."

That night several pranksters from lower-class families got into the seed-beds in Motovilov's garden. The Dylin sisters and brothers were there, Valya herself was too. It was dark and quiet. The pranksters kept giggling softly to one another. Suddenly one of them screamed desperately. The rest were over the fence in an instant.

Motovilov himself had heard the rustling in the garden, crept up on one of the uninvited vistors, and seized him by the hair. The little boy struggled desperately, but Motovilov was dragging him toward the house and summoning the servants with a loud shout.

"Eh-hey! Why, I know you, you good-for-nothing!" said Motovilov when he had had a good look at the boy. "Ah, you beast, you were even in my school!"

It was Ivan Kuvaldin, a fourteen-year-old boy. He was a native of a nearby village but lived in town as a cobbler's apprentice. He had formerly attended the town school, but did not finish it. The pranksters had posted Vanka as a look-out while they went about their business. The little boy had begun "star-gazing," and had got caught.

Voices were heard as people came running from the house to help their master. Vanka manoeuvred himself around and bit Motovilov's right hand, right on the thumb. Motovilov cried out and let him go. In one instant Vanyushka was over the fence and bolting after his comrades. He soon caught up with them and boasted of his good luck.

Laughing, shouting, and squealing, the crowd of little boys, little girls, teenage boys and girls went about the town. Ragged, barefoot, wild, they flashed by in the whitish mist of the dawn that was barely appearing in the air. They flashed by like frenzied specters fleeing the vicinity at the cock's crow. The dogs raised a loud and troubled barking. Windows were hurriedly open in the houses. The disturbed inhabitants ran outside in their night clothes. The police were alarmed. Like a damned fool, the watchman, who had started dozing up in the fire station's watch tower, sounded the alarm bell. Panic spread through the whole town. Fearful cries resounded:

"Fire!"

"The balloons have come! The bastards are dropping cholera!"

"The English tried to drop some extermination in our well, but our lads caught it and are beating it."

It was especially crowded and noisy in the market place; the people were summoned there by the alarm-bell and driven there by habit. A drunken peasant made his way headlong through the crowd, desperately made use of his powerful fists and elbows, and yelled:

"No one is equal to God! Don't give up, good Christians!"

But the perpetrators of the disturbance kept running about the town, shouting, hooting, and delighting in the commotion.

Later a crowd also gathered near Login's home. They did not go close to the house, and there was no shouting here. The windows were all dark. Login was asleep and did not hear the hubbub. Certain ones in the crowd would be replaced by others. Only towards morning did they all disperse.

165

CHAPTER TWENTY-TWO

The picnickers had arrived for their May Day celebration. They had settled on a site about six versts from town, on a wooded meadow near the road. It was by a stream behind which rose hills overgrown with pines and fir-trees. On the other side of the road the unharnessed horses were grazing around the tarantasses. The picknickers were laughing and talking, sitting and lying on rugs or directly on the grass, around the campfire, on which something was cooking.

Here were Login, the Motovilovs, Claudia, Anna, Mr. and Mrs. Baglayev (and with them Eulalia Pavlovna), Andozersky, Bienstock, Gomzin, Brannolyubsky the young assistant-prosecutor (a thin little gray-faced man with slicked-down hair), Miss Ivakin, Valya and her sister, and the actors Pozharsky, Gutorovich, and Miss Tarantin. There were several more ladies, girls, young men, and schoolboys. All this company seemed tiresome to Login: there were just a great many unnecessary people.

Miss Ivakin looked at Login with horror, but she was drawn to him for some reason; she would babble timidly about ideals and hearts of gold. Login peered at the consumptive flush that covered her face, at her terrified little eyes, at her gray dress with the tiny pleats on the chest, and it seemed to him that Miss Ivakin was sick and was raving. However, he smiled cordially to her: Anna was sitting across from him, and her eyes were radiant. She took off her black straw hat with yellow flowers and a high bow, put it down next to her, then smoothed her dress at the knees. It was a wide-skirted, lilac-colored dress of light, patterned material. It seemed to Login that Anna enjoyed sitting there, being silent, and smiling—and her joy was communicated to him. Miss Ivakin summoned up her courage and decided to touch upon the matter that was troubling her.

"Do let me ask you," she began, "about a certain subject which in the last few days has extremely interested and even troubled me."

"Do me the favor," Login said, frowning.

His gray eyes grew stern. Miss Ivakin lost her nerve. But he was annoyed at Anna—an experience that he often had nowadays: Andozersky was making eyes at her, and she was talking merrily with him. His red cheeks shone from under his wide-brimmed straw hat. Login did not understand how she could even look at that fop without revulsion, much less smile at him. Growing excited, Miss Ivakin was saying:

"When I had the honor of visiting you last time, you deigned to mention balloons."

"Balloons?" Login replied in amazement.

"Of course," he thought, "Anna just couldn't be directly impolite to him, but why the bright trustfulness in her eyes? Is it indiscriminate towards everyone? Why her sunny smile for that rodent?"

"At the time, I didn't quite understand," Miss Ivakin babbled on. "That is, I did understand, but I should like to know about the time. You were saying that the arrival of the balloons would soon follow, but couldn't you define more accurately just when this will occur?"

Miss Ivakin's little eyes stared at Login with exasperating anticipation.

"Excuse me, somehow I don't remember," Login said with a gentle smile.

"Oh-ho!" he was thinking. "How cruel Anyuta's little eyes can be! The poor suitor, it seems, has sat on her pretty hat-pin and is making a pitiful face. That's how it is. But it was inexcusable of me to think that Anna doesn't see through him!"

He took off his soft gray hat and fanned himself with it. This movement of the air stirred the thin lock of blond hair over his high forehead. Miss Ivakin whispered:

"Excuse me, I understand that it's a secret, but, I assure you, I shall not betray it. I shall warrant your confidence."

Finally Login remembered.

"Why, I just stated it vaguely. I meant to say that not everyone nowadays has access to rapid means of communication—there are too few railroads, blimps have not been perfected. But if the inhabitant of each tiny hamlet could easily contact whomever he wished, then life would be changed."

At first disappointment, then suspicion was reflected on Miss Ivakin's face. In a hurt tone she said:

"No, I see, you don't want to trust me. But you're making a terrible mistake. Of course, I don't belong to any radical group, but I deeply despise those abuses which keep our poor, neglected region fast in the clutches of the darkness of ignorance and superstition. And if any sudden acts that will advance the cause of civilization and progress are anticipated, then I, like any sincere friend of the people and of enlightened culture, shall sincerely rejoice."

"What a damned annoying fool she is!" thought Login. "She wants me to hand her some sort of nonsense. Well, all right, then!"

And he said to her in a whisper:

"They could overhear us here." He said loudly: "Look at the wooden ruins on the other side of the river, something like a mill." He whispered again: "I'll be there in half an hour."

He walked away from Miss Ivakin. His eyes had a weary and somewhat mocking look.

Miss Ivakin got excited and began making her way toward the bushes. She took so much care not to be noticed that everyone noticed how she wanted to slip away. But she looked so unhappy, that no one hindered her, and only Baglayev, choking with laughter, sought to explain it by whispering

167

something in Andozersky's ear. Andozersky heard him out, guffawed, slapped Baglayev on the shoulder, and shouted:

"Oh, you liar, what an idea!"

Baglayev panicked and mumbled in dismay:

"All right, all right, please don't repeat it out loud; there are ladies present."

"Then don't you even mention such things when ladies are present, you web-footed goose."

"Come, come now, you were sloshed before daybreak, then you act disgracefully as well. You should be ashamed."

"Yushka, brother, we'd better have a drink," Andozersky said in a conciliating spirit.

"Why, that's just the thing! What's the use of standing here with your mouth wide open, your tongue on your shoulder, when we can really tie one on."

"Even when there are ladies present?"

"Brother, we can do that any time. Why, even the monks permit it."

Eulalia Pavlovna was quietly conversaing with the young assistant-prosecutor. Her cheeks were flushed, and Brannolyubsky was in a state of tender elation. Bienstock looked at them and was furious. When Branno-lyubsky had gone away, Bienstock began whispering urgently to her about something. He pushed his head right up to Eulalia's ear, right up under her broad, fancy hat. She leaned away from him in annoyance and said softly:

"Oh, leave me alone—what kind of suitor are you!"

"What do you mean! I, er... Suppose that I don't have a big salary right now; still, I rank higher than some at the office."[1]

Eulalia laughed caustically.

"Than some! I dare say! So who was kissing Josephina?"

She walked away from Bienstock. She looked angry and began smiling ironically. Login walked up to Bienstock, who said angrily:

"Damn the people here! They're an abomination!"

"Why?"

"The gossipers, the slanderers! Do you know, for instance, what Bran-nolyubsky says about you?"

Login frowned and asked:

"Do you remember what you yourself said about me?"

Bienstock rolled his eyes in embarrassment.

"What do you mean, Vasily Markovich? When was that? Who told you that? Believe me, I've always stood up for you, but, now, Andozersky..."

"I don't care to know that," Login coldly cut him short, then walked away from him.

Bienstock stuck out like a sore thumb in the middle of the glade and smiled in embarrassment.

Meanwhile, as they waited for breakfast, the company would stroll off in groups from the meadow into the woods. The young ladies thought of swimming: Valya promised to show them a splendid place. But just as they were quite prepared to go, Anna said something in Claudia's ear. Claudia blushed and sat down again where she had been sitting.

"What's the matter, aren't you going?" Anna asked her.

"Of course, I'm not going."

"I'm not going either," said Anna, and she too sat down. The others also stayed. Claudia quietly said to Anna:

"Then, you yourself say..."

Anna glanced at her with cold, clear eyes, shrugged a shoulder, and casually replied:

"I don't know for sure. I only thought so. Besides, does it really matter?"

Valya and Varya tried in vain to persuade others to go with them; they stamped their feet, giggled, then went by themselves. As she watched them go, Anna smiled indifferently and said:

"Everyone else has gone off a little way; let us also go somewhere."

Walking between the bushes and the road, she went in the opposite direction from the stream. Claudia and Neta followed her.

"How fed-up I am with these ladies and gentlemen!" Claudia was saying. "How deadly-dull it is with them!"

Anna started thinking about something. Almost unconsciously she broke off a thin switch, stripped the leaves off of it, and lightly beat against her dress with it.

"It seems, he ventured upon that at the wrong time," she said suddenly.

"Of whom are you speaking?" Claudia asked in surprise.

"I am thinking about Login."

"You haven't fallen in love, have you?" exclaimed Neta, and she broke out laughing. "Now there's a real joy! Someone so uninspired."

Anna blushed and said:

"And you, you're the one who's inspired..."

"Why, of course, I certainly am," Neta said with a wry face.

"But what's he going to do?"

Neta quickly looked around—there was no one else nearby.

"I don't know how it's going to be," she whispered. "We might even have to elope, since my parents wouldn't marry me to him for anything."

"How poetic!" Claudia said derisively.

"Not at all—it's just a terrible problem! How nice it would be to do everything in the proper way!"

"With a bridal veil, flowers, bridesmaids, choristers..." Anna said, smiling gently.

Login stood on the little bridge that dolefully stretched its half-rotten

169

planks over the merry stream. The day was cloudlessly bright; Login's heart felt hopelessly melancholy.

Andozersky and Baglayev walked up to him. Both of them were gleefully excited about something. Andozersky said with a laugh:

"The young ladies didn't go swimming—what a pity! It's all Anyutochka's fault."

"Why, were you looking forward to ogling them?" Login asked, almost with hostility.

"Should I just stand around yawning, or what? A fine thing to do, when those two sisters aren't at all bad-looking, and sleek as otters."

"And they can jump and dive around like real frogs," Baglayev said with a giggle. "Let's go; you'll say thank-you."

"They won't be offended," Andozersky said, trying to convince him. "They deliberately chose a conspicuous spot."

They both tried to pull Login after them, but he flatly refused, and the two of them went off together to ogle the bathing girls. The sisters were splashing around in the stream at an open spot where the channel was wide. Their shouts and squeals and the splashes of water made by their feet were barely audible from a distance. Andozersky and Baglayev stopped behind the bushes and watched the bathers. Then they squatted down and crept a little closer to the bank.

Valya caught a furtive glimpse of them, felt a thrill of joy, and pretended not to notice anyone. She quietly said something to her sister. Varya took a look in the same direction, and also pretended not to have seen anything. The sisters laughed and swam, and sprays of water rose up from under their nimble feet with a loud, glassy splash. Under the cheerful, bright sun their strong, shapely bodies stood out like bright, rosy-golden spots amid the white spray, the almost transparent blue water, the forest's cheerful greenery, and the narrow strip of beach, where their clothing lay. Their thick black hair made a fine contrast against their suntanned faces with provocative eyes and richly crimson cheeks.

"Gomzin should have come here," Baglayev giggled. "He would really click his teeth over this!"

"Why, there's Valya's boyfriend feasting his eyes on them," said Andozersky. "Hey, doesn't have much for a face, does he!"

"A real clown!" Baglayev rejoined. "He looks like the goalie for a dart team.[2] See him gawking away!"

Yakov Sezyomkin's curly head was peering out from behind the bushes on the opposite bank. It was obvious that he did not see the others, who were standing opposite him: for the time being, his eyes dwelled only on Valya—as though he were memorizing every feature of her beautiful body. The sisters saw him and were glad.

Login stood for a while on the bridge, then crossed the stream and began to make his way up the high bank along a narrow path. But when, from the top of the hill, he heard the laughter and the voices of the bathers and saw that they were splashing around in an open place, he turned back—and suddenly ran into Josephina Baglayev. She was out of breath from walking fast. She had a worried and exasperated look on her face. Quickly she asked:

"Where is my husband?"

"I really don't know."

"Oh, you're hiding him!" Mrs. Baglayev screamed furiously, and her dark eyes flashed angrily at Login. "But don't worry—even without your help I'll find him."

She ran past Login. He stopped and listened. Soon he heard her angry shouts and the loud squealing and laughter of the Dylin sisters.

He remembered that Miss Ivakin had already been waiting a long time for him. Now ascending, now descending the steep slopes of the bank, he made his way to the mill which he had indicated to Miss Ivakin. Sometimes he had to grasp the resinous boughs of young fir-trees in order to keep from sliding downhill.

He caught sight of a loving couple in a secluded little spot behind some bushes: Neta and Pozharsky were sitting together, pressing themselves close to each other, exchanging looks of love, and talking. He passed behind them—they did not notice. A loud, sweet kiss resounded behind him and filled him with the languor of desire.

Finally Login got to the deserted mill. Miss Ivakin was sitting on the doorstep of an abandoned hut. Her burning face was almost pretty—her little eyes shone with such fervid impatience. Login said:

"So that's where you are! Let's go down, and perhaps they'll serve us some stew."

Miss Ivakin timidly gave him her hand, and they quietly walked toward the bridge. Login said:

"Now then, my very kind Irina Petrovna, you want to know when exactly. If you don't mind, first you must swear that you will keep this a secret."

"I swear," Miss Ivakin said solemnly.

Login stopped, released her hand, and, peering darkly at her, said:

"Swear by the salvation of your soul."

Miss Ivakin was astonished and even wrung her hands.

"But... mercy, that's an irrational oath. Ever since Darwin proved..."

"Well, it doesn't matter," Login said condescendingly. "Each gives a promise in conformity with his own convictions. Maybe, then, you're a Tolstoyan?"

"Naturally, I regard the great Russian writer with the deepest respect; however, I find that his notorious doctrines of inaction, or non-resistance to Evil, are the errors of a brilliant man. When unalloyed Evil reigns everywhere, when the two-legged parasites and kulaks in tight waistcoats and frock-coats suck the people's blood, every honorable citizen's duty is to toil and struggle against them. Besides, in our age of psychology and electricity I deem references to such a dated source as the Gospel irrational and behind the times: the principles presented alternately with legends in that remarkable book were, of course, useful in their time, but they have long outlived their service to humanity."

"Hence, the commandment: Thou shalt not swear..."

"Under the ordinary conditions of life, I spurn the oath, as a manifestation unworthy of self-respecting people, a manifestation of mutual relationships of distrust and petty suspicion. But in exceptional instances, when the matter concerns social and progressive interests and, likewise, sublimely ideal aspirations, I consider it my duty to acknowledge the obligation of an oath."

Meanwhile, Login was thinking: "A plague on your tongue, you long-winded old scab!"

"So then," he said, "swear not to betray to anyone the secret which I shall reveal to you; swear by science, progress, and the general welfare."

Miss Ivakin solemnly raised her right hand and exclaimed:

"I swear, by science, progress, and the general welfare, not to betray to anyone the secrets which will be revealed to me by you!"

"Two weeks from Thursday," Login said in a mysterious tone of voice and again offered his hand to Miss Ivakin.

Miss Ivakin trembled.

"How? But what exactly...?"

"Something drastic will occur: balloons of a secret design will fly here, and they will bring a Constitution straight from Hamburg."

"From Hamburg!" Miss Ivakin whispered in reverential terror.

She walked along quite upset, not noticing the road. Login continued:

"I can say nothing more. And remember: there's a death penalty for betrayal: one gets tied in a bag and drowned."

"Oh, I know, I know! I took an oath, and I shall keep it!"

"Irina Petrovna, don't you devote some time to literature?"

Miss Ivakin smiled slyly and asked:

"Just why do you think so, Vasily Markovich?"

"Well, you have such a literary way of expressing yourself."

"Indeed? You find it so? Oh, I read a very great deal: to say nothing of the fact that not one detail of the conditions at school escapes my notice, I do read a lot, even in the area of general literature. But imagine! In my out-of-the-way village, where, instead of people, one can only meet Mr. Volkovs and county clerks completely devoid of intellect, I have no one, positively no one with whom I can exchange vital and fresh ideas, which are disseminated by reading books of an upright tendency. Yes, you guessed right: I am somewhat occupied with literature. That is, you see, I have composed an alphabet according to a genetico-synthetic, syllabo-tonic method, and a collection of dictations set forth according to an analytically inductive

172

method and with contents of a popular, practical, scientific nature."

"Very useful works; they have, of course, been accepted in many schools?"

"Alas! We have such routine reigning everywhere, such striving to hold fast to the beaten path: they don't even want to know anything original. That alphabet of mine is used in two schools of our province; imagine, only in two! And in one school in the district of Tetyushi; in three schools altogether. My collection of dictations has been overtaken by a still more lamentable fate: I could not even find a publisher for it, and I can use it only in my own school."

"That's very sad."

"But I do not lose heart. I am inspired by the thought that, in the great process of elevating the masses of common people, I too am being of some use, even though my contribution may be only a small one. I am now bringing to its conclusion a certain grandiose undertaking that has cost me many sleepless nights, a moral and mental struggle, and several years of intensive toil and tireless research."

Login tried hard to keep from laughing. He said:

"That's very interesting. Just what sort of undertaking is it?"

"It's a reader for the public schools, with the object of making the children fully aware of those ideal individuals, of whom there are so many in our land, that the children should have models to honor and imitate."

"You believe that there *are* ideal individuals?"

"Absolutely! I am setting forth literary examples of the ideal priest, doctor, footman, nurse, the ideal school-mistress, the ideal landowner, the ideal policeman—in a word, the ideal individuals of all classes."

"Well, but simply the human being, the living human being—is he in your book?"

"They're all human beings, and the best at that!"

"And you want to cram little country children with all these saccharine ideals? To what end? Why deceive them," Login said heatedly.

"To what end? Why, then, in your opinion, should children from their earliest days be shown everything bad in life and have their faith in the good destroyed? No, a school is obligated to give children positive ideals of goodness and truth."

"The ideal is God, the ideal person is Christ, but you would give them rotten petty idols for models, would train them to set up all sorts of hypocritical self-seekers on a pedestal, to bow and scrape like serfs—and before whom?"

"You deny that there are ideally good people?"

"I haven't met any."

"I feel sorry for you. I have."

"Any lousy oaf imagines that he virtually showers heroic acts of love at every step; but take a good look: even the very best people are vain, only they're useful to others."

"What? You deny that there is any selfless love, that hallowed force that sometimes ennobles even a villain?"

"Selfless love, Irina Petrovna, is as absurd a concept as magnanimous starvation. If I really love, then I love for my own sake."

"I must tell you that you have either not met good people or have failed to appreciate them. But I deeply believe that there are pure, sublimely ideal individuals, and I am convinced that we must show children such ideals embodied in living people. Whoever could think otherwise, excuse me, are only those of a callous nature or people who want to flaunt their assumed nihilism."

Miss Ivakin was highly indignant; all the wrinkles in her little face rippled and quivered. Login looked at her with a smile but also with annoyance.

"Look, she may be consumptive, but what a brave spirit she has!" he thought.

By this time they had come to the meadow where the rest of the company were already sitting at breakfast in the shade of the ancient elms and birches.

"Why, old friend," Andozersky shouted, "Irina Petrovna must have been giving you a good scolding for your nihilism?"

Login laughed. He said:

"Indeed we didn't come to a meeting of the minds on ideals."

"It is immoral and irrational not to acknowledge ideals," Miss Ivakin said passionately.

"I am fully agreed with dear Irina Petrovna," Motovilov said imposingly. "The principal shortcoming of our time is the eclipse of moral ideals; unfortunately, our *young people* have distinguished themselves in this."

"Unfortunately, what you so graciously said is absolutely true," Gomzin confirmed, grinning respectfully.

Motovilov gave a long, imposing, and thorough oration on ideals. Some listened respectfully, others talked in a subdued tone. Andozersky entertained Neta and surreptitiously cast piercing glances at Anna.

"You were with her at the mill?" Claudia asked quietly.

"Yes," said Login; "it's nice there."

"Nice? Talking with *her* in that beautiful wild place? And she rambled on endlessly to you about ideals with that woolen tongue of hers! What a pity!"

Login laughed.

"You like her?"

"No, I'm just astonished at her. How silly for anyone to be so deadly-dull, to talk about writing samples and ABC books, then to combine such talk with tirades about ideals! The ideals of a fixed pattern!"

"She likes to talk about what she doesn't comprehend," said Anna, "about her own business. So she speaks in words that seem studied, polished, and sound. And besides that, appealing and incontrovertible."

She spoke softly, but to Login her words and her bright smile and the slow movements of her hands seemed cruel.

Brannolyubsky was surreptitiously tossing off glass after glass and was rapidly becoming intoxicated. Suddenly he shouted:

"I don't agree! To hell with ideals!"

But immediately he "grew weak and lay down." Bienstock and Gomzin picked him up, and he made no further display of himself. Eulalia Pavlovna pretended that she was happy, but she was extremely vexed, and pitilessly made fun of Gomzin. Bienstock did not approach her, and watched gloatingly.

Baglayev was sitting next to his wife; he looked ashamed. The Dylin sisters returned with a look "as though nothing had happened," and merely kept shaking their wet braids. Andozersky winked at Valya, Valya coyly lowered her eyes. Baglayev carefully kept from looking at the sisters. Neta's cheeks had a deep red glow, and her face was happy.

Some high school boys arrived; they told Andozersky something with a laugh. Andozersky guffawed. He shouted:

"That's the way *children* act!"

Everyone turned toward him.

"Our young fellows have just seen an interesting sight."

"Imagine!" Petya Motovilov said, showing his decayed teeth and slobbering. "Some little boys were playing 'county court': there one of them was supposed to have been a drunk; they sentenced him to a birching. And they had all this done as in real life; they even carried out the sentence then and there. And little girls stood there too and feasted their eyes."

The ladies blushed, the gentlemen laughed. Mrs. Baglayev said scornfully.

"What crude Russian muzhiks!"

"Well, and what happened then?" asked Bienstock.

"Why, we left: the way they performed it was quite elaborate, even revolting."[1]

Josephina Antonovna was grumbling angrily at her husband, flashing her dark eyes at everyone, and casting wrathful glances at Valya. Quite suddenly she declared:

"A certain wife just might scratch out the eyes of a shameless tart, the trash who goes around tempting other women's husbands."

"You just try it!" Valya snapped.

"Oh, so you admit it?" Mrs. Baglayev stormed at her. "Evidently, as your Russian proverb goes, the cat knows whose meat she has eaten."[2]

Valya would have liked to make a retort, but Anna checked her sternly. Valya blushed furiously and in her confusion began telling the ladies what was being said in town about the cholera. Anna laughed, took her by the elbow, and quietly told her:

"Valya, you need a good whipping."

"But what for, Anna Maximovna? How on earth did I know that he would go there?" Valya said, trying to justify herself.

Varvara watched her sister with a gloating look. In a low and imposing voice, Motovilov said:

"You know, I've been getting complaints about you, Miss Dylin."

Valya sat on pins-and-needles and maintained a dismayed silence.

"Yes ma'am, the peasants are complaining," Motovilov continued after a slight pause.

"But why?" Valya asked timidly.

"In general, they are dissatisfied. In general, they do not like the idea of having a school-mistress. Why, you quarrel with your colleagues and also are spoiling the children, yes ma'am! And everything in general about your job is getting out of hand."

"But, Alexey Stepanych, I..."

"Well, young lady, I have warned you, but thereafter it is no concern of mine. However, I do agree. In my opinion, a woman or a lass in the classroom will only spoil the children."

"Why, what's going on here!" Baglayev started to interfere.

But his wife stopped him immediately.

"What right do you have to step in? Did anybody ask you? Could it be, you're a lover of someone here? You're out of your mind over every pretty little flirt. You'd better realize that you have a wife, and let that be enough for you."

"I know, I know, dear, I'm sorry!"

"There now," Gutorovich said didactically, "don't argue, wine-guzzler;

176

the wine is not yet dry on your lips."

The young people laughed.

"What? Did they give your head a dusting?" Varya asked her sister in a caustic whisper. "It's just what you needed!"

Login and Pozharsky stood off to the side. Login said:

"Will we soon be feasting at your wedding?"

"What wedding!" Pozharsky said dolefully.

"What's happened?"

"The girl herself is fine, honors me, what more can I say? But here's the rub: her rich but ignoble father doesn't even want to hear of me—he's laid his cards on the table."

"That's bad. But you keep trying all the same."

"Why try? I made a formal proposal on the way over today. They made me feel like a fool. But you, most esteemed Signor, have certainly gone after the ancient *ingenue,* Miss Ivakin. But that's a barren object! You'd do much better to touch the heartstrings of the ladies' rival—the merry little girl."

"She's spoken for, my friend."

"Falstaff?"

"No. That's Josephina's false alarm; Valya has a suitor."

"So then, Helen the beautiful worries for no reason?"

"Absolutely for no reason."

With an ingratiating smile, Bienstock addressed Motovilov:

"Alexey Stepanych, Constantine Stepanych here wants to read you a poem."

"A poem? I am not an enthusiast for poetry: what people write in verses is mostly rubbish."

"But this," said Ogloblin, the author, "is not at all that kind of poem. I have taken the liberty of writing it in your honor."

"Very well, we shall listen," Motovilov graciously consented.

Login peered in amazement at the unexpected author of the verses in honor of Motovilov; Ogloblin had not been at the picnic earlier, and Login had not noticed how he had turned up here. Ogloblin struck a pose, put one hand inside the breast of his overcoat, and, making absurd gestures with the other hand, recited from memory:

A worthy citizen of late,
A teacher skilled, a friend worth trusting,
Hath been o'ercome by cruel fate,
By slander foul and most disgusting.
Who caused the first vile slanderous ripple?
His own colleague, by envy stained,
The sly, conniving moral cripple!
His goal he might well have attained.
But then, for justice, unexpected,
A valiant boyar, fear despising,

His fellow citizens collected,
And with his wrathful speech arising,
Proposed a most sagacious plan
Of public protest to assail
The outrage that an honest man
Must suffer being put in jail.
And the wise boyar, never stopping,
Unwearyingly hath attested
In behalf of him who, sobbing,
Hath wept e'er since he was arrested.
All pains our boyar gladly faces,
Dauntless for innocence and truth.
He'll show the ones in higher places
Who is the culprit here in sooth.
Boyar distinguished, praise to thee!
Prosper and live so long that rather
The reverent children on thy knee
Call thee not Grand- but Great-grandfather!
For us, 'tis time to hail thee: Ah!
Hurrah! Hurrah! Hurrah! Hurrah!

The poem, read in a voice trembling with emotion, made quite an impression. Motovilov stood up and shook Ogloblin's hand warmly. His face was a mask of the grandeur of spirit to which, he perceived, the praises were entirely appropriate. He said:

"I thank you very much for the feelings that you have expressed in relation to me. But in other ways too they are very profound verses. Such thoughts do you honor."

Ogloblin pressed a hand to his heart, bowed, muttered something of deep feeling. People crowded around him, kept shaking his hand and praising him for his fine feelings. Baglayev exclaimed:

"Skillful lad! Really talented!"

There were some on whom the recitation had made a different impression. Paltusov smiled caustically. Login listened with annoyance. Claudia quietly broke out laughing at the words "moral cripple"; thereafter she listened with a bored and disdainful look. Anna knit her brows, smiled vaguely; the accent on the word "great-grandfather" struck her as hilarious, and she laughed for a long time. Neta felt awkward: she liked the poem, but Claudia's disdainful look and Anna's laughter made her blush.

Claudia asked Valya:

"Well, Valya, did you like the verses?"

"Excellent little verses," Valya said with conviction. "But nowadays there's another fine poet hereabouts, a Mr. Fofanov, altogether like Pushkin. They say that at one time he was forbidden to write."[3]

"But why?"

178

"Well, now, you really haven't heard?"

"No, I haven't."

"Well, nowadays, they say, he's writing again. Very fine verses too, they say."

Anna stood alone by the stream. She gazed pensively at the quiet-flowing water, at the wide, dark-green leaves of the water burdock. They swayed and slumbered, but Anna knew that a time would come when large white flowers would open up over them. The sharp tapping of a woodpecker was heard from afar.

Login came up to Anna. He asked:

"And why are you here?"

Anna smiled. Login continued:

"All that company is so banal! However, let them be, it's fine here, right here, where we're alone."

Cautiously he took a look at her glowing face. Her eyes were sad and affectionate. Their hands sought and held each other's tenderly, and a sensation of joy shot through both of them like a sudden pain.

Suddenly Login was all but overcome by the passionate desire for something impossible. He looked at Anna, and he felt annoyed that right now she was elegantly attired like everyone else. He asked her in a tone of mock-tenderness:

"Are you wearing a new dress again today?"

"There's a time when even fish get dressed fancily," she replied. "I love joy."

"Only joy?"

"No, everything else in life. It's good to experience different things. The richness of Moet and the pain of the rod—there's a richness of feeling in all of it."

It hurt Login to think that Anna suffered pain. But she said calmly:

"It's good to feel the barriers fall away between me and the external world, to feel akin to the earth and the air, to all this."

With a sweeping gesture of her arm she indicated the water in the stream, the forest, the distant sky—and to Login everything distant seemed near.

A drunken peasant was stamping down the road. He grew bolder and bolder as he moved nearer and nearer to the ladies and gentlemen who were making merry. His bruised face, his bewildered eyes, the dull, constant smile on his dry, bluish lips, his disheveled hair, his wretched attire, the reek of vodka—all confirmed the impression of a man irrevocably gone the way of hopeless drunkenness.

Baglayev started giggling. Softly he said to Login:

"There's going to be a little scene—my heart tells me so—a lovely little

179

scandalous scene."

Login looked at him inquisitively. Baglayev explained:

"Do you see that character? Well, in a certain way, that's Alexey Stepanych's rival."

"How is that so?" asked Login.

"Why, that's Spirka, the husband of Ulyana, the girl, you know, who lives at Motovilov's, as his housekeeper, you understand? Motovilov has cuckolded Spirka, and Spirka keeps getting drunk out of sorrow."

"Watch out for that wretched muzhik!" Bienstock said in warning. "It'll get awfully sloppy if he squeezes against you."

By now Spirka was quite close, and suddenly he said:

"If, for instance, a gentleman gets any girl of our class in trouble, then she goes away for her confinement, and then, brother, oh-ho! She's sent to be treated at a warm-water spa.[4] Well, but if someone has a go at one of our married women, then, for doing it with him, he won't, I suppose, give her even so much as a pat on the back."

"Spirka, you're drunk again," said Gomzin.

"Drunk? That's something else! An important point! Even gentlemen drink. Here, in our little school, a teacher's an expert at drinking, and where did he learn how? At the institute. He was taught in the finest form—all the sciences, both how to drink, and, of course, how to go after the girls."

"Spiridon, go away before you get into serious trouble," Motovilov said sternly.

"Why go away! Where will I go to? If my wife now... You just give me my wife," Spirka roared furiously, "or else, Sir, I'll obtain satisfaction myself. Yes, even from you, you devils..."

But here Spirka was seized by Motovilov's coachmen and footmen, whom the nimble Bienstock had managed to run and fetch. Spirka struggled free and shouted:

"You just remember me, Sir: I'll do you a good turn, I'll burn your damned house down."

But soon his shouts died away in the distance. The company vigorously took up their amusements. Everyone pretended that no one had noticed anything out of place. Miss Tarantin struck up a merry little song, and the rest began to accompany her. The discordant but loud and cheerful singing carried through the forest and mocked it with its resounding racket.

Bienstock kept thinking that he ought to say something agreeable to Login, to prove that he was not slandering Login but sympathized with him. He walked up to Login and, assuming a serious expression, said:

"That Spiridon is an unfortunate man. I feel very sorry for him!"

"Indeed?" Login asked in reply.

"Really! And I do think that all the woes of the common people stem from their ignorance and lack of culture. I often dream of a time when everyone will be equal and well-educated."

"And the muzhiks will strut around in starched collars and top hats?"

"Yes, I'm convinced that such a time will come."

"That will be fine."

"Yes, indeed! Then there won't be any of this miserable provincial life: society everywhere will be great. In general too we have al lot of prejudices. Why, just look at marriage. Adam's children married their sisters, why are we forbidden to?"

"Really, what a shame!"

"Or, the ancients took pleasure with boys, why don't we?"

"Yes, all the prejudices, just think!"

"But progress conquer them, and then as a result we'll have everything: free marriage, everything, even free prostitution."

"Exactly."

"What a poem he slapped together!" Bienstock said, grinning.

"You like it?"

Bienstock snorted.

"I could hardly stand it!"

"Well, what's this, you rascally little seducer?" said Gutorovich, who had come up to him. "Why, have you forgotten the ladies? Come on, Eulalia Pavlovna, pretty as a picture, has gotten bored to distraction!"

"Oh, blast her!" Bienstock said peevishly and walked away.

Drunken Baglayev was going up, first to one person, then to another, and whispering secretively:

"Login, you know, put Spirka up to it; nobody but him; brother, it's true. Certainly I know: I'm friends with him."

"You're lying, Yushka," said Bienstock.

"Ah, you don't believe me? Me, the mayor? Oh, you German so-and-so! Hey, boys!" Baglayev yelled. "Let's baptize Bynka, the German! Into the water with him!"

Laughing, the tipsy young men surrounded Bienstock and dragged him toward the stream. Bienstock clutched at the bushes and cried:

"You'll spoil my nice clothes, a whole new three-piece suit! That's abominable!"

CHAPTER TWENTY-FOUR

It was the Tsar's Day.[1] By the end of the Mass the Church was completely full. The civil servants of important status in town strutted to the
front of the nave in their uniforms and decorations. Off to the sides, near
the choir, stood their wives. Both these men and their wives thought little
about the prayer; the men crossed themselves with dignity, the women with
grace, and in the interval between making the signs of the Cross, they gos-
siped in whispers—*that* was permitted. The young ladies affected piety and
knelt often—out of weariness. One of them prayed very zealously; pressing
her middle finger to her forehead, she remained kneeling motionlessly for
several minutes, with her eyes looking from under her hand straight at an
icon; then she finished making the sign of the Cross, and pressed her forehead to the dusty floor.

Next stood the middle-class congregation: civil servants who were a
bit younger, and beautiful girls of petty-bourgeois stock. Still father back
were the people of last and least distinction: muzhiks in tarred boots, peasant
women in many-colored kerchiefs. A gray-haired old man in a coat of coarse,
undyed wool intruded among the middle-class congregation; he was devoutly
doing full prostrations and whispering something. Two clerks—one being
small, dry, and slender like a pencil, the other rather tall and rather stout,
with the white and rosyface of a Palm Sunday cherub,—would elbow each
other, stare at the old man, and chuckle, covering their mouths with their
caps.

In front, on the left, little boys—pupils from the town school—were
standing in formation. They stood at attention, and pinched each other
surreptitiously. At the proper time they would cross themselves and kneel
in unison. From a distance the children's faces looked lovable, and their
genuflecting ranks were very handsome, especially to nearsighted people,
who would not notice their misbehaving. Krikunov stood behind them. His
face was contorted in prayer; his mean little eyes peered tensely at the
iconostasis and at the little boys; his little head reverently swayed back and
forth. His new uniform—recently made for him (at state expense) for the
occasion of the high-ranking personage's passing through town—choked his
neck and very poorly became his unimposing figure.

A boy about twelve years old who had come with his parents prayed
very zealously and did frequent full prostrations. Whenever he got up, it was
evident from his face that he was pleased with his own piety.

The choir, made up of students from the seminary and of pupils from
the primary school attached to it, was excellent. In the gallery they sang like
angels. And there was their precentor,—a red face, a fierce exterior, a heavy
fist. The little sopranos who started day-dreaming and the little altos who

182

played pranks would repeatedly feel the force of the precentor's palm on the back of their heads. Therefore they misbehaved only when the precentor's back was turned. The congregation did not see them, only heard their angelic singing, and had no idea that the singers who mysteriously resembled cherubs had their ears in constant danger.

The day turned out hot and dry. It grew stifling inside the cathedral. Login stood in the crowd; his thoughts kept wandering, and only occasionally did the singing rouse him. The sweaty faces of those surrounding him brought a lethargy upon him.

The Mass was over. The prominent gentlemen and their ladies were kissing the cross; men and women alike tried not to yield precedence to anyone who did not have the right to it by virtue of status.

In a beautifully tailored uniform, Andozersky came up to Login and asked:

"Well, brother, is it hot enough for you? What do you think of my new uniform? Good-looking, eh?"

"Why, not bad."

"Notice the embroidery, old friend: it's a uniform of the fifth rank, almost a general's! It isn't like the wretched little stitching you'll find on some uniform of the eighth rank. But why aren't you in uniform?"

"Well, all right," Login answered with a smile, "my uniform is of the eighth rank. What does it have? Wretched little stitching."[2]

"Yes, brother, I've outstripped you quite a bit in the service. Why don't you try harder?"

"You mean, for a uniform?"

"Indeed, for a uniform! Or for anything in general. But, then, old friend, you *have* fixed yourself up like a lord."

"Just how is that?"

"I'll tell you: you've got yourself, as it were, something like a serf, your very own page-boy—and what a pretty one at that!"

A mean, irritating note came out in Andozersky's voice. Login grinned wryly. He asked:

"You aren't jealous, are you?"

"No, brother, I'm not a boy-lover."

"You, my dear fellow, are, as I see, a rubbish-lover, and of quite vulgar rubbish too."

"Oh, please, not really."

"You just tell me one thing right now: Did you make up this rubbish yourself, or did you borrow it from someone and repeat it?"

"Excuse me, but I, er, you know, didn't mean any offense."

"Oh, to hell with you," Login cut him short and turned away from him.

Andozersky grinned spitefully and thought caustically:

"He didn't like that, you can see!"

183

He had heard the page-boy remark from Motovilov, considered it extremely witty, and repeated it to everyone that he met, repeated it even to Motovilov.

At home Login found an invitation to Motovilov's for dinner; it was Neta's name-day.[3] On the way, he met Pozharsky. The actor was sad but tried not to seem downcast. He said:

"Magnanimous Signor! You, I must assume, are directing your feet toward the very place where my darling lives?"

"Right, my friend!"

"Consequently, you're favored to behold with your own eyes my charming Juliet! But I, miserable..."

"Why, come along, congratulate the name-day girl."

"A most brilliant, delightful piece of advice! But, alas! I cannot apply it,—they won't let me in. I have been formally asked not to visit them and not to bother them."

"I sympathize with you for your sorrow."

"Well, as yet it's a half-sorrow, but sorrow lies ahead."

"So much the better; so, then, sleep it off, make a new beginning, and don't fret about anything!"

"But my magnanimous friend will somehow manage to do me a slight service, won't you?"

Pozharsky grasped Login's hand, pressed it firmly, looked him in the eye ingratiatingly, smiled beseechingly. Login asked:

"What service? Maybe we can handle it."

"Be a friend, hand this impetuously passionate epistle to the loveliest of maidens—but in some inconspicuous manner."

Pozharsky pressed Login's hand again—and Login suddenly felt in his hand a little note folded into a small triangle. Login broke out laughing.

"Ah, you Lovelace! You're crossing my friend's path, and yet you want me to help you."

"Friend? That Don Juan Andozersky is your *friend?* You're pulling my leg, my dear sir,—don't play Hakim the Simple—Andozersky doesn't care a rap for you. I'm sure you must be indulging in irony. So, then, I may have hope!"

When Login greeted Neta, he deftly stuck the note in her hand. Neta blushed but managed to hide the note without anyone's noticing. Then for a long time she kept looking at Login with grateful eyes. The note gladdened her—she found time to read it through, then her cheeks glowed so that she did not need to pinch them.

The town's leading citizens were sitting in Motovilov's study and having a discussion before dinner. With an air of redoubled self-importance, Motovilov was saying:

"Gentlemen, I want to call your attention to the following deplorable

184

circumstance. I do not know whether you happened to notice, but more than once I have had occasion to encounter facts of this sort: After the Mass, the junior civil servants, our subordinates, go out first, whereas we, the foremost people in town, are compelled to walk behind, and sometimes even happen to get jostled."

"Yes, I too have had that embarrassment," said Mokhovikov, the headmaster of the pedagogical institute, "and, by the way, I fully agree with you."

"Isn't it the truth?" Motovilov addressed him. "It *is* embarrassing, you know: our subordinates don't care a farthing for us."

"Yenonder-shish, it's free-thinking," said the police chief. "Libertie, egalitie, fratiernitie!"

"We must put a stop to it," Dubitsky resolved sullenly.

"Yes, but how?" asked Andozersky. "After all, we have different departments of the government services here. It's a ticklish business."

"Gentlemen," Motovilov raised his voice, "if everyone agrees... Do you, Sergey Mikhailovich?"

"Oh, I also fully agree," Pavlikovsky, the headmaster of the high school, replied with a lazy grin, not tearing himself away from contemplating his pudgy palms.

"That is excellent indeed," Motovilov continued. "In that case, I think we can then take action. Let each issue an order in his own department, that henceforth the junior civil servants not allow themselves to leave the church before their superiors. Isn't that as it should be, gentlemen?"

Exclamations of "Yes! Yes! Splendid!" were heard.

"Then let us do so. Otherwise, gentlemen, it is absolutely disgraceful, the uttermost lack of discipline."

"What discipline we'll establish around here, yenonder-shish! Soon we'll have to say *vy* to every tramp.[4] He shouldn't even open his mouth, the rascal; yet you have to... Lord! To hell with *ty!* And good riddance!"

"Yessir," said the inspector of the public schools, "you should just see my teachers: one's from a peasant family, his father plows the land; he himself lives on some fifteen rubles a month—poorer than Job's turkey in other words; but you have to treat him so nicely, even shake hands with him! What kind of a gentleman is *he!*"

"No!" Dubitsky spoke up in his hoarse bass. "I don't let them take it for granted. For that reason they're as afraid of me as devils are of incense. I drive up to a certain school. There's a young teacher. 'How many years have you been teaching?' I ask. 'This is the first,' he says. 'Exactly,' I say, 'the first. You don't even know how to talk to people; I'm a general, I'm addressed as "Your Excellency." ' He blushed but didn't say anything. 'Oh-ho, my dear boy,' I'm thinking, 'you need to be drilled, and thoroughly, in case you don't know "ate" from "eaten." ' So I give him an examination: 'What was the name of Lot's wife?' The boy doesn't know..."

"What *was* her name? I don't know either," said Baglayev.

185

Up to now he had been sitting rather modestly in a corner and longing for vodka.

"I must say, I've forgotten. But, after all, I went to school a long time ago, while they... Well, all right, that was on Scripture. But in the other subjects? 'Read!' I say. I had a newspaper with me, *The Citizen;* I handed it to him. He reads poorly. 'What's a stick good for?' I ask. They don't say anything, the scum; nobody can give me an answer. Fine! 'Write!' I say. He writes, making mistakes, spells "spank" with an *e!* 'What is this, my dear fellow?' I say. 'What *do* you teach them? What are you getting paid for? I'll fix you, you scoundrel!' 'By what reason,' he says, 'can you?' 'Reason? You damned blockhead! By reason of the dictatorial power invested in me, I'll make you clear out of here! And so fast that as of this very day, you so-and-so, there won't be any more of your carcass in this school, not even a whiff of you around here! How do you like that?"

Loudly and suddenly Dubitsky started laughing. Svezhunov shouted:

"Now that was clever!"

"You made it hot for him," said Motovilov.

The rest laughed heartily and in accord.

"So what do you think? I look, my teacher's trembling, he looks awful, and suddenly he's at my feet, blubbering, and he howls at the top of his lungs: 'Have mercy, Your Excellency, spare me, don't ruin me!' 'Well,' I say, 'all right, get up. God will forgive you, but you remember this for the future, you so-and-so, hah-hah-hah'."

Approving laughter drowned out Dubitsky's final words.

"Now that's our style, yenonder-shish!" the police chief exclaimed in rapture.

When the laughter had slightly abated, Father Andrey said obsequiously.:

"For all of us, Your Excellency, you are like a beacon in a storm. There's only one thing we're afraid of: that you might be taken from us to some post a bit higher."

Dubitsky bowed his head majestically.

"They'll do all right without me. I'm not pursuing that. After all, why should I!"

"Yessir, gentlemen," Motovilov said firmly, "discipline is the foundation for everything. The reins have been let out too far; it's time to draw them in tight."

"Why, look, gentlemen," said Father Andrey. "I have a maid named Zhenka. Perhaps you've seen her?"

"The one with such a dark complexion?" asked Svezhunov.

"Uh-huh! She was such a rude rascal. Then I threatened to thrash her: 'I'll summon the deacon,' I said, 'we'll take you to the woodshed, and there I'll give you such a treat that you won't forget it before new switches have grown again.' Now she's become so meek! Hee-hee!"

"Mind you, she doesn't want a taste of that, yenonder-shish!"

"It's certainly practical," said Motovilov. "Afterwards she herself will thank you for it. Discipline, discipline before everything else. Unfortunately, it must be admitted, we ourselves are largely at fault."

"Yes, we have been much too humane," Andozersky remarked in a melancholy tone.

"Yes," said Motovilov, "deeply deplorable phenomena are occurring even in our midst, so to speak. Let us just consider a recent fact. Gentlemen, you know in what exemplary order the local alms-house is maintained through the efforts of Yury Alexandrovich, what care and shelter the elderly receive there, and what a highly moral upbrining children are given there in an atmosphere of good morals, modesty, and industriousness."

"Indeed, I can say, I don't regret my great toil and concern," Yushka interjected.

His dirty face beamed with self-satisfaction.

"And God will reward you for your truly Christian works! Yessir, so then, gentlemen, a little boy ran away from the alms-house, ran away for the second time, mind you: last year he was found, punished, that is to say, as he would have been by his own parents; but, mind you, he was not denied shelter, and was again lodged in the alms-house. And just how does he repay the blessings rendered him? He runs off, lounges around in the woods; a man that we all know finds him there, takes him to his home, and what does he do with him? Does he return him to the place where the boy received an upbringing corresponding to his status? No sir! That boy, who should have gotten the devil thrashed out of him for running away a second time, he takes to his home and makes him into a little gentleman! Some nobleman's son born of poor parents could literally envy that dolt's new status. I ask you: Isn't it disgraceful?"

"It's immoral!" Dubitsky decided.

"Definitely immoral!" the treasurer chorused. "And who knows why he needed to take on that little swine?"

"You know," said Andozersky, "there are some people who find little boys appealing."

"Precisely, they find them appealing," Motovilov agreed, "But I ask you: how should we deal with such disgraceful phenomena?"

Everyone's face portrayed the highest indignation.

"Humaneness!" Dubitsky said with contempt. "In my opinion, the brat should be taken away from him, flogged, and sent away."

"Yes, yes, sent away," Vkusov chorused, "to Siberia, assigned to the society of *paysants* somewhere."

"At least his morals might be safeguarded," said Motovilov. "Login is organizing some sort of secret society! But the idea that anything hereabouts might be concealed is so stupid that it simply cannot be believed."

"Arrogance, sophistry," Father Andrey said didactically, "but God will punish him for it. No, he has to devise something of his own in order to live like everybody else!"

"Gentlemen," said Andozersky, "I must stand up for Login: in actuality he is a fine fellow, although, of course, not without great eccentricities."

Motovilov interrupted him:

"Excuse me, we do understand you! It's entirely natural and goodhearted on your part, that you want to intercede for your old schoolmate. But whatever you say, it's not good to associate with a dubious gentleman."

"That's right," said the police chief; "of course, c'est nie pas joli."

"But, nevertheless, kind Anatoly Petrovich, you will never convince us of that."

"But, after all, gentlemen, I, er," Andozersky tried to justify himself: "Of course, I know he's got a screw loose somewhere. After all, he and I've known each other for a long time. I know how arrogant he can be. But in essence, that is to say, at heart, he's a fine fellow. Of course, he's spoiled, but what's to be done about that! You yourselves know: ours is a neurotic age!"

"Yes," said Dubitsky, "more than once you'll miss the good old days."

"The good old days of the Nobility," Motovilov chorused, "when they did not tolerate individuals like Yermolin, who has brought up his own children in such a wild manner."

"Yes," Vkusov said worriedly, "he lives peaceably, but it's always made me uneasy: God knows what he's really like."

"A dangerous man!" said Father Andrey. "He's an atheist and doesn't even deem it necessary to conceal it. A man who doesn't believe in God—why, what else might he be besides that? If there's no God, then is there also no soul? Why, such a person is no better than a dog, worse than a Tatar."

"What do you mean 'a dog?' " said Dubitsky. "*Any* dog is better than *some* people."

"And his daughter," Vkusov continued to lament, "behaves altogether indecently. Is it proper for a girl of the Nobility, a well-to-do, marriageable girl, to run about the countryside—if you'll pardon my saying it—*barefoot?* It's not good, yenonder-shish, not good! Altogether mauviais ton!"

"Rotten little bitch!" declared Father Andrey.

Meanwhile, in a sitting room, the ladies were eagerly questioning Login with great concern, about the foundling boy.

Raising her eyes toward the ceiling, Anna Mikhailovna Svezhunov, the treasurer's wife, said:

"You have acted so generously, so like a true Christian."

"Oh, yes, it's such a noble act!" Alexandra Petrovna Vkusov echoed Mrs. Svezhunov's sentiments.

Cleopatra Ivanovna Sazonov, mother of the zemstvo chairman, wanted to show the other side of the coin and said with sad compassion:

"Yes, but people are so base! You can bestow blessings upon them, but do they really appreciate it?"

"Oh, that is so true, Cleopatra Ivanovna," said Mrs. Svezhunov. "Some gratitude you can expect from them!"

"Common rogues," Mrs. Vkusov said, grew embarrassed, then added: "Pardon the expression."

"Now just look at what happened to me," Cleopatra Ivanovna went on to say: "I adopted an orphan, reared her like my own daughter, and what then? Can you imagine, she married, chose her own husband, some merchant, a Glinyany or Fayansov or something of that sort—and she doesn't even care to think of me.^{5} It doesn't mean anything to her that she became such a part of my life!"

"Astonishing ingratitude!" Mrs. Vkusov exclaimed. "Watch out, Vasily Markovich, the same thing will happen to you too."

"Oh, undoubtedly," the other ladies agreed.

"Please, what does gratitude have to do with it!" said Login. "After all, it we do something good for others, it's only because it brings us pleasure ourselves..."

The ladies exchanged eloquent glances.

"Why then the question of gratitude?" Login continued.

"Here I just don't understand what pleasure it is to trouble yourself over people when you know in advance that you can't expect any gratitude from them," said Mrs. Sazonov.

"Ah, Cleopatra Ivanovna, everyone has his own tastes; to each his own, you know," Mrs. Vkusov said, tightening her lips wryly.

At this time Motovilov and his guests emerged from the study. Motovilov, having heard what Login had said, regaled him with a didactic speech:

"I must tell you, Vasily Markovich, that our common people do not understand being paid delicate attention. It is not possible, is it, that they are the same sort of people as we? You grant them a favor, even a blessing, and they take it for an obligation."

"Oh, that's absolutely right, the absolute truth!" sympathetic voices resounded.

"In general, I think that in dealing with the common people simple and immediate measures are needed. Apropos of this, let me tell you of an incident that occurred the other day. Marya, our cook, a very fine woman lives here in my house. True, she likes to drink sometimes, but who does not have some weakness? Only God is without sin! But, I must tell you, she is a very good cook, and a respectful one. She has a son, Vladimir. She treats him sternly, and, well, he is a quiet, obedient, obliging boy. He goes to the town school. Of course, why shouldn't he go to school? I maintain the opinion that literacy in and of itself is no harm if good morals go along with it. Well, now, one time I'm standing by the window and see Vladimir coming

189

home from school,—and by that time it was quite late. Well, then, either he'd been up to mischief with his friends, or he'd been punished—I don't know. Then, I see, there are other boys with him. Suddenly I see Marya go trotting through the gate, right up to her son, and—pow! Right on one cheek; then—pow! On the other one! Then she took him by the hair! Right there on the street she gave him such a scolding that it was a real pleasure to behold."

Motovilov's story struck the company as a very jolly and delightful anecdote.

"She parted his hair!" Andozersky said, savoring it fully.

"I can imagine," cried the treasurer, "what his face must have looked like."

"Yessir," continued Motovilov, "right there on the street, in front of his friends: his friends were laughing, and he was both hurt and ashamed."

"The height of outrage," Login said in disgust: "Slinging him around by the hair like that out on the street, and the little boys' laughter, vile laughter at a comrade—what a base scene!"

Everyone looked at Login sternly and disapprovingly. Mrs. Vkusov exclaimed:

"You're just too fond of little boys!"

"In my opinion," said Motovilov, "it was a very moral scene: a mother punishing her child. That's good, and the laughter was corrective. Consequently she has him walking the straight and narrow."

Login smiled. A strange thought had come to mind: he looked at Motovilov's gray-flecked beard and felt an almost insuperable urge to stand up and yank Motovilov by his curly gray locks. He grew dizzy, and with a great effort he turned his head in another direction. But against his will his eyes turned toward Motovilov, and the silly thought hammered at his brain like an obsession and evoked a strained, wan smile. Then suddenly a wave of anger rose up, and stopped in time. He sighed in relief; the silly thought was drowned, taking with it the wan, needless smile.

"Killing you would be a good deed!" he thought.

His eyes sparkled with a cold glitter. He remarked curtly:

"Your theory does have one unquestionable advantage: that is—consistency."

"I am very glad," Motovilov said sarcastically, "that I managed to please you even in that respect."

At that point Anna appeared in the doorway. The rustle of her light-green dress calmed Login.

"How silly of me to feel such anger!" he mused. "To rage at the night birds when you know that the sun is as bright as ever!"

And he answered Motovilov calmly and gently:

"No, excuse me, I altogether do not favor such consistency. I'm used to feeling differently... Everyone has his own ideas... I don't think I can

190

make you change your mind..."

"Altogether rightly," Motovilov said coldly. "By now I have a gray beard. Learning things over again hardly agrees with me."

After that conversation, the company was utterly convinced that Login's relations with Lenya were not moral.

"What shamelessness!" Mrs. Svezhunov said later, when Login was in another room. "He himself admitted that that little boy gives him pleasure."

"I can just imagine what sort of pleasure," said Mrs. Sazonov. "A fine fellow indeed!"

Among the men—also, of course, when Login was not around—Bienstock attested that he had long known just what sort of acts Login was performing with the boy, and that he, Bienstock, knew this for certain and had known it long before anyone else: he himself, he said, had seen it, that is, he had almost seen it, had almost caught them at it. Apropos of this, Bienstock recounted, quite mal a propos, how a certain lady in Petersburg had seized him on Nevsky Prospekt and enjoyed his services for a whole week, and had then paid him very handsomely. Bienstock's story aroused general delight.

Incited by Bienstock's success, Andozersky became inspired and made up the story that Login had had a very young and very beautiful mother, a very sensual woman.

"Well, do you understand then?"

The indignant gossipers chorused:

"Not really!"

"That's just too much!"

"How vile!"

"And then, imagine," Andozersky continued fantasizing, "one time his father caught them!"

"Well, I'll be damned!"

"Yenonder-shish, c'est tre mauviais!"

"I can just see it!"

"A terrible situation!"

"The mother faints on the spot. The father's in a blind rage. But the son says coldbloodedly: 'Not a word about this, or I'll let it out about your carryings-on with my sister!' Well, then the father turned tail, can you imagine!—tiptoed out, and that evening he brought his wife a broach as a present, and a hunting rifle for his son!"

Loud laughter resounded, exclamations went around:

"Now that's some family!"

"Oh, what a papa!"

"A real mess!"

"Of course, gentlemen," Andozersky said worriedly, "that's strictly between us."

"Why, naturally!"

CHAPTER TWENTY-FIVE

The dinner, cheerful and boisterous, seemed a dull, drawn-out affair to Login. They all kept eating, drinking, talking vulgar nonsense. He had not even had a chance to talk with Anna today.

Motovilov addressed a question to Login:

"Well, Vasily Markovich, what do you intend to do in the future with that—er—with your ward?"

All other conversation stopped immediately, the knives gripped in the diners' hands came to a halt, all heads turned toward Login, and everyone pricked up his ears to what Login was going to say. The silence fell so suddenly that Login did not manage to adjust his voice to it, and his answer sounded inordinately loud:

"I shall send him to high school."

"To high school?" Motovilov asked in reply with a look of astonishment.

The ladies broke out laughing; the men smiled derisively, and their faces showed the sort of expression that says: "Now, just what should you expect from him but nonsense?" Motovilov assumed a stern expression and said:

"Well, I must tell you that you will hardly succeed at that."

Login was surprised. He asked:

"Why is that?"

"Who on earth will admit him? I shall be the first against it. And I am sure that our esteemed Sergey Mikhailovich agrees with me; isn't that so?"

Pavlikovsky smiled apathetically and silently bowed his head. Login said:

"He'll be prepared, he'll pass the examination—then why shouldn't he be accepted? There's plenty of room in our school."

"High school is not for muzhiks," Motovilov objected. "You have made the mistake of overlooking that fact."

"*Both* high school *and* college are for everyone who really wants an education," Login insisted.

"Even college?" Andozersky said with a chuckle. "No, old friend, the overproduction in education is making itself felt as it is, but you'd even drag the little muzhiks through college; and then they'll even wangle scholarships. Well, and, of course, with their peasant-like industriousness..."

"All those scholarships," Dubitsky declared, scowling terribly, "are an overindulgence, a corruption. I'd tell 'em: 'You have no business studying. March straight to the country, plough the land, and don't beg off.' Some studying they do! They just fool around a while, and then get into the civil service, just so they can make off with thousands. That's how the lower orders are, aren't they?"

"Yes," said Pavlikovsky, "you just leave that path open to the children of proper society, but for the rest... well, they have their own little schools; that's enough for them, you know. What more do they need?"

"It is wrong to think that we have enough adequately educated people," Login objected. "Ignorance can be strongly felt in our own society."

"Oh, I daresay! Ignorance? In *our* society?" Mrs. Motovilov said touchily.

The ladies exchanged glances, smiled, shrugged their shoulders. Only Anna looked at him affectionately, as she straightened the wide bow on her light-green scarf. Her gentle smile said:

"It's not worth getting angry!"

"Excuse me," said Login. "I didn't mean that at all. I'm talking about Russian society in general."

"Now look here," Vkusov interrupted. "I wasn't ever in no university, so what does that make me, a ignoramus? Why I can even parley-Franciais!"

"You and I are fools, the eggheads have decided," the treasurer cried out.

Login looked around the table: the mean, stupid faces, the baseness, the gloating. He wondered:

"And after all, they really can keep Lenka from being admitted to high school!"

Never before had Pavlikovsky's apathetic face seemed so disgusting. Motovilov's solemnly self-satisfied mien aroused powerless but furious indignation from the bottom of Login's heart.

At the end of dinner, an unexpected and even scarcely believable scene occurred. By some means unknown, the drunken Spirka appeared in the doorway. Ragged, dirty, hideous, he stood before the astonished guests, raised his huge fists, shouted in a wild voice, and peppered his words with unprintable abuse:

"You're all in the same gang! He ruins our women! Give me my wife, you hear? Give her to me? I'll smash everything! You'll remember what a friend I can be!"

The women and girls jumped up from the table and fled; the men assumed defensive poses. Only Anna sat calmly.

They soon managed to have Spirka dragged away. Order was completely restored. Motovilov made a speech.

"There, we have plainly seen just what a muzhik is. He is a dull-witted beast when sober, and a savage beast when drunk—but always a beast in need of restraint. You, the members of the foremost class of society, must not forget our high calling in regard to the people and the state. If we withdraw or weaken, that is who will come forth to replace us. And in order to fulfill our mission, we must be strong, not only in unanimity, but also in that which, unfortunately, gives anyone power nowadays: we must be rich, we must not squander, but gather. And in that case we shall be the true gatherers of the Russian land. That is a great service to the state, and the state must show us more essential support than it has up to this time. It's time that *we* looked homeward!"

"What's true is true!" Dubitsky corroborated. "Look homeward! We have strayed far enough!"

"Gentlemen," Motovilov continued, "I sometimes dream that our holy Russia will again be covered with landowners' estates, that every village will again have a center of culture—as well as policemen—and will again have its master and his family..."

"The Russian Nobility—that's a myth," said Login, "and believe me, nothing will come of the Nobility's feeble impulses. Such is the lot of our Nobility: to flare up and burn out, to vanish in the dust and smoke of a general debacle."

When dinner was over, Baglayev quietly led Login aside and whispered with a tongue thick from having drunk too much wine:

"I did that, you know!"

"Did what!"

"Spirka—got him drunk and put him up to it—I did!"

"How did you do that? And why?"

"Sh! Tell you later. Well? Huh? Wasn't it funny? Didn't I fix Motovilov's wagon? What a fellow that Spirka is!"

Finding a minute when Login was alone, Neta went up to him. She said:

"Pardon me, but you're such a good man!"

And again there was a small piece of paper in his hand. Login grinned, stuck the letter in a side pocket of his coat, and began talking about something else.

It was already evening when Login left Motovilov's home. Stars dotted the sky. The streets were crowded with people, more people than usual on holidays. The murmur of troubled talk swept through the streets. Everyone looked in one direction, at the sky, where a bright star was shining. There was talk of a balloon, of Prussian officers, of an Englishwoman, and of cholera. Someone confidently kept telling people that right at midnight a balloon was going to "drive up" to the jail window, Molin was going to take a seat "in the balloon" and ride away. The women moaned and sighed. The men listened more attentively to the old women's gossip and were enraged.

Login heard an insolent voice behind him:

"Why, look, if it isn't the most evil son of the Evil One himself!"

194

He looked around. A bunch of tradesmen, some ten people, was standing in the middle of the street. In front of them stood a young fellow with a pale, mean face. There was something uncanny about the way he looked. His hair, pushed to one side, stuck out from under his wretched cap, which was soaked through with oil, like a rye pancake; it was like a uniform for him, even in its color. His lips were dry, thin, blue, contorted. His eyes were a dull tin color. His big, thin nose seemed like cardboard. His threadbare jacket, tattered trousers, coarse, down-at-the-heel shoes—everything stood out awkwardly as on a garden scarecrow. He was the one who had said the words that had made Login stop.

Login stood and looked at the tradesmen. They stared glumly at him. The fellow with the tinny eyes spat, cast a sidelong glance at his comrades, and said:

"He puts the mark of the Antichrist on people, that is, anyone he takes into his covenant. Every night he flies around on balloons, drops poison for the Germans; that's why there's the cholera."

The rest all maintained a sullen and angry silence.

Login's field of vision suddenly narrowed: he saw only the pale face, blue lips, tinny eyes—all somewhere far away, yet strikingly distinct. He felt a certain tightening in his chest, as though for joy. Something imperious and exultant drove him onward. The pale face, on which his eyes were riveted, was drawing near with amazing swiftness, and Login's field of vision was narrowing just as swiftly: all that he could see now was the tinny eyes—then suddenly those eyes shifted around helplessly and timorously, began blinking, grew watery, and darted somewhere out of the way.

Login came to his senses. The tradesmen made way for him. He walked on away from them without looking back. The tradesmen stared after him.

Someone in the crowd said:

"If he knows a magic word, then you can't catch him."

"No," said another. "If you give him the back of your hand, then that'll be the end of it, and we won't hear a peep out of him."

"Give him the back of your hand, that's right," agreed the rowdy with the tinny eyes.

Login's burning curiosity kept him from going home. He walked the streets, watched, listened. A wry smile, slow and sad, which he himself did not notice, would sometimes steal over his lips. The townspeople who saw this smile and heard the soft laughter coming from his throat at times, would look at him with malice.

He walked for a long time and began to gather certain impressions.

"What wild, malevolent faces!" he thought. "No, nonsense—it's an illusion. I'm just drunk, that's all."

On one street he met the headmasters Pavlikovsky and Mokhovikov. They were standing on the wooden sidewalk, supporting each other arm-in-arm, swaying slightly, and looking at the brilliant star. Mokhovikov addressed Login:

"What amazing ignorance there is! Why, tell me please, how does *that* resemble a balloon?"

"Why, hardly at all," Login agreed.

Pavlikovsky continued gazing apathetically at the sky. A drunken smile hideously contorted his bloodless lips. Mokhovikov continued stating his views:

"I, incidentally, think that it's a comet."

"Why do you think so, Nikolay Alexeyevich?" Pavlikovsky inquired. From his face it was obvious that the urge to have an argument had come over him.

"For the simple reason," Mokhovikov explained, "that it has a tail."

"Pardon me, I don't see a tail."

"It's a small little tail."

"I don't even see a little tail," Pavlikovsky imperturbably continued to insist.

"That one, you know, like a hook," Mokhovikov said very persuasively, but by now a note of indecision and doubt could be heard in his voice.

"No, I don't see it."

"Hm, strange," Mokhovikov said slowly, feeling confused. "Well, then, what is it in your opinion?"

Pavlikovsky assumed a pompous air and said:

"How should I put it? I think that it is Venus."

Mokhovikov tried to give his wine-flushed face an expression of even greater profundity, and he said:

"And I want to tell you the following, Sergey Mikhailovich: In my opinion, if it isn't a comet, then it's Curmery!"

"What?" Pavlikovsky said in surprise. "You mean Mercury?"

"Why, yes, incidentally, I do mean Mercury."

"You think so?"

"Indeed without a doubt," Mokhovikov said ardently and with conviction. "Why, judge for yourself. How can it be Venus! There cannot be the slightest doubt that it is anything but Mercury."

"All right," Pavlikovsky agreed, "perhaps it is Mercury."

By now his stubbornness had subsided after being satisfied by the initial victory; it bored him to argue, it no longer mattered. Mokhovikov strutted for joy at having prevailed over him at last.

A spry little peasant woman who had scampered out of the crowd and dashed about near the gentlemen while they conversed, now rushed to her friends and informed them in an excited whisper:

"D'ye hear? That balloon up there's got something either *heinous* or *murdering;* the gentlemen couldn't make out exactly."

Fearful exclamations and whispered prayers were heard among the women who had crowded around.

Login left the town and walked along the highway. It was quiet and dark. He walked rapidly. The wind rustled softly in his ears, kept singing damp and doleful songs. His thoughts and fantasies came in disconnected bits and fragments, like tiny chunks of spring ice. He walked on several versts, returned to town, and almost lost his feeling of weariness.

By now it was long after midnight. The town was asleep. There was no one on the streets. When Login crossed a certain street paved with small stones, a little rock that had come loose from the pavement rolled out under his feet. Login looked about. Andozersky's house was not far away.

Login picked up the rock and, smiling, walked to that house. Its windows were dark. Login raised his arm, swung it forward, and hurled the rock through Andozersky's bedroom window. The sound of broken glass was heard.

And Login quickly walked away. He turned the first corner and quickened his pace all the while. His heart was beating violently. But not for one minute did his thoughts dwell on that strange act. Only the persistent tinkling laughter of the windowpane—flying into smithereens—rang out incessantly in his ears. And it was the laughter of despair.

CHAPTER TWENTY-SIX

A plan was developing in Konoplyov's disturbed mind, a plan which, by his reckoning, could be carried out immediately, even before establishing the society of which they had conceived: Savva Ivanovich wanted to set up a printing press. As Konoplyov figured it, they would get plenty of business: there were quite a few establishments in town that placed orders for a great number of printed forms. All the orders went to the press in the provincial capital, the only press in the province. It was a long way to that press; theirs would be close at hand. Here indeed was a chance to take over all the printing work in town.

One beautiful morning Login, Shestov, and Konoplyov were discussing this matter at Login's place while having something to eat and drink. None of them had the money for a printing press. But that was no obstacle: Konoplyov was sure that they could obtain and organize everything on credit; Login agreed (he was convinced beforehand that, all the same, nothing would come of it, somebody would interfere with or slander the operation, but, nevertheless, for the time being it *would* offer a spectre of life and activity); Shestov took the others at their word because of his youth and complete ignorance of how business is done.

An argument arose, a very heated one, and it became impossibly strained: Konoplyov was reckoning on printing his own work for free; Login raised the objection that Konoplyov would have to pay. Konoplyov began running around the room, stupidly waved his long arms, and shouted in his rapid, sputtering speech:

"For heaven's sake, if the printing press is mine, then why should I have to pay? For what reason? I don't give a damn about the press then!"

"The press isn't yours personally, but is mutually owned," Login objected.

"Then what use is it to me?" Konoplyov seethed.

"There's the advantage that it's cheaper than using someone else's: part of what you'll pay will come back to you in the form of the profits."

"But I'm never going to pay you: the paper, all right, I'll buy; I'll pay for the type, as much as I wear out; what else is there?"

"What about the labor?"

"But the workers get a salary; that's from our common resources."

"Right! So wouldn't you want remuneration for the capital that is expended by your partners?"

"Why, the devil knows what to make of that! Butter wouldn't melt in your mouth. You're looking at the matter from a narrow, mercantile perspective; you have no more soul than a dirty penny!"

"Savva Ivanovich, watch your language."

"Why, yes, yes, just a cheap dirty penny of a soul. You have the most bourgeois views! Your words are hypocritical: you talk one way, act another!"

"In a word, we can't agree with you; at least *I* can't."

"Nor I," Shestov added, then blushed.

Konoplyov looked at him savagely and scornfully.

"Hey, so you're following suit! And I *had* considered you a decent fellow. Have you lost your mind or something?"

"Go look for other partners," said Login. "*We* can do without your abuse."

"What? You don't like it? Apparently, the truth hurts."

"What truth? You're talking nonsense, my dear sir."

"Nonsense? No sir, it's not nonsense. If you were an honorable and consistent person..."

"Savva Ivanovich, you are becoming insufferable..."

But Konoplyov continued to shout, rushing in a frenzy from corner to corner:

"Yessir, you should have taken the chance to put your ideas into practice. If I've written something, then I've already done my job, and you're obliged to print it for free if I have a share in the press."

"Savva Ivanovich, you wouldn't teach your classes without being paid for it, would you?"

"That's a different matter: that's labor, but this is capital. Oh, you contemptible bourgeois! Now I understand your sordid little affairs!"

"Indeed? Just what sort of affairs do you mean?" Login asked, forcing himself to be calm.

"Such deplorable affairs that they shouldn't even be mentioned! They really are telling the truth that you're a very immoral man, that you're so jaded that you've actually gotten sick of girls, that you acquire little boys for your amusement."

Login paled, scowled, said sternly:

"Enough!"

"Shameful, ignoble matters!" Konoplyov continued to shout.

"Be quiet!" Login shouted, approaching Konoplyov.

"Oh, no indeed! You can't gag or smother the mouth of another."

"Wouldn't you care to take back your words?"

"No sir, I wouldn't care to; you can keep them!"

"You prefer a challenge?"

"A challenge?" Konoplyov drawled out contemptuously. "What kind do you mean?"

"Do you prefer, then, a duel?"

Konoplyov guffawed. He shouted:

"You must take me for a fool! With a wife and children to look after, I'm going to let some rascal take a shot at me!"

"In that case, you're invulnerable," Login said, turning away from him. "I'm not about to sue you."

"On principles, you mean? I just thought that it was simply out of cowardice."

"For whatever reason, it's purely my concern, only..."

"Only nothing. I would have put you to shame in court, I would have done you up brown. Now I understand perfectly that your society is only a subterfuge, and your aim is something ignoble too. The devil knows, you may even be planning a rebellion! Motovilov apparently is right in calling you an anarchist. Only, your society won't succeed; you needn't worry about that; Motovilov and I shall open everyone's eyes that need opening."

Finally Konoplyov was exhausted from his jabbering and came to a halt. Login took advantage of this respite and said:

"And now I ask you to relieve us of your presence."

"Don't worry, I'm going, and I won't set foot in your house again. I'm not so blind to you as Yegor Platonych, whom you've taken in completely."

And Yegor Platonovich burned with embarrassment. Blushing, he took refuge in a corner of the room, and from there he looked with outraged eyes at Konoplyov. But the latter shouted all the louder, spurting forth his rabid saliva:

"But in parting let me tell you the whole truth. You won't delude me any longer, Sakhar Medovich![1] I have a farewell song to sing to you."

"No, do spare us."

"No, I shall not be silent. And what if your neighbors talk—after all, they may very well know! Why, you'll be turned out of the school!"

"Listen, if you won't leave my place, I myself shall leave."

"No, you're wrong about that; you can't get away from me! I'll follow you down the street, at the crossroads I'll graphically describe what sort of person you are! You have scabs everywhere; soon your nose will fall off. And yet you even hang on to respectable girls, you make dates with them at the summer-house!"[2]

Login walked toward the door; Konoplyov blocked his way.

"You lure schoolboys to your house and debauch them!"

Trembling with almost uncontrollable rage, Login tried to thrust Konoplyov aside with his hand—he could not speak, he clenched his teeth: he felt that, instead of words, a howl of fury would have come forth from his throat—but Konoplyov grabbed him by the sleeve and poured forth foul language.

"What do I have to do, then, beat you?" Login said quietly through his teeth.

He stared gloomily at Konoplyov's face, which was trembling all over in angry contortions and kept leaning insolently toward Login: Konoplyov was taller in stature, but he maintained a rather stoop-shouldered posture, and in a heated argument he had the habit of bringing his face down toward

200

that of the person with whom he was talking. Now he roared at the top of his lungs:

"What? Beat? Me? You? Why, I'll grind you into powder."

The anger overflowed in Login's heart, like a great wave causing a dam to burst—and at the same instant he felt an extraordinary relief, almost joy— a headlong, insuperable feeling. Something heavy, seized by his hand, raised that hand with unexpected force and drove him forward where, through a rose-colored haze, an evil face showed whitely with its eyes rolling in panic.

Shestov screamed something, then rushed forward toward Login. A heavy cushioned chair fell against the wall with the sharp crack of splintered wood, and the springs in its seat twanged briefly in alarm. With a dismayed and pitiful-looking face, Konoplyov, stunned by the blow on his back, moved back the coffee table with trembling hands. Login kicked aside the armchair on the other side of the table; again Konoplyov saw before him Login's face, crimson, with the veins standing out on the forehead. Konoplyov turned utter coward, got down on the floor, and scampered under the sofa. From that close and dusty place he shouted:

"Help! Murder!"

Login came to his senses. He walked up to Shestov and said:

"What a disgraceful thing a man is capable of doing! You chuck him out of here. Tell him he can crawl out from there."

He made an effort to smile. But he felt himself trembling as in a fever and was ready to burst out sobbing. Hurriedly he left the room.

Shestov soon came upstairs to him and said:

"I'll stay for a while; even though he is leaving, he's still going to curse all the way."

From the window Login soon caught sight of Konoplyov, moving with that special guilty and embarrassed walk typical of people who have just been beaten up.

"That's what society is like here!" Shestov reflected sadly. "So much slander and gossip!"

"All right, there is slander here," said Login, "but you know the saying, don't you: 'Where there's smoke, there's bound to be fire?' "

"How is that so?" Shestov asked in surprise.

"In that we ourselves are to blame. We've been acting as though we live in a desert. Or like that devil who sheared a pig: he got a lot of squealing, but no wool. But there are people around us, with their vices and weaknesses. They want to live *their* way for *their* sake; they're right. And we're right, as long as we act for our own sake. But as soon as we step even a pace into the realm of another soul, we assume a responsibility for others, and here there's no point in climbing the walls when we hear criticism."

"Slander, gossip—what kind of criticism is that!"

"Then would you wish that we went without even gossip and slander?" Login asked morosely. "Whatever they may be, they are still public opinion, the first steps toward public self-consciousness."

"Fine steps they are!"

"What's to be done? Everything good evolved from, as we see them, very foul phenomena."

Shestov had gone. Bitter feelings oppressed Login. Bursts of anger would flare up, and at such times the corpulent figure of Motovilov would rise up again, from behind the embittered face of Konoplyov.

Finally his thoughts dwelled on Anna. A state of tranquillity settled over his mind. Anna's image sparkled, abounded with delicate smiles and trusting looks. But Login could not bring himself to visit her today in the dusk and shame of his incoherent thoughts.

Like an evil obsession, the absurd slander often came to mind—and evoked the cruel desire to torment someone weak and helpless and to delight in his torment. Sometimes Login thought about just getting up, going downstairs, and giving Lenka a beating, just like that, for no reason. But he would sternly suppress this desire,—and then Anna's eyes would smile at him.

Late in the evening he sat by the little boy's bed and looked at him with unusual attention. The boy's tan face, with his mouth slightly open as he breathed in his sleep (a mouth with lips the rich red color of dried raspberries), and the shadows over the slight, convex roundness of his closed eyes, and the short curly hair over his round forehead which was half turned upward, while one ear and the back of his head were buried in the pillow—all this seemed a forbidden beauty. The cord to the cross that Lenya wore around his neck could be seen at the spot where his collar was unbuttoned. It was like a seal that must be broken in order to take possession of something, something that he would crumple and mutilate. Login pondered:

"It's the slander. It's made me indignant. But why should I have been indignant at it? If *that* is a delight, then why should I spurn it as immoral? Because of religion? But I have no religion, and, instead of religion, *they* have hypocrisy. Because of purity? But my purity foundered long ago in dirty puddles, and the child's purity will inevitably founder in those same puddles. Does it matter? Sooner or later it will perish! If *that* is a delight, should I spurn it because of an extraneous law? Yet, to the extent that it is extraneous to me, to that same extent it is not binding; and as for them, the others, the slanderers and spreaders of slander... to *them* a law is something that may be broken as long as no one finds out. Should I spurn *that* because of hygiene? But I doubt that that vice would shorten the span of my life; why, in any event its boundaries would merely be broadened by the risque experience. It's just that I wouldn't want to impose any abnormalities on the child.

"The main thing is that I would have to have him constantly in my sight, we would have to hide, then he would condemn me,—and the thought

202

of all that is humiliating.

"And he would become cynical, rude, lazy, dirty. That would be disgusting. His paleness and thinness would evoke pity and distaste at the same time! But that would not stop *them,* the others, if *they* dared!

"Yes, a healthy body—he needs it—if he's going to live. But does he need life? What does life have in store for him?

"I think that life is an evil; yet, I myself live, mechanically, without knowing why. But if life is an evil, then why is taking it away from others not permissible?

"After all, he would have died anyway if he had lain there in the woods for a few more hours.

"And if I had to choose between this child's life and satisfying my desire, then why would I have to prefer *saving* another's life to *using* it even if for only one moment of real enjoyment?

"Besides, it's impossible to look at a person without desire. Each looks longingly at his 'neighbor'—that's just inevitable; we're predators, we worship conflict, we enjoy tormenting someone. That's why we so hate the aged: we find nothing worth taking from them!"

He raised the cover slightly: the boy's thin little body seemed pitiful. A tender feeling that had suddenly arisen stood between him and his torrid desire. He walked away from the bed. Anna's tender eyes gazed affectionately at him.

But later the storm clouds descended on his consciousness again, the wild fantasies again crowded in upon him. And long hours he suffered, swinging like a pendulum between temptation and pity for the child. Fatigue and drowsiness won out over temptation, and he fell asleep with tender thoughts, and Anna's eyes again smiled to him.

In the morning Login had been asleep for a long time. Lenya quietly went up to the bed and thought:

"He needs to be awakened."

The murmurs of the wakening day reached Login and roused him to a vague state of awareness. He dreamed of a gloomy wilderness: a mountain, and a cave at the foot of it; the entrance to the cave yawned gloomily in the shade of sullen pines. In the heart of the weary wayfarer there was a thirst for unknown happiness. There was no slaking it. Though a spring of water flowed from the bare cliffs, his thirst made it seem like turbid blood and bitter tears. Someone said:

"Go to sleep until man's never-fading happiness shall awaken you."

And Login saw how, in clothing worn and dusty, he entered the cave and lay down with his head on a mossy stone. Then a long, long deep sleep. Through his sleep he sometimes heard the wild howling of a storm, the loud noise of a falling pine—sometimes the carefree chirping of a bird. His heart felt a terrible anxiety and longing for freedom and life. It kept driving the warm blood through his body, and that blood was pounding in his ears, whispering hotly, hurriedly:

"It's time to get up, it's time!"

He tried to open his heavy eyelids a little. The doleful pines sadly shook their tops and said dully:

"It's too early."

Again his eyelids closed, again his heart sank and beat anxiously. Ages were passing, long ages, like a sleepless night.

And then he sensed the fragrance of carefree childhood; vernal, white lilies-of-the-valley began to give forth a silvery ringing; a mischievous ray of the rising sun broke out in resounding laughter and began playing on his chest, which was weary of sleep; little songs of unknown birds burst forth in golden fires, and a clear brook began to babble with a purl like the sound of tinkling crystal.

"It's time to get up!"

Lenya stood there for a minute, touched Login's shoulder, and said:

"Vasily Markovich, it's time to get up!"

Login opened his eyes. It was bright and cheerful in the room. Lenya was smiling. His face was fresh with that special morning freshness that children have, a freshness that will not be seen on *anyone's* face in the afternoon or evening. Login stretched, yawned, and stuck his hands under his head.

"Ah, you've already gotten up?"

Lenya drummed his palms on the edge of the couch. He said:

"The samovar's ready."

"Well, fine, I'll get up too in a minute," Login said lazily.

Lenya gathered up his hands in the sleeves of his shirt, stamped around by the bed, then ran downstairs. The stairs creaked faintly under his bare feet.

Login got up, then sat down on the bed. He felt slightly dizzy. He sank down on the pillows again. He closed his eyes and peered at dark little figures that whirled swiftly and presented a whole kaleidoscope of grotesque and laughing faces. Then the rotation slowed; a ruddy-cheeked, white face stood out, a broad, solid figure, and it became brighter and brighter, more and more lively. Finally a smiling boy appeared distinctly before his closed eyes. He was robust, tall, much more sizable than Lenya; he was outlined in blue. Login opened his eyes—the same image remained for a single instant, even more distinct, but pale; then it quickly began to grow dim and lose shape, and in half a minute it disappeared.

Lenya was lively and cheerful that morning. With a blushing face he suddenly began to tell about how he had run away from the alms-house last year, how they had found him in the bushes in the Summer Garden, taken him back to the alms-house, and punished him. Login drew the little boy to him and hugged him. Lenya trustingly told how painful and shameful it had been. A picture of the ordeal arose in Login's mind: the bare, thin little body, and the blows, and the red stripes, and blood. This picture did not seem revolting; in fact it induced a cruel desire to put it into reality again, to hear the cries of terror and pain at his own hands.

He began speaking in a stern but failing voice:

"Listen to me, Lenka; why did you knock the books off of the book stand in my room yesterday? And you put them back in all upside down."

Lenka raised his eyes, open and pure. His expression of habitual alarm flashed in those broad windows to his soul. He smiled guiltily and whispered softly:

"I didn't mean to."

His thin little fingers started trembling on Login's knee. Login grasped the sense of capriciousness and the ugliness of his thoughts. Pity touched his heart. His lips formed just as guilty a smile as Lenka's. With embarrassment and affection he said:

"Well, all right, it's nothing serious. But, look, isn't it time for you to be going?"

There was an examination in the town school that day, and Lenya hoped to pass it.

At dinner Login asked Lenya:

"Well, brother, how are things? Did you fail?"

"No, I passed," Lenya said, but somehow without enthusiasm.

After a brief silence, he began:

"Only..."

Then he stopped and looked inquisitively at Login.

"Only what?" Login asked.

"They asked each person in a different way," Lenya replied.

"How do you mean 'in a different way?' "

"It's true. Yegor Platonych treated everyone equally, but the rest treated each one differently."

"Why, who were the others?"

"Who? The esteemed supervisor was there, Father Andrey, and Galaktion Vasilievich. They were nice to the rich boys, and easier on them, but they were rude to the poor boys."

"Lenya, I think you're making this up."

"Now, look, why should I be making it up? Ask the others. At our school the rich boys can just give incredible answers—one boys stands there, doesn't say a thing, doesn't know one word about it, but Father Andrey or Galaktion Vasilievich will just tell it all to him. But when a poor boy even hesitates, right away Galaktion Vasilievich will curse him blue: 'You rotten little brat," he says, 'all you do is play around.' And his eyes get like nails. And the supervisor also has something to say: 'Such good-for-nothings,' he says, 'need to be thrown out. You're just kept here,' he says, 'out of kindness.' That's how they're going to give the prizes too."

"What nonsense you're talking, Lenka! Now, judge for yourself: Why should they act that way?"

"I'll tell you why: Those that have are those that get."

"Well, now that's..."

"And they themselves say, the rich boys, they boast: 'We'll get through without even studying; what do we care!' But we had some young ladies at the examination today—some teachers from the junior high school for girls. Well, it was easier with them around. In fact I was questioned when they were there."

"And did you succeed in answering only because of that?"

"But then, even so, I would have..."

"Look, you have to realize, nobody's going to hurt you."

"But, all the same, why is there such unfairness?" Lenya said, losing his temper. "In fact, how *won't* they hurt us? They think up such words... Here, they asked one boy at our school today: 'What are barbarians?' 'We'd read it in a book about savages. Well, but he really doesn't know how to define barbarians. So then the Father says, 'Well, how come you don't know what barbarians are—and your own father's a barbarian!' The boy's father lives in the country. He said that on purpose to make he ladies laugh. It was funny to them, but it hurt the boy's feelings—he burst out crying when they let him go. Why is that? It's just not right! Barbarians don't pray to God, they go around naked, they don't cultivate the earth, they eat carrion. And, just like that, the Father always likes to amaze himself at our expense."

"To amuse himself?"[3]

"That's it, to amuse himself," the boy said slowly.

"And then, of course, you regret that Alexey Ivanovich wasn't at your examinations?" Login asked.

"Now, *that* I certainly don't regret. He's the meanest. You'll cry your eyes out just being in his classes. I've had to stay on my knees seventy-two times in his classes—and most of the time he's made me kneel on my bare knees."

"Why, what a lot of mischief you got into! That's not good, brother."

"Yes, but, if it weren't for our pranks, most of the time we'd get punished for no reason at all."

However strange what Lenka was saying may have been, Login believed it and had reason to do so: the town school had a bad reputation in our town. Besides, acts of injustice were committed even in the high school, where Login taught, albeit they occurred in forms that were much milder, almost unnoticeable to the students. The teachers at the high school did not go after a bribe as desperately as those at the town school; they valued agreeable acquaintances more. Likewise many of them had the desire to please the headmaster, and therefore even a teacher's relations with one student or another would be modeled on the headmaster's relations with the respective student. It was noticeable how some teachers strove to convince the poorer parents that they had made a mistake in thrusting their sons into the school.

When it began getting dark and Login was upstairs by himself, a vague uneasiness again possessed him. The boy that he had dreamed of in the morning had stood before him whenever he would close his eyes. When reading, Login would often put down his book in order to close his eyes and behold the boy. The little boy teased him unbearably with his persistent, rosy smile. It seemed that he was now more rosy and more carnal than he had been previously—as though, while hovering over Login, he assumed the properties of flesh and blood. When Login, after snuffing out the candle and getting under the cover, put his head down on the pillow, the boy's lips trembled, began moving; he began saying something rapidly but indistinctly; suddenly he became particularly bright and lively, then, as he drew closer and closer to Login, he began falling toward some point off to the side; faster and faster he tumbled, then vanished. Login fell asleep.

In the morning the boy's red hair shone again in the mote-filled and provocative rays of the sun; again his smile appeared, and the words, ringing but indistinct; and he stood before Login's open eyes longer than he had on the previous day, and he faded away more slowly.

In order to save himself from this unholy fascination, Login tried to envision Anna, and he was drawn once more to see her and hear her.

CHAPTER TWENTY-SEVEN

Login left the house. The streets were deserted; only, in one spot he did encounter a crowd of tradesmen and the same fellow with the tinny eyes; they made way for him in silence. He passed beyond the town, spent a full hour on the winding paths in the woods near the Yermolins' home, but he could not bring himself to go there. He was thinking:

"What do I, who am immoral, have in common with her, who is chaste? It's such torment for me to be with her nowadays: a hopeless wandering by the locked doors of a lost paradise!"

Then he suddenly caught himself secretly hoping that he would accidentally catch sight of Anna, that he would meet her on these paths that were so familiar to her. He grew annoyed and embarrassed, and quickly set off for home. At the Summer Garden he encountered Andozersky. Andozersky smiled glumly and said insincerely:

"Let's go shoot some balls around at the billiard parlor, old friend."

"I don't care to," Login replied, shaking his head.

The touch of that hand was unpleasantly warm and soft.

"Why so? Were you going hunting, brother? Watch out, don't miss!"

Andozersky laughed in a self-satisfied way, then disappeared into the garden. Login stood on the dusty road and gazed after him in annoyance. A light wind arose, drawing dust and bits of straw out of the town, and in their wake walked Login.

Clouds of dust danced before him, teased him, made themselves look like Andozersky; both the way he talked and the way he looked—*everything* about Andozersky was disgusting. Login made an effort not to think about Andozersky, and he succeeded. But not without a price.

The dust clouds kept dancing and dancing around him, and nearby there shone a persistent smile; two cunning eyes flashed, then faded out. A hot, gray shadow was suddenly cast by the dust. But there was something insidious in its appearance. Login grew sad.

He walked along the highway with his head bowed as he meditated dolefully; then he turned onto a path through the rye field. He had gone for half a verst amid the whispering rye, then suddenly he encountered Anna. She was wearing a light, short, yellowish-pink sarafan. A fine web of gray dust softly enveloped her feet that were animated by such light and free movement. Her pink-ribboned, light straw hat's broad brim, turned down at the sides, shaded her tan face. She smiled to Login and said:

"What a place to meet you! You're taking a stroll here, right? But I'm on business."

"Where to, may I ask?"

"There's a village here called Ryadki. I have work to do there. My

208

father's sent me."

"For charity?" Login asked with a harsh smile as he let Anna walk ahead and he followed.

Anna laughed and asked:

"You don't like good works?"

"For heaven's sake, what sort of *works* are they? They're an amusement for people who have everything," he answered, staring morosely at her sarafan's narrow straps that lay against the light yellow background of her open blouse.

"I think that there are some genuine 'good works.' Only the term is poor; it's bookish. And it's used too much, indiscriminately. But they are acts of helping... And there almost cannot be any other occupation for us people who have everything, as you call us."

"There's something better."

"What?" Anna inquired, glancing at Login.

"Seeking the truth."

"That's an abstract matter. But truth is neither in good nor in evil, it's in love for people and for the world and for everything. It's good to love everything, both a star and a toad."

"There's hardly much truth in love," Login said quietly.

"But it's true, nevertheless. People seek truth and arrive at love. I imagine that that's how the matter went in fact. At first people lived by hope. Hope often was deceiving and always kept moving farther away, like a mirage: the Jews wait for the Messiah, the Christians put their hope in a life after death—and so people began to live by faith. But the age of faith is ending."

"Yes, it's ending. The old gods are dead. But, nevertheless, the need for faith is strong. The new deities have not yet been born, and there lies our whole problem and the whole solution to the riddle of our pessimism."

"But in fact, new deities will not be born," Anna said with calm conviction.

"They'll be invented!"

"No, that cannot be. The future belongs to love."

"Apparently, you think that love is hindered both by faith and by hope?" Login asked.

"Yes, I think so. Here's how it seems to me: Hope is so disquieting, so egoistic, it leaves little room for faith and love. Faith is too precise; in its presence hope melts away and love submits to commandments and dogma. However, people hope only in a situation where things can be either one way or another, and then everything's plain, as in the fairy-tale: You go to the right, and you'll lose your horse; go to the left, and you'll save your head; just choose the good or the bad. But what's there to hope for in that? And one can only love freely, not according to commandments. Next people will have love, and it will be as free and as vital as air."

209

"And it will form an earthly paradise?" Login asked derisively.

"I don't know. Perhaps it will be harsh. It will be received by a world that has nothing to hope for, nothing to believe in."

Login listened absent-mindedly. He was again bothered by sensual arousal and was troubled by the nearness of her bare shoulders and arms and her half-revealed bosom; the sun-tanned calves of her legs that walked so lightly through the dust of the road teased him as they peeped out from under her short sarafan. Suddenly he felt a burning desire to bare this shapely body that gave off the sultry fragrance of amber and rose, and to take possession of it. In a languid voice he said:

"Love is an impossibility. It is non-being, an attribute of God, who created the world and then lay down to sleep forever. Our love is only vanity, only an aspiration to broaden one's own self—an unrealizable aspiration."

"Have you experienced it?"

"I long for it!" Login exclaimed miserably. "Oh, tell me, Anna Maximovna, do you believe in this future of love for all mankind?"

"I do," Anna replied, smiling.

"But, you know, faith prevents love, doesn't it? You're inconsistent! But how worthy you are of love!"

Anna started laughing.

"There's an unexpected compliment!"

"No, no! I meant to tell you.. But all words are so pitiful! Oh, if you only..."

Anna turned toward Login and looked at him. Her flushed face burned in joyful expectation with wide-open eyes. Login fell silent and walked along beside her and gazed at her trembling red lips.

"Well," she said in confusion, "perhaps..."

"Oh, Nyuta!" Login exclaimed passionately.

Anna's lips, red and trembling, were so close. A sultry cloud of desire hovered and passed over them.

Remote, unclean memories flared up in his mind, crude words began ringing in his ears. Something imperious like a conscience stood between him and Anna's immaculate smile. But a youthful joy, a thirst for happiness drove him toward her. The earth and dust clinging to Anna's feet reminded him that she was of this earth, dear to him and near to him, that she had arisen out of the gloomy mundane through a joyful blossoming, through a striving for the sublime Fire of the heavens. He hesitated in agony.

Her lips trembled haughtily and their smiled faded. A sorrowful expression flashed in her eyes. Anna turned away and laughed softly. Login felt a chill. He recalled the laughter of the mermaid at the mill-pond, that laughter which he had heard on one of his difficult nights. Anna said wistfully:

"You've started day-dreaming under a clear sky, and I have to hurry; otherwise my father... I heard that you've fallen out with Konoplyov."

Login told her about the quarrel. Anna listened through quietly, and then said:

"You should have expected that. Some man he is! The wind blew from the West, and he was a Nihilist. A breeze came from the East: he became a Domostroy fanatic. And he could even have become a fanatic of the simple life. Perhaps he will too. With him it all depends on the occasion. He has no mind of his own. He's a complete weathervane, changing direction with every breeze that comes along."

"It's strange," said Login, "that he doesn't refer to anyone but Motovilov."

"Motovilov! There's a man who doesn't have the right to live!"

Login glanced at her face. It was all ablaze with anger and indignation. Login smiled timidly.

Login's heart felt joyous and sad as he returned homeward. The oblique rays of the sun smiled in raspberry-red reflections on the window panes of the little gray wooden houses. By evening the streets were becoming more crowded. Sometimes one would encounter noisy little gangs of tradesmen.

All of a sudden, a crowd appeared in the middle of the street; it had come around the corner, down the road from the fortress. It was something like a procession. The windows along the way opened in a hurry, the residents stuck their heads out to look, passers-by would stop, and the street urchins ran along behind the procession with a look of the utmost amazement.

Finally Login discerned who they all were. Right down the middle of the street walked Motovilov with his wife, Krikunov with his snuffbox, both headmasters, the treasurer, the pawnbroker and his wife, Gomzin (his magnificent teeth sparkled joyfully in the distance), a few more men and ladies, and, in the midst of this crowd,—Molin, the teacher who had recently been arrested. Evidently, he had just been let out of jail.

Login guessed that they were giving the "innocent victim" an ovation; they were leading him in honor about the town, to show everyone that Molin's reputation had not suffered. Their faces were solemn and (as it often happens on unexpectedly solemn occasions) really quite stupid-looking. The hero of the triumph maintained an expression of gloomy despondency *and* deep gratitude on his face as he strutted along. He was about twenty-seven; his face was covered with pock-marks and pimples; he had the red nose of an inveterate drunkard. His felt hat could hardly fit over the shock of curly hair on top of his head. His forehead was narrow, whereas the back of his head was well-formed; this made him look thick-skulled. His huge cheekbones gave his face the look of a Tatar. His dull, near-sighted eyes were concealed by blue-tinted eye-glasses in steel frames. There was a huge bouquet of flowers in his hands.

Login tipped his hat as he came alongside this company. Motovilov said:

"Why, you're just in time, Vasily Markovich; do come join us!"

Login stopped on the wooden sidewalk and inquired:

"Are you taking a stroll, Alexey Stepanych?"

The triumphal crowd came to a halt in the middle of the street. Everyone looked at Login with a defiant sullenness.

"Yes, we're taking a stroll," Motovilov answered significantly.

"Why, that's nice. But I beg you to excuse me; I'm tired. I have the honor of bowing farewell to you for now."[1]

Login tipped his hat again and went on his way. Pozharsky caught up with him and asked:

"How come you didn't hitch on to our triumphal procession? You've angered the gray-haired adulterer by that, you know."

"That's silly, my friend. Those people—I mean, they're civil servants of one sort or another—well, they have connections, maybe they're afraid; ultimately they're just pawns. But why you? You're an independent man, to some extent an artist, so to speak,—and then, all of a sudden!"

Pozharsky laughed good-naturedly.

"Don't be malicious, most honored Signor: I have only done so out of pure motives."

"Just what do you mean?"

"Well, now, I study mimicry. It's indispensible for anyone like me. Well, and then besides, much as I regret it, you yourself know the reason: 'Flattery, my friend, flattery...' "

"But if you don't want to play the part? What then?" Login concluded.

"Look, look, that's just how it is. That is, it's not what's in the part, but always the box-office returns we have to consider, and then there's the benefit performance.[2] Ah, most honored Sir, all of us in my profession are as dependent as serfs on all of you, I swear to God! But, you know what, old man? You didn't see the main attraction; you missed a lot, by God! By the gates of the holy cloister—that is, in front of the jail—that's where the spectacle was! Motovilov made a speech in the middle of the street; the ladies cried; the young ladies brought flowers to him, our hero,—you saw them, a huge bouquet! Nata and Neta presented them in fact. On one side, you know, angelic chastity; and, on the other side, insulted innocence."

"And on all sides stupidity and vulgarity," Login said angrily.

Pozharsky burst out laughing.

"Rage on, most honored Sir. But I'm glad that I encountered you. Now that I've gotten away from them, I'm going to take the opportunity to study the geography of the town. The Motovilov girls have gone for a swim, so I need to head off in that direction."

"To ogle them?" Login asked with a note of distaste.

"Nothing of the sort! I'm going to meet Neta on her way back—and that's all."

212

"You don't mean to say that Netochka's yours now?"

"The purest ardor! The sweet nonsense of love! I play the 'jeune-premier' in the open air: a devilishly successful role."

"Things are all right, then?"

"The girl and I reached an understanding long ago—oh, I should say we did! A perfect joy of a girl: spirit and soul—oh, what a dear soul! But Tartuffe himself—alas and alack! I'm afraid even to go near him: I might get hanged."

"Well then, elope."

"It'll probably come to that. Only, where can you get a priest to perform the ceremony? Aye, there's the rub! Oh, love, love! Poetry, rapture! Drunk without wine, the heart all but bursting with inspiration! It seems, I could bring the moon down from heaven for her."

"But you can't get a priest!"

"I'll get one, most honored Sir; I'll get one, without fail."

For the time being, until he could find other quarters, Molin resided at Father Andrey's. His things were still at Shestov's.

When all those escorting him had departed, Molin stood before Father Andrey, bowed low, and declared:

"Why, Archbishop,[3] you and Motovilov have saved me."

"Why, what of it! You're one of us!" Father Andrey put him off.

But Molin went on:

"I shall never forget it. Thank you. But I don't know how to: I'm not much of a talker, but what I feel, I say straight out: You saved me! I would have been sent to hard labor like a stinking dog—and there I would have rotted."

"Now, enough of that; you don't have anything to lament now."

"Ah, yes,—now, that is! So, Father, my benefactor, let me have some vodka: I'll toss off a whole glass to your health."

Vodka was served. The host and guest drank, embraced, kissed each other, drank more and more, got high and wept. Then guests arrived. They sat down to play cards, and drank again.

On the next day, when Shestov had left the school, he ran into Molin. Molin walked up to him and held out his hand. They walked side by side. Molin remained silent, with the same look that he had had yesterday, that of a man who has suffered innocently. That exasperated Shestov. Shestov was at a loss for words, although this was the first time that they had met since Molin's arrest.

Molin stuck out his thick lips and spoke up sullenly:

"You and your little aunt had signed me over to life as a convict at hard labor: well, you can hold off your rejoicing for a while."

Shestov blushed and said with a trembling voice:

"I've wanted very much for you to be extricated from this affair; and there's been nothing joyous about it."

Molin cleared his throat in disbelief, assumed an expression of pathos and resentment, and was silent. In silence they reached the home of Father Andrey. Without saying a word or bidding him goodbye, Molin turned off toward the gateway. Shestov walked on without turning around. His heart began beating violently from a feeling of bitterness and from the awkwardness of his embarrassment: they would see him—and they would laugh at him.

Molin entered the dining room. Father Andrey was getting ready to have dinner.

He owned the house that he lived in, a rather small wooden house with five windows facing the street; it was a one-story house with a basement. The dining room was in the basement, next to the kitchen. Father Andrey's dining room never got enough light from its two small windows, which were set in one of the shorter walls; in fact, since the room was three times greater in length than it was in breadth, the far end of it was gloomy even in midafternoon. At that end there was a sideboard with liqueurs. Near it stood an oaken barrel of vodka of a particularly pleasant flavor and of considerable strength. Father Andrey ordered this vodka straight from the factory for himself and for certain friends who chipped in with him to buy it. Through the windows one could see the street's surface, overgrown with grass, and, occasionally, someone's feet. A narrow bench, covered with soft cushions and, for greater comfort, provided with an ample quantity of soft bolsters, extended the length of the long wall that was opposite the door to the kitchen. The long dining table stood alongside the comfortable bench. At one end, by the window, it was covered with a white tablecloth. It was obvious from the many spots, that this was by no means the first day that the cloth had been spread there.

Father Andrey was reclining on the bench, with his head toward the window. He kept shouting at Eugenia. Eugenia was intermittently going from dining room to kitchen and back with plates and knives, making the floor shake with the heavy tread of her bare feet, and answering Father Andrey's angry shouts with angry looks.

The priest's wife,[4] Fedosia Petrovna, a nimble little woman about fifty, puttered about the table. She frequently would dash into the kitchen, there she would quietly nag Eugenia, and, obviously, she was worried about the dinner preparations. Her fussy exclamations were heard coming from the kitchen:

"But you know the Father doesn't like that. You complete idiot! Now, you know that Alexey Ivanych... Oh, you damned fool!"

Molin took a seat at the table, smiled bitterly, and said:

"I'm through with him!"

Father Andrey looked at him attentively and asked:

"Of whom are you speaking?"

"Why, that fellow, Shestov."

The priest's wife jumped out of the kitchen with a curious look and asked Molin:

"You've run into him, then?"

"I should say I have!" Molin replied.

He set his stoop-shouldered torso swaying, forced out a strange, awkward laugh, and set about recounting the incident curtly, as though he were angry even at the people with whom he was talking:

"He came out of the school, bounced up to me, fawned, and held out his hand. I could hardly control myself! I just wanted to let him have it right in the teeth!"

"And you should have," the good father said with a gleeful snicker. "Hey, Eugenia, bring the dinner!"

"Why, indeed you should have!" the priest's wife agreed. "Eugenia, you clumsy fool! Where are you hiding?"

"But God damn him to hell!" Molin said angrily. "He'll start crying again, and run around slandering me, the damned little squirt!"

"Wife," exclaimed Father Andrey, "where the hell's the vodka?"

"Eugenia! Eugenia!" the priest's wife began fussing. "You unimaginable fool, do you have *any* kind of noggin on your shoulders?"

Eugenia brought a steaming pie into the dining room. She shouted:

"I can't do everything at once."

The priest's wife rushed to the sideboard and pulled out the vodka and glasses in an instant. Eugenia dashed away to fetch the soup, and Molin muttered to himself:

"He came fawning after me. Sidled along as far as your front door... Well, but I didn't pay him a bit of attention. He bit his tongue, and took off like a scalded dog."

Father Andrey let out a stentorian laugh. The priest's wife filled the glasses with vodka and passed one of them to Molin. She looked on him with tender, loving eyes. Father Andrey and Molin drank up, and the priest's wife in the meantime served Molin a huge piece of beef pie and filled his bowl with the soup, which was still steaming hot.

"Clever!" said Father Andrey. "You just have to teach them, the scoundrels. Why, say, brother, people can't wet their whistles on the first drink. Eh, Alexey Ivanych?"

"Now you're talking!" Molin said in approval. "I must admit, I'm going to do some drinking,—I really had to keep the fast in that damned jail!"

They poured a second one each and drank up. Bitter memories haunted Molin. He spoke up:

"If he'd been a real friend, the beast, he should have had that bitch's tail between her legs immediately. They should have had an accounting!"

215

"Of course!"

"Why, if she hadn't up and informed on me to the investigator, I would have been completely in the clear—I didn't pay her off, why should I? It just wasn't the thing, for *me* to offer *her* money!"

"Why, naturally. Besides, it seemed fishy to me. I just kept thinking that they had it worked out with the aunt. And you see what they did."

"The basest creatures!" the priest's wife yelped.

"But then, it's all right, I'll be rid of them, and without having to pay them anything."

Father Andrey suddenly broke out laughing and asked Molin:

"Have I told you what happened at the examination?"

"No. What?"

"Yes, yes, imagine, what a mean trick!" the priest's wife said, getting all excited.

"He pounced on Akimov," said Father Andrey. "Said he doesn't know geometry. Gave him an F. He said he'll have to take a reexamination. Well, so we'll see again. Why should you have to know what you don't know?"

"Shestov did it out of envy, you know," the priest's wife explained. "Akimov's father gave Father Andrey a contribution for a new cassock, but he didn't give Shestov a damn thing. Akimov is a merchant who's respectful, but respectful, of course, only to whom he should be; after all, anyone can see who's worth what. Good Father, Andrey Nikitych, now why don't you serve him? You see, the glasses are empty."

"They are at that," said the good father, and he filled them.

"Hey!" Molin shouted. " 'Drinking is the joy of the Russes; we cannot exist without that pleasure.' "[5]

"Eugenia!" Father Andrey shouted through the open door to the kitchen. "Who is it you're jabbering with in there?"

"Why, Father, it's my brother," Eugenia replied.

A little boy about twelve years old huddled warily in a corner of the kitchen. He was afraid of Father Andrey: he was a pupil at the town school.

"Your brother? Well, just at the right time. Let him stay there a while. I need to send him on an errand." Then Father Andrey turned to Molin and said: "I only wonder why it is that our little boys won't fix up a surprise for Shestov for giving those F's. Somebody should lay for him and get him with a rock—the perfect thing! Hah-hah-hah!"

The priest's wife squealed in delight.

"Right in the back of the neck!" she shouted, then let out a hearty laugh.

Molin nodded his head at the open door to the kitchen. Father Andrey shouted:

"Eugenia, fasten the door! Look at the smoke you've let in, you mare!"

Eugenia swiftly slammed the door shut. Father Andrey started laughing quietly.

"How about that!" he said.

"Still, it's uncomfortable—the schoolboy right there and all that."

"Don't be silly; why, I did that on purpose," whispered Father Andrey: "Let him hear. He'll tell his friends; there'll be some prankster who's daring enough, and he'll let Shestov have it."

Again Father Andrey guffawed, then he poured a fourth round. Sharing his sentiments, Molin giggled, showing his tobacco-yellowed teeth. He gulped down the vodka and shouted:

"Ah, pack up your troubles!"

"He's always going to see Login," said Father Andrey.

"Ah, to the blind devil! Oh, Login, you empty-headed agitator! He found one fool and charmed another crooked mug into going along with him. But, then, he's a past master at talking nonsense."

"He and Konoplyov had a row and fell out completely," the priest's wife informed them.

"Why, the hell you say! Where did you come on to that? It must have happened over money."

"It doesn't matter; their whole undertaking, that damn-fool society of theirs, will come to naught," Father Andrey said gloatingly.

"Why?" asked Molin.

"Motovilov will just pick them apart."

"He'll pick them apart!" the priest's wife exclaimed in excitement.

"It would certainly take Motovilov to do that," Molin agreed: "A rascal of the first degree."

"Yes, brother," Father Andrey explained, "he's not to be trusted. Call him your friend with high regard, but never fail to be on guard."

"A rascal, a rascal, the only word for him!" the priest's wife said in delight.

"But a clever rascal," Molin added.

"Why, I say the very same thing: a first-class rascal, a fine fellow," the priest's wife continued. "Now, my Andrey Nikitych is sly—oy, is he sly! But that one is even slyer!"

CHAPTER TWENTY-EIGHT

Login came home from the school early and in a sluggish state of mind. He sat down at the table, lazily set about eating lunch. The vodka stood before him. Login looked at the bottle and thought that the habit of drinking vodka was a foul one. He leaned back in his chair and recited in a low voice:

"Goodbye to wine the first of May,
And in October, goodbye love!"

Then he pulled up the bottle and a vodka glass, filled the glass, and drank it up. His thoughts became light and cheerful.

At that point he heard the unpleasantly sharp sound of a cane knocking against the sill of his open window. Login shuddered. He frowned in annoyance, wiped his lips with a napkin, and walked up to the window.

"Are you home, old friend?" Andozersky's voice resounded.

Login pretended that he was very glad, and answered:

"I'm at home, I'm at home. Well, what are you doing there—come on in!"

"Do you have vodka?" Andozersky asked emphatically.

"Why not?"

Andozersky quickly ran up onto the porch. His ruddy face seemed haggard. His little eyes were sleepy and could hardly stay open. Today his voice was hoarse. Turning his neck in the tight collar of his judge's uniform was an agony.

"Eh-hey, you have cucumbers! Splendid! And a radish—even better!"

Login poured a glass of vodka for each of them.

"Do you need to take the edge off of a hangover from yesterday?" he asked.

"I took the edge off, old friend, but not well enough; I got up late, had to drag myself to the conference—there was a court session today.[1]

"Where was it you stayed so long yesterday?"

"That's just the problem, I wasn't anywhere. I sat at home and guzzled vodka."

"With whom."

"By myself, brother, like a sergeant-major. I put away so much that I hate to think of it."

"From sorrow or from joy?"

"From trying to make up my mind, old friend."

"You don't mean...?"

"Yes, yes, I've decided, I've made a choice... Well, but that's for later... I'll tell you all about it tomorrow."

"Well, then, what did you impartial judges do today?"

218

"We handled a lot of cases! Today, brother, we decided to make an awesome judgment."

Andozersky poured himself a second glass of vodka and began laughing gleefully.

"Correction was administered today! You know Spirka? The comic Othello."

"I ought to know him! Only, what sort of Othello is he? He's a Hamlet."

"Spirka, a Hamlet? Well, you can just tell me anything now!"

"But, then, that's precisely what he is, a Hamlet: he thirsts for vengeance, then he hates vengeance, and then, you'll see—he'll get revenge in any way that he can. Well, so what did you do with him?"

"You see, the county court sentenced him to fifteen strokes with the birch rod: Motovilov complained about him, and he also got it for his prodigality and drunkenness, which were wrecking his household."

"It was Spirka's household that was being wrecked!"

"Why, absolutely! So he made an appeal to us. Well, then, we as a proper court heard the case and decided to increase the punishment for him, the scoundrel; we decided to give him twenty!"

"But, now, why on earth should you increase it?" Login said in amazement.

"For this reason: you should know better than to appeal!"

"Perfect Solomons you are! Well, what *else* did you do?"

"Furthermore, old friend, we convicted a little boy. You can feel sorry for him, brother; you're sympathetic toward little boys."

"Just what little boy was it?"

"Why, Kuvaldin, the one who got caught in Motovilov's garden. The county court also sentenced him, to ten strokes, and he also got the idea of appealing the sentence. Well, we just threw on an extra five for him."

"But, after all, you know that he just happened to get caught in a prank that's a custom hereabouts."

"So why should he bite people? Besides, it's an awful custom."

"But, after all, you couldn't sentence a boy to more than half of the standard penalty, could you? As it turns out, *you've* broken the law."

"Broken it? Well, the letter of the law, that is; but we... We, brother, are the new breed of the magistracy. We are without sentiments."

"A heartless breed, there's no denying it!"

"Heartless! Why, you'd have it that every rascal should get a pat on the back! No, brother, we bear a great responsibility on our shoulders: to take matters in hand and set them straight. It's no use being soft-hearted: give them an inch, and they'll take a mile. Being firm is particularly imperative nowadays in our provinces: there's a ferment among the common people—I'm just afraid we'll be faced with a riot over the cholera.[2] As it is, the devil knows what rumors are going around."

219

"Well, then, you want to make the people conscious of what's right and wrong?"

"Of course! It's high time. After all, just *living* in our villages is getting impossible: there's no respect left for the authorities, for the Nobility, the right of property, or the law."

"Wait a minute, brother; just how is it you think you can hammer into the people an awareness of what is right or wrong, when you yourselves break the law?"

"We need to inculcate obedience and discipline in the muzhik. We, the noblemen, are his natural guardians."

"But, tell me, then, did your assistant prosecutor protest?"

"Why should he have protested?"

"It was, after all, illegal."

"Why, let the boy himself take his complaint to the court at the provincial capital. Only, the boy wouldn't dare: he'd be afraid that they'd add on still more to the sentence."

Andozersky chuckled.

"Can it really be, that no one of you even dissented? Can it be, that there wasn't a single decent man among you?"

Andozersky chuckled again, in a gleeful and carefree manner.

"There *was* one, brother, the same type as you. An idealist, with a pudding-soft heart—Uklyuzhev, the young head of the zemstvo. He got the urge to agonize over the boy. It's too funny! He was so moved to pity over the little hellion, that he almost cried himself! Well, we shamed him. 'Go ahead and cry,' we kept saying. Well, he was embarrassed and tried to take it all back; he mumbled; 'I was just speaking,' he says, 'about things in general.' We embarrassed him so that he then had to make an excuse: 'It was just because,' he says, 'I'd taken a little swig before court.' He's lying of course: taken a swig—in a pig's eye he had!"

"There was only one, and he turned out to be a gutless wonder!" Login said scornfully.

Andozersky laughed gleefully. He continued his account:

"It's too funny! We came out of the conference room, Dubitsky read the decision, the boy at once burst into tears, fell at our feet: 'Oh, dear fathers, merciful sirs, please don't!' However, you could see from his face that the boy's a scoundrel: he needed to have his hide tanned but good!"

"What a cruel, savage, Tatar way you have of doing all this! You're all such heartless wretches!" Login said with revulsion.

It was disgusting to look at Andozersky's smiling face, and Login felt like saying something rude in order to insult him, to anger him. And Andozersky did in fact take offense and sulk.

"Just why are you standing up so for the brat? Have you seen him?"

"I have."

"Well, all right, he's not a beauty, you know; your Lenka's a lot prettier. He's nothing for you to get excited over."

Login's face turned crimson, and in his chest he felt that particular sinking feeling familiar to anyone who has ever been crudely and unjustly insulted.

"Listen, Anatoly Petrovich," he said, "you have said this sort of thing to me more than once, so that I am compelled to ask you: do me a favor, say plainly what you mean to say."

Login felt that he was getting too excited, and reproached himself for it, but he could not control his agitation.

"What do I mean to say?" Andozersky repeated the question with a mean smirk. "No more, it should be assumed, than what everybody else is saying."

"Namely?" Login asked in a harsh, metallic tone.

"A lot of rubbish, you see, is being bandied about. Your society, so they say, is a front for anti-government propaganda. People are jabbering that you gather students together in order to instill harmful ideas in them. They say you're carrying out some sort of plot; some sort of balloons will fly to your house... They say you're leading a life of depravity with little boys."

"That's vile, vile!"

"But our people just thrive on it, old friend! It's vile to you of course! But our people find it piquant. The young ladies hereabouts are simply transported by such tid-bits. You should hear how Claudia talks about it— she's in ecstasy!"

"Yes, I remember what a fling you were having at my expense in front of Claudia."

"Why, that's just your... I stick up for you everywhere."

"Absolutely to no avail."

"Silly, I can't stand to listen to slander and not object. But they don't believe me—they'll listen, shrug their shoulders, and stick to their own opinions. You yourself ought to know what blockheads run around in our blessed town. Don't feed them bread, but smutty news instead. What else can they do? They only talk about trivia, they only read bawdy novels—there's idleness, boredom, no spiritual concerns whatsoever. And you yourself provoke them. You aren't careful. You tease the geese and don't give a damn what might happen to you."

"You don't say!"

"Yes, brother; 'If among wolves you prowl, like wolves you'd better howl.'[3] Just consider Molin's case. Maybe it is ugly, but just why do you have to make it appear that it is, as you say, a case of scoundrels' having taken up for a scoundrel. Shestov's a fool, a little boy; he angered people by his stupidity, and whoever isn't wanted around here gets slandered. You're friends with him—well, then, so you get slandered too. Well, even if we actually are all scoundrels, nevertheless, old friend, we don't like—oh, how we don't

221

like—to be despised to very openly."

"Are you going to get revenge through slander?"

"I won't, but they will!" Andozersky corrected him didactically. "What can be done about it? All human beings are people, and everyone has his own personal outlook on things. Here we made a judgment according to conscience, and you condemned us as heartless wretches. I bet, if you had the power, you'd even send us into penal servitude."

Login laughed softly and malevolently. His face grew pale.

"Indeed, Anatoly Petrovich, some of our associates are such that even penal servitude would hardly be good enough for them. Poisonous vipers have to be exterminated."

"Why, I daresay, it's not good the way you're laughing," Andozersky said gloomily. "Your nerves, old friend; you need to see a doctor. Well, anyhow, I've chatted too long with you."

He departed, and he left behind a resentful, vindictive feeling in Login's mind. And again, as before, this dark feeling was focused on Motovilov.

" 'There's a man who doesn't have the right to live,' " he recalled.

Pale and angry, Login gripped the back of a chair with his hands and struck the chair against the wall several times—the absurd action calmed him. Again Anna came to his mind—her eyes watched reproachfully.

News in our town travels amazingly fast. Andozersky had not managed to reach Login's place before the sentence pronounced at the morning session of the appellate court was already known to Valya—and Valya hastened to make use of it.

She was convinced that Andozersky was courting young ladies of the gentry, was choosing a bride, and had only been amusing himself with *her*. She decided to make up with Sezyomkin again. In his joy poor Yashka felt that he was in the seventh heaven. But Valya was annoyed because of her disappointed hopes. She longed for the chance to repay Andozersky.

Valya well knew that, of all Andozersky's prospective brides, only Anna would be displeased by the heavy-handed sentence passed today; Neta sincerely believed that muzhiks were savages; and such vile things as the court cases of muzhiks could be of no interest whatsoever to Claudia. And so Valya ran, barefoot and red-faced with gleeful excitement, to the Yermolins' estate.

Anna had just come back from somewhere and was changing into a house dress from her riding-habit. Valya stood before her and told the news. Anna looked sternly at Valya and knit her brows. She said:

"That's not good, Valya. You were there also—and now..."

"But, Anna Maximovna," Valya said, trying to excuse herself, "that has nothing to do with him: for some reason he didn't pay attention, and then he bit Alexey Stepanych's thumb."

"Oh, Valya, that's not the point—he got caught in someone else's garden, that's what! You should have restrained the children, and yourself along with them."

"But, after all, it really wasn't stealing, but simply a prank."

"A lovely prank indeed! It's not the little boy, but you, who merited that punishment."

Valya started crying. Amid her sobs she said:

"I know I'm at fault, only why did they punish him so cruelly?"

"Why blame others, Valya! You did wrong in rushing here to tell me this."

Valya cried even harder, knelt before Anna, and clutched at her hands.

"I swear to God, I won't do it any more," she said. "Don't turn me away—I'd rather you punished me, as you know."

That same day Andozersky finally decided to confirm his choice for a bride. Not for nothing had he been sitting at home with the door locked and drinking: he had been pondering the great step that he was about to take.

Of all the marriageable young ladies, the richest was Anna. Andozersky decided that he loved her. It was time to propose. He was almost sure that he was being anxiously awaited.

It would have been wiser to postpone it until tomorrow in order to conduct the matter with a clear head. However, he was driven onward by the vodka and by his annoyance at Login.

"He's gotten the idea of flirting with her, it seems," Andozersky mused. "I'll show him what a friend I am!"

He took a bath. It seemed that his head was clearer than ever. "Clean as a whistle," he recalled Baglayev's saying. Suddenly he felt cheerful and pleasant. He wondered if perhaps he smelled slightly of liquor, but that was no problem, he decided: He sprinkled his clothes with perfume and then felt sure that its fragrance would cover up the aroma of alcohol.

He rode quickly to the Yermolin estate. Fate was kind to him: Anna was at home reading, sitting on the terrace. Her black braids were arranged in a low bun. Her close-fitting, high-waisted, golden yellow dress went well with the lovely tan of her bare feet.

"May I have a look at that?" Andozersky inquired.

Anna handed him the book. Andozersky read the title, looked surprised, and said:

"What do you want to read such books for?"

Anna smiled faintly and asked:

"Why not read such books?"

"Those books are only fit for someone who has had a lot of worldly experience. Tender-hearted, inexperienced souls only become needlessly embittered upon reaching such books and grow steeped in false opinions, and tried and true experience has no antidote for it."

223

Anna looked carefully at Andozersky. She grinned slightly and said:
"But what can I do? I've started it, so I just have to finish it."

"Oh, I wouldn't advise it! However, let's not waste precious time.
I've been wanting to impart something to you; may I?"

"Please do."

Andozersky fell silent, as though he were searching for the right words.
Anna waited for a little while, then she said:

"I'm listening Anatoly Petrovich."

"You see, it can't be said in just a few words. And besides, maybe there
are no words adequate for it: every expression is so old and hackneyed. Right
now, you see, it's spring, the flowers are blooming, everything is so idyllic,
you grow young again in the spring."

"Your spring has already passed," Anna said slyly.

"Yes, it passed, furtively, imperceptibly, but now it's returning, and
how beautiful it is! My soul rejoices, grows finer and purer."

"And *how* have you noted this return of your spring?" Anna asked
quietly.

She was looking past Andozersky, off into the distance. Her eyes had
turned sad.

"I still don't know yet," said Andozersky, "but I think that I've noted
it in the way I feel."

"You say that you've become better, finer? That's not, of course,
merely a phrase?"

"No, no, it's true!" exclaimed Andozersky.

He saw Anna's face only from the side: she had turned in her chair,
and, it seemed, she was looking carefully at something in the distance, where
the gilded crosses of the town's churches could be seen through the bright
green foliage of the garden. Slowly, pensively she said:

"That happens rarely, so rarely that somehow one simply cannot believe in such holidays of the heart. Better, finer—how good that is, what
spiritual illumination! That's how religious people feel after Communion.
But now, tell me, how has this been reflected in your work, in your public
service?"

Anna quickly turned toward Andozersky and scrutinized him carefully. Her face suddenly grew flushed, reflecting the rapid shift of her
thoughts and feelings.

"That, Anna Maximovna, is a dull and coarse subject, my work,—it's
absolutely of no interest to you."

Anna's face suddenly became indifferent. She said coldly:

"Pardon me, I took it at face value: I thought that you actually wanted
to tell me about your *renaissance.*"

"Anna Maximovna, how can I talk about business when I have something entirely different on my mind! But, tell me, for God's sake, can you
really not have noticed the tender feeling that I nurture for you?"

Anna rose abruptly. Blushing scarlet, she turned away from him.

"Tell me," Andozersky said, approaching her, "have you, after all..."

Anna cut him short:

"Look, you've been telling me about your inner revival, but you don't want to tell me what you do at work. I know that a session of the district court was scheduled for today, and you must have been there. Tell me, did the court change that boy's sentence? Kuvaldin, I believe, his name is?"

"Yes, it changed it."

"The boy was acquitted?"

"How in the world could he be acquitted!"

"The sentence was not commuted? No? It was increased, then? Yes? Not really, not really?"

"Oh, Anna Maximovna!"

"But you, you disagreed with the others, didn't you? No? Even *you* shared their opinion? With spring in your heart, you endorsed such a stupid, cruel, pitiless sentence? and *that's* what it means to be *revived?* You like to joke, Anatoly Petrovich!"

"Why do you feel that way about it, Anna Maximovna? After all, it's my job, a matter of conscience."

"All life is a matter of one conscience, not two... However, talking like this is pointless of course. Only, you did start talking about your inner revival. I can't endure idle phrases."

"My love for you is not a phrase. Anna Maximovna, just tell me..."

"Even if I were so unfortunate as to have fallen in love with a man who loves what I hate and hates what I love, I would nevertheless refuse to be so stupid as to wreck my own life. Besides, I have no feelings whatsoever for you."

"But I nurtured such hopes, and it seemed to me that I had grounds..."

"Enough of that, Anatoly Petrovich, please! You were mistaken."

Anna quietly walked down the terrace steps into the garden, which laughed greenly before her. The merry red blossoms in the flower-bed whirled about in a light and joyous round-dance.

Andozersky looked furiously at Anna. And now everything about her suddenly became loathsome to him—the prettiness of her simple attire, and the way that she wore her hair, and her poised and easy manner of walking, and the brazen tan of her bare feet.

"For a guest she should at least have put her shoes on!" he thought with furious annoyance.

CHAPTER TWENTY-NINE

Login walked along the streets. The sense of sleepiness and idleness depressed him. It was not as though everyone were asleep: the sun was still high, people were moving about, dogs were yapping, children were laughing— but everything was dead and dull. Here and there near fences the tall nettle hid its evil sting; dust was turning gray on the unpaved earth.

Login stopped on the bridge over the stream; he leaned on the railing. The turbid water lazily flowed by in its narrow bed; springy little smoky-blue eddies undulated about the piers of the bridge; wood-chips and litter fluttered around down there. A little boy and girl, each about eight years old, were wandering near the bank and splashing the water that churned with white foam under their sun-browned bare feet. Their antics were phlegmatic.

Login walked on. A five-year-old boy, the son of an excise official, rolled along on a scooter. He did not smile, nor did her shout. His face was pale, his muscles flaccid.

He encountered peasant women with their obtuse faces; young girls with empty eyes, clutching something from a shop in their tenacious hands; a red-haired shopkeeper with a ledger under his arm; a barefoot and dirty "holy fool" begging a copeck from everyone and cursing when he did not get one. He encountered drunken muzhiks, hideous and torn up from a fight. They were reeling, bawling. Occasionally a "lady of fashion" would sail forth in tawdry attire, waddling like a duck, with a lemon face and goldleaf eyes.

Login went by the cholera barrack. A white-jacketed chubby lad, a medic, was standing on the porch. Login inquired:

"How are things, Stepan Matveich?"

"Why, I declare, things are in a bad way!" the medic answered in distress.

"How so in particular?"

"Would you believe, I've completely worn myself out, just worn myself out... Why, you just look, look at this jacket..."

The medic drew out the slack in the front of his jacket.

"See how it fits?"

"You've lost weight," Login said with a smile.

"And it's simply inconceivable how much riff-raff hangs around here! Every day you hear such awful things said! My heart just sinks down to my boots and stays there. One way or another, I just wish it were over!"

"It's all right, it'll pass."

"I just don't know how God will carry it through."

Suddenly the medic flinched for some reason; he turned pale, hastily bowed to Login, and darted inside the barrack. Login looked around. The rowdy with the tinny eyes was standing across the street from the barrack. He curled his lips in contempt, spat, and spoke up:

"Amazing! Just like that, in broad daylight! Pah! No shame nor conscience nor fear! Fine people! Must have gotten desperate."

Login stood there and looked, then he ascended the rampart. That encounter had a bad effect on his mood, but in his conscious mind it slipped by without much notice: he was thinking about something else.

He liked being on top of the rampart. It was open and bright all around him, the wind blew and swept by boldly and freely—and his thoughts became purer and freer. In fact his chest expanded with a feeling of joy and freedom after ascending the steep flight of steps.

But today it was bad even up there: the breeze was still, the sun shone wth a dead motionless quality, the air was sultry, heavy. At times the dusty shadow would dance about, a little boy with laughing eyes. At times he would hear the patter of bare feet in the grass—what was it? Anna's step? Or the gray shadow?[4] He turned his head—there was nobody.

Even his thoughts about Anna were bitter today:

"Will I ruin her, or will she save me? I am unworthy of her and ought not to go near her. And besides, can she love me? Me myself, and not, as the case may be, some false image created in her mind and adorned by virtues that aren't real?"

Andozersky came riding by the rampart in a hired carriage. He caught sight of Login, got out of the carriage, and quickly made the ascent to the top. Drops of sweat were streaming down his ruddy face. He spoke up angrily:

"Tell me, for Christ's sake, what do you rootless idealists live by?"

"What's the matter?"

"What sort of principles do you have when they're such as destroy your own well-being? Just like a cat, she falls in love, keeps luring me on with tender looks,—then suddenly she thumbs her nose at me: 'I won't marry you,' she says. 'You don't acquit scoundrels!' "

"Why, what happened to you? Did you propose to her, or something?"

"I made a fool of myself, offered that natural-born fool my hand and heart, and what then? In reply she gave me an entire lecture that didn't have one drop of sound reason! The devil knows what! However, I just know for sure that she's in love, like a kitten."

"You and she are no match: marry Netochka."

"No match! Look, you haven't been up to something, have you? You fell in love with her yourself, so then you made her fall in love with you, didn't you? The devil take it, there'd be some excuse for it if she were a beauty! But she's got a bill like a swallow!"

Andozersky shouted all this, almost choking with anger. Login calmly objected:

"There's no reason for you to get so excited. Obviously you don't feel any particular love for her."

"Well I'm certainly not about to shoot myself over her; let her be at ease on that score. You can even convey that to her."

"I can certainly convey it, if you want me to. After all, you know, you do have two other prospective brides, if not more."

"Oh, don't worry, I won't cry over it—to hell with her!"

Andozersky spat and ran back down. Login gazed after him with a smile.

An invitation from the high school's headmaster was waiting for Login at home; it asked that Login report to him for an interview on official business.

Pavlikovsky looked worried and even embarrassed. With an amiable smile he moved an armchair for Login up to his desk upon which many groups of photographs stood out vividly in different directions. The pictures, in sculptured upright frames of walnut and bronze, were presents from colleagues and students. Pavlikovsky settled himself in another armchair and offered Login a smoke. Login did not smoke, but Pavlikovsky up to now could not remember that. He was an absent-minded man. The story was told that once in the hall he stopped a student who was up to some mischief and who accidentally ran smack into Pavlikovsky's stomach with his head.

"What do you mean by acting up like this! What's your name?" the headmaster had asked sluggishly.

His eyes were gazing off in the distance, but he had put his right hand on the student's shoulder. The boy, who happened to be his son, had looked up at him in surprise and smiled.

"Why are you silent? I'm asking you: what's your name?"

"Pavlikovsky," the boy had answered.

"What? Oh, that's who it is!" the headmaster had said, discerning at last.

"Ah, yes, yes," Pavlikovsky now said, "I'm always forgetting that you don't smoke. So then, I asked you to pay me a visit. Excuse me for troubling you. But it was imperative for me to have a talk with you."

"At your service," answered Login.

"Here, you see, there are certain... Excuse me for touching upon it, but it's, unfortunately, imperative... You have embarked upon, so to speak, a career of public activity. How will the authorities look upon that?"

"Why, if it proves embarrassing, they won't allow it, and that's that."

"All right, but... You see, the students visit you... And that runaway is living at your home... I, of course, understand your magnanimous motive, but all this is awkward."

"All this—excuse me, Sergey Mikhailovich—is more my personal business."

228

"Why, you know, that's not altogether so. But, in any event, I ask you not to gather students together at your home."

"Why, in fact I don't gather them together—they come of their own accord, whoever needs to or whoever wants to."

"In any event, I ask of you that they not come in the future."

"Is that all?"

"Next, I would ask you not to associate with suspicious characters like, for instance, Serpenitsyn."

"Pardon me, I must decline this suggestion of yours."

"That certainly is your privilege. I told you what I considered my obligation, but thereafter it's your business. However, I do hope that you will think it over carefully."

Pavlikovsky grinned slyly and lazily.

"The answer for me is clear even now," Login said resolutely.

"So much the better. Next... You see, there are a lot of rumors in town. And your name is involved. Certain statements are ascribed to you—I really don't know, something about balloons, and then suddenly some sort of constitution. And therefore I earnestly entreat you that for the future you refrain from any conversations on such themes. For us to become involved in politics, you see, is... Finally, you weren't compelled by force to work at your job, consequently..."

"I understand that very well, Sergey Mikhailovich, and I'm neither thinking nor speaking about politics at all..."

"However..."

"It's some sort of stupid gossip, absolutely groundless in every way."

"Yes, nevertheless.. Next, I would ask you to attend church more often. Well, and finally, I would ask... You see, at Motovilov's, I remember, you deigned to speak of the Nobility with a certain irritation, well, and later... about other subjects... and in general, such a tone... you see, it's inappropriate."

"In other words, when talking with Motovilov, it's required that one automatically say 'yes' to him?"

"No, why on earth? Anyone may have his own opinion, but... You see, one must respect another's opinion. Now, for example, you were so demonstrative in declining Alexey Stepanych's invitation when we all were escorting that unfortunate Molin. After all, that wasn't in actuality an obligation to anything, but simply an act of Christian charity—and it was inappropriate of you to stand apart there."

"Permit me to tell you, Sergey Mikhailovich, that I also understand this requirement of yours perfectly well, but that I cannot acquiesce in it."

"You're making a mistake."

Login returned home tired and sad.

"There's going to be a struggle," he thought, "but with whom, and with what? A struggle with something nameless, a struggle for which there are no weapons! Both the question about Lenka and being respectful toward Motovilov, and the talk about my being suspected of 'disloyalty'—all these are trifles: it won't be difficult at all for me to win out in these matters. But there's one thing that isn't a mere trifle: that my *plan* has been ruined merely because Motovilov doesn't like it, because Dubitsky finds it useless, because Konoplyov was merely seeking personal advantage in it, and the rest were waiting to see what would happen. The ruin of my plan; after that, life is empty!"

Login could not sleep that night. He left the house about twelve o'clock. He was drawn to the place where Anna was. He knew that she would be asleep, that it was hardly the time for visiting. He neither thought of seeing her nor even thought of where he was going—a dream depicted the familiar pathways and the gate and the house immersed in midnight somnolence in the clear, cool stillness and fresh, moist fragrance in the midst of the slumbering garden.

There in fact was the last gloomy hovel, the last low wattle fence. Login had left the town.

The wide road with its tiny little peaks of crushed and rut-pressed gravel gleamed in the moonlight—a quiet night road enchanted by the invisible passage of *her* who wandered by the crossroads at midnight. The small woods ahead were mysteriously silent. A light silvery mist was rising. The outlines of the lonely trees and bushes that stood motionlessly here and there along both sides of the road were growing misty under the spreading haze. Light clouds were sailing over the moon and playing around it with irridescent colors. It seemed that the moon was running across the sky, while everything else—the road and the forest and the meadows, even the very clouds—had stopped and, enchanted by its mysterious green light, stood rapt in contemplating the magic flight of the moon.

A throng of vague, indistinct dreams and thoughts filled Login's mind. Agonizing, sweet languor, a restless narrow-winged swallow, hovered over his heart. And his heart beat so, and his eyes gleamed so, and his chest heaved so, and he was parched with the thirst of spring, the captivating thirst that can be slaked only by love, or, perhaps, only by the grave.

Login walked a little beyond the driveway to the Yermolins' estate. From the broad expanse of the road he turned off into the woods on a narrow, familiar path. Something cracked under his foot. The damp boughs of a hazelnut tree brushed against him gently and tenderly and descended behind him with a soft prattle.

The path wound like a capricious little snake. Here it was fresher and cooler. The stillness came to life, the forest shades dispelled the moon's charms; the bushes conversed in a barely audible tone with the scarcely trembling leaves. The light rustle and murmur of the forest brook could be heard. The logs of its narrow little bridge began creaking and shaking under

Login's feet.

Something quiet and timid buzzed by in the air. Suddenly, somewhere off to the side a nightingale brightly and gaily drew forth the golden thread of its song: the tender, ringing peal poured forth with enchanting, intoxicatingly sweet sounds. Wave after wave, the languid peals rang out under the low arches of the boughs. All the forest fell silent and listened, avidly and timidly. Only the young little leaves would quiver at times when the tremulous ring of the languid song would suddenly reach its resounding height, then suddenly grow still, like a musical string that has been forcibly stretched and suddenly bursts. With these songs, it seemed, an incomprehensible magic poured forth and was borne up and away into the unknown distance.

And there indeed was the familiar fence, there was the gate, and it was open: and in it something showed whitely in the flickering moonlight. Then suddenly everything foreign and extraneous faded away, and it grew quiet all about: the sounds and the light and the magic—everything came from the spot where Anna was standing by the gate. She had her shoulders wrapped in a white shawl, and she was smiling, and in her smile sounds and light and magic—all the external world—and the world of the soul—flowed together.

Perhaps the nightingale's song or the moist charm of spring had called her out into the garden—perhaps she had been unable to sleep and had tossed and turned restlessly in her virginal bed, had laughed and wept and thrown off the light but nevertheless stifling cover, had kept putting her shapely hands against her burning head and looking with blazing eyes into the nocturnal darkness—maybe she had been sitting by the window for a long time, fascinated by the silvery night, and was already preparing for sleep and had already thrown off all her clothes and walked quietly to her bed, and then, quite unexpectedly, seized by a sudden urge, had hastily thrown on some clothes and some shawl, then had walked out into the garden and up to this gate. In any case, here she stood now by the gate. Her thick braids were spread out in loose locks against her white clothing. Her feet appeared white on the dark sand of the path.

Login quickly walked up to the lattice-work. He said something.

Anna said something.

They stood and smiled and looked trustfully at each other. Moonbeams fell across her face, and under their light it seemed pale. Her eyes were trustful, but a troubled, timid expression flickered in them. Her fingers were trembling slightly. She pulled the lattice toward her. The gate creaked faintly, and then closed. Anna said:

"There's a nightingale singing."

Its quiet voice rang out softly.

"You must be cold," said Login.

He grasped her slender fingers. She smiled gently and tenderly, and did

231

not take them away. She whispered:

"I'm warm."

He pressed and squeezed her long fingers. He said something simple and joyful about the nightingale, about the moon, about the air, about something else just as close and innocent. She replied to him in the same manner. He felt that his voice was growing faint and trembling, that something new, uncontrollable seized hold of his breast. Their hands slipped apart, came together. Then a white shoulder flashed before his burning gaze and trembled under a cold hand resting on it. Then her face suddenly turned pale, then moved up so close—so close were her wide eyes. Now her eyes gazed with a troubled, frightened look and suddenly were lowered, then covered by her eyelashes. A kiss, quiet, tender, long...

Anna moved back. Login stood there awakened from sweet oblivion. Against his chest was the hard grill with the flat top, and behind it was Anna. Her eyes were lowered as though they were looking for something in the grass or as though she were listening keenly to something: so quietly did she stand there. Quietly he called her:

"Anna!"

She started, clung impulsively to the grill. He kissed her hands, kept repeating:

"Anna! My love!"

"My own! My darling!"

She grasped his bowed head in her hands and kissed his high forehead. Instantly there was a feeling of lovely intimacy. Suddenly, with a slight rustle, her body recoiled from his impatient arms. Login raised his head. Already Anna was running down the path toward the house, and her white clothing fluttered as she ran.

"I love you, Anna!" he said softly.

She halted at the terrace steps. She had heard him. Once more in the misty dimness of the garden—her dear face with its happy, tender smile... And then he saw only her feet on the gently sloping steps, and then she had disappeared—a nocturnal vision.

He did not notice and did not remember the journey homeward. Time stood still—all his soul dwelled on one instant.

"Was it not a dream," he thought, "the wondrous night, and she, incomparable? But if it is a dream, let me never awake. The visions of waking life are dull and insipid. And I would rather die in my enchanted dream, on the moon-charmed stones!"

The rickety steps of his porch roused him with their tiresome creak. In his room Login again found the dark and unavoidable. The cruel doubts stirred again; troubled, oppressive forebodings were as yet only dimly realized. A strange coldness enveloped his heart, but his head was burning. Suddenly, a bitterly ironical thought:

"Nothing threatens me now: I can retire—I'll have a rich wife."

He turned pale with anger and despair; for a long time he walked about the room; his face was gloomy. Anna's image turned pale, grew hazy.

But then, the sun through the clouds, Anna's radiant, trustful eyes again shone through the swarm of gloomy and resentful thoughts. Anna was gazing at him and saying:

"Love is stronger than anything that people have created to heap up barriers between themselves—we shall love each other, and, like gods, we shall create, and we shall build a new heaven and a new earth."

Thus Login wavered and shifted from anger and despair to bright, joyful hopes. All night he was unable to fall asleep. Torment both sweet and bitter drove away his nocturnal slumber. The solitude and darkness were alive and deceptive. The hours flew by.

The rays of the early sun fell through the window. Login walked up to the window and opened it. The sounds of the morning came up to him—voices, racket. Front doors banged,—then a resounding, slatternly voice,—then a barefoot, shaggy-headed girl ran along down the rickety wooden sidewalk with a loud patter under the windows. A chilliness pulled at Login's shoulders. Ordinary life was beginning, empty, tiresome, unnecessary.

CHAPTER THIRTY

Andozersky felt that he had to get even with Anna, to prove that her refusal had not distressed him in the least. The very next day Andozersky set out to win Claudia's hand.

Claudia was pale and ill at ease. The open summer-house in the garden, where she sat now with Andozersky, exuded torrid memories. The sun was hot, and the air was sultry, and the first peonies were too bright, and the late lilacs irritated one with their cloying smell. The sand of the paths sparkled annoyingly in the sunlight. The trees' foliage seemed unbecomingly glossy. The distant smell of the town's dust beat its way through the smells of greenery and flowers.

Claudia crossed her hands in her lap, looked out into the garden, listened absentmindedly to Andozersky's eloquent declarations: Finally he said:

"Now I await your decision."

Looking upset, Claudia turned toward him and said with a wan smile:

"You've been mistaken about me. What am I to you? I can't bring you any happiness."

"Your consent alone will be the greatest happiness for me."

"It certainly doesn't take much to please you. *I* have a different concept of happiness."

"What do you mean?" asked Andozersky.

"That life be complete, if only for an hour; thereafter, perhaps, there's no need for it."

"Believe me, Claudia Alexandrovna, I'll know how to make you happy!"

Claudia smiled.

"If that were so... I doubt it. And besides, you mustn't, believe me, you mustn't. I cannot give you happiness. It's the truth!"

Claudia stood up. Andozersky also stood up. His head began to whirl. He experienced such a sensation as if a gaping abyss had suddenly opened up before him. He exclaimed:

"Why think about my happiness! My only happiness is that you be happy, and for that I am ready to sacrifice anything. Without you I am only half a human being."

Claudia looked at him with a smile that he found inscrutable but intoxicating. At that moment he was convinced that he sincerely loved Claudia. The thirst to possess her was beginning to blaze within him.

"Indeed?" Claudia asked in a cold voice.

The coldness of her voice aroused his passion even more. In his dismay he repeated:

"To sacrifice anything, *anything.*"

And he found no other words. In the same cold tone Claudia said:

"If that is so, then, truly, I do not deserve such love. For my happiness you would have to make *only one sacrifice,* which I would accept with gratitude."

She said it quite sarcastically.

"Oh, you have only to say the word!" Andozersky exclaimed in joyful excitement.

Claudia turned away, fixed her wandering eyes on the garden, and said softly:

"Indeed, I'm very grateful. If you could, if only you *could* make this sacrifice!"

"Tell me, tell me! I'll do anything," said Andozersky.

He showered her hand with kisses, and her hand trembled in his hand and was as pale as the hand of a marble statue.

Claudia hesitated. A cruel smile played on her lips. Her eyes stared gloomily at something far away. She spoke up—and her voice rang with overtones that sounded sometimes cruel, sometimes timorous:

"Here—take me, but only to give me up to another. That's the sacrifice! After all, you were talking about sacrificing *anything.* That's a sacrifice indeed! So then, if you are able... or don't, as you wish. Well, why are you silent?"

"But that's so strange!" Andozersky said in confusion: "Truly, I don't understand."

"It's simple. We'll get married. Then I'll go away. That's what I really need: I'll be independent, and then I'll live with the one I... well, I can't marry him. In a word, I need that. And *that,* you say, will bring you the greatest happiness."

Claudia's face had turned quite pale. Her voice had grown mean and cold. She looked at Andozersky with cruel eyes, and she smiled a wicked smile, and Andozersky burned and shuddered at that smile.

"What the hell is this!" he wondered.

He passed a hand over his damp forehead. His pudgy fingers trembled.

"Do you agree, then? For such a favor on your part, I'll even share with you a small amount of happiness and a large amount of wealth."

Claudia's eyes opened wide and shone with a wild exultation. She broke out laughing, threw back her supple and shapely torso, and held her trembling hands back perpendicular to her wrists above her head. Her dress's wide sleeves slid down and bared her arms. Her pale, gloating face looked out from a living frame, from behind her slender arms that had suddenly grown rosy—two trembling, supple snakes intertwined and laughed tremulously over the green summer-lightning of her naughty eyes.

"Ah! What are you saying!" exclaimed Andozersky. "You're really a seducer! Give you up to someone else—what an absurdity! Why? Oh, how I love you! But I love you for myself, for myself."

Claudia turned toward the doorway of the summer-house. Andozersky rushed toward her and held out his hands in a beseeching gesture. Her face assumed an immovably cold expression. She said curtly:

"There was no point in even talking about sacrifices."

And she walked past Andozersky toward the exit. She stopped near the doorway, turned toward Andozersky, and said:

"You will excuse me, please, but you see for yourself, there can't be anything between us, and there never can be."

She walked out of the summer-house. Andozersky was left by himself.

Several steps away Claudia stopped, absentmindedly plucked the leaves from a lilac bush and crushed them in her pale fingers.

"Damned bitch!" thought Andozersky. "Enticing, wild—isn't it for the better? But, God damn it, what a situation! I'd better get out while the getting is good!"

He walked out of the summer-house, walked up to Claudia.

"What a disagreeable smell!" she said. "That smell when the lilacs fade seems stifling to me."

"There are a lot of lilacs in your garden," he said. "They have such a luxurious smell."

"I prefer lilies-of-the-valley."

"Lilies-of-the-valley smell too innocent. The lilac is fascinating, like you."

"With whom, then, would you compare the lily-of-the-valley?"

"I'd take Anna Alexeyevna Motovilov for an example."

"No, no, I disagree. What scent, then, would you ascribe to Anyuta Yermolin?"

"It's... it's... I find it extremely hard to say. But, of course! What's the matter with me! No doubt, it's the violet, Anna's little eyes!"

Claudia broke out laughing.

When Andozersky said goodbye, Claudia, smiling coldly, said quietly to him:

"Farewell."

"Oh, Claudia Alexandrovna!"

"The lilacs are fading, and let them; give it up. Go look for lilies-of-the-valley!"

Paltusov (he was right there at the time, in a nearby hallway) watched them in amazement.

Claudia returned to the garden, picked a sprig of lilac, brought her pallid face down to it. Quietly she strolled through the lanes. She was alone; there was no one else in the garden. Zinaida Romanovna, as usual, was lying undressed on the couch in her room, stretching lazily, lazily skimming the spicy, languid pages of a new book in a yellow jacket. And Paltusov—what was he doing?

Claudia walked past his study (the room on the first story at the corner facing the garden), glanced in the direction of the open windows, and, on a sudden impulse, threw the sprig of lilac through the window. Then she abruptly wheeled about and swiftly set off towards the summer-house in the middle of the garden, where she had been talking just now with Andozersky.

Paltusov was gloomily pacing about his study. He kept recalling the troubled face of Andozersky and the pallid face of Claudia and surmising that something had occurred between them, and he was tormented by jealousy. With a light rustle the sprig of lilac fell through the window onto the floor behind him. Paltusov turned, looked about him, caught sight of the lilac, and quickly went up to the window. Claudia was walking away from the house and did not turn around.

Paltusov quickly came out of the house and hurriedly overtook Claudia. She quickened her pace and finally ran into the summer-house. He entered behind her. She sank down onto a bench, raised her hands to her breast. Green-eyed, out of breath, she looked frightened. He rushed to her, got down at her feet, and exclaimed:

"Claudia, Claudia!"

And he embraced her knees and kissed her dress at her knees.

She put her hands down onto his shoulders and smiled both tenderly and bitterly. She said:

"Let us live for life, only for life!"

Paltusov's face was lighted by a triumphant smile. Claudia felt her virgin body held in strong and passionate embraces. The floor of the summer-house receded from under her feet, the ceiling rocked and disappeared. Paltusov's burning eyes blazed with a wonderful brightness. An eerie and sharp sensation swiftly passed through her, and she began writhing and trembling. Rosy circles swam in the darkness. In an abyss of selflessness she blazed with utter and complete happiness...

Claudia suddenly freed herself from Paltusov's embraces and cried out fearfully:

"She was here!"

Paltusov looked in bewilderment at her pallid face with its burning eyes. In a voice dry with excitement, he asked:

"Who?"

"Mother," Claudia whispered. "I saw her."

She sank down helplessly onto the bench. Paltusov said in annoyance:

"Nonsense! It's your imagination, just nerves! What would your mother be doing here! You just thought she was here."

Claudia listened carefully but did not hear anything. In a faint voice she said:

"No, she stood in the doorway, laughed, and then sneaked away."

"Nothing but nerves!' Paltusov said in annoyance.

"No," she laughed, and covered her mouth with a handkerchief.

"Let's go away from here, let's take a stroll. You have a headache."

They went out of the summer-house. Paltusov felt Claudia shudder. He peered at her: she was looking hard at something. In the direction of her gaze Paltusov caught sight of something white on the grass right by the path. A white handkerchief stood out like a glaring stain against the bright green.

"The handkerchief!" Claudia cried. "She's the one who dropped that handkerchief."

She let go of Paltusov's hand and rushed to the handkerchief. Paltusov heard her laughter and saw how her shoulders were quivering. He walked up and cautiously asked:

"Claudia, what's the matter?"

Claudia stood over her mother's handkerchief and laughed and wept uncontrollably.

Strange, somber days dragged by. Claudia and Paltusov would get together surreptitiously in the afternoon for brief moments, sometimes in his study, sometimes in her room, and they would give themselves over to the delights of love, with no word or thought about the future. When they met in the presence of outsiders, they looked at each other coldly; in fact they even seemed to show a marked hostility in their behavior towards each other.

Zinaida Romanovna spied on them. Occasionally she would smile at certain thoughts of her own. Her calmness surprised them but did not trouble them much, although they did at times wonder what was hidden beneath this veneer of imperturbability. Claudia was indifferent, Paltusov coldly polite to Zinaida Romanovna.

The nights—the nights were strange!

On the first night Claudia quietly left Paltusov's room after one o'clock. In her own bedroom she heard a rustling, caught sight of a white shade in the corner, but, being tired out, she hastened to lie down, and had hardly put her head down on the pillow before she fell asleep.

She had a bad dream. She dreamed that some dark and ugly thing landed on her chest and was crushing it. It turned into a vampire with luminous eyes and wide gray wings; its long, misty torso twisted and coiled endlessly; its tenacious hands held Claudia's body fast; its sticky red mouth bit into her throat and was sucking her blood. It was agonizingly frightful. She dreamed that her muscles were strained and trembling—if she could just turn away a little, just evade those horrible lips—but her body remained motionless.

Finally she awoke with a start and opened her eyes. Her mother's eyes were shining over her. Her mother's face, pale, contorted with hate, was looking with burning eyes straight into Claudia's eyes, and she was coming down hard with all her weight on her daughter's chest. Claudia sprang forward, but her mother threw her back down onto the pillows.

"Why?" Claudia asked in a broken voice.

Zinaida Romanovna was silent. She took a long look at Claudia, put her cold hand over Claudia's eyes, and got up from the bed. Claudia felt her chest free and at the same time felt weariness and dejection throughout her body.

Claudia got up from the bed with difficulty. The door was half open; there was no one else in the room. Claudia lay down again but could not go to sleep. For a long time she lay with her arms thrown up over her head. She stared into the gray half-light of the breaking day. Her thoughts were dim and muddled. Pale, evil faces, monstrous hands with flowing mane drifted before her eyes.

Upon meeting her mother in the afternoon Claudia looked carefully at her. Zinaida Romanovna's face was inscrutably calm.

On the next night Claudia retired to her room early and locked the door with the key. About midnight, Paltusov knocked at her door. She let him in reluctantly.

He left after about two hours. She locked the door after him.

When she had lain down again and was already beginning to fall asleep, she suddenly remembered that the door had remained unbolted all the while that Paltusov had been there. She felt annoyed for a minute, but somehow she did not dwell on this thought, and soon dozed off. Again her mother fleetingly appeared before her, like a pre-dawn shadow, and again clouds of pale, menacing faces swarmed in her wake.

The third night came. Claudia carefully inspected the corners of her room, bolted the windows, locked the door, and went off to Paltusov's room. She returned towards dawn, drew the curtains at her windows, walked up to the bed. When she threw back the cover to lie down, she suddenly felt that someone was looking at her from behind. She turned around—in the corner behind a cabinet something, resembling a dress that had been hung up, showed up a dim white in the semi-darkness. Claudia approached it and saw her mother. Zinaida Romanovna stood in the corner and looked at Claudia in silence. Her face was pale, tired, expressionless, like a beautiful mask. Claudia scrutinized her mother, and her mother's figure began to seem a transparent shade. It was becoming frightening. Claudia made an effort to suppress her terror and asked:

"What sort of comedy is this? Why are you here?"

Zinaida Romanovna was silent.

"Why do you come to my room?" Claudia continued asking in a failing and broken voice. "What do you want? Do you want to talk with me? You're silent? What on earth do you want from me?"

Her mother's silence and stillness in the gray semi-darkness made Claudia feel afraid in spite of herself. She took her mother's hand. Its cold touch made her shudder. Claudia stared into her mother's face: it was quivering all over with mute, exultant laughter—every tiny feature of that pallid face laughed gloatingly. It seemed to Claudia that her mother's green eyes shone with a phosphorescent gleam, and that her whole face had become blue. This cold laughter on the blue face with the shining eyes was so horrible, it effused such unnatural malice, such hopeless madness, that Claudia shuddered, covered her eyes with her hands, and backed away from her mother. Vaguely, from behind her trembling hands, she saw the white fabric flash by downstairs. She lowered her hands and saw that there was no one else in the room.

She walked up to the open door, stood for a long time by the door-jamp. She peered into the dark corners of the corridor, thought brief, troubled thoughts. Her bare shoulders felt cold, and her body shuddered from the morning chill.

CHAPTER THIRTY-ONE

Claudia did not tell Paltusov about her nocturnal terrors. When she recalled them in the daytime, it would all seem funny to her, a feeling of gloating would take possession of her, and she would grow annoyed at herself for her cowardice at night. But with the approach of night, she would again feel frightened.

She spent the fourth night in Paltusov's room. By the time that Claudia left Paltusov, the sun was high and people were waking up. Her eyes squinted, wearied by the sleepless night. She wanted to sleep, but her soul exulted in an intense feeling like that of children who have just escaped from some danger. By the door to her room Claudia encountered Zinaida Romanovna and glanced at her with mocking eyes. But her mother's face effused such vindictive exultation, that Claudia's heart sank. Full of terror and foreboding, she went into her room.

She slept for a long time. Her sleep again ended with a nightmare. Suddenly she felt strong fingers on her shoulder, and then she saw her mother on top of her. There were blue shadows on Zinaida Romanovna's face. Her eyes were half-closed. She was heavy, like a cold corpse.

"Ah, you've awakened," Zinaida Romanovna said calmly. "It's after one o'clock by now."

She got up and went out of the room.

Claudia sat up in bed.

"How stupid!" she thought. "What am I waiting for? I must get away—with him, without him, it doesn't matter—I must get away!"

This thought had occurred to her even before now, but it had not remained for long. In that state of sweet reveries and oppressive nightmares that she was living through, her head was not working very well. She had not yet managed to talk with Paltusov about getting away; their meetings were still spent in passionate ecstasy, and she could not leave the house without him—that she perceived. It seemed to her that her life was inseparably bound to Paltusov's, that a new future, an infinity of love and freedom somewhere far away in a new land under new skies, lay ahead for them both.

Finally she resolved to talk with Paltusov that very day as to how they should settle their fate. But not for one moment did they manage to meet alone that afternoon: sometimes outsiders, at other times their mother prevented it.

Night came, the fifth since the day that had determined their lot. Claudia was in Paltusov's room.

"Listen," she said, "we finally *have to have a talk.*"

"What's threre to say?" he answered lazily: "You're mine, and I'm yours, and that's decided once and for all."

"Yes, but... to live here, near to *her*... to keep hiding, to keep pretending..."

"Ah," he drawled, then yawned.

He was unusually sluggish today.

"Strange," he said, "my whole body feels heavy. Yes, so you're saying..."

Claudia passionately pressed herself against him and said ardently:

"We can't live like this any longer, we can't!"

"No, no, we can't," Paltusov agreed.

He livened up and spoke with enthusiasm:

"We'll go away, and the farther away, the better."

"Quite far away, so that everything will be novel and done in a fresh way," whispered Claudia.

"Yes, my dear, far, far away. To somewhere in America, to the far West, or to some unknown country, to Bolivia, where no one knows us, where we'll meet none of those from whom we're fleeing. There we shall begin a new life."

"Completely new!"

"The two of us, by ourselves. And if, when we're getting old, we want to have a look at our dear native land, then we'll come here as two Brazilian monkeys. Yes, yes, and tomorrow we'll consider how to arrange it. We'll take care of the details tomorrow."

Paltusov smiled lazily and sleepily. He repeated softly:

"Tomorrow the details, today let's be happy with the present, happy with the moment."

Their burning kisses and passionate embraces intoxicated Claudia and drove away her care. Suddenly Claudia felt Paltusov lying heavy and cold in her arms. She glanced at his face: he was asleep. She tried in vain to awaken him: he only mumbled semiconsciously, then dozed off again. She turned away with a scornful grimace, stood up, and walked up to the window. She was again filled with melancholy. Claudia pushed back the blinds with her hand and stared with wistful eyes into the nocturnal gloom. The branches of an old maple stuck out of the darkness and shook their sullen leaves with a mysterious murmur of reproach. Terror stole over Claudia— the sleeping man was absolutely immobile.

Claudia shuddered. A resounding laugh rang out behind her. The eerie anticipation of something horrible made her stiffen and feel cold. Overcoming her terror, she turned around—and let out a little scream.

Zinaida Romanovna's face, deathly pale, again quivered with exultant, vindictive laughter. Claudia scowled, bowed slightly, and leaned, with one arm bent, against the back of a chair. Her eyes blazed with daring determination.

Several long moments went by in eerie anticipation. The folds of the white dress on Zinaida Romanovna hung down straight and motionless. All white and pale, she seemed a menacing specter, and Claudia, in the depths of her troubled consciousness, harbored the felicitous hope that she only imagined seeing her mother there. Suddenly it seemed to Claudia that Zinaida Romanovna wanted to put her hand on Claudia's elbow. Claudia seized Paltusov's arm and shook it. Her mother's curt, cold laughter filled the air. Zinaida Romanovna said softly:

"Leave him alone! He won't soon awaken."

"What have you done?" Claudia exclaimed.

Menacing green lightning flashed in her eyes.

"Enough of that!" her mother answered in a harsh tone. "He's alive and well, only he's drunk some sleeping medicine. You made him too tired—that's what I think; let him have a good sleep. Let's go for a walk!"

Her voice was quiet but commanding. She took Claudia's hand. Claudia followed her half-consciously.

"Leave me alone," she said weakly when they had gone out into the corridor.

Her mother turned and stared coldly at her. A bluishly pale face suffused with terrible laughter again arose before Claudia's eyes. Claudia felt that that laughter was depriving her of her will, was clouding her reason. Without a thought in her head, with no ability to resist, she obediently followed her mother.

They went out onto the terrace, descended the steps, and wound up in the garden. The night's damp coolness enveloped Claudia from all sides; the damp sand of the paths was unbearably cold and harsh on her bare feet. She stopped and jerked her hand free from her mother's.

"Let me go—I'm cold!"

Again her mother gazed at her with a fixed, empty look, and again her mother's face was suffused with silent laughter and deprived Claudia of will, and again she followed her mother.

And when once again the cold, dampness, and the sand, brittle and hard under her bare feet revived her, then she would halt stubbornly. But the malignant face with the exultant laughter would turn toward her again at such times, and it would again deprive her of her will. Zinaida Romanovna was squeezing Claudia's fingers hard, but Claudia did not feel the pain.

Thus they reached the summer-house and ascended its steps. With a sharp movement of her arm Zinaida Romanovna flung Claudia onto a bench. Quietly, distinctly, she began speaking:

"You lay here in the embraces of another woman's husband, whom you took away from your own mother, and I stood here and watched you. And here I curse you, on this spot which you have defiled. Run where you will, take your lover with your, get yourself a dozen new lovers,—damned as you are, nowhere will you ever find happiness!"

Claudia reclined on the bench and laughed convulsively.

"Come along, come along with me!" said Zinaida Romanovna.

She raised Claudia up by the arm and led her out of the summer-house.

"Every lane of this garden has heard your profane discourses; your shameless kisses were heard on each of them."

She pulled her daughter after her—and Claudia followed her along the sandy paths, and was growing numb all over from the cold and damp-ness.

"I'm not afraid of your curses," she told her mother. "Utter them as much as you like and where you like, I am not afraid of them. And why have you been tormenting me at night?"

"At night? Because you tormented me both night and day."

They stopped by the pond. A thick, damp mist was rising from its smooth surface.

"Right here," said Zinaida Romanovna, "you caressed him again, and I stood behind the bushes and cursed you. When you had left and I remained, standing over this pond, I thought of death, of vengeance. Here I realized that there's no need of death, no need to worry about vengeance: you, damned as you are, will never see a single joyous day! You stole your mother's happiness, and for you there will not be a shadow of happiness nor a shadow of joy. Your lover will rend your heart, your husband will insult and betray you, your children will turn their backs on you—anguish will haunt you. You're familiar with it: already you drink in order to attain oblivion from it. And I pitied you—after all, I am your mother, you wretch! I thought it would be better for you to drown in this pond than to live with my curse."

"I'm not afraid of your curses," Claudia said sullenly, "and happiness—what do I want it for? Anyhow, I *am* happy!"

"No, you're shivering in terror, you damned wretch!"

"I'm cold."

Claudia tried to break out of her mother's grip. Zinaida Romanovna held on to her.

"Wait, listen to my final word. Look what a fine grave you have in this black water. Die while he has not abandoned you—*now* he would even weep over you. Would you like that? I'll help. Are you afraid? I'll give you a push!"

Zinaida Romanovna dragged her daughter toward the bank. Claudia fought back in horror. Finally Zinaida Romanovna gave up. She whispered malevolently:

"No, you want to live? Then live, live, you damned creature!"

Zinaida Romanovna's voice began to ring with fury.

"Live, suffer to the end of your strength, know despair, jealousy, horror, people's contempt, every woe, every sorrow, complete shame, shame as naked as you."

She seized Claudia's gown by the collar in both hands and yanked it apart; the thin fabric parted with a faint ripping sound. Furiously she tore it to pieces and threw the pieces far away. She shouted:

"You damned and shameless creature, now go to your lover!"

And she pushed Claudia away.

Claudia ran down the garden's dark paths. Behind her the quiet, malicious laughter rang without ceasing—the ecstasy of wild exultation.

It was quiet and empty in the garden and in the house. No one heard or saw Claudia carefully making her way through the dark rooms to her bedroom and freezing with shame when the floor boards creaked under her bare feet.

Cold all over, she flung herself into bed and wrapped herself up in the covers. She felt a thrill of joy: like a bird that had made its way through a storm to its nest, she warmed herself, luxuriated, and rejoiced.

"The comedy is over!" she would whisper, laugh softly, roll herself up into a ball, and stick her cold hands under the pillow. Soon she fell asleep.

In the morning she felt that she was having trouble breathing. She opened her eyes. The room glanced back dolefully. The sun's rays were mournfully bright. A sorrowful thought was slowly forming inside her head, but it was difficult to translate it into words. She shook her head, and this movement made her head throb with pain.

"Yes," she answered her thought aloud.

Her voice sounded weak and decrepit, and her throat was sore. Indifference and weariness held sway over her, and she felt sick at heart. Claudia recalled the night she had gone through, and smiled wanly and submissively. She thought:

"The curses won't come true,—my life will be cut short!"

She no longer thought about how she needed to get away, or of the fact that she was sick, or of how her sickness would end. Somehow she felt at once that she had no strength. She was beginning to die, it seemed. It was as though she had read her own death sentence and lost heart.

It seemed that someone was standing by her pillow. With difficulty she turned her head and beheld the transparent figure of her mother. She was not surprised that the window was clearly visible through her mother's chest. Then she saw that another, identical, transparent figure had come through the closed door. Both stood around her and demanded something. She listened keenly, but could not understand. It did not surprise her that her mother was standing before her in two forms. She only was afraid because the one that had come in later had a wicked face and wild eyes and rapid utterances on its desiccated lips. This image was drawing nearer and nearer, and growing every greater in size.

Her terror kept mounting. She wanted to scream but had no voice left. The image with the wild eyes bent down quite close, came down heavily on Claudia's chest, and split up into a whole crowd of ugly gnomes, black and hairy. They all kept making frightful grimaces, sticking out their long, thin, bright-red tongues, and savagely rolling their blood-shot eyes. They danced around and waved their hands, faster and faster; the walls, the ceiling, the bed were drawn into their wild dance. Their hordes kept growing denser and denser: new crowds of gnomes, ever more ugly, poured forth from all sides. Then they began growing smaller, moved away from her, and turned into a cloud of rapidly revolving black and red faces; then that cloud merged into one bright-crimson, fiery glow—the glow spread out widely, flared up in a brilliant flame, then suddenly died out. Claudia had lost consciousness.

CHAPTER THIRTY-TWO

When he awoke in the morning, Login felt that the day, so bright and permeated with sunbeams, was sad and unnecessary. His heart sank in melancholy, and his lungs could hardly breathe—all that light stifled him with its clear, hot weight. The flowers on the wallpaper gazed out brightly, tiresomely. He kept recalling how he had met with Anna at night; that encounter was like an impossible dream.

Login leaned his shoulder against the window frame and looked at the town streets, where the distinct shadows of houses and fences fell across the light-gray, dusty earth—and his dream of *her* was alien to all that appeared before him. She was as from another world, from a distant and impossible world. It was strange to think that she lived on the same earth and breathed the same air as *these* people in this nightmare of stagnation. Yes, impossible and incomparable as she was, perhaps she did not really exist? Perhaps he himself, the inveterate dreamer, had created her for his own enjoyment.

He passionately desired to see Anna—but nagging doubts distressed him on the way to the Yermolins' estate. His head ached dully. Through his blurred eyesight everything appeared dusty, dilapidated; the details of objects escaped his notice. The wind would spring up in gusts, the dust devils would whirl along the road, rise up, and fall down. It was hot and quiet. The people that Login now and then encountered seemed sleepy.

There was no one in the Yermolins' garden, and neither voices nor other noises were to be heard. Login quickly ascended the terrace steps. The doors into the house were open. He hurriedly went through all the rooms on the first story and did not meet anyone. He returned to the terrace. There was nobody for him to ask about Anna. How frightening the empty dwelling seemed!

"A dream, an insane dream!" he thought.

Suddenly the stillness was broken by the loud, sharp sound of—Anna's voice, coming in resounding howls, long and rhythmically... Then they stopped.

Login stood and listened. Had he heard real howls of pain somewhere nearby, behind the wall—or phantom howls?

Login hastily withdrew from that house, toward the hateful town.

Restless streets. A distant racket. A black wagon with white edges suddenly flew by at the crossroads. It was without its usual cargo. The driver, a tall, swarthy fellow with a black eye, was whipping the horses on furiously: evidently, some people would not give up a patient to him, and he was even afraid that they might beat him within an inch of his life.

At home Login called Lenya to him and asked him:

"Why, Lenka, do you like Tolya Yermolin?"

247

Lenya spoke up enthusiastically:

"He's so smart and entertaining—he knows anything you ask him."

And he went on talking about Tolya for a long time, with gusto. Actually, Login was waiting anxiously for what Lenya would say about Anna. But the boy shifted from Tolya to other subjects and did not mention the name that Login was expecting. Finally Login asked indecisively:

"And what would you say about Anna Maximovna?"

Lenka's eyes twinkled, he laughed joyfully—then was silent. Login asked with a scowl:

"Well, how do you feel?"

Lenya thought it over, twiddled his thumbs, then spoke up slowly:

"She's like this—you can talk with her right away—and it's always as though—as though she were one of the family. You could tell her anyting."

"You mean, she's nice?"

Lenya thought again, looked up at Login, and said:

"No. And not mean. She's just herself. Being with her is like being with someone just like yourself—only like the good part of yourself."

On the previous day Login had received an invitation to the town school, to the public speech-day, a celebration held annually, by custom, at the end of the school year.

By the time that Login entered the main hall of the school, the prayer service being held there was almost over. By a table that was covered by a red cloth with golden fringe, Motovilov swayed heavily, and made little signs of the cross at the proper times. Quite conspicuous behind him was Krikunov, in his new little uniform: its tight collar was choking him; his closely cropped little head, which protruded so roundly in back, was trembling from an ecstasy of religious feelings. A piteous expression was frozen on his wrinkled little face; that face, in its color, reminded one of a lacquered wooden doll; his low, brown forehead was creased by seven wrinkles. Still farther back, Shestov, in his teacher's uniform, huddled by the table, embarrased that he had to participate in the ceremony. He kept trying to hold himself erect and look independent. He hardly succeeded: he looked as though he were standing on a brazier. His face was flushed. He perceived this, blushed even more, pretended that it was hot and stifling, and kept wiping himself with a handkerchief.

And in fact, it *was* hot and stifling, even though the windows were open. Students were standing in files along one side of the hall. Their faces were anxious. The rest of the space was completely filled by the audience, which today was a large one, as it had not been in years past. There were ladies and young ladies here—Neta had managed to send a note to Pozharsky, and therefore she was cheerful and listened graciously to Gomzin's silly whispering. Nata was making eyes at Bienstock; everybody that one

248

might meet at Motovilov's home was here. Next were the parents from the merchant class. In the front of the audience it smelled of perfumes; farther back, the odor of sweat mingled with these fragrances; in the rear, it smelled of sweat and tar from greased boots. Close to the doors it was becoming quite crowded, while in the front there was open space, even rows of chairs for the "ladies and gentlemen."

The pupils went in line to kiss the cross. Father Andrey hastily and carelessly held out the cross and did the sprinkling. The little boys would quickly cross themselves and walk away with drops of holy water on their sweaty noses.

Login made his way forward. Baglayev poked him in the side with his pudgy white fist, giggled, and asked:

"Some crowd, eh?"

"Yes, a lot of people. And it's hot besides. Has it always been like this?"

"No, that's the point! They've assembled now because they smell a scandalous scene in the air; who'd be here otherwise! As it is, all sorts of characters have showed up."

"All of a sudden, a scandalous scene inside a school! What nonsense!"

"A scandalous scene can occur anywhere. Any little boy can tell you that. Was Molin released?"

"All right, he was released—so, what of it?"

"Well, that's just it, silly! Everyone's dying to see whether he'll come here."

"Why, has he come here?"

Baglayev whistled.

"He can't come, my good friend,—he's in retirement, and it's awkward enough for him as it is. But the audience hasn't considered that—it's still dying to get to see some scandalous little scene."

"But *what* scene? Speak plainly!"

"Motovilov's going to deliver a speech on the topic of the day."

"And where do you know that from?"

"I don't *know*, I *foresee* it, brother. That's why I'm the mayor: I know my own flock down to the last detail. Brother, I know all there is to know. Yes, brother, you ask me who's having what for dinner today, and I'll tell you just that!"

They had finished kissing the cross; Father Andrey removed his cassock. The audience were taking their seats. Motovilov took the central place at the table; Krikunov sat down at one side of him, Father Andrey at the other.

"Take your seat, please," Motovilov said pompously and condescendingly to Shestov.

Shestov blushed in annoyance and seated himself in the chair next to

Krikunov.

"The insolent creature! He's running things just as he would in his own home," Shestov thought of Motovilov.

The audience was nervous, was obviously expecting something—Login clearly saw this now from their uneasiness and the gleeful excitement of their faces. The somewhat older prominent people assumed expressions of indifference; occasionally they grinned and exchanged significant glances. Those who were a bit younger and a bit more innocent kept their eyes wide open and avidly looked toward the table covered with the red cloth, looked toward the place where Motovilov towered heavily and majestically with an expression of wisdom and virtue on his face, Krikunov wrinkled and contorted his face, Father Andrey sat respectably and looked about, and Shestov, being watched by everyone, was burning up with embarrassment. The dull part came first. The pupils sang the hymn to Saints Cyril and Methodius loudly and out of tune, Krikunov read a review of school activities, then the pupils bawled out two extremely merry folk songs, then Father Andrey read the list of pupils who had passed, or not passed, their examinations. The pupils who were awarded books and certificates of merit came up to the table and received theirs from Motovilov's hands, and he pronounced words of favor over them. Then the pupils broke into song once more. It was tiresome—the audience languished in impatience and suffered from the heat and humidity.

At last Motovilov stood up. Currents of excitement ran through the hall—then, suddenly, silence descended, and such an avid, anxious silence, that it startled people who were high-strung. Motovilov spoke:

"I congratulate you, children, upon the conclusion of your annual labor. Hereupon I cannot help but express to you my observation: I note a trace of sadness on your faces. I shall not ask you the reasons for this sadness, since it partly concerns us ourselves as well. We do not see in our midst your teacher, our colleague, Alexey Ivanych Molin. I do not have the right to go into a discussion of the reasons why we do not see him here. But public opinion speaks loudly of his innocence—and we are convinced that the law and the social conscience will remove from him the stigma laid upon him by the accusation. And we can hope that we shall again see Alexey Ivanych in our midst as the same useful figure as he indeed was formerly. Goodbye, children! Go home!"

Everyone began moving about. Chairs began sliding back. Pupils left with their parents. The guests began talking noisily. Some young lady kept asking:

"Was that all?"

Many were disappointed—they had been expecting something big. The treasurer was saying:

"That wasn't the thing—wasn't strong enough. He should have taken that Shestov to task but good."

250

The police chief stuck up for Motovilov:

"No, buddies, he's a fine fellow, all the same, yenonder-shish! He's never at a loss for the right word."

"He strikes deep and cuts clean," said Dubitsky.

Krikunov was utterly content: his little eyes shone gleefully and he looked gloatingly at Shestov. Motovilov was surrounded: people kept congratulating him and warmly praising his speech. He beamed and said in a self-satisfied way:

"Ladies and gentlemen, I am a fiend for the truth. I speak like a Russian, without constraint; I speak the whole truth."

He invited them to stay and have lunch. A place was being cleared for a luncheon in the same hall: several pupils were moving the chairs aside, the watchmen were dragging in tables, setting them together, and covering them with tablecloths. Once the extra people had left, it became fresher and cooler inside. From the street came the merry shouts of children, the chirping of birds, and streams of warm air.

"Are you going to stay?" Shestov asked Login.

"I've no desire to—I'll slip away inconspicuously."

"Well, then, I'll leave with you."

However, they did not manage to leave unnoticed: Krikunov was running about the school, all huffing and puffing, and he ran into them as they were looking for their coats.

"Vasily Markovich! Yegor Platonych! My dear fellows, where are you off to?"

"Excuse me, Galaktion Vasilievich, I can't stay," Login said firmly.

"Good heavens, how *can* you do this! You must want to hurt our feelings. Do stay, if just for a little while."

"I would gladly do so, only I can't, I haven't got time! Do excuse me."

"No indeed, I shan't let you go. And you, Yegor Platonych, why, you just absolutely can't: after all, you belong here—so how *can* you do this!"

Shestov grew embarrassed and blushed.

"No, really, I just can't stay, pardon me," he blurted out, and pulled at his overcoat.

"Why, enough, enough of that, take off your overcoat!" Krikunov said, speaking more and more firmly.

Shestov now was on the verge of turning back to the coat rack. He cast pleading glances at Login.

"My regards, Galaktion Vasilievich," Login said firmly and shook Krikunov's hand. "Let's go, Yegor Platonych," he said in just as firm a voice, took him by the arm, and swiftly set off toward the exit.

Shestov sighed in relief. But Krikunov grumbled after them:

"Why, how on earth can you do this! Ah, gentlemen, what in the world are you doing!"

Shestov laughed merrily: he felt that he had reached safety.

251

When they had come out onto the street, Login said:

"But for me, you would have had to spend several hours in that hornets' nest!"

"Yes, what can I do? My character is such that I cannot refuse anyone."

"And indeed don't refuse if you can help it: just go about your own business."

"Only," Shestov drawled plaintively, "it's not all that simple."

"How do you mean it's not! You just think less about what they think of you and how they regard you, and you keep watching carefully and listening. Here, would you like me to repeat Motovilov's speech to you from memory?"

Login repeated the speech word for word. Shestov said:

"You have a splended memory!"

"I've simply developed the habit of resting my attention on given objects and putting everything else out of my mind during that time in order not to be distracted. But, it seems, you're beginning to lose your nerve?"

"Why, no, I'm all right."

"Ah, youth, it's high time to decide: either complete submissiveness or complete independence—of course, within the limits of what's possible: you have to be either a man or a mouse. There's just such *scum,* you know, everywhere around us!"

Wines and vodka graced the table in the hall of the school. A chicken pie was brought in. The guests took their seats at the table. The glasses rapidly tossed their contents into dry gullets. The choir of pupils in the adjacent room kept up a lively performance of folk songs.

Motovilov slowly took a look around the table, then asked:

"And just where is the young teacher, Mr. Shestov?"

"He left; he didn't care to share our meal," Krikunov replied meekly.

"You don't mean it!"

"Yessir, and Mr. Login also did not care to stay," Krikunov reported, "he literally even saw fit to lure away our colleague."

"Now then, ladies and gentlemen," said Father Andrey, "just now Alexey Stepanych graciously expressed the hope that we would again see Alexey Ivanych in our midst. Some time from now he will be formally acquitted, but I think it must be painful for him to sit at home now, while his friends have assembled within these walls, where he was, so to speak, a disseminator of goodness. So, shouldn't we console him, eh?"

"Yes, indeed, we should invite him here," Motovilov seconded. "I think that that would be just: if he could not participate in the official part, then, nevertheless, we can show him once more how we love and appreciate him. How about it, ladies and gentlemen?"

252

"Yes, yes, splendid!" was heard from all sides.

"It will be the nice thing to do," said Motovilov. "Our innermost heart will say so to each of us."

"You see to it, then, Galaktion Vasilievich," Motovilov said, turning to Krikunov: "After all, he really doesn't live far away, and we'll wait with the following courses."

Running busily, Krikunov headed for the watchmen to send them for Molin. The company again became gleefully excited: they waited for Molin like children waiting for a present. He showed up as quickly as if he had been expecting the invitation—Krikunov had sent Motovilov's carriage for him. Molin was dressed as though he were trying to appear foppish. On his thick neck he wore an embroidered white tie with ruffled edges; he had on a new jacket that looked like a horse-collar on him; besides vodka, Molin reeked of pomade.

There was an uproar of salutations. Molin made his way around the table, bowing clumsily, shaking hands, and making his pock-marked face grin, not unpleasantly. He kept mumbling:

"How you've consoled me! I was sitting at home and was so bored. To confess frankly—though with some embarrassment—I even cried a little."

"Ah, you poor soul!" the ladies exclaimed.

"I'm ashamed of myself; I know I went limp, but what was I to do with my nerves? I broke down completely—sitting and crying. All of a sudden, I'm invited. I arose, and off I fly. And here I am with my friends again!"

"With your friends, Lyoshka, you rascal, with your friends!" Svezhunov cried out and embraced Molin. "It's all right, don't be sad, just be one of us."

"Congratulations, yenonder-shish," said the police chief: "It's downright touching how you're loved in society!"

Everyone tried to say something comforting and pleasant to Molin. They gave him a seat facing the ladies, fed him pie, poured him more vodka one minute, more wine the next. And the little boys kept up their lively performance of merry songs. In the intervals between songs they would drink tea and eat sweet rolls—all provided through the munificence of Motovilov.

The ring of a knife tapping on a glass was heard. Someone shouted:

"Sh! Alexey Ivanych wishes to speak!"

All fell silent. Molin rose and began rocking toward the place where Motovilov was. He spoke up:

"Alexey Stepanych! I shall say frankly, for me you have wrought a blessing. Well, I'm a person of no great guile, I don't know how to speak eloquently—what I feel, I say straight out, like a muzhik, like a simple soul... But what can I say here! Ah, to put it frankly: you have saved me! God bless you! For many a year! A toast to Alexey Stepanych—hurrah!"

All joined in the shout, jumped up from their seats, clinked their glasses

253

together. Motovilov and Molin embraced and kissed each other.

After the luncheon a harmonium was hauled out; the pupils sang to its accompaniment and started dancing—noisily, with much laughter, mischief, and silly pranks: the boys put on airs and led their partners around roughly; the girls kept squealing. Two lively little ladies overwhelmed a bashful youth, a village schoolteacher. He did not know how to dance; they had given him a partner, told him that they were dancing a quadrille, then began pushing him back and forth from one partner's arms to the other's. The youth was burning up with embarrassment and kept stamping around clumsily. It was a gay time for drunk and sober alike.

In the intervals between dances, the little boys would continue their boisterous concert. They enjoyed watching the merry dances: they were not bored, and gladly swallowed the dust that drifted into their innocently open little mouths. Their faces shone, their eyes laughed. Then too, their precentor, the deacon, had gotten tipsy. He had gotten into a good humor and was not harassing the choristers. During the singing and during the dances alike, he would wave his arms just as senselessly and shout good-naturedly:

"Alas, your mother spoiled you rotten! Go ahead, go ahead my dears, act up all you want to! Why *won't* your mother take a switch to you!"

Pozharsky and Gutorovich walked about with their arms around each other and sang silly songs.

Even Krikunov had softened up. In his weak, thin, disgusting little voice he was telling no end of smutty stories, slurring them over with his frail little laugh. It turned out, he had a vast store of such rubbish. He did have a good memory, especially for trivia and nonsense.

Molin, drunk from the vodka and an excess of feeling, went up to the choristers, exchanged kisses with them, mumbled touching words. At this, the children's faces would grow scared, stony. As he approached to kiss them, one by one they would open their eyes, purse their lips, assume a stupid, dumbfounded look; afterward, they would straighten their smocks, look around guiltily, twiddle their thumbs in embarrassment, and involuntarily wrinkle their noses at the revolting, burnt-out smell of vodka and at that peculiar, rather warm, chemical odor with which Molin was saturated, as are all men who, like him, perpetually fool around with medicines for their secret diseases.

From the boys Molin went over to the girls and uttered awkward compliments to them with a tongue that he could hardly control. Valya got the idea of flirting with him. *That* struck a responsive chord in Molin and whetted his appetite for more. He put his sweaty arm around her waist. She drew away with a loud laugh. Molin suddenly stuck his wide paw inside Valya's bodice. Her bodice began to split. Valya let out an unnaturally loud scream. Her voice drowned all the sounds of boisterous merriment. She ran

254

off into the other rooms to straighten herself up. Molin would have pursued her, but others restrained him.

Molin did wander from room to room for a long time yet. Finally he weakened, crashed to the floor in the main hall, and fell asleep instantly. Gomzin spoke to the watchman, who was also extremely drunk:

"Listen, Mikhey, you get him a pillow."

"I don't have any pillow right now," Mikhey replied.

"Well, look! You go to Galaktion Vasilievich and ask him for one," Gomzin said, trying to persuade him.

"What good's a pillow going to do him now?" Mikhey said sensibly. "Really, should I go sticking a pillow under his head at such a time? He's out cold as it is! I can't go bothering him at this point, can I? God help him, let him sleep it off."

"We shouldn't do it, you say?" Gomzin asked.

"Of course, you shouldn't. You yourself happen to know—when a man's sozzled, what does he need a pillow for? Why, mercy, he's a lot better off as he is 'cause he can get the coolness, being next to the floor."

The little boys struck up the song, "Oh, Awaken Her Not at the Dawn." Someone finally had the sense to send them home.

CHAPTER THIRTY-THREE

In the afternoon, when Shestov was not at home, Molin came. Mitya answered the doorbell. Molin inquired:

"Is Shestov at home?"

The boy looked warily at him and replied:

"No, he isn't. Mama's at home."

Molin entered the living room, sat down in an armchair. Mitya went to the kitchen to get his mother. Molin stamped his feet in impatience. Alexandra Gavrilovna came at last; her face was red from the kitchen heat. Molin did not rise, and he did not greet her with any amenity. He said hoarsely:

"I brought you the money for the room."

"You needn't have worried; we certainly could have waited: you might need that money nowadays."

Mitya stood in the next room. He looked through the doorway. He was wearing an old smock and was barefoot.

"Well, that's just none of your business," said Molin. "I brought it, so take it."

"As you wish."

"And you give me a receipt."

"Mitya," Alexandra Gavrilovan called, "bring me the ink-pot and paper."

"Right away," Mitya responded, and disappeared.

"Otherwise," said Molin, "you'll say you didn't get it."

"You're quite mistaken there."

"No, I'm not mistaken; I know what you're like, damn you!" Molin shouted irascibly.

Mitya brought a sheet of stationery and a glass ink-pot like a turnip on a wooden saucer. The ink-pot had a cork with a tin top. He did not leave, but stayed by the table. In order that the tiny spaces in the knitted tablecloth would not hinder her writing, he pulled it back from that half of the table where his mother was sitting. Molin stretched his legs and came down hard with his heavy heel on Mitya's foot. Mitya turned red and stepped away quietly, trying to keep his mother from noticing. Alexandra Gavrilovna inquired:

"Kindly tell me what I ought to write."

Grinning spitefully, Molin dictated:

"Write: 'I have received for the room ten rubles from the convict Alexey Molin.'"

Alexandra Gavrilovna wrote down the first words, but then she looked in amazement at Molin.

"Well, now, you did want to have me sent into penal servitude, so write it."

"Why, think what you will, I certainly won't write that: you tell me seriously what to write next."

Molin was adamant and raised his voice:

"No, you write 'from the convict.' "

Mitya intervened:

"Mama, write: 'From Alexey Ivanych Molin,' then the date of today, then your signature. And that's all."

Alexandra Gavrilovna handed Molin the receipt. He read it, grinned hastily, put the receipt in the side pocket of his wrinkled, dusty coat, then stretched himself in the armchair.

"You really did me a fine turn, Alexandra Gavrilovna!"

Alexandra Gavrilovna sighed and said:

"Well, it isn't determined yet who did the fine turn to whom."

"You haven't given me back all my things."

"I certainly have as far as I know: you asked that your things be sent to Father Andrey, and you didn't come for them yourself. Well, Yegorushka did send all your things to him."

"One deck of cards is missing," Molin insisted sullenly.

"Then, you ask Yegor about that—*I* don't know."

"You pocketed them. And maybe you swiped something else of mine from my carrying case for your little ragamuffin son."

"You're forgetting yourself, Alexey Ivanych. You came here when I'm alone..."

"You're not alone, Mama," said Mitya.

There was a grimace of revulsion and annoyance on his face as he looked at Molin. His mother put her hand on his shoulder. She said:

"Oh, come now!"

Molin broke out in a nasty laugh.

"And besides, I've handed over quite a lot of money. I doubt,—There's just something unfair about it. You swindled me."

Molin sprawled out still more in the armchair and put his feet up on the sofa.

"Sir, what is the matter with you!" Alexandra Gavrilovna said reproachfully: "Have you gone crazy? Come to your senses; you ought to be ashamed of yourself!"

"Robbers! Damned fiends!" Molin grumbled.

Mitya began shaking with rage in his mother's hands. He rushed forward. He shouted clearly:

"How dare you behave like that! Take your feet off of the sofa! Take them off right now and get out. You deliberately came here when Yegor wasn't at home, just so you could act like a bully. Get out, or I'll throw you out the window."

257

Molin stood up and glared spitefully and cravenly at the boy. Alexandra Gavrilovna pulled Mitya back by the shoulders and tried to calm him with a whisper. Mitya broke away.

"Leave me alone, Mama. He's a coward, he's just acting like a bully. He wouldn't dare fight."

Molin made a pathetic grimace, brought his face down to Mitya's, and said plaintively:

"Why, go ahead, swear at me, beat me, spit in my face; after all, you can do that to me—I'm a *convict.*"

"If you don't want to leave," Mitya said, "I'll send for Yegor; you can have it out with him, but don't you dare be rude to Mama. Wait if you like, and sit up properly."

"Why, of course, I'll wait for Yegor Platonych, and you'll abuse me to him until I'll really be in a fix! No, to hell with you. I'd just better leave. Farewell; I thank you for your *great kindness.*"

Molin turned around abruptly and headed for the door. Walking with his arms bent far out to the sides (a gesture expressing his sense of personal dignity), he accidentally banged one elbow against the doorjamb. With a crash he tumbled out of the room; he fooled around for a while in the entrance hall, fumbled with the outside door, slammed it loudly behind him, and made a heavy rumbling down the steps with his boots. His loud cursing and swearing came up from the yard through the open windows.

"Ah, you Anika the Warrior!"[1] Mitya's mother said to him. "Now, wait and see, he'll complain his heart out to Motovilov, and you'll really catch it."

"How do you mean?"

"Like so: they'll call you into the school and whip you so that you won't forget it before a new crop of switches has grown, and what's more, they'll expel you."

"Why, they can't do that."

"They can't? Who can forbid them? It's very simple; they'll just up and give you a tanning with a dry besom."

"Ah, Mama, the things you say... There's none of that in the rules."

"They won't look in the rules, but they will look up under your shirt-tail and then start beating the daylights out of you. Then you won't forget that Kuzka's mother's the strictest yet.[2] You know: 'Quarrels with the strong you don't begin, nor sue the rich and hope to win.' "[3]

The next morning Gomzin and Ogloblin showed up at Shestov's. Their solemn looks and lined faces showed that they had been drinking heavily all night. In voices hoarse from their excessive drinking, they inquired as to whether Shestov was at home. Shestov heard them and came out into the entrance hall. They exchanged hasty, perfunctory handshakes. Gomzin, angrily flashing his teeth, declared:

258

"We've come to you on business."

Ogloblin silently rocked his fat body back and forth on his short legs. Shestov invited them into his study. Gomzin and Ogloblin took their seats, remained silent for a moment, then each glanced at the other, and both said at once:

"We..."

And they stopped and again exchanged glances. With downcast eyes Shestov sat opposite them, alternately opening and closing a pen-knife with four blades in its ivory case.

Finally Gomzin said:

"We've come from Alexey Ivanych."

"Listen," Ogloblin spoke up suddenly, "please give us each a glass of vodka so that we can 'take a hair of the dog that bit us.' "

Gomzin glared sternly at Ogloblin. Shestov stood up.

"And if you would," Ogloblin continued in an ingratiating tone, "something tart: a salted cucumber or some red whortleberries."

"Yes, precisely, some red whortleberries," Gomzin said, livening up suddenly, and his white teeth smiled cheerfully: "My head's been aching off and on for some reason."

"We've been drinking a few toasts, you know," Ogloblin explained.

Shestov tried to make his face look amiable and went off for the vodka. When he had gone out, Gomzin said in an undertone:

"We ought not to drink at his place: any way you look at it, he's a scoundrel."

Ogloblin grinned slyly and said:

"Well, all right, my dear fellow, as far as I'm concerned, if that's how you feel, then we shouldn't drink. To hell with him, really and truly!"

"But *now,* by this time, once we've asked for it, we *have* to drink *one* glass each..."

Shestov returned and sat down at his place. He said:

"It'll be here in a minute."

"Alexey Ivanych sent us," Gomzin declared. "You wrote him a letter yesterday."

Shestov blushed suddenly and became agitated. He said:

"Yes, I wrote him, and I almost regret it."

"Do you wish us to tell him so?" Ogloblin asked mockingly.

"No, I said that strictly for you, but as regards the letter..."

The outside door banged in the entrance hall, the slapping of bare feet was heard, the door to the room was opened by a strong blow from an elbow—and in came Dasha, the ragged, stupid-faced maid in a dirty calico dress. In one hand she had a bottle of vodka; in the other she was holding a warped tin tray with a picture etched on it. On the tray were a plate of herring and one of pickled red whortleberries and apples. She set all this on the green felt of the desk, flew out of the room, came back half a minute later with three vodka glasses, two spoons and forks, set all this down on the table with a clatter, then disappeared. During this time Shestov and his guests were silent.

"It seems to me," Shestov spoke up, "I wrote to Alexey Ivanych yesterday in no uncertain terms. Just what does he intend to tell me now?"

"He's very angry," answered Ogloblin, "fit to be tied."

"Yes, he's highly irritated," Gomzin confirmed.

"Well, it seems to me," said Shestov, "*I* rather have the right to be angry and irritated."

Gomzin began to explain didactically:

"You ought to bear in mind how aggrieved and upset he is at present. It's perfectly natural that he said something blunt. But he told us positively that he said nothing insulting."

"Definitely nothing insulting," Ogloblin joined in. "However, shouldn't we drink the tear of the grain?"

"Pour it," Gomzin said curtly; then he asked Shestov: "We don't understand—why exactly are you disgruntled?"

Ogloblin filled all three glasses, took one, clinked it against the edges of the other two, then cried:

"Look out, soul, here it comes!"

And he drank it up. He wiped his lips with his wide palm, took a spoonful of whortleberries, and said:

"Why, gentlemen, what's the matter? Don't lag behind."

Gomzin drank up, made a face as though he had swallowed carrion, and muttered:

"What rot-gut!"

He reached for the whortleberries.

"You don't understand?" said Shestov. "He behaved disgracefully in my home. I wrote him that in fact."

"No, excuse me," Gomzin objected angrily, "you ought to say what you took offense at. Otherwise, for heaven's sake, what'll be the point of it?"

"Yes, of course," said Ogloblin, "we need to know, anyhow, as he intructed us, we must... well, and all that. Otherwise, why make such a mountain out of a molehill?"

"And precisely *what* message do you bring?" Shestov asked in vexation.

"Just this," Gomzin explained: "Alexey Ivanych is very irritated and desires some explanation from you for your letter."

"What do you mean *he* wants an explanation? After all, *he* was insulting, not I."

"Then what reason is there to dawdle!" Ogloblin said resolutely. "Do you challenge him to a duel?"

"What, then," Shestov thought to himself: "do I want to fight with him, with *that* fellow? Fie, what a vile thing!"

He wrinkled his face in disgust, and then answered:

"That's clear, apparently. Now it's up to him to accept the challenge or apologize or choose some other course of action."

"In that case," said Gomzin, "we have to know what it is exactly that you have considered offensive."

Shestov lowered his eyes. He felt ashamed to talk about yesterday's rude scene. He said:

"I have asked Vasily Markovich Login to handle the negotiations on this matter. I ask you to consult him."

Gomzin and Ogloblin exchanged glances.

"Why, we can't do that," said Gomzin. "We haven't yet been authorized by Alexey Ivanych."

"Then why have you come?" Shestov asked.

He began pacing nervously around the room.

"We, er, strictly *had* to know in what namely..."

Shestov spoke in a furiously calm voice:

"Namely in that he came yesterday when I wasn't here, sat in our armchair, put his feet on the sofa, and uttered insulting words to my aunt. Is that clear?"

"Excuse me," said Ogloblin, "why do you feel that way about it? Why, he just had too much to drink yesterday,—well, what of it?"

"I hope, however, that you now have what you need to tell Alexey Ivanych; do consult Vasily Markovich about the rest."

"All right, we'll tell him that," said Gomzin, "But once more I say, Alexey Ivanych is irritated. Moreover, I'm convinced that now he will endow us with the sufficient authority. I would therefore advise you to make haste to end this matter. Alexey Ivanych is not fond of joking. So, then, we suggest that you take back your letter."

"Gentlemen, I would ask you to stop this: everything has already been said, you know."

"In that case, I have the honor..."[4]

Gomzin bowed ceremoniously.

"I have the honor," Ogloblin chorused, just as ceremoniously; then, suddenly, he added, "but you haven't taken your drink, have you? Is it too much for you? Perhaps you don't use this hooch in the mornings? I'm the same way, you know, but..."

"Constantine Stepanych!" Gomzin called sternly.

He was already at the door.

"In a minute, in a minute. But, you see, I have to treat this hangover with a drink. So I'll just gulp yours."

"Why, what the hell is this, anyway?" muttered Gomzin. "Listen, Constantine Stepanych!"

Ogloblin held the glass fast to his lips.

"Eh?" he replied.

"What the hell do you mean, lapping it up by yourself, pig!" Gomzin swore vehemently. "Pour me one too, for company."

"Now you're talking," Ogloblin said approvingly.

He poured Gomzin a drink and said instructively:

"There's no better drink than water—once you distil grain alcohol in it."

The two friends drank and partook of the snacks. Shestov watched them morosely.

"What good whortleberries!" Ogloblin said approvingly.

"Eh-hey!" Gomzin responded.

Ogloblin again addressed Shestov:

"Really, my dear fellow, you should let the matter drop. Ah, why be insulted! Take back your little letter—look, we brought it along with us. Won't you take it back, eh?"

Ogloblin gently pushed the letter, which he had pulled out of his pocket, into Shestov's hands. Shestov silently moved away from it.

"Well, do as you please. Only, he is very angry."

They said goodbye and left.

Near evening on that same day, Vkusov called on Login and declared that he would not tolerate a duel.

CHAPTER THIRTY-FOUR

Neta was standing on one end of the swing-board, Andozersky on the other. They were swinging back and forth. In that awkward situation Andozersky had managed to make a declaration of love—and had received a negative answer.

"Stop the swing," said Neta.

"I love you," Andozersky repeated.

He began letting the swing go more slowly, but he did not stop.

"I feel sorry for you," Neta said derisively.

Holding on to the ropes and swinging back and forth, they kept exchanging fragmentary remarks.

"I would give you everything!" he exclaimed passionately.

"Let me go!" Neta cried angrily.

"I'll win your love."

"Enough of that!"

"Love is a great force."

"Let me go!"

"You'll be mine."

Neta suddenly shook the swing violently. She and Andozersky stood with flushed cheeks and burning eyes and sent the board rocking ever more violently, as though they were competing with each other in daring.

"You will be mine."[1]

"Never!"

They fell silent. The swing flew up as high as its suspending ropes would allow. The huge points of Neta's lace collar flew back and beat against her face. Suddenly Andozersky noticed that Neta had turned extremely pale; her eyes blazed; she had moved all the way to one edge of the board and was moving her arms in a rather strange way.

"She's going to jump!" Andozersky guessed.

With a mighty effort he stopped the swing from swaying. Neta made a move, but before she could get ready to jump, Andozersky was already standing on the ground and holding the board. Neta took a step toward the middle of the board. Andozersky took hold of her by the waist, took her off of the board, and stood her on the ground. Neta was breathing heavily. She repeated:

"Never!"

"You'll see!" he replied.

She turned away, she wanted to get away. He again took hold of her. His lips almost touched her cheek. But she whirled out of his hands and ran away.

"Ah, this one's not going to get away!" thought Andozersky.

He headed for the house and sought out the head of the household. Their conversation in Motovilov's study was brief. After about two minutes Motovilov went out and Andozersky remained. Then Motovilov came with Marya Antonovna.

As Andozersky left, he had the look of a conqueror.

"Sit down and listen," Motovilov said to Neta when she had come into his study.

"And be grateful to your father," added Marya Antonovna.

Neta sat down in a chair made of animal horns, got the splendid bow of her sash caught, and set about disengaging it. She disliked this room with its uncomfortable furniture.

"He should be sitting here himself!" she thought concerning her father.

But Motovilov lounged quite comfortably on a low sofa. His short little wife pompously hung around next to him.

"Look here, mother o' mine," Motovilov said to his daughter:[2] "There's good fortune for you—you're going to be a general's wife."

"I haven't the least desire to," Neta answered willfully.

"I have news to tell you, pleasant news to us, your parents: Andozersky has asked us for your hand."

"He's pleading absolutely in vain!" Neta said resolutely.

Motovilov looked at her sternly, and Marya Antonovna said didactically:

"Don't be wilful, Neta—he's an excellent young man."

"And on such a fine path upward in the world," Motovilov added.

"But I love someone else," said Neta.

"Nonsense, my dear! Get that foolishness out of your head: you can't marry Pozharsky!"

"And I *won't* marry Andozersky!"

"Listen, Neta," Motovilov said imposingly, "I seriously advise you: think it over."

"Think it over, Neta," said Marya Antonovna.

"Otherwise, it will go badly for you. I'll knock the foolishness out of you, don't worry. And the actor won't come off well either."

Neta was subjected to incessant nagging at home. Her father would call her to his study, usually twice a day, and would lecture her at length—she had to stand and listen.

"I'm tired," she said angrily during one such dressing-down.

"Well, *kneel,* then!" her father shouted.

Then she had to listen to him for a long time after that, on her knees.

Her mother nagged her in small but more frequent doses. Julia Stepanovna badgered Neta constantly. Neta did not get to see Pozharsky—but she did manage to send him a note.

In the morning some two days later, Pozharsky appeared and asked to be announced to Alexey Stepanovich. The maid, a rather young, pretty girl, all red and stocky, red-haired, red-faced, red-bloused and white-aproned, with large red hands and red feet, brought the answer: He could not be received. Pozharsky said:

"Tell Alexey Stepanovich that it's on business of some importance to him."

The maid went off reluctantly. Pozharsky pulled a visiting card out of his pocket and wrote with a pencil:

"My business is not complicated; should you not wish to hear me out, then I shall convey it verbally through someone else—only, you might want to avoid publicity; the matter is a delicate one, and any publicity would ruin *your* plans."

The main returned and, grinning as though rejoicing at something, she said:

"He's sorry. You simply cannot be received."

"Well, then just hand him this."

A minute later the maid came out again to Pozharsky. Her red face was frowning in annoyance. She said:

"You are invited to come in."

"It's high time," grumbled Pozharsky.

Motovilov was waiting in his study. He locked the doors carefully. He inquired coldly:

"In what am I obliged to you?"

"Venerable Alexey Stepanovich!" Pozharsky said solemnly: "I have the honor of asking you for the hand of your daughter Anna Alexeyevna."

"Is *that* all you came here for?"

"That depends on your answer."

"You know the answer," Motovilov said curtly.

Pozharsky smiled insolently. He said:

"Circumstances have changed since that time, and therefore I take the liberty of..."

"Your circumstances?"

"No, not mine personally."

"I've already told you...," Motovilov began.

Pozharsky interrupted him with undue familiarity:

"Believe me, Alexey Stepanych, it will be better if you consent."

"In one word: No. That's final."

"In that case, I have to tell you—albeit with regret—that, in asking for your daughter's hand at this time, I am only fulfilling the duty of an honorable man."

"What?" shouted Motovilov.

He turned crimson.

"Alas!" sighed Pozharsky: " 'In erring, youth is never free!' *That,* in fact, is the circumstance..."

"That's a lie! A foul lie!"

"I can prove...'

After several minutes of arguing violently, Pozharsky found himself on the street. He thought in dismay:

"How disappointing! What a hard-hearted man! I wasn't expecting that—I just cast aspersions on my Juliet to no avail. Alas, what if they give her a beating!"

He called on Andozersky, and with just as little success. Andozersky believed him but pretended that he did not believe him. It was obvious that he would not give her up.

Pozharsky's aspersion cost Neta dearly. Her father summoned her to him. He kept shouting furiously. Neta did not understand it at all and could not vindicate herself. To her father, her answers seemed confessions. He grew more and more savage. His shouts filled the entire house. He kept slapping Neta's face. Neta sobbed bitterly. Finally Motovilov grew weary. He remembered that he had to tell his wife. He drank some water, paced about the study, then said:

"You, young lady, are going to be the death of me. But you're still in my power. Go to your room and await your birch kasha."[3]

Neta went out. Motovilov and Marya Antonovna talked for a long time. Then Marya Antonovna went to her daughter.

Neta was sitting by herself. She was weeping inconsolably. She did not doubt that her father would carry out his threat. But she was completely unable to understand what had happened. Her mother sat with her for a long time.

Finally Neta said:

"He's a scoundrel!"

Her eyes flashed.

Marya Antonovna went off to comfort her husband. Motovilov said:

"Well, thank God indeed! I am very glad. But, all the same, Neta is at fault, and, wish what you may, I am going to punish her. She's just too hard-headed for her own good! She picked out whom she was going to love, I daresay!"

Neta was again summoned to her father.

Near evening, people in town were already gossiping about how Neta had been whipped. Molin was in ecstasy. Gleefully he kept telling his friends about it, making up silly and vulgar details as he went along. They had a grand time—Gomzin kept clacking his magnificent teeth, Bienstock kept giggling.

CHAPTER THIRTY-FIVE

Every morning nowadays Login woke up feeling somber, gloomy. It was sultry inside his room. The ruddy-cheeked, red-haired little boy that had appeared to him on that unhappy morning had become so corporeal that he had begun to cast a shadow when he stood in the sun's rays. But Login had only to think of Anna—and the little fellow would vanish, as though he did not exist.

Login recalled the affairs of the last few days, both his own and others' affairs. The wicked slander's cruel venom kept burning his heart ever more painfully. And now Login knew from whom the slander was coming. Others' affairs too—at his recollections of them he would seethe with indignation and contempt.

One hateful image was connected with all his bad thoughts and memories, the image of —Motovilov. His malice toward Motovilov would arise like a diabolical power, and his feeling for vengeance would struggle furiously with the reproofs from his intellect. In vain did he recall the precepts of forgiveness. In vain did he make himself remember Anna's bright eyes. Indignation held sway over his memory; he would even remember Anna as indignant and would hear her impassioned words:

"There's a man who doesn't have the right to live!"

He was parched with the thirst for vengeance, like the parching thirst in the desert. It was grievous to think that Motovilov, this walking insult, this sin incarnate, was still living and breathing the same air as Anna and was poisoning this air with his putrid speeches. Sometimes he would imagine that Motovilov might hurt or insult Anna—and acute pain would stab through Login.

"But am I in fact not as bad as Motovilov?" he asked himself, and he judged his own past harshly for the vice with which it was laden.

"I have to separate myself from the hateful past, I have to kill it! I must remain alive with only the pure half of my soul. This life is insufferable. There must be a solution, whatever it might be. Even if it's as agonizing as being tortured or executed."

The more Login thought about this, the more strongly within him raged the malice, frightful even to him, and wild, beastly; and the more unbearable the situation was, the more imperative was the demand for a solution. It would perhaps be something cruel—Login did not know what exactly, would not even think about it, and was afraid to—but he did feel, ever more strongly, the necessity for some solution.

At times the recollection of Anna's trustful eyes would bring him tranquility, and a festive and idyllic feeling would fill his heart. But the bright moments flew by swiftly; another man, vengeful and malicious, would come forth and complain bitterly of his injuries.

And after each happy interval, this other man that he was became ever more hateful to Login, and his malice was ever more grievous. It was imperative that he put an end to this, that he do away with the sad necessity of being dual.

Seeing his gloomy and pensive state, Lenya sometimes would say:

"It's time you went to the Yermolins. These books, why, you must have read them all, and so you'll even manage to reread them later."

Login would smile and reply:

"Is that your business, Lenka?"

"Just why isn't it?" Lenya would answer.

Login would go to the Yermolins. On the road, as the grasshoppers chirped tiresomely, he kept thinking how he needed to have a talk with Anna and tell her that he was not worthy of her, tell her to forget him. If he did not find her at home, he would go look for her in the field, in the village, or at the farm-stead, even though he knew that he would find her at work and might prove a hindrance.

But just let him catch sight of her in the distance—and gloomy thoughts were forgotten. He would come up to her as a different man: meek, trustful Abel would awake, and sullen Cain would hide in the innermost recesses of his heart. But sensitive Anna detected the cold breath of Cain in the serenely gentle words of Login, and she was unhappy. She was obsessed with an idea: how could she melt the ice? How could she destroy the Cain? How could she restore in Login's troubled soul the unfading light that that sacred place so needed? Did she need to make a sacrifice?

In fact, she had decided to make a sacrifice, but nagging doubts would not leave her: would her sacrifice do any good? Would she not be unleashing a wild beast?

She and Login talked a great deal about their future life and about town affairs. Cholera had flared up in the town. The common people were vaguely uneasy. Everything irritated the ignorant people: the sanitary precautions, and the bright star, the cholera barrack, and the release of Molin, the slanders about Login, and the rumors about the leaders of the zemstvo. Drunkenness had increased, and fights kept occurring in the taverns and on the streets. Some of the well-to-do people began moving out of town: they feared the cholera; they also feared riots.

Anna came to her father in the evening, knelt before him, and trustfully huddled against him. Her face glowed in the rays of the sunset, and over it lay an indefinite evening expression, a happy wistfulness. She had let her hair down, had nothing on her feet, and her plain white dress hung down in broad folds like a tunic. The sweet smell of birdcherry came through the open windows.

"So, my friend, you've decided your fate," Yermolin said softly.

"Yes. And it's strange at first. It's as though you're swimming about midnight and can't see the shore."

"See that you *both* don't drown."

Anna's cheeks flushed.

"Don't worry. He has no foundations, he could perish uselessly and thanklessly. But there are great possibilities within him. Together, we'll be fertile ground for something."

"But will you be happy with him?"

Anna smiled meekly and looked up into her father's eyes. She said:

"If there's sorrow, then we'll live with sorrow too. You trained me not to fear that which the weak fear."

"Life's sorrow, dear, is a bit more terrible than running around barefoot in the snow or howling in pain during a flogging."

"We'll struggle through," Anna answered softly.

She smiled tenderly, but large tears were slowly falling from her eyes.

Late at night Baglayev was visiting Login in his study. Before them stood a whole battery of bottles, empty, full, and not-yet-empty.[1] Baglayev was afraid of getting cholera and therefore redoubled his heavy drinking. Login was quite in the mood for a drinking bout. There was something fantastic in what loomed before Login's eyes. The small room seemed suffused with a red glow. Yushka's flushed face looked drunken and absurd. Login felt the blood pounding agonizingly in his temples, and he felt an agonizing dizziness. Yushka, with his tongue thick and crooked, was babbling:

"But then, I know I'm a swine! Even worse, in fact,—simply a filthy flea, an insignificant creature. On the other hand, I don't have any great tricks behind me: 'Even a flea has little fleas on it.'[2] Me? I'm just a drunk—and that's it! But you, brother, you've got something on your conscience. You're a proud and a weak man: your eyes are bigger than your stomach! You're always pulling tricks; for a trick you'd gladly kill a man!"

"You're an inveterate liar, dear fellow," Login said morosely.

"No, brother. Yushka's no inveterate liar! Yushka Baglayev's not a fool! And maybe I am in fact an inveterate liar, but it's all the same as if I'm not. You don't like anybody, you think everything's vile, and, brother, you despise us. Well, damn you, go ahead and despise us—it serves us right. But I love you, all the same; you're a cordial fellow, even though sometimes one can't figure out anything about you. Come on, brother, let's get potted. You know, Motovilov's a scoundrel; I'll tell him that to his face."

With trembling hands but with great enthusiasm, he filled the glasses. Login had been strangely silent for a long time by now. He took his glass. Yushka babbled on:

"Let's clink, then drink, brother."

They drank up. Yushka continued:

"Yes, I love you even though you're a hypocrite; you're a secretive, arrogant man. You always keep to yourself. Any sore of your own you want to scratch raw and gobble up. You're a fantastical and mischievous man. Vasya, my friend, I feel sorry for you! Vasyuk!³ You can't feel at home among us!"

Yushka burst out crying and started to lean over to kiss Login. But his tousled and sweaty head suddenly lolled, fell back, came to rest on the back of his armchair. He sobbed once more, snored, brought his head down on the table, onto his crossed hands, and fell asleep. Login closed his eyes: an abyss opened in the pit of his stomach; it felt eerie and pleasant, and he sailed off to some place, then flew off into the abyss, faster and faster, and the feeling grew ever more pleasant and more eerie. The fall ended—and he opened his eyes. It was dismal and ugly in the room.

Login took his hat, went downstairs, and quietly opened the front door. At the same time, the door opened to the room where Lenya slept. Lenya gazed out into the hall. Login looked, but did not notice him.

He swayed slightly as he walked along the streets. The full moon sweetly tormented him. It peered so intently and inquisitively—was it expecting or fearing something, or foreboding something? He could not grasp the meaning of its pale, angrily immobile beams, but the meaning that was in them had a biting, heart-chilling portent.

Disjointed fragments of thoughts and feelings kept flitting around in Login's mind. Somewhere just beyond the threshold of his consciousness two mysterious visitors were standing importunately, side by side. It was like knowing by certain signs, that someone is standing at a door, even when he has not come in. Login tried in vain to open the door of his consciousness to them. One was the likeness of someone that he knew, a child's face, frightened eyes, something else familiar—but he did not know what it was. The other visitor was something strange and amorphous, a foreboding or a command, something angry and vindictive, connected with the image of someone that he deeply hated. This vague and persistent thing lay heavy on his chest, made it hard for him to breathe.

At times it seemed that he had a goal and that he knew where he was going and why. He did not notice the road, his gaze wandered, and the moon kept staring at him. Its pale, wicked beams kept saying that everything was as it should be, as it had to be, that everything was decided and now had to be fulfilled.

Halfway across the bridge, he stopped, leaned on the railing, and gazed into the water. The water glistened dully. With a soft murmur the dark, smooth eddies kept rushing against the shaky foundations. The horror of his half-forgotten childhood nightmare awakened in his mind. Login stood there unable to decide. He wanted to go back. He raised his anguished eyes up to the sky. Something that had been smashed and trampled and buried in his mind now rushed forth from its grave with a desperate effort. The longing

270

for prayer and humble resignation stirred pitifully in his heart. But up in the sky, empty and quiet, the green disk of the moon hung dead and malevolent, and with its dead beams it froze his heart.

Login went on farther. Insane threats broke loose from his tongue. He knew that what his childhood nightmare had portended was now about to come true. The wilderness of the heavens, and the dead moon with its dead smile and cold light, and the sparse, pale stars were saying that the nightmare which had tormented him in childhood was now coming true. The wind murmured plaintively in the branches of the willow bending over the river and repeated with a doleful howl that the nightmare was coming true. The ancient lindens of the Motovilov garden looked hard over the fence, at the road, where a pale man with wildly-staring eyes was coming toward them, a man whose nightmare was now coming true. The windows began to glitter with a dull gleam from the moonbeams and spitefully rejoiced that the nightmare was coming true.

The garden gate, through which the young ladies went to go bathing, was locked. But the flimsy lock yielded to force. Login entered the garden. There was no one in the garden. In the house everyone was asleep. Only in Motovilov's study was a light shining.

Past the windows Login cut across the garden and went out into the yard. He stopped in the shadow of the stacked firewood and considered how he might most easily get into the house.

A door banged on the terrace in the garden. Login shuddered and jumped back between two piles of logs. He stumbled over something—under his feet was something hard, like a smooth log. He kicked it forward and timorously looked into the garden, while trying not to stick out too much from behind the woodpile. His heart was beating violently.

Motovilov was walking through the garden, Login gathered that he wanted to go to the vegetable garden, which was on the other side of the yard. In that case, Motovilov would have to go past the place where Login was hiding.

Login looked at the object encountered underfoot. An axe. He quickly moved it back into the shadows with his foot, quickly picked it up, took it in his right hand. And by now Motovilov was coming into the yard.

Login stood still in agonizing suspense. Motovilov's footsteps were drawing near. Then he passed Login and did not notice him. Login quietly moved out from behind the woodpile, then swung the axe. Motovilov had opened the gate and taken a step into the vegetable garden. At that point the heavy blow fell on his curly head. A dull thud was heard, also a slight crack.

Motovilov lay face downwards.

"Is he dead or unconscious?" Login wondered.

He leaned down—the blood-stained back of the head was hideous. Login was overcome with anger and hate. Again he swung the axe, another

271

time, and another. The crunch of bones being broken was disgusting. The brained head was revolting.

"He won't get up now," Login thought maliciously.

He dropped the axe, stood up straight, and quickly crossed the yard into the garden. He felt amazing relief, almost joy. The thought that he might be seen had not yet entered his mind.

Then he went up to the garden gate; drunken muttering was heard on the riverbank. He stopped in the shadow of the fence and listened.

Spiridon was walking by the fence, was cursing and muttering;

"No, brother, don't try that on me; you're not going to give me a flogging and get away with it!"

Spirka saw the open gate and tumbled heavily into the garden. He stopped for a minute with his face in full view to Login—and Login felt a horror. The face of a witness... No, it was not that alone that was horrible. It was the face itself, contorted by inordinate suffering, despair, shame,— the face, almost blue in its pallor, with the lost look of its frightened eyes, with its trembling lips—every feature of this face trembled in terror as though before an inescapable calamity. He was not as drunk as it seemed from his voice, but all over, from head to foot, he was trembling with a minute, pitiful, cowering quiver.

Login's gaze shifted to Spiridon's hands, and a new wave of horror shook Login. A length of cord could be seen in Spiridon's trembling hands. He held on to this length tenaciously. Login did not quite realize what the logical connection was between the cord and Spiridon's appearing here at this time, but he did perceive that there was a connection, and a horrible one at that. He leaned against the fence and watched as Spiridon fitted a noose to a thick bough of a tree directly opposite the terrace...

A merry, lively tune was heard somewhere far away. It made Login start trembling again.

"Run! Far away from this accursed spot!"

Again he met no one on the road, and only the moon watched him, and its cold beams brought tranquility.

"The vicious past is slain; do not resurrect it!" the moonbeams whispered to him. "Do not repent of what has been done. Be it bad or good, you had to do it.

"And what is bad, and what is good? Is the death of an evil man an evil or a blessing? Who can determine? You are not your neighbor's judge, but neither are you your own judge. Submit to the inevitable.

"Do not go to the court of *men* with what has been done. What do you care for the moral side of retribution? Will you accept a great lesson of life from *them?* And the material side—bondage, the burdens of hard labor, and deprivations, sufferings, disgrace—all this falls at random to the lot of the good and the evil. Who need for you to add to permanent sorrow and human disgrace your sorrow, your disgrace, and the sorrow of those who love you?

272

"Let the dead rot; think of the living!"

He walked with rapid steps along the streets, but his face was calm and peaceful. If anyone had met him, who would have recognized the murderer? He did bear drops of blood on his clothing, but his clothing would burn up tomorrow, along with this evidence.

And Yushka was still asleep. Login changed clothes, hid the blood-stained clothing, and sat down at the table. Suddenly it seemed that he had not gone out of the room, and that it had all been only a bad dream.

"But I shall never forget that dream," he thought sadly.

Melancholy gripped his heart. Then suddenly Anna's redeeming image arose before him. He seemed to hear her firm, assured step beyond the wall. Login felt strong and youthful. He had something to strive for! He had that for which no struggle is too fearsome!

Yushka began saying something in his sleep. Login tapped a bottle against a glass. Yushka began to stir and opened his lackluster eyes.

"Well, well, Yushka, did you have a good nap?"

"I never heard such nonsense! I wasn't even thinking of sleeping. You've drunk yourself silly."

"Well, let's have a drink while we're half-awake."

"I won't even *drink* for such a damn-fool reason as that. Just look what he's made up! That Yushka Baglayev would fall asleep in front of vodka! What's the matter with you? Come to your senses!"

"But, all the same, Yushka, you did have a nap. I managed to go for a walk during that time."

"Why are you trying to fool me right to my face? You yourself were the one who went to sleep."

"Really?"

"I swear to God, you were asleep. Snoring to beat the band."

"But it seemed to me that you were the one who was asleep, Yushka."

"Why, look here. You even started raving in your sleep, so I wet your head with water."

"Then, thank you for that, brother."

"There now, Yushka Baglayev knows when something's so or not."

In the morning the town was incensed by a brutal crime. Motovilov was found slain in his yard. His head had been completely chopped to pieces with an axe. Evidently, the murderer had inflicted senseless blows on the already lifeless body. And, not far from the victim, the murderer too had been found: on the tree in front of the terrace hung the now cold body of Spiridon. Bloody stains were visible on his tattered shirt.

People were crowded around in front of Motovilov's home. The motive for the murder was clear to everyone: revenge by Spiridon for his having been sentenced because of the late Motovilov's complaint.

"God's judgment!" they said in the crowd. "God sees."

The prevailing mood was an austere, profound one. True, certain rowdies would shout from time to time:

"Certain *other* people ought to get it the same way!"

But they were hushed up. However, had anyone carefully observed the faces of the townspeople here in the crowd and in other spots in town when conversation turned to the topic of the murder, he would have noticed traces of cruel, bloodthirsty thoughts in these faces. The bloody event mysteriously excited the people and, as it were, helped incite the crowd to a vicious act.

CHAPTER THIRTY-SIX

Near evening Anna went down the terrace steps into the garden and unexpectedly ran into Login face to face. Her heart all but stopped beating. Login looked at her with sunken eyes. His pale face expressed suffering and anger. He forced a smile. He squeezed her hand so hard that it hurt. He asked:

"I did, I believe, hinder you from something? You were about to go somewhere."

"No," Anna replied, smiling in confusion, "I just wanted to go..."

"Anyhow, I won't detain you," he interrupted. "Just for a moment. I need to say... But let's go somewhere farther away."

He said all this in a hoarse, failing voice, as though he were short of breath. Not waiting for a reply, he turned around sharply and set off quickly, without looking at Anna. She could barely keep up with him. Thus they came to the bench on the shore of the little lake, where yellow Florentine irises swayed slowly in the breeze. Login stopped. He abruptly seized both Anna's hands and for some reason drew her to the very edge of the shore. He began by saying:

"Listen—I don't love you."

"That's not true," Anna said, growing pale.

"No, no, I don't love you, even though you are dearer to me than anything in the world. I don't know what it is. I'm such a depraved man for you, and I want to possess you. I hate you. I would like to torture you with an unendurable pain and shame, to destroy you—and then die because I just can't live without you. You have enchanted me, you know magic charms, you have made me your slave—and I hate you—agonizingly. So, then, while you are still free—banish me; you see, I'm wild, I'm evil, I'm depraved. Tell me to leave."

He pressed her hands and peered intently into her eyes, sad eyes, but calm.

"You feel miserable," she said gently, "but I love you."

"Oh, my dear one! Oh, my hated one! And my hatred doesn't frighten you? Then, do you want to be my wife?"

"I do," Anna said without hesitating.

Her eyes peered calmly and firmly at Login, and he saw in them a strange combination of gentleness and cruelty. A cruel, vicious feeling welled up inside him, made him see through a crimson haze, made his head whirl sickeningly.

"You do? Here, then!"

He raised his hand to strike Anna. Her eyes, frightened eyes, opened wide, but she stood motionless, with her hands at her sides. Suddenly Login's

275

hand dropped powerlessly, and he quietly bowed down to the sand of the path at Anna's feet.

Calm, serene, she stood over him and silently looked into the distance. She saw that much sorrow and madness still lay ahead, but the future did not frighten her, but drew her on with a strange fascination.

"Anna, leave me to my fate! I am a ruined man," Login said sadly as he slowly got up.

"Never! Don't lose hope as long as you are alive."

"I had hope for happiness with you. But can you love me after what has happened?"

"Nothing will separate us. I am bound to you with all my heart."

"Nothing will separate us? Not even a crime, a bloody one?"

Anna shuddered.

"Nothing can separate us!" she exclaimed. "I would follow you to penal servitude, or I would help you keep the secret."

She looked up at Login: her eyes, full of tears, expressed her suffering. Tears rolled down her cheeks, and that tore Login's heart.

"Nyutochka, my poor soul, do you know something?"

"I know that you feel miserable. Tell me your secret: let us have nothing unshared between us."

"Listen, Nyutochka,—I killed Motovilov."

Again he felt her tremble. He was afraid to glance at her; he looked to one side. But the silence was unbearable. Their eyes met. Anna's gentle eyes shone with compassion. Login felt joy rise up again in his heart.

"It was a deed fated for me. It began long ago, and it kept tormenting me. When I killed him, I felt—however savage it may have been—joy and relief. It seemed to me that I had killed a beast within myself. But I ought to tell you everything. Would you care to listen to me?"

"Yes, tell me everything," Anna said softly. "And only me. Don't you tell *them* all this."

Even Login himself did not anticipate that the story of his relations with the man that he had killed would be so long. He recounted it and did not feel his former malice. But how hard it was to talk about the murder! How cruel it had been—that bloody deed—and, apparently, how pointless!

Finally he reached the end and looked at Anna in anxious anticipation. She took his hand.

"You killed the past," she said firmly; "now, together we shall forge our future—we shall live a new and different life."

She quickly bent down and kissed his hand.

"Nyutochka! My pure one!" Login exclaimed. "How poor I am before you, my priestess and lamb!"

He knelt before her and covered her hands with kisses.

"We shall go onward and upward," she said. "We shall not look back, lest we meet the fate that befell Lot's wife."

Login stood up before Anna and asked her in a quandary:

"Need I confess it publicly?"

"No," Anna replied firmly. "Why should we put our own necks under the yoke. We ourselves shall bear the weight of our own burdens and our own audacity. What do you need a convict's fetters for? Here, you have me, a sweet burden: take me and carry me."

She stood up, put her hands on his shoulders. He picked her up in his arms.

"No, don't carry me away," she whispered softly. "Sit here with me."

He embraced her. He sat down on the bench and held her in his lap. She put her head on his shoulder and half closed her eyes. Her breast was heaving violently. Login felt the hot trembling of her body. But her uneven breathing and the hot flush of her face did not arouse lust in Login, and he looked at her with calm eyes, as at a baby. But she trembled agonizingly and turned her misty eyes away in embarrassment.

"What a heavy one you are!" said Login.

Anna looked at him quickly and smiled.

"Why is her smile so bashful?" Login wondered.

Login returned homeward with uncertain feelings. At first when he had left Anna, after saying goodbye with a tender kiss, a peaceful mood had come over him. But as he approached the town he felt mentally uncomfortable, as though he had vaguely remembered something forgotten, despised, but essential—as though something that had to be done had not yet been done. And in the wake of this first strange feeling that something was amiss, vague, irritating reminders began to arise in Login's mind.

And in the town it was wild and noisy. Throngs of drunken and sullen riffraff loitered about the streets. In one place opposite the doors to a tavern, a small band of tradesmen had surrounded a police inspector as they badgered him with questions of why were only the poor dying, and why had the cholera barrack been set up. The inspector, pale with fright, tried to get out of the crowd, babbled impossible promises and tried to get the townspeople to calm down and disperse; however, he could not even remember what he was trying to say. A fierce lanky fellow, snapping to attention and saluting crookedly, hung around in front of the inspector and, mocking him, constantly bawled out for some reason neither here nor there:

"Yes, sir, Your Honor! At your service, Your Honor! Very good, Your Honor!"

The police official had no hope of getting off alive. However, a droshky came jingling up, a puny policeman, with a cockroach mustache and a fierce soldier's face, jumped down from it, and, advancing on the tradesmen as on an empty space, he announced that the police chief was demanding the inspector and wanted him *this minute*. The tradesmen fell silent and made way, while the inspector and the policeman sat down in the droshky and rolled away. As the droshky started off, someone from the crowd shouted to the strong-willed policeman:

"When the revolt starts, we'll kill you first, Tochilov."

And these words reminded Login again of something, but what exactly he did not know.

At home his anxious bewilderment increased. Suddenly, by chance he noticed Lenya's look of perplexity at him. Login looked attentively at the boy. Lenya quickly looked away, but it seemed to Login, that the boy was pale and confused.

Then Login suddenly remembered whose eyes had looked at him on the night of the murder. A new anguish burned within him.

"I was drunk at the time," he thought bitterly, "and didn't understand anything. I went where my feet and my drunken good-fortune bore me. Committing murder while drunk! And I didn't tell *her* that I was drunk! I omitted the simplest and principal reason and tried to inspire her with some strange respect for my drunken act of murder. I omitted it, like any vulgar fellow who tries in every way possible to make himself look good in front of his favorite little girl in order to dazzle her with the brilliance of his 'superiority.' And she, the silly girl, kissed my hands! What heroics!"

"But, really, what a reverential attitude I have toward that little girl: I made a confession to her, tried to be sincere, and then I didn't tell her the main thing!"

He sat alone and languished in gloomy, evil thoughts. Sometimes, when worn out by their malice, he would, with an effort, summon up the image of Anna in his memory—and when she thus stood before him calm and beautiful, his mind would briefly submit to and admire this serene vision of her. But the tenderness would burn out quickly and be replaced by torrid, depraved lust. He asked himself:

"Why *was* she so timid, and then burned so when I embraced her? How identical, how tiresomely identical everyone's life is! That passionate breathing, just the way it is with everyone else, and eyes misty with desire. *She* has to travel the same paths as countless generations of her ancestresses. Actually, this way of life, so clearly defined in our motives, is always plain and clear, always pure, like spring water. Simple fleshly love is like spring water and mountain air,—but human institutions and unclean thoughts befoul it.

"Why did she choose world-weary me? Is this really love? Others too are attracted to me. I'm a mass of temptations. The leaden weight of them presses me to the ground—aren't her shoulders too weak to bear this burden?

"And why are sacrifices made? Does unsated passion perhaps require suffering? Love united with the desire to possess is a cruel love, and perhaps it has derived from the frenzy with which the wild beast pursues its prey."

Strange thoughts kept developing in Login's mind. And as they accumulated, his feelings grew ever more wild and wicked. It seemed to him that he loved Anna, not with a love, but with a hate. And he thought how sweet it would be to cause her much cruel suffering and then console her with tender caresses. "Russian women love to endure beatings from their beloved."

Near evening, as Anna was returning home alone from the farmstead, she encountered Serpenitsyn at the garden gate. He doffed his ragged cap and said quietly:

"I take the liberty of asking for your attention."

Anna stopped. She looked attentively at Serpenitsyn. She thought that he was about to beg for something for himself, and she considered how she might help him. Serpenitsyn continued:

"Although I see you in the footwear conferred by nature, as maidens of the lower class are in the habit of walking about; nevertheless, on certain grounds I conclude that you happen to be the noble daughter of the owner of this richest estate."

"Yes," said Anna.

"I have something to convey to you, something pertaining to one of the personages who have the honor of enjoying your father's hospitality."

"To me..." Anna began, knitting her brows, but Serpenitsyn interrupted her:

"No gossip or slander whatsoever, but something important in the most sublime sense. Gentleman's word of honor!"

Serpenitsyn struck his chest with his fist and looked very earnestly at Anna.

"But you," she began again, and again Serpenitsyn, guessing what she meant, quickly cried out:

"Serpenitsyn!"

Anna opened the gate, let Serpenitsyn into the garden, and walked on ahead of him. She stopped at a little area covered by thick bushes. Serpenitsyn spoke up:

"You may have deigned to know of those events that have agitated the town's population, especially the ignorant part of it."

Anna bowed her head in silence. Serpenitsyn was silent briefly, hemmed and hawed a little, then resumed speaking:

"Certain of the gentry residing hereabouts have deigned to get out of town to places more or less remote, in order to avoid unpleasant matters. But meanwhile, Mr. Login has not left town, even though the summer vacation has begun. Let me be so bold as to call your gracious attention to the fact that Mr. Login is excessively negligent of certain disconcerting eventualities that might occur."

"Is there anything that you know of?" Anna inquired.

She was growing pale, and her eyes opened wide in alarm. Serpenitsyn replied:

"It's utterly impossible to know the future, but then I was only thinking that your prudent counsels directed to effect a timely absence of Mr. Login from the town could have a beneficial effect. But hereupon I have the honor of bowing goodbye to you."

Serpenitsyn again doffed his cap, bowed goodbye while holding it in his outstretched hand, then turned to go.

"Listen," Anna stopped him.

Serpenitsyn halted. Anna wanted to say something; he again anticipated her words and said:

"Anyhow, don't let yourself worry; in case any immediate danger arises, I shall consider it my sacred duty to forewarn my noble creditor."

"Right now," said Anna, "maybe you could use..."

"Kind lady!" Serpenitsyn exclaimed, smiting his chest. "Not a word more! I may be in a state of misfortune, but I am a gentleman!"

Solemnly and respectfully he bowed once more and then departed, leaving Anna in a state of acute anxiety. For a long time she stood there pale and motionless, with her trembling hands crossed on her heavily-breathing chest, and she listened carefully to her own thoughts. She saw how greatly disturbed and greatly ravaged was Login's mind, and she knew that it would be better for him to die than to live like that. But she could not let him go alone to his death, and she knew that only through something extraordinary, only through some cherished sacrifice, could his salvation be procured.

That evening she had a long talk with her father.

"You have some strange thoughts," he said finally. "And where have they come from? You used to be completely different."

"Even a linden grows," Anna replied, smiling and blushing. "You tell me yourself, should I turn my back on him now?"

"You ought to be together. But can you help him? And how will he live with such a disturbed mind, with such depraved thoughts?"

Anna walked up to the window and gazed at the dark sky and the faintly twinkling stars. Her face took on an inexorable expression. She spoke quietly:

"Whoever is incapable of being regenerated is bound to die. He must have his dark thoughts burned away. There *is* delight in life, miracles do happen. And I must do it. He will see that love at its heights is stronger than passion and vice. I'm frightened, but still, it's better to let us both burn. Don't you forbid me, then."

She quietly walked up to her father, and an unwonted timidity shone in her eyes. He said:

"Do as you think best, but I find it strange what you want to do."

Again it was a hot, clear day when time seems to stand still. Anna and Login were sitting on the bench in the remote garden lane. Before them lay the quiet lake within its low-lying banks which were overgrown with coarse grass. Florentine iris blossoms were turning yellow on top of the water. Gusts of wind would spring up, and the flowers would sway. Their slow, shaky movements were reminiscent of something private, their yellow color induced bitter thoughts, and the sun's heat aroused burning desire in Login's blood.[1] Anna's bright eyes did not bring him peace. And she seemed remote; her attire—a white dress buttoned at the left shoulder and so short that it left her legs bare, even partly above the knee—seemed to transport her into other times.

Login was thinking that he needed to leave, in order to keep from bringing sin into Eden. And so they sat there, side by side, and talked sadly. Login was saying:

"I've been having nightmares, such ominous ones. Listen: last night it made me miserable. Some ungainly, hideous thing landed on my chest. Its eyes burned a reddish-gray color. Do you know the superstitious ritual?"

"You have to ask whether it stands for good or evil," Anna replied.

"Yes, I asked it."

"And then what?"

Login laughed bitterly.

"Look, if I knew, then I would have heard. No, it only mumbled. If it had been a ghost, it would have been in a complete quandary. It would hae seen two souls in me—so which of them would it take?"

"Our love may be for good or for evil," Anna said firmly, "but let us go together and bravely!"

She pressed herself to him trustfully and laid her head on his shoulder.

"Where can I go!" Login exclaimed sadly. "My burden doesn't let me go!"

"All right, then, let us bear it together. Or better, let's get rid of it, just as trees shed their leaves in autumn,—then we shall be free: Look ahead, speak to me of the future!"

The evil smile stole over his lips. He said bitterly:

"Like everyone else, we too will start living quite an ordinary sort of life. We'll go to a church, which we don't need, and we'll get married before the altar of that God, in whom we don't believe. Despicable concerns over personal happiness will fill the emptiness of our days, but will not quench the thirst. And then I'll be mean to you and idle. Trifles will irritate me; I'll carp at you, and then, repenting of it, I'll come crawling to you with kisses, like everyone who leads that philistine sort of life. The tender nicknames, so vulgar! And what will you start calling me? Vasya, Vasyenka? And then all the squealing of children, and the smell—all that will recur even with us. An abomination of vulgarity!"

Anna listened to him with her blushing face bowed low. She said:

"No, even on the beaten paths there is the unexpected, that which is scorned by other people and welcome to us. We shall walk this road, not as slaves, but free, without terrors. We shall resurrect the happiness of old, and

281

it will become the happiness of new generations."

"Nyutochka, if you only knew! The debauchery, the drunkenness, the sleepless nights, the dull days. How can I rid myself of the past? It would take a miracle—and I don't believe in miracles."

"My darling, love works miracles. It is the fire in which impure thoughts will be burned away."

Her bosom was heaving with excitement. Her eyes blazed with rapture. Login looked at her sadly and morosely.

"I don't know any such fire," he said gloomily.

"Let us endeavor to rise," Anna said, speaking still more softly. "Let us see whether we can reach the heights of happiness—love without desire. If we cannot reach them, it's better that we die."

The terrible word as she uttered it sounded gentle and tender.

"Dear priestess, you will kindle the flame, but where shall we get a victim for the sacrifice?"

She stood up. Login rose behind her. She stretched out her arms to him. She said:

"Let's go. I want to present a gift to you, and it is ready. I want you to be splendidly happy with it."

Silently they entered an enclosed summer-house. Login was feeling an incomprehensible excitement, like a presentiment of some important event. He looked out the windows at the cheerful greenery; it had grown up so thickly here that one could not see either the house or the paths. Sultry and sonorous, the air poured into the summer-house through the tangled branches.

Login saw that Anna too was strangely agitated. She stood all a-tremble before him and first would lower her hands, then raise them to the place where her dress was fastened. The color quickly fled from her dusky cheeks. Suddenly an expression of firmness and great tranquility came over her face despite its momentary pallor; she slowly raised her calm hands, quietly unfastened the metal clasp at her left shoulder, and said in an impassive voice:

"My gift to you is—myself."

Her dress fell to her feet. Bare and cold, she stood before him, and her chaste eyes watched him with anticipation.

"My dear one," Login exclaimed, "we are at the height! What happiness! And what sadness!"

He drew Anna's strong, shapely body to him, kissed her rosy cheeks, and said tenderly:

"My darling, my eternal sister, I shall take your gift, I shall merge your soul with mine, and I shall fill your body with joy and rapture."

A happy smile lit up Anna's face. She was silent. Her eyes were humble. He bent down to pick up her dress. Their hands met. He helped her get dressed.

Returning homeward, Login felt that his dark thoughts had been burned away; a new and free man rejoiced in that which is more sublime and more meaningful than life and death. White, beautiful Anna stood before his eyes, and he knew that, with this serene vision in his soul, he could not go to sin and depravity. He did not think about happiness and life; thoughts of death and torture would sometimes occur to him; but, with this unashamed and chaste image of her in his soul, he could no longer turn from the path which *her* feet would travel. This beautiful vision brought him great tranquility,—and all life's opportunities became equally desirable.

That evening, in the quiet of his room, he sometimes seemed to hear her soft footstep,—and that reminded him that the evil spells had been broken.

Early in the morning Login was awakened by a noise coming from somewhere not far away. Lying in bed, he listened carefully. A wild racket was heard in which the furious cries of individuals could occasionally be distinguished. Such shouting was heard in various place, sometimes quite nearby. But around Login's home itself it was quiet—only, one could at times hear people exchanging hushed and frightened remarks as they ran along below the windows.

Login had a confused and depressing feeling of anxiety, a premonition of the spiritual uplift that comes over people in moments of general excitement. Trembling nervously and hurrying, he set about getting dressed. A sudden wild howl below his windows made him shiver in surprise. A crowd was passing by with much racket and whistling, and some individual was yelling furiously:

"Don't give up, boys! Beat the doctors!"

Login walked up to the window and stood by the sill. The crowd consisted of little boys and quite young town lads. That rowdy with the tinny eyes, whose face Login so well remembered, was walking at the front of the crowd. He in fact was the one yelling, as he waved his arms absurdly and kept rolling his eyes upward and from side to side in a strange crooked way. When they had passed, it became quiet again on the empty street, except for the incoherent fuss at the Dylins' (the refrains of which came up to Login from the yard) and for all that other racket, which had awakened Login.

Login went downstairs, and he bumped into Serpenitsyn in the entrance hall. The latter had just come up the stairs from the kitchen and had a mysterious and worried look on his face. He said:

"Kind Sir, forgive me for showing up unannounced, but your Dulcinea of Toboso has deserted you, as you should judge from the fact that the doors downstairs are wide open, and she is nowhere to be found.[1] I beg an audience with Your High Honor."

Login went into the living room and invited Serpenitsyn to sit down. The tramp coughed in surprise, seated himself carefully in a cushioned chair, then whispered:

"Let me be so bold as to report that your further presence in this town, kind Sir, may have very dangerous consequences."

"Well, all right," Login said glumly, "what consequences do you mean? And why are you whispering? There's no one here to eavesdrop."

"What about that character?" Serpenitsyn asked, using his chin to indicate someone behind Login.

Login looked around; Lenya, who had just hopped out of bed, peered out at them from the dining room.

"Why, that character isn't dangerous," Login said with a smile.

Serpenitsyn spoke louder:

"If I may express it in literary style, the problem is that the lower classes of our town have raised an insurrection against the power of cholera and have now gathered together under the leadership of the wench Vasilisa the Loud-mouthed, with hostile intentions toward the cholera barrack. And since Your High Honor has happened to incur suspicion in the eyes of the venerable local lower middle class, the suspicion, that is, of your belonging to a gang of criminals who have dropped something fatal into the wells, therefore devastation threatens your peaceful dwelling as well. And therefore I shall be so bold as to recommend to you, kind Sir, that, before it's too late, you make a decent retreat, even if, for instance, only as far as to the most esteemed Mr. Yermolin's estate, which the fury of the people would not encroach upon under any circumstances."

"But what if it does?" Login wondered.

In his imagination there instantly arose the image of Anna, and in front of her—an enraged mob. The thought that Anna might be exposed to danger made him shudder: he almost felt physical pain at imagining how a heavy blow might fall on Anna's beautiful body.

"The devil is not as black as he is painted,"[2] he told Serpenitsyn. "I'll stay here: running away is useless: if they wanted to, they'd find me even there."

"Do get away while the getting is good," Lenka said in a troubled voice.

Login laughed, walked up to the little boy, and hugged him.

"Get away yourself if you want to," he said. "They won't chase after you."

Login was left by himself. He had seen Serpenitsyn to the door all right, but he had somehow failed to notice where and how Lenya had disappeared. He sat down by the window in the living room—and new and meaningful thoughts surged around him. He gradually became immersed in the flood of these thoughts. Longing, then a cold tranquility, clear like the frosty air, stole over his mind.

He saw the irremediable evil of life, felt a great weariness, and, without sadness and without joy, he waited for rest. He recalled his life in snatches—minor and supposedly forgotten incidents flashed by in his mind like the bright-colored, fleeting images of a kaleidoscope; a procession of living and eternally departed people passed by; currently familiar and long-forsaken places came to mind. As an impartial judge he appraised without wrath and without self-pity the evil and falsehood of his own actions as they now passed by in his mind. He knew that a form so defective had to be destroyed, and the clay from which so much evil had been moulded had to be crushed. He did not like to think that he himself was the one who had been molded from that clay; calmly he gave himself over to the Will that eternally creates and eternally destroys, and he fearlessly awaited the completion of his life.

The image of Anna, white and chaste, reigned over his thoughts. It gladdened him to think that *she* would remain. He did not regret having caused her suffering—and he did not wish her happiness. Classical and eternal, she stood before him in her solemn nakedness—she was perfect, and there was nothing else to wish for her.

He recalled without bitterness his childish, naive dreams and plans for happiness and well-being—and he did not laugh at them. And his fear of the past appeared like a remote and unfamiliar suffering, a needless and futile languor.

He realized that both the beaten paths and the roads not yet traveled by anyone are equally significant and interesting for the restless spirit that thirsts for novelty and finds it everywhere. A promise of the future life appeared to him in an endless variety of possibilities—but for Login himself the present age had become utterly superfluous and insufferable.

About an hour had passed. It was becoming noisy outside. A crowd was gathering below the windows of his house. Shrill female shouts were heard over the turbulent uproar. Login raised his head and listened.

"I saw him, I saw him myself with my own eyes," a woman shouted fiercely.

The end of her sentence was lost to Login in the general commotion. A tinkle of broken glass was heard in the dining room: ragged urchins had begun flinging rocks through the windows. Upon hearing the tinkle of glass the crowd quieted down. Login walked over into the dining room, opened a window, and, scowling sternly, peered at the crowd. The little boys rushed away, the crowd backed up fearfully. It became quiet for a moment. Then, somewhere in the rear ranks, a woman's furious shout was heard:

"Why, what are you afraid of, you blockheads!"

The despicable wench, in a tattered dress, bare-headed, and pock-marked, elbowed her way through the crowd, jumped forward, and shouted to Login:

"All right, you witch-bear, come out of your den, come out honestly. You've done us wrong long enough—now you're going to get it!"

The crowd broke out in a harsh and chaotic racket. Rocks—flung by the momentarily emboldened brats—came flying at Login.

"Hail Death!" he said quietly and walked away from the window.

He passed unhurriedly through the rooms and down the stairway that lead to the street; then he came out calmly onto the porch. At his appearance the shouts redoubled, the crowd advanced toward the porch—Login caught sight of the screaming women's red faces, and what was happening seemed pointless and absurd. Both this thought and the panic that had seized him for an instant quickly vanished; he felt that his time was up, and, starting to rush somewhere, he began descending the steps. He did manage to see a heavy stone hit him in the shoulder and roll down his body; he even managed to hear somewhere a close, familiar voice that cried out something desperately; then, after a brief, aching sensation of dull pain in his head, he fell down bleeding on the steps.

The crowd rushed back from the porch. Anna bent down over Login as he lay there wounded in the head by a rock.

Lenka had known the right place to go to, and Anna would have come in time, had she not been delayed by the crowd rioting in the streets.

The mob violence did not continue for long after Login was injured: the cholera barrack was wrecked; the medics fled; the doctor ran away too and hid in a deep ditch in someone's back yard; and then the crowd had nothing else to do, so the people just went on rioting together, chasing policemen, and smashing things in the doctor's place and in various other homes. But soon after midday a pouring rain fell and dispersed the rowdies. Toward evening a squadron of dragoons, summoned by telegraph, arrived in town; but there was no longer anyone who had to be suppressed, and the legal investigator had no trouble in jailing those charged with the riot.

The town took on a woeful appearance. Patrols of dragoons rode about the deserted streets. The cholera increased, and the mournful wagons contrived by Yushka dashed about town with their wheels making an ominous clatter—but only the deceased were borne away on them.

Login lay sunk in a deep coma. And he lay motionless for a long time, filling the stillness of his room with the hoarse, labored breathing of a person critically ill. Anna would not leave his bedside. She would not think of his dying. Even during the most difficult days she did not lose confidence that he would get up; she even had great confidence that he would get up a new man, free and fearless, for a new and free life, the man with whom she would go onward and upward into a new land under new skies. And so death departed from Login's bed and yielded its object to life.

Vague, fragmentary impressions began to reach Login's mind—familiar smells and voices. Sometimes he would see Anna's face as through a milky-white haze, and he would vaguely remember something. At times he would get brief flashes of thoughts, but his brain would tire quickly and lose them.

His first return to coherent consciousness was agonizing. Near the evening of the fourth day after his eyes had first made out dim shadows passing before them and Anna had seen his semi-conscious gaze not yet focusing on anything, Login suddenly saw himself in his own room, and the flowers on the wallpaper began jumping around and laughing. There was a sonorous buzzing in the air, and at times grayish-crimson waves of mist would rush by from corner to corner. Something amorphous began swirling by the wall,

287

began to come together and stretch itself upward as it divided in places and formed members for itself like the limbs of the human body; and then the hideous, slippery apparition came away from the wall and, slowly circling in the air, moved closer and closer to Login. More and more distinctly Login began to make out the details of the specter's naked body, blue, dead, half-decomposed, with black bones sticking out here and there. A strand of half-rotten cord flapped at its neck, and then, in the terrible face of the corpse, Login recognized the face of the hanged Spiridon. That face was deathly still, but strangely its features were somehow changing, as though with tinges of dull light. And then, in the dead face of the approaching apparition, Login saw, as in a mirror, his own features; and suddenly he had a feeling that it was he himself who was swirling and circling about the room—his old self, afflicted by the dead, impotent, Cain-like malice. Login grew faint with horror, and his weak, barely audible voice called someone.

Shielding Login from the dead man, Anna came from somewhere and stood in front of Login. Both the bright-colored flowers and the crimson mists disappeared from sight, and the dead man, hurled back by something, disappeared when Anna bent over the sick man and smiled joyously as she met his eyes that recognized her.

"Has he gone?" Login asked softly.

"He's gone and will not return," Anna said in the same soft tone, deftly guessing his thoughts.

Login was silent as he slowly pondered something.

"Have you been here all the time?" he asked Anna next.

"We're together now," she said joyfully as she lowered her head onto his pillow. "I won't leave, but don't talk: it's bad for you right now. Close your eyes and go to sleep."

Login obediently closed his eyes and fell asleep.

His illness ran its course; a new life began for Login and Anna. The renewed heavens have turned blue above them, but what will become of them, and what will they come to?

Neta was really quite on the point of bringing herself to marry Andozersky, but suddenly she changed her mind, and, to the surprise of everyone, even Pozharsky and herself, she finally married the charming actor. She has discovered certain dramatic talents in herself and intends to appear in our municipal theatre in the role of Ophelia.

As soon as Claudia began to recover from her illness, she and Paltusov left suddenly. Shortly thereafter, news came that Paltusov had drowned in Lake Geneva. That is not believed in town. It is said that he is living very quietly under a different name, that he has married Claudia, and that they have been seen in a certain fashionable and popular spot abroad. Zinaida Romanovna soon found consolation. General Dubitsky visits her often.

Molin's case was dropped, and to the great sorrow of his drinking companions, he left to drink his way to another town, where he had been given the same sort of teaching position. The town to which he was assigned is far from ours, so along the way Molin stopped in towns great and small where he was met by friends in the teaching profession who hailed him as an innocent martyr. He would weep in his cups, and he repeated his slanders against Shestov everywhere. In one town, because he felt the need for money, he stole a watch from a friend but got caught. However, he was allowed to go in peace, since it was decided that he had acted so because of his misfortune and that it was Shestov's fault.[3]

And so everything goes on as before, in the usual way, and only Login and Anna think that a new life has begun for them.

THE END

NOTES

Chapter One

1. *Gimnazia*—a school where boys, usually from ages eleven to eighteen, received a classical secondary education. Although in tsarist Russia all legally recognized schools were operated, as all teachers were employed, by the government, education was at no level by any means compulsory; however, members of the middle and upper classes, boys moreso than girls, were generally expected to finish their secondary schooling. The enrollment of a gimnazia in many cases appears to have been restricted largely to sons of the landed gentry, the service gentry, or of well-to-do merchants. Hence, while not actually a "private" institution, it did tend to be a rather "exclusive" one.

2. Login, like the young Sologub, appears strongly impressed by the poetry of Fet and Tyutchev, wherein the confluence of the senses, synesthesia, is commonly employed. Frequently in this novel verbs and adjectives of sensual perception are applied to some sense other than that with which they are logically associated.

Chapter Two

1. Verst—the standard unit of measure for long distances in tsarist Russia. One verst was equal to approximately 3500 ft., or slightly more than a kilometer.

2. Zemstvo—an elected and representative rural district assembly. Such assemblies existed in tsarist Russia from 1864 until 1917.

3. Tolka, Nyutochka—affectionate, familiar forms of *Anatoly* and *Anna*. Most Christian names have acquired such "diminutive" forms in Russian, but, apart from the common people, Russians use these forms of the Christian name almost exclusively to address relatives, close friends of the family, childhood friends, lovers, or servants. Otherwise, addressing or sometimes even referring to someone in conversation by such a form may have a slightly condescending or even insulting force.

Chapter Three

1. *Sazhen*—a Russian measure equal to 2.13 meters or slightly less than seven feet.

2. Protocol in the Russian civil service required that when officials shook hands, the one of higher rank held out his hand to the junior official. As one may deduce from Yermolin's account in this chapter and from Login's conversation with Dubitsky in Chapter Eight, a junior official's holding out his hand first to a senior official could be construed as an act of gross insubordination.

3. *Volost*—In tsarist Russia the administrative divisions of the realm in Russia proper were the *gubernia* (province), the *uyezd* (subdivisions of a gubernia), which we shall call "district" and the *volost*, (somewhat like the American or Canadian county).

Chapter Four

1. Andozersky is a member of the circuit court for the *uyezd*. This was an appellate court, where cases appealed from the *volost* courts were reviewed and the former verdict either sustained or overturned by the majority vote of the council of judges.

In Chapter Twenty-Eight one gets a first-hand account from Andozersky, telling just how efficient he and Dubitsky are in this capacity.

2. The system of grading in Russian schools is similar to that in America, except that, instead of the letters A, B, C, D, and F, the numbers 1-5 are used, with 5 as a mark of excellence, and so forth down the scale to 1, the mark of flat failure. Petya Motovilov is earning 2's in Login's classes, a mark comparable to a D in an American school.

3. Irina Avdeyevna Kudinov is the town matchmaker. She does not appear in the novel until Chapter Sixteen. Both she and her characteristic expressions are indeed "syrupy."

Chapter Six

1. It is not easy to find a suitable English equivalent for the Russian word *bratets*. Etymologically a diminutive of *brat* (brother), the word has assumed the principal meaning of *chum, fellow, pal, old man, buddy,* etc. Though "buddy" may sound too American for dialogue in a translated Russian novel, in certain places it seemed to fit better than any of its synonyms. One may be consoled by the knowledge that "buddy" originated as an infantile diminutive for *brother,* and even as such, is the only existing diminutive form for *brother* in English.

2. Mrs. Kudinov—see Note 3, Chapter Four.

Chapter Seven

1. Arshin—a Russian measure equal to 28 inches.

2. In the Russian text it is implied rather than stated explicitly that the visiting dignitary was the Tsar; however, it seems doubtful that the local officials would have gone to the trouble of building and preserving this structure for any lesser occasion, and also the Russian terms, vague though they would be in literal translation, do tend to indicate that the visitor was the Tsar.

Chapter Eight

1. Vkusov's affected speech is a patois of none too grammatical French garbled even more by the frequent addition of Russian diminutive suffixes, plurals, and occasionally other Russian inflectional endings. The expletive "Yenonder-shish" does not seem to have any meaning, but sounds derogatory in French and vaguely obscene in Russian, where *shish* means the "fig," an insulting gesture. The word "Yenonder-shish" is discussed briefly by the characters in Chapter Fourteen.

2. Birch kasha—colloquial term for a switching.

3. "Freedom for the free..." etc. One of the many popular Russian proverbs that Sologub skillfully puts into the mouths of appropriate characters in his novels. Pushkin in *Boris Godunov,* one may remember, has a dissolute monk take the same proverb and quip: "Freedom for the free, heaven for the drunk!"

4. Merchant-benefactor—possibly referring to Motovilov, who helped others when it served his own advantage.

Chapter Nine

1. Russian proverb: "A thread from everyone in the *mir* will make a shirt for the man who has none." The *mir* was the old Russian village community.

2. Another Russian proverb: "Just get a trough, and a pig will soon turn up."

3. Danilevsky, Nikolay Yakovlevich (1822-1885)—Russian naturalist and historical philosopher, according to whom Russia and the Slavs should remain indifferent to the west and concentrate on the development of political absolutism, their own special cultural heritage. His two-volume work criticizing Darwinism was published posthumously.

4. Domostroy—The book of rules for domestic order, and its sect of followers, which dated from the sixteenth century and lasted in Russia until the Bolshevik revolution and the assumption of Soviet power. The Domostroy cult appears to have been arch-conservative, narrow-minded, highly legalistic and ritualistic. Grim portrayals of the Domostroy way of life are to be found in the works of Ostrovsky, Nekrasov, Pylnyak, and many other Russian writers. Among other zealously followed rules, the Domostroy book prescribed in great detail when, where, how, and why one should use corporal punishment on one's wife and children. Before looking askance at Russia for this, one should note that similar phenomena occurred in England, France, and elsewhere during the fifteenth century, which was generally a period of cultural and moral decline in much of Europe.

Chapter Ten

1. Glupov—"Stupidton," fictitious setting for a satire by Saltykov-Shchedrin.

2. Collegiate registrar—lowest of the fourteen ranks for officers in the Russian civil service; perhaps comparable to the rank of warrant officer in the army.

3. *Kaputt-kranekn*-"irreparably demolished," from the German "kaputt" (broken) and "krank" (sick).

Chapter Eleven

1. A quote from Gogol's *The Inspector General*. In the first act there is an account of a schoolteacher who got so excited in telling his class about Alexander the Great, that he picked up a chair and smashed it. The mayor, who tells this story, adds: "Of course Alexander of Macedon was a great man, but why smash up the chairs?"

2. For the benefit of and in consideration of any readers not generally familiar with the significance of Russian names, this note is added: Orthodox Russians have three names. The first is the given name or Christian name; the second (ending in -ovich, -evich, -ych, or -ich for males, and -ovna or -evna for females) is dervied from the father's Christian name, hence is called the *patronymic;* the third is, of course, the family name and, like family names elsewhere, usually is derived from some ancestor's Christian name, occupation, or outstanding physical characteristic. Hence, Peter (Pyotr) Petrovich Petrov would be like the name Peter Peterson Peters in medieval England. There is a word equivalent to "Mister" in Russian, but its use has remained relatively rare. For centuries the most common manner of respectful address among Russiansx has been the combination of a man's first name and his patronymic. If we use the above example, *Peter Petrovich* sounds just as respectful but less stilted to a Russian's ear than does *Mr. Petrov.*

3. Yegorushka is the endearing form of Shestov's Christian name. (See Chapter Two, Note 3) Perhaps, when and where Sologub wrote *Bad Dreams,* pronouncing a man's patronymic without the *v* (i.e. Platonych instead of Platonovich) lent a degree of affection of familiarity to the address; however, this seems unlikely. In spoken Russian the tendency has long been not to pronounce the *v* in male patronymics unless the vowel preceding it is stressed, as in *Petrovich*. Platonovich, Shestov's patronymic,

is normally pronounced: "Platonych." In serious, respectful conversation, one does not use the patronymic with diminutive forms of the Christian name. Hence, Krikunov's addressing Shestov as "Yegorushka" (overly familiar) followed by "Platonovich" (stilted form) must have sounded very strange indeed to the young man.

Before leaving the subject of names it might be of interest to remark that many of Sologub's characters like those of Dostoyevsky and Gogol, have utterly fantastic surnames. Molin, for examples signifies "moth" in Russian, Krikunov means "screecher," and Motovilov means "reel." Dubitsky bears connotations of great physical strength, but limited mentality. Login, conversely, is apparently derived from the Greek *logos* ("word, study, reason") and sounds also somewhat like Russian words for "den," "couch," "to lie down," etc.; hence the hero's surname seems to have connotations of mental magnitude enslaved by physical torpor and concupiscence.

Krikunov's distasteful sweetness and feline manners seem reminiscent of the Cat of Kazan, a satyrical figure in early 18th century folk verse, who sweetly ate and drank and even "farted sweetly."

4. Russia, like the United, States has long had currency based on a decimal system; the Russians also tend to call certain coins by their lowest common denominator as fractions rather than by their percentile value of the basic unit of currency. A twenty-five copeck piece, for example, was and is most commonly called a *chetvertak* ("Quarter"), as a 25 cent piece in this country is rarely spoken of as anything other than a *quarter*.

5. Literally: "Whoever cooked the kasha must eat it." "To cook kasha" is an idiom meaning "to stir up trouble."

Chapter Twelve

1. Ivan Krylov—fabulist, satirist, and humorist of the late eighteenth and early nineteenth centuries. A great many of "his" fables were skillful adaptations from Aesop and other foreign sources.

2. The pun does not come out very gracefully in English; the actual expression for inebriation used here is "to pack it behind one's tie." This, of course, has no equivalent in English.

3. Aranzhuyets—mispronunciation of Aranjuez, the city built near Madrid under Ferdinand VI in the mid-eighteenth century. Used for a time as a summer residence for the Spanish royalty, the town has many palaces, parks, and formal gardens. Charles IV abdicated there to the Fernandista party in 1808. Soon thereafter Charles as well as Ferdinand, his son, abdicated to the Bonapartes.

Chapter Fourteen

1. Atheists suffered political oppression at this time. Since the Russian monarchy still operated theoretically on the principle that the Tsar's power was received from and justified by God Almighty, it is hardly surprising that the status quo of such a state would doubt the political loyalty of any suspected or manifest atheist. Schismatics from the Russian Orthodox Church at various times and places fared little better than atheists in the treatment that they received from the state. Religious toleration was not legally granted in Russia until 1905.

2. *Mauviais*—Vkusov, in his "French" dialect, pronounces both e and ai like the Russian palatalized e, i.e. a *ye* sound as in *yellow*.

3. Aside from the other atrocities that Vkusov inflicts on the French language, such as barbarisms and mispronunciation, his grammar is terrible. Here he uses the third

person singular (future) form of the verb with the first person singular pronoun.

4. A *bertha* was a special kind of collar worn by women. It was a deep collar falling over the shoulders from a low neckline. A *chou* (pronounced *shoo*) was probably a kind of pin with a pompon or ribbon cluster attached.

5. "Knock-off"—in Russian, *stukolka;* a card game.

Chapter Sixteen

1. This is one of several places in the novel where Sologub has apparently put malapropisms into the mouths of certain of his characters. The Russian adjective that Mrs. Kudinov applied here to Login is "raznorechivy," a strange compliment indeed, since the word means "contradictory" or "conflicting." It seems likely that she meant to say "krasnorechivy," which means "eloquent" or "expressive."

2. "Kalachny ryad"—literally "Baker's Row"—has acquired a meaning similar to that of Easy Street in English, especially in referring to one who had found his way into a higher class than that in which he was born.

3. In Vkusov's actual language, which might be called "Frussian," the line is: "Frerchiki, je suis nalimone!"

4. Second form in the gimnazia—roughly comparable to the fifth and sixth grades in a modern American school.

5. You-roach-ka—anglicized drawl for Yurochka, diminutive of Yury. In Russian the jest is heightened by the fact that this diminutive form of Baglayev's Christian name rhymes with the diminutive of the Russian word for "cigar butt" as used here in the genitive case.

Chapter Nineteen

1. While this paragraph does not actually contain these two oft-quoted lines of Kipling and Shakespeare, the translator feels that they render best in English Sologub's derogatory description of Sergey Yakovlevich's wife in rather aphoristic colloquial Russian.

2. *Batyushka*—"little father," a term once commonly used by Russians in addressing most male elders; since the middle of the nineteenth century, however, the term has been applied less and less to anyone other than Russian Orthodox priests.

Chapter Twenty

1. Kamarinsky song—a lively type of Russian folk song.

2. "A though once uttered is a lie."—This is a famous line from the poem "Silentium" by Fyodor Tyutchev.

Chapter Twenty-One

1. "Children are nothing but trouble, etc."—an old Russian proverb.

2. *Shapka-nevidimka*— in Russian folklore, a hat that gave its wearer invisibility.

3. Svetlana—the meaning of this is uncertain; the name may at this time have been a brand name or slang term for vodka.

Chapter Twenty-Two

1. Bienstock says literally: "... but I do have a *protege.*" That, of course, does not make sense in the context, and the translator has tried a freer interpretation here that might make some sense. The only conceivable alternative, apparently, would be to consider this clause of Bienstock's a malapropism resulting from a russified German's attempt to use a gallicism. In that case, he may have said *"protege"* while meaning *"protektsia"* ("patronage").

2. Literally: "The devils played *svaika* on his mug." *Svaika* is a Russian game like ring-toss or horseshoes, where at least one sharpened stake is driven into the ground. Andozersky and Baglayev are making fun of Sezyomkin's acne.

Chapter Twenty-Three

1. Although Sologub may have refrained from mentioning the explicit details of this game out of artistic restraint, there was little need for Andozersky to mention here (or in telling of the actual court procedure in Chapter Twenty-Eight) what was common knowledge to Russians of his day. However, readers in our supposedly more humane and enlightened age may not be aware just how cruel, degrading, unfair, and (even worse) how prevalent corporal punishment still was in Russian courts at this time (c. 1885). In "Shameful!"—written in 1875—Leo Tolstoy vehemently protested the fact that, in a day when such punsihments had been discontinued in the schools and were coming to be frowned upon in the better homes,—in the courts and police stations men and women, and children, if convicted of a misdemeanor, were compelled to undress completely, lie face downward on the floor, and be beaten a prescribed number of times on the buttocks with rods. Tolstoy found particularly galling the inequity of this punishment: certain people were exempt from it, those who belonged to the Nobility or who had attained a higher formal education.

2. Mrs. Baglayev apparently is either French by birth or of French descent.

3. Constantine Fofanov, minor 19th century Russian poet.

4. "To a warm-water spa," to get her out of the community and thus appease the public indigation during and after the time of her delivery.

Chapter Twenty-Four

1. Apparently this was a national and religious holiday celebrating the anniversay of the reigning monarch's coronation.

2. In the judicial branch of the civil service, Andozersky holds the rank of Councilor of State; in the education branch, Login holds the rank of Collegiate Assessor, comparable to that of Major in the army; this, apparently, is also the rank held by Motovilov (that Motovilov is only a "major" in the civil service is indicated by Ryabov's remark in Chapter Twenty-Eight). Motovilov's power in the community and in the school system rests largely on his wealth, prestige, and personal influence over others, rather than on his rank.

3. Name-day—her saint's day and the anniversary of her christening, more significant to Eastern Orthodox Christians than one's birthday.

4. Russian, like French, German, and some other European languages has a "formal" second-person pronoun *(vy)* used for politely addressing all except one's family and close relatives, close friends, children, animals, and the Deity, for any of whom the second-person singular, familiar pronoun *(ty)* is applied. Vkusov objects to the fact that the more common and simple folk have always been prone to address individuals

by the familiar rather than the formal pronoun.

5. Glinyany or Fayansov—Clay or Potter. Surnames in Russia became universal much later than Western Europe; hence those names derived from family occupations were at this time much more likely to reflect peasant or bourgeois family status than are names of comparable meaning in English.

Chapter Twenty-Six

1. Sakhar Medovich—literally "Sugar Honeyson," an expression for a deceitfully alluring person.

2. Konoplyov's insinuation that Login is syphilitic appears to be no more than his own psychotic fantasy.

3. Lenya has said "izdivlyatsya" instead of "izdevatsya" (to mock). Login then politely corrects his malapropism.

Chapter Twenty-Seven

1. Literally: "I have the honor of bowing." This is a very formal and by now very archaic expression for taking one's leave. Of course, it hardly fits gracefully into English; however, the translator finds it necessary to preserve the expression because Sologub uses it in Chapter Thirty-Two, in comic word play like that which was masterfully employed by Gogol.

2. Nineteenth century Russian actors were usually paid, not a regular salary, but a certain percentage of each performance's "take" at the box-office. In addition to this, theatres allowed their most popular actors each year a certain number of evenings when they could have the entire proceeds from the show in which they participated. This is what Pozharsky means by his "benefit performance."

3. Here Molin is being obsequious. Father Andrey is only an archpriest *(proto-pop)*, not an archbishop (arkhierey).

4. Like "batyushka" in its application to men, the word "matushka" ("little mother") applicable to any older woman as a respectful or endearing term of address—in standard Russian now means primarily "a priest's wife" when it appears in non-vocative usage.

5. " 'Drinking is the joy of the Russes...' " This is a quotation from the *Russian Primary Chronicle,* wherein these words are attributed to St. Vladimir, first Christian prince of Kievan Russia (978-1015).

Chapters Twenty-Eight and Twenty-Nine

1. The Russian word *syezd,* which in this sentence may be translated literally as "conference," is hereafter translated in this chapter as "court" because it seems to be used in the sense of "the court as composed of the judicial officials having convened for a particular session or series of sessions."

2. Literally: "They'll present us with a cholera *bunt."* Andozersky's pun is difficult if not impossible to simulate in English. In Russian the word *bunt* means either "riot" or "packet."

3. An old Russian proverb, somewhat similar in meaning to the expression used in English: "When in Rome, do as the Romans do."

4. *Moroka*—evidently another Russian word without any satisfactory equivalent in English. Like *mrak,* to which it is related etymologically, it suggests darkness, dimness,

gloom, confusion, etc.

Chapter Thirty-Three

1. Anika the Warrior—subject of Russian folk songs and oral poetry for centuries. Ultimately the tradition derives from a Byzantine epic. Anikes (the name means "unconquerable" in Greek), a Byzantine knight, boasted that no one had ever beaten him in combat or ever would. Death appeared in disguise to him and rebuked him for his boasting. Anikes challenged Death to combat, wherein he eventually weakened and repented of his boasting, but Death was implacable and slew him. Anika the Warrior in his battle with Death was a favorite secular subject frequently depicted in the old wood cuttings and block-printed pictures of Russia.

2. Kuzka's mother—a colloquial, folk expression meaning a severe beating.

3. Russian proverb: "S silnym ne boris, s bogatym ne sudis."

4. "I have the honor.. (of bowing)." See Chapter Twenty-Seven, note 1.

Chapter Thirty-Four

1. Here Andozersky uses the familiar second-person pronoun.

2. In prerevolutionary Russia, the Russian word with the primary meaning of "mother" was also used, especially in rural and lower-class society as a respectful or endearing form of address to any woman. Here, moreso perhaps than at any other point in the novel, Sologub brings home to the reader the irony and absurdity of Motovilov's oppressive, often ridiculously stiff and dated mannerisms and phrases. Elsewhere in the novel, when the Russian word *mat* ("mother") is used in its secondary meaning, it has seemed more natural to translate it as "my dear," "young lady," etc.

3. See Chapter Eight, Note 2.

Chapter Thirty-Five

1. An interesting military metaphor, more apt, it seems, than the one in English usage. After all, for their shape, it seems far more natural—and far less morbid—to call bottles cannon, rather than call them "dead soldiers" when empty.

2. Baglyaev's quip, "Even a flea has little fleas on it," is a Russian proverb. One is reminded of the age-old English verse long in the public domain:

> Man has rats and rats have fleas
> Upon their backs to bite 'em;
> The big fleas have smaller fleas,
> And so *ad Infinitum...*

3. Vasya—the least informal and most common Russian diminutive form of Vasily, Login's Christian name. "Vasyuk" is more common to the Ukraine than Russia. At several places in the novel Baglayev's speech includes certain rare words and peculiar pronunciation of standard words; this may indicate that he is supposed to be of Ukrainian or Belorussian origin.

Chapter Thirty-Six

1. The yellow Florentine iris ("kasatik" in Russian) is the flower commonly represented in heraldry and design as the fleur-de-lis. The flower's Russian name is also

a term of endearment for males in Russian folk poetry. Plagued as Login is with guilt feelings over his penchant for self-abuse, erotic fantasizing, and occasional erotic indulgences with others (as with Spiridon's wife, Ulyana, in Chapter I), he is bothered by the phallic resemblance in the flowers.

Chapter Thirty-Seven

1. It is Praskovya, Login's ugly, sullen housekeeper, that Serpenitsyn here facetiously refers to as Dulcinea of Toboso, the beloved of Don Quixote.

2. Another Russian proverb.

3. Molin, nevertheless, does not go unpunished forever. In *Smoke and Ashes,* the last book in Sologub's trilogy *The Created Legend,* Molin reappears in the year 1905, by which time he has finally lost his job as a teacher, supports himself principally by thievery, and has finally been allowed to sink to the level of his natural element, the utter dregs and outcasts of society. In this book he steals a suffragan's gold watch and is not caught. However, after he and three cronies steal a "wonder-working icon," strip it of its jewels and precious metals, and burn the remains, the thieves then fall out over how the valuables should be divided, and a fight results in which Molin, like his "benefactor" in *Bad Dreams,* finally gets his head split by an axe and dies instantly.